Mama Namibia

MAMA NAMIBIA

BASED ON TRUE EVENTS

Mari Serebrov

kamel press

Visit us at

www.KamelPress.com / Serebrov

to see more from this author!

ISBN-13:   978-1-62487-053-8 - Paperback

                978-1-62487-054-5 - eBook

Library of Congress Control Number: 2017934595

Published in the USA.

*To the Herero and Nama grandmothers,
the "mamas" of Namibia.*

May their legacy never be forgotten.

Mama Namibia

From old Mother Africa she sprang
In that moment when yesterday touched tomorrow,
Born of rusted sands and salted tears
Into a land of bones and strangers.

White cows graze on the sacred graves.
The homestead longs for its holy fire.
The ancestors call, but no one hears,
For their future sleeps in the sand.

Dancing in the ancestral flame,
Singing the praises of yesterday,
Mama Namibia.
Mama Namibia.

– Mari Serebrov

BOOK 1

Jahohora

FIRST DAY

I wave at the morning sun peeping over the mountains.

"Jahohora!" Mama calls.

I run to the kraal to help her get sour milk. Mama's belly is big with a baby so she walks slowly. Her bangles and iron beads make music when she walks. I want bangles. But I have to wait until I'm a woman. I have beads on my skirt. And in my hair. They don't make music like Mama's beads.

Mama smells the milk in the gourds. I smell the gourds, too. Sour fills my nose. It makes my belly hungry. Mama puts the ancestors' gourd on my head. I put my hands up to hold it still. I walk very, very, very slowly to omuriro omurangere, our holy fire. I hold my breath so no milk spills. Tate and brother Ramata are sitting by the fire. Mama carries our gourd to Tate. Her big belly gets in the way when she tries to set the gourd on the ground.

Tate smiles. I see his pointed front teeth. His tate and mama filed his top teeth and knocked out his bottom teeth when he was a little boy. I don't want Tate and Mama to do that to my teeth. It would hurt.

Tate takes the gourd from my head and sets it by the fire for the ancestors. He drinks from the gourd Mama carried. "Ahhhh," he says. "It is good omaere. The ancestors will smile."

Mama and I sit on the ground by Ramata. When Tate is done drinking the sour milk, Mama, Ramata and I drink from the gourd. My belly is happy.

Yellow cow calls to us. It's time to milk. I help Mama stand up. Tate laughs. She makes a funny face at him. She pats her belly and smiles. "Soon," she says.

I pick up the empty gourd.

"I'll race you to the kraal," Ramata says. He's already running.

"That's not fair," I tell him. "You started first. And you're not carrying anything."

Ramata gets to the kraal first. He's bigger than me so he always wins. He runs over to help Tate fix a broken rail. We have many cattle. But only the cows that give milk live in the kraal. Yellow cow is my cow. She gives lots of milk. Tjikuume gave yellow cow to me when I was a baby. Tjikuume is Mama's tate.

Mama milks the cows. Clang, clang, squirt. Her bangles sing as her hands pull milk from red cow that belongs to the ancestors. I watch the milk fill the jar and then run to get another jar for Mama.

"Slowly, Jahohora," she says. "Stand tall. And walk slowly. Only servants rush through their work." She pats red cow and then stands up straight and stretches. I put an empty jar under brown cow with white spot. Mama's belly hangs low to the ground when she bends to milk brown cow. Clang, clang, squirt.

A fly buzzes my head. I shoo it away. "Mama, tell me a story," I ask. "About first day."

"I want to hear, too," Ramata calls.

Mama closes her eyes to think. Her hands keep pulling milk from the cow. Clang, clang, squirt. Clang, clang, squirt. Mama opens her eyes. She's done thinking. She doesn't look at me. She sees many yesterdays.

I sit on the ground as Mama begins the story. "On first day, Njambi Karunga called the first ancestors from the trunk of the omumborombonga tree. One by one, they stepped from the sacred tree. Mukuru and Kamangarunga, the first Herero tate and mama, stepped from the tree. Then the first Berg-Damara tate and mama. The first Nama tate and mama. The first tate and mama of the Ovambo. The first tate and mama of every tribe on earth."

"And the first tate and mama of cattle," I say. "Don't forget the first ancestors of cattle! And kudu!" We're from the kudu clan. That means we can't eat kudu meat or wear the brown color of kudu.

Mama smiles. "On first day, Njambi Karunga also called out the first tate and mama of cattle. The first tate and mama of kudu. Of lions and leopards. Of wildebeest and baboons. On first day, the first tate and mama of every living thing stepped from the omumborombonga tree."

"Did the lions eat the others?" I ask.

"Shhh!" Ramata says. "Let Mama tell the story."

I know the story about first day. Mama has told it to me many times. But I like asking questions.

"The lions couldn't see the other tates and mamas," Mama says. "First day was darker than a night with no stars or moon. All the ancestors hugged the omumborombonga tree and each other so they wouldn't get lost in the darkness."

I close my eyes tight. I try to make it dark like first day.

"The first tate of Berg-Damara made a fire. That made the first tate and mama of lions, kudus, giraffes, and other wild animals run away." Mama makes a loud noise like many animals running over the veld.

"Why?" I ask.

"The fire scared them," Ramata says. He thinks he knows everything.

"But not the tate and mama of cattle," I say. "They weren't scared."

"No. The first ancestors of cattle were brave and loyal," Mama says. "They stayed with Mukuru and Kamangarunga, the Herero tate and mama. But it was hard to see, even with the fire. So Njambi Karunga sent light. For the first time, the ancestors saw each other and the animals that stayed."

"They saw cows!" I shout.

"And horses, camels, goats, and all the other animals that live with people until now," Mama says. "When the first ancestors saw the animals, they chose which ones they wanted. Mukuru and Kamangarunga chose wisely...."

"They chose cattle!" I clap.

Ramata shakes his head at me and makes a face. I look away from him.

"Yes, but the other ancestors wanted them too," Mama says. "They argued and shouted so much that different languages were born. They no longer understood each other, so the ancestors walked separate paths. Mukuru and Kamangarunga came here with the first tate and mama of cattle. And until now, the Herero take care of cattle. And cattle give us milk, skins, and meat."

Mama stops pulling milk from the cow and stands up slowly. "That's why we give the ancestors milk – to thank them for giving us life, and for choosing cattle. And to thank them for talking to Njambi Karunga for us. When we give the ancestors sour milk at the holy fire, they know we remember them and we remember Njambi Karunga."

"What if we forget the ancestors?" I ask.

"They would give us bad luck." Mama carries the full jar over to the gourds that hold the sour milk. I help her pour the fresh milk from the ancestors' cows into the ancestors' gourd. We mix the new milk with the sour. We fill the other gourds with milk from our cows.

"Then the ancestors are bad," I say.

"Why do you think that?" Mama asks.

"They give bad luck."

"No. The ancestors only give bad luck to make us remember them," Mama says. "They know if we forget them, we will forget Njambi Karunga. And we will lose who we are."

THE BABY

Tuaekua Ehi and I pick up cow dung and carry it to Mama, Tjikuu, and Mama Vitjitua. She's Mama's sister. They mix it with sand and put it on the hut they're building for Mama. It's the house where baby will come. They need lots and lots of dung.

Tuaekua Ehi and I start to play. "Bring some more dung," Tjikuu tells us. Tjikuu is Mama's mama. "Baby is coming soon. The hut must be ready."

Tate and Ramata kill an ox so Mama, Tjikuu, and Mama Vitjitua will have food while they wait for the baby to come.

At last, the baby house is done. It's round, like our house. "A round house keeps snakes away because it makes no shadows where snakes can hide," Tjikuu says. "Herero who build square houses like white people are foolish. Round houses bring good luck. They're like nature."

I laugh. I think she's teasing.

Tjikuu points up at the sky. At the trees. And at the mountains. "Do you see anything that Njambi Karunga made that's square?"

I think hard. Sun, moon, trees, berries, seeds – they're all round. I can't think of anything square.

"What about a rock?" Tuaekua Ehi asks.

"Rocks are only square when they've been cut or broken from the mountains," Tjikuu says.

I nod. Tjikuu is right. She is very, very wise. That's because she's old.

Mama Vitjitua goes in the baby house. I want to go in, too. But Tjikuu stands in the opening. "No, Jahohora. Only your mama, Vitjitua, and I can go in the baby house. We have to keep the house clean so the baby won't get sick."

"I won't make the baby sick," I say. "I want to be with Mama. And I want to see the baby when it comes."

Tjikuu smiles. "You must be a big girl and go home. You have to take care of Tate."

"When will Mama come home?"

"When the baby is named," Tjikuu says. "Now go home with the others."

"Come on, Jahohora," Tuaekua Ehi calls to me. She is walking toward our village.

I tell Mama goodbye and try not to cry. Then I run to catch up with my cousin. Tuaekua Ehi puts her arm around me. "It's all right. Your mama will be home soon with the baby," she says.

I like Tuaekua Ehi. She's as old as Ramata, but she isn't mean to me like he is.

Many days pass, but Mama doesn't come home. I miss her. Ramata makes me play stone echo with our cousins. Ramata hides. I hear him throwing stones to show where he is. He thinks he can trick us. When the others go to find him, I don't look for him. I cross the veld to the baby house instead.

I'm tired when I get there. The sun is hot. I sit by a camelthorn tree close to the hut. It makes a little shade. Not enough for snakes though. I look at the ground anyway. Just to be sure.

I wait a long time. No one comes out of the hut. I am almost asleep when I hear crying. I open my ears. It's baby! Mama sings to the baby. It stops crying. I want Mama to sing to me. But I don't want to make the baby sick. I sit under the tree till the sun makes long shadows. I listen to Mama sing. I pretend she's singing to me.

Many days later, Ramata and I go to Tjikuu's house. Mama, Tjikuu, and Mama Vitjitua come with the baby before the sun wakes up. It's baby's first time outside the baby house. The bright sun could hurt the baby's eyes. So Mama must bring the baby when the sun is still sleeping. Tjikuu spreads a goat skin on the ground by her house for Mama to sit on. Mama holds the baby. Her big belly is gone. Ramata is happy that the baby is a boy. I wanted a sister. But seeing Mama again makes me happy.

I sit close to Mama and watch the baby while he drinks milk from Mama. Like the baby calves drink from their mamas. The baby's hair and skin are red. Mama says Tjikuu rubbed ochre on him when he was born to make him smell nice and to keep his skin soft.

The sun is waking when Mama's brothers and their families come to see the baby. We sit by Tjikuume's holy fire. He drinks water from the ancestors' cup, but he doesn't swallow it. He spits water on Mama and the baby. Tjikuume is older than Tjikuu. He's the oldest person I know.

Tjikuume takes out a special knife to cut a piece of the baby's hair. The baby doesn't have much hair so Tjikuu tells Tjikuume to be careful. "I know what I'm doing," he says. "How many grandchildren do I have, woman?"

Tjikuu laughs. "It's been many seasons since we've had a newborn," she says. "Your eyes are older now. And your hand isn't as steady."

Tjikuume cuts a piece of hair and gives it to Tjikuu. She puts it in a skin pouch.

"What's that?" I ask.

"This will make medicine for the baby if he gets sick," Tjikuu tells me.

"His hair?" I think she's teasing.

"Not just his hair. His ongua is in here, too."

"Let me see. What's ongua?" I ask.

Tjikuu opens the pouch wide so I can see a fat dark string. "It's the cord that joined baby to Mama when he was in her belly." She nods her head toward Tjikuume. "It's time for Tjikuume to give baby a name."

Tjikuume looks closely at the baby. He closes his eyes to think. Naming a baby is important work. Tjikuume's mouth gets big with a smile. "Karemarama!" he says. He pulls the baby's legs straight. Everyone laughs. The baby's name means "long legs."

Tjikuume's smile goes away. "He may need these long legs to help him run far from the Germans."

The laughing stops. Uncles say Tjikuume is right. Tjikuume holds Karemarama up. He tells the ancestors about his new grandson and asks them to bring the baby good luck.

The uncles follow Tjikuume to the kraal to get the cow he has chosen for the baby.

"What are Germans?" I ask Tjikuu.

"They are white people," she tells me.

"Why must the baby run from them?"

"They take our land and cattle," she says. "And they dig up our graves."

I look up when I hear a young cow calling. Tjikuume is leading the baby's cow. It's a red cow with spots all over its back. It has long legs like Karemarama. Uncles are laughing. It's a good choice, they say.

Tjikuume brings the cow close to Mama and the baby. Mama holds the baby up so his head touches the cow's head. The cow sniffs him. Karemarama puts his fingers in the cow's fur.

"Baby likes his cow," I tell Tjikuu.

"She is the sister of your cow," Tjikuu says.

"Come," Mama says. "It's time to go home so Tate can meet his son." She carries the baby across the veld to our village. I walk close to her. Ramata brings the baby's cow. Tjikuu, Tjikuume, uncles, and their families join us. I smile and smile and smile. We will have a feast in our village!

When we get home, Tate puts a big goat skin on the ground for Mama and the baby. I sit next to Mama. Uncles and aunties from Tate's and Mama's clans give the baby presents. Mama Vitjitua and the other aunties all want to hold the baby. But Mama says I should hold him first. I sit very tall and straight. Mama puts the baby in my arms. She shows me how to hold his head. The baby's eyes are closed. I try to sit still. I don't want to wake him. Mama smiles at me.

I look down at the baby. Tjikuu says I'm a little mama. I feel important. I hold the baby a long, long time. My arms are hurting. The baby is heavy. Like a big rock. I move my arm. The baby wrinkles his eyes and cries. Loudly. It scares me so I cry too. Mama takes the baby from me.

"I'm sorry, Mama. I didn't mean to make him cry," I say. I'm still crying.

The baby drinks from Mama. He's quiet now. "It's all right, Jahohora," Mama tells me. "You didn't do anything wrong. Babies cry. It's the only way they can talk. But you have words so you don't need to cry."

I rub the tears from my eyes and smile at Mama. I pat the baby's soft head. He keeps drinking. He must be very, very thirsty.

Finally, it's time for the feast. Tate has killed two oxen, so there's lots of meat. I eat and eat and eat. Ramata and the cousins start to play stone echo. Tuaekua Ehi wants me to play. But my belly is too full. I lie down next to Mama and the baby. I close my eyes and sleep. The sounds of my family talking and laughing join my dreams. They are good dreams.

Mama wakes me. "The sun is telling earth goodnight," she says. "It's time for Tate's ancestors to meet Karemarama."

Tate's mama and tate live with the ancestors. Tate is the oldest son, so he is the keeper of the omuriro omurangere for his family. The holy fire is a gift from Mukuru, the first Herero tate. It reminds us that the ancestors gave us life. And that they watch over us. The fire must never go out. Sometimes Tate lets me put wood on the fire to keep it burning.

Tate sits by the fire, near the branch of the omumborombonga tree. The sacred branch can't be burned. When I see it, I think about Mukuru and Kamangarunga climbing out of the omumborombonga tree on first day.

Mama and the baby sit next to Tate. Then Ramata and me. Uncle Kozondanda and Auntie Uajoroka sit behind us with Tuaekua Ehi and all their sons. The other uncles and their families also sit behind us. Tate stands up and drinks water from the ancestors' gourd. He spits water on the baby and on me and all the little cousins. We laugh. He hands the gourd to Mama. She drinks and spits water on the ground three times. Then she gives the gourd to Ramata. He drinks and spits and hands it to Uncle Kozondanda. I watch as Tuaekua Ehi drinks from the gourd and spits. Soon I'll be big enough to drink from the gourd like Ramata and Tuaekua Ehi. Then Tate won't spit on me.

After every uncle, auntie, and cousin drinks and spits, Tate tells the ancestors who is at the fire. He starts with Mama. He says her name, "Tutejuva of the Omukuatjivi clan. Tutejuva of Koroe. Koroe of Hiruku. Hiruku of...."

Tate names all Mama's ancestors.   Back to Mukuru and Kamangarunga. I try to sit still, but it's hard. Naming Mama's ancestors takes a long time.   When he's done with Mama's ancestors, Tate looks at my brother. "Ramata Eliphas Mutihu, son of Mutihu and Tutejuva," he says. Mutihu is Tate's name.

I sit tall. I'm next. I don't want the ancestors to think I'm not listening.

"Jahohora, daughter of Mutihu and Tutejuva." Tate smiles at me. Then he takes the baby from Mama and holds him up so the ancestors can see him. "Karemarama, the newest son of Mutihu and Tutejuva," Tate tells the ancestors. He names the ancestors of all the others sitting around the fire.

When the food is gone and the sun sleeps, everyone goes home. I look up at the big round moon. It seems close enough to touch. I remember Tjikuu saying Njambi Karunga made only round things. I look at the stars glowing with the colors of fire. They're round, too.   I yawn and follow Mama into our round house.

I'm tired. But I can't sleep. I hear the baby cry. Mama picks him up to feed him. I crawl next to Mama. She pats my head. "Do you like your baby brother?" she asks me.

I nod. I touch his little bare foot. "Tjikuume gave him a funny name," I say.

Mama smiles.

I think about my name. Jahohora means "our home is getting weaker."

"I don't like my name," I tell Mama. "It's sad."

"My name is sad, too," Mama says. "Tutejuva means 'we die day by day.'"

"Why do we have sad names?" I ask her.

"Our names tell about the days when we were born. I was born when the Witboois were fighting the Herero. Many people died."

"What about my name?"

Mama is quiet. Her eyes close. I think she's sleeping. But then she opens her eyes and speaks. "Your name is like Tuaekua Ehi's name. When she was born, the white people began taking more and more Herero land. Her name means 'our land was taken away.' And when you were born, white people took the land where our cattle grazed. And they dug up the graves of our ancestors to plant maize and calabashes." Mama's eyes look to a faraway place.

The baby kicks his legs out. Mama laughs quietly. Her sadness is gone.

"He does have long legs," she says.

* * * * *

The baby's loud cries hurt my head. I put my hands on my ears, but I still hear him. Tate has a big smile. He holds a special knife in one hand and a piece of baby's skin in the other. "Now Karemarama is a true Herero boy," he says.

Mama wipes the blood from the part that makes Karemarama a boy.

"Why did Tate cut the baby?" I ask.

"It's a Herero tradition," Mama says. "It's what makes Herero men different from all other men."

"I'm glad I'm a girl. I don't want Tate to cut me."

Mama laughs. "It doesn't hurt much," she says. "See? Karemarama is already playing."

I watch as Mama cleans the baby. He makes baby noises. And plays with his feet. Mama puts her finger on the baby's chin. He smiles at her. "Look. He has his first tooth," she says. "It won't be long before he is truly a man."

I go outside to play with Ramata. "Let's race," he says. I like running. I don't like losing. We run and run and run. He wins every time. But not by much.

"You're getting faster," he says. "But you'll never beat me."

We lie on the ground, looking up at the blue sky. The sun warms my skin. I think about Tate cutting the baby. "Does it hurt where Tate cut you?" I ask Ramata.

"Of course not. That was when I was a baby," he says. "I'm nearly a man now." He puffs his chest out.

I laugh at him. "You're still just a boy." I stand up and run. "I'm going to beat you this time."

"No fair! You started first."

I run as fast as I can until I reach our house. I breathe hard and look back. Ramata is a long way from the house. He's walking.

"I won!" I shout when he gets close.

"No, you didn't," he says.

"I got here first."

"But I wasn't racing." He makes a face at me.

Before I go to sleep that night, I sit by Mama while she feeds the baby. "What makes Herero women different from other women?" I ask her.

"Lots of things," Mama says. "Our skin skirts. Our pointed headdresses. The red ochre we put on our bodies. The way we take care of the cattle. How we remember the ancestors." Mama looks down at me. "There are other things you'll learn when you become a woman."

"When will that be?" I ask sleepily.

"When you're ready."

I close my eyes. Mama sings to the baby and me about a special cow.

WHITE PEOPLE

Tate frowns. He says too many white people come to Hereroland. They are all called German. But they have other names, too – Missionary, Trader, Farmer, and Soldier. Tate says they are bad for the Herero. They make the Herero forget their ancestors.

Tate is an omundu uonduko, a healer. He brings peace to Herero families. But German Missionary says Tate is evil because he talks to the ancestors. That bad spirits make him trick the Herero. Tate laughs. But his face isn't happy. "Missionary doesn't know the ancestors, so Missionary medicine poisons the Herero soul," Tate says. Some Herero believe Missionary. They put out their holy fires and forget the ancestors. Even our chief listens to Missionary.

Tate is surprised when the chief sends headmen to him. They say the chief wants to see him. It's important. We all go with Tate to Otjimbingwe, the chief's village. It's a long, long walk. Karemarama wants to walk with Ramata. But he gets tired and sits down. We have to take turns carrying him. We reach the chief's village after the sun sleeps. We stay at the house of Tate's cousin.

The next day while Tate meets with the chief, I walk by Missionary's square house. It is the biggest house I've seen until now. It's bigger than the brick house of the chief. Missionary must have lots of wives and children to need such a big house. But why do wives want to live in the same house? I shake my head.

I stop when I see Missionary daughter digging in the dirt. She must be hungry if she's digging for uintjes there. I am sorry for her because her family is very poor. They have few cows in their kraal. And no holy fire. No ancestors. They don't know who they are.

I stare at the girl. She's not white. Her face is red. Like a baboon's bottom. And she has lots and lots of yellow hair. Like the grass in dry season. She's covered in cloths. She looks very hot. Maybe she's sick. "Uri naua?" I call to her, asking her if she feels all right.

She looks up at me. Her mouth falls open as wide as a lion's when it yawns. I tell her to close her mouth before she eats a fly. But she opens it wider. And screams. The wall of the house opens. Missionary wife runs out to her daughter. The girl talks in her mama's ear. She points at me. Missionary wife looks at me. I stare back. She's not white either. She has a yellow face and yellow hair. And she's fat with many cloth skirts. She has no beads or bangles. Missionary wife shoos me away. She hurries her daughter into the house. Maybe she isn't Missionary wife. She runs like a servant. She doesn't walk tall like an important wife.

I find Mama and put my head on her legs. I watch Karemarama play in the dirt. The hot sun makes me sleepy. My eyes close, but I see Missionary girl with the yellow hair. She shouts at me with the sound of thunder. She chases me across the veld. I run faster than I've run until now. I run until I can't run anymore. Then I fall to the ground. It hurts to breathe. My mouth needs water. I look around. There's no water. I'm alone. And I don't know where I am. "Mama! Mama!" I cry.

"Jahohora." I hear Mama calling me. I run to her voice, but I can't find her. "Mama!" I cry again. Something shakes me. I wake up. Mama's face fills my eyes. I smile. I am safe.

We wait a long time for Tate. Mama walks with Karemarama and me so we can see more of the chief's village. It's a big village with many big houses. They are all square. Even the houses of the Herero. The village has lots of white people. They stare at us and point their fingers. Some laugh. They sound like hyenas howling.

"Why are they laughing?" I ask Mama.

"They don't know better," she says. She lifts her head higher and walks slowly. She pushes my back. "Is your mama dead?" she asks. "Walk tall. You are Herero."

I stand straighter. I try not to look at the white people faces. I smile when I see Herero women. But my smile goes away. They don't look like Herero. They don't wear skins. Or beads. Or headdresses. They are covered in cloth like white people. Mama sees me looking at them.

"They follow the Missionary," she says. "They have forgotten what it is to be Herero."

Mama suddenly stops walking. I bump into her. She picks up Karemarama and puts his head against her shoulder so he can't see. She looks across the path. Many people stand there. More people than I've ever seen. Two white men are pulling the clothes from a Herero man. They push him down and tie his hands and feet to a wood bench. One white man hits the Herero with a stick made from skin. The other white man calls out a strange word: "Eyns!"

Mama pulls me against her with her free arm so I can't see either. But I hear the skin stick slap the man's back again. "Tsvy!" the white man says as the Herero man screams. I cover my ears with my hands. I can still hear him screaming.

Mama turns around, pushing me toward cousin's house. The man's screams – and the shouting of the white man – follow us. Mama talks with cousin's wife. "Why are they beating Hijatjikenga?" she asks.

Cousin's wife shakes her head. "He paid Trader," she says, "but Trader wanted more money. Hijatjikenga said no, he had paid what he owed."

"So they beat him?" Mama looks like she doesn't believe cousin's wife.

"White people beat Herero for no reason," cousin's wife tells her quietly. "It happens too often. Sometimes they beat Herero until they die."

"I thought white people promised to protect the Herero," Mama says. "They made a treaty."

Cousin's wife laughs. Her laugh isn't happy. "They never protect the Herero. When the Witboois take our cattle, the German soldiers watch them and then drink tea with them."

"But what about the treaty?" Mama asks.

"The Germans use it to make the chiefs do what they want. And to take our land," cousin's wife says. "If the chiefs don't do what the Germans tell them, the soldiers kill them with thunder sticks."

Mama sees me listening. She tells me to play with Kare-marama.

Tate joins us after the sun wakes the next day. He looks tired. And sad. Tate is quiet for many steps after we leave the village. Then he talks. "We must go to the house of your tate," he tells Mama.

"Is something wrong?" she asks.

"The chief wants me to talk to him. Sick oxen pulling a trader's wagon passed through your family's village. Someone said one of the cows in the village got the sickness. By now, more cattle could be sick," Tate says. "The Germans said they must kill all the cattle so the sickness doesn't spread."

"Even the ancestors' cattle?" Mama stops walking. So we all stop.

"Yes, even the ancestors' cattle," Tate says quietly.

"Tate would never do that," Mama whispers.

Tate sighs. "The chief is afraid that if he doesn't, the Germans will kill all Herero cattle. They are looking for a reason to kill our cattle so they can make medicine for theirs. And they think if we don't have cattle, we will give up our land and work for them. It's what the Germans want – to make us their servants and to take more of our land."

"What are you going to do?" Mama asks.

"I told the chief I would talk to your tate. We will do what we have to do." Tate looks across the veld. "But that may not be what the Germans think should be done." He begins walking again. We follow him.

THE SICKNESS

When we get to Tjikuume's house, we see him sitting by the holy fire. Tate goes to his kraal. Tjikuume joins him. "I hear your ancestors' red cow has the sickness," Tate says.

"She isn't eating. But that doesn't mean she's sick. Maybe she's not hungry," Tjikuume tells him.

Tate nods. He looks at red cow. Her bones stick out. And her eyes sink deep into her head. "How long has she not been eating?" Tate asks.

Tjikuume shrugs. "A few days."

Tate checks red cow's mouth and nose. She stumbles backward and lifts her tail. Instead of dung, sticky black blood comes out. "She has the sickness," Tate says.

Tjikuume looks at the ground. He is very sad. "I will talk to the ancestors. Then I'll put red cow down. But I won't kill the other cattle." He shakes his head. "Our cattle never had sickness until the white people came," he says softly.

Uncles come out of their huts. When they hear Tate and Tjikuume, they say it is Kahamemua's curse. Mama takes Karemarama and me to Tjikuu's house. Tjikuu looks worried when Mama tells her about the cows.

"Who is Kahamemua?" I ask Mama.

"He was a Herero chief," she answers.

"Why did he curse Tjikuume?"

Mama doesn't answer my question. She pretends to be busy. I ask again.

Mama and Tjikuu look at each other. Mama shrugs. "He cursed all the Herero and their cattle."

"Why did he curse his own people?" I ask.

"Because they let the white people kill him. They had no choice. Now no more questions," Mama tells me.

Tjikuu shakes her head. "Watch out for white cattle that come to the village," she sings quietly. "Then the homestead misses its fire."

I laugh. "We don't have white cows, Tjikuu. And what if a white cow comes? We can't chase away cattle."

"I know," Tjikuu sighs. "That's the problem. Ever since Missionary came to Hereroland, the white people take more and more. We can't chase them away. Soon, all our holy fires will be gone."

I tell Tjikuu about Missionary daughter with yellow hair like the grass and a face the color of a baboon's bottom. "I don't like Missionary," I say.

"Why is that, little one?"

"Missionary says we don't need the ancestors. Missionary says the ancestors are bad."

"What do you think?" she asks me.

"I think the ancestors are good."

"And why do you think that?"

"The ancestors give us life. They watch over us and guide us. Those are good things, aren't they, Tjikuu?"

She pats my head. "Yes, they are."

"So if Missionary says the ancestors are bad, then Missionary must be bad. Missionary tells us things that aren't true."

"Missionary thinks he's telling the truth," Tjikuu says. "But he doesn't understand the ancestors because he has forgotten his own. We should feel sorry for Missionary. People without ancestors are people without yesterday or tomorrow."

"How can we feel sorry for people who lie to us?" I ask.

"It is up to us to choose what is right. No one can make us eat a lie," she answers.

I hear the cows crying. I want to go outside.

"No," Mama says. "Let the men do what they must do."

"But Ramata is out there. He's not a man. He's a boy!"

Mama doesn't answer. She and Tjikuu sit quietly. They look sad. I play with Karemarama. He laughs. But even he can't make Mama and Tjikuu happy.

The cows finally stop crying. We go outside to wait for Tate, but he doesn't come. The sun is sleeping, so it's too dark to see the cows. But we see an orange light far off in the veld.

"Something stinks," I say. I cover my nose. I can still smell the stink.

Mama looks over at Karemarama and me. "It's time to sleep," she says. "We will sleep in Tjikuu's house tonight."

We follow her and Tjikuu inside. Tjikuu spreads a skin for us to sleep on. She sprinkles herbs on it. The skin smells good.

When the sun wakes, I go out to help Tjikuu and Mama milk the cows. The kraal is empty. We look everywhere, but there are no cows. Tjikuu's eyes are wet. She turns away from me so I can't see her face.

My belly wants sour milk. Mama says no. "We will get omaere at home," she tells me. "Tjikuu has no cows to milk. She must keep the omaere she already has so she and Tjikuume will have enough to eat and to give to the ancestors."

We wait and wait for Tate to come back so we can go home. My belly growls with hunger. I tell it to be quiet, but it doesn't listen. "I want to go home," I tell Mama. "I'm hungry." I watch Karemarama drinking milk from Mama.

Tjikuu gives me uintjes. But I want omaere. Mama tells me to hush and eat the wild onions.

Mama and Tjikuu talk softly. I open my ears, but I can't hear their words. Tjikuu is very, very sad. She sees me looking at her. Her mouth smiles. But her eyes don't. Something else is in her eyes. I don't know what it is. It makes me want to cry.

Tjikuu stands up and claps her hands. "There's work to be done," she says. Her voice is too happy. "We should patch the house while we still have dung."

She takes me outside to show me the holes in her hut. She sends me to the kraal to get cow dung so she can fill the holes. "Stay away from the dung of the sick cow," she tells me.

I look at the ground and walk carefully. I don't want to step in sick cow's dung. I find good, dry dung and carry it to Tjikuu. I want to make her happy, so I walk like a Herero woman – tall and slow. Tjikuu's eyes look at me, but they don't see me. I go back to the kraal to get more dung for Tjikuu.

"What will you do when the dung is gone?" I ask her as she fills the holes in her house.

Her eyes come back from a faraway place. "I will use something else," she says.

When I go to get more dung, I see Tate and Ramata coming across the veld. "Tate is back!" I shout. I run to meet him. Tate looks tired. And his smile is gone. I follow him back to Tjikuu's house where Tjikuu and Mama are waiting for him. He tells them that Tjikuume and uncles are moving their cattle into the mountains away from the other cattle.

"The milk cows?" Tjikuu looks at the empty kraal.

"Some of them had the sickness, so we had to put all of them down," Tate says. "The cattle in the fields were still eating. If they go into the mountains, they might not get sick, and the Germans won't find them."

Tjikuu nods and goes into her house.

As we walk home, I ask Ramata what happened to Tjikuume's milk cows.

"We had to kill them," he says.

"That's lots of meat. What will they do with it? Will they have a feast?" I wait for Ramata to say something mean.

He doesn't. "The cows were sick, so the meat is bad. No one can eat it," he tells me.

"Where are the cows? I didn't see their skins or horns."

"We took them away from the village. The white people said they had to be burned to keep the sickness from spreading. Tate started a fire that burned everything. Even the skins and horns. The fire smelled bad. It was hard to breathe." Ramata is quiet.

I think about the awful smell from last night and the orange light across the veld. I am quiet, too.

As soon as we get home, Tate goes to the kraal. He checks our milk cows and looks at their dung. "They don't look sick, but we must watch them. If they get sick, they won't eat. So make sure they're eating," he says. "Keep strange cows and other animals away from them. They can get the sickness from eland, kudu – even the Germans' horses."

When the sun sleeps, Tate sits at the holy fire. Some uncles and aunties join him. "Where were you when the cattle of the Herero became sick?" Tate asks the ancestors. He tells them about Tjikuume's cattle and says he's sorry for having to kill so many cows. He asks them to keep the sickness from our cattle.

Mama and I bring omaere for the ancestors, Tate, Ramata, and the others. Then I eat omaere. But my belly isn't happy. I think about Tjikuu and Tjikuume. What will they do without milk cows?

"Can we take yellow cow to Tjikuu?" I ask. "She needs a cow to milk."

"You can take omaere," Tate says. "But you can't take a cow. The Germans would kill it. They say even the dirt in Tjikuume's kraal would make cows sick."

Tate talks with his brothers about the cattle sickness. The ancestors told him to move our cattle from the field into the mountains, far from the other herds.

Mama and I put food in a bundle for Tate and Ramata. They will be gone for many days. Uncle Kozondanda will stay in the village while the other uncles help Tate move the cattle. Tate takes Mama and me into his secret healing garden to show us a special plant that is medicine for the milk cows.

"Look at the shape of the leaves," he says. He makes me feel the stalk. "See the color? When these plants are gone, you can find more growing in the veld, but you must get the right plant."

He takes us into the veld to find the plant. I look and look. "Is this the plant for cow medicine?" I bend down to pull a plant from the earth.

"No, Jahohora. Don't touch that." Tate pulls me back. "That is a bad plant. If you touch it, you will get sores all over your body. It could make you very sick." He shows me the medicine plant again. "See the difference?"

I look hard at the two plants. Then I hunt again for the medicine plant. "Here's one, Tate!" I shout.

Tate looks at it. "Very good, Jahohora." He smiles at me. "Now don't forget what it looks like."

We pull several plants from the earth and take them back to the village. Tate shows Mama and me how to prepare the roots of the plant to make medicine. "Mix this in the food for cows so they don't get sick. But just a little. Like this." He shows us how much medicine plant root to put with grass for the milk cows. "Don't let the cows eat the whole plant. It will make their belly hurt," he says. "Then they won't eat or give milk."

While Tate and Ramata are gone, I watch the milk cows. When the sun wakes each morning, I go to the kraal. I check my cow first. I look at her mouth, eyes, and nose. Just like Tate did. "You don't have the sickness, do you?" I ask yellow cow.

She moos and rubs her head against me. I scratch her ears and give her food with the medicine plant. She eats. I check the other cows. They don't look sick either. I make sure they eat.

Every day, Tuaekua Ehi and I go into the veld to get more cow medicine. I show my cousin what the medicine plant looks like. When she finds some, I make sure it's the right plant. We put the medicine plant outside the kraal so the cows won't eat it.

One morning, yellow cow won't eat. I look at her mouth, her eyes, and her nose. She looks all right. I check her dung. There's no blood. I try and try to get her to eat. She hangs her head. "Please eat," I tell her. "I don't want you to die."

But yellow cow won't eat.

"Mama!" I shout as I run toward our hut. "Mama! Yellowcowwonteat!" I'm crying, so my words fall together.

Mama comes out. "What's the matter?" she asks.

"Yellowcowwon'teat. Shecan'thavethesickness. Igavehermedicineeveryday." I talk too fast.

Mama doesn't understand. "Slowly," she says.

I take a deep breath. "Yellow ... cow ... won't ... eat."

"Did you give her the medicine plant?"

"Every day. But not today. She won't eat it today."

Mama goes to the kraal with me. She looks at yellow cow's mouth and eyes. She tries to feed the cow. But yellow cow hangs her head. "I don't see anything wrong with her. Maybe she's not hungry today," Mama says.

Uncle Kozondanda comes over to the kraal. He checks yellow cow, too. Then he looks at the dung in the kraal. "Where is the medicine plant?" he asks me.

I show him where Tuaekua Ehi and I put it next to the kraal. It's all gone. "Where did it go?" I ask.

Uncle smiles. "I think it's in yellow cow's belly. That's why she isn't eating." He tells Mama to put yellow cow by herself for a few days. Until we know she doesn't have the sickness.

A few days later, the chief's headmen and two white men ride into our village on horses. They want Tate. Uncle Kozondanda tells them to keep their horses far away from our kraal. They take their horses into the veld and let them graze. The men walk toward Mama and Uncle Kozondanda. The headmen ask for Tate again.

"He's not here," Uncle Kozondanda says.

"Where is he?"

Uncle shrugs.

"When will he be back?" the headmen ask.

"I don't know," Uncle says. "Maybe in a few days."

The headmen say the white people are angry because Tate told Tjikuume and uncles to move their cattle. Moving cattle won't stop the sickness, they say. Only killing cattle will end the sickness.

The white men point at the milk cows in the kraal. They make strange words with the headmen. "Why haven't they been killed?" one headman asks Mama and Uncle Kozondanda.

"They're not sick," Mama says quietly. "Why should we kill cows that aren't sick?"

The white men check the cows. They see yellow cow. The headmen ask Mama why yellow cow is by herself.

"She ate too much medicine plant, so her belly hurt," Mama says. "But she's better now. She's eating."

The white men make more strange words with the headmen. One reaches for a small boom stick in a pouch strapped to his belly. The headmen tell Mama the white men want to kill yellow cow so they can make medicine for the white people's cattle.

"No, that's my cow," I shout.

The headmen look up at the sky. They look down at the ground. They look across the veld. But they don't look at me.

Mama pulls me to her. "They can only make medicine from sick cows," she says. "Yellow cow isn't sick."

The headmen make strange words with the white men again. One of them points at Mama. I hear the headmen say Tate's name. The white man puts the boom stick back in his pouch. Anger covers his face.

The headmen turn back to Mama. When Tate returns, they say, he must come to see the chief.

Tate comes home many days later. Ramata and uncles are staying in the mountains with the cattle. Mama tells Tate about the headmen. He sighs. "I will go to see the chief tomorrow," he says.

Tate wakes up before the sun and goes out to the holy fire. Yesterday touches tomorrow in early morning and when the sun goes to sleep. That's when the ancestors are close. So that's when Tate talks to them. I put wood on the fire to keep it burning. I hear Tate telling the ancestors about the headmen's visit and his journey to see the chief. He asks the ancestors to help him. Tate looks very tired.

"Can I come with you to the chief's house?" I ask when Tate is done talking with the ancestors.

"Not today," he says. "But you can get more medicine plant for the cows. I will give it to the chief."

I smile. Getting medicine plant for the chief is important work. I go into the veld and pick lots of medicine plant. I like helping Tate.

PEOPLE SICKNESS

Many seasons pass before the cattle sickness ends. Ramata and the uncles finally bring our cattle home. "The ancestors were good to us," Tate says. "None of our cattle got the sickness. But the Herero who live near Germans had to kill all their cattle. Even if they weren't sick."

Tate is sitting by the holy fire. I hear him talking with his brothers. "They forgot the ancestors," Tate says, shaking his head. "They followed the way of the white people. Now they have no cattle."

"I think more trouble is coming," Uncle Kozondanda says. He has just come from the chief's village. "Many Herero chiefs lost their cattle. Now they are selling more and more Herero land to white people so they can buy new cattle."

"But land is a gift from Njambi Karunga," Tate says. "It's not theirs to sell."

Uncle Kozondanda nods. "The white people don't know that. They think a paper signed by a chief gives them the land. So the chiefs take their money. When Herero cattle become many again, they will graze on the land as our cattle always have done."

Tate frowns. "The Germans will never let that happen. Once they take something, they hold it tightly to their chest. Even if they don't need it."

After the cattle sickness ends, the people sickness comes. Tate heals many people. But many die. And some Herero refuse to see him. They want the medicine of the white people. "Germans brought the sickness," Tate says. "How can they heal it?"

"How did they bring the people sickness?" I ask Tate as he sits by the holy fire.

"Germans brought many cattle from other lands. Sick cattle. And when the sickness spread to the Herero cattle, the Germans made the Herero kill them — even the cattle of the ancestors. Taking care of the ancestors' cattle is a sacred duty for the Herero. By killing their cattle, the Herero made the ancestors angry. Now, many Herero have no food. Without omaere, they get weak and die," he says.

"Can we give them food?"

Tate smiles, but he looks sad. "We have given omaere to your mama's clan and the chief. We do not have enough to feed all the Herero."

Mama asks me to help her tan a goat skin. She lays it out near the holy fire. I take fat from a jar and rub it deep into the skin. I work hard as the sun shines down on me. The sun makes me too hot. I have to sit down. My belly hurts. It pushes up toward my throat and spills out of my mouth.

"I hurt," I tell Tate. "Do I have the sickness? I don't want to die." I hold my belly.

Tate touches my belly and then my head. He looks at my skin. He shakes his head. "It's not the sickness. Your body is just cleaning itself."

A few days later, Mama's brothers come to Tate. Tjikuume is very sick, they say. He needs a healer. Tate must hurry, or it will be too late. Tate goes into his secret garden and wraps many herbs in a skin. Mama, Ramata, Karemarama, and I go with Tate to Tjikuume's village.

When we get there, Tjikuu cries and hugs Mama. Tjikuume has already gone to the ancestors, she tells us. We look at Tjikuume lying on a cow skin. Big sores cover his body. His eyes are closed. He looks like he's sleeping.

"Mama, wake Tjikuume," Karemarama says. "I want to talk to him."

Mama is crying. "We can't wake him," she says softly. "He's sleeping his final sleep."

"Why?" I ask. "We gave Tjikuume omaere. He had food."

"Tjikuume had seen many, many seasons," Mama says. "He was growing weak. Then his soul got sick when he had to kill his milk cows and the cows of the ancestors."

"Tate helped kill the cows," I remind her. "Is his soul sick?"

"Tate is a strong man. He has many seasons before him."

I play with my cousins while Mama, Tjikuu, Mama Vitjitua, and the other women take care of Tjikuume. I race with Uapiruka. He slows down so I can catch up with him. I like Uapiruka. He is Ramata's age mate, but he doesn't tease me like Ramata does.

Just before the sun says goodnight to the day, we sit at the holy fire. Tate doesn't sit with Mama and us because he keeps his own fire. Uncle Horere – Mama's oldest brother and Uapiruka's tate – tells the ancestors who is there. He names the ancestors and reports that Tjikuume has joined them. He puts out the holy fire of Tjikuume. Uncle Horere will start a new fire. He is now the keeper of the omuriro omurangere for the Omukuatjivi clan.

Tjikuume's favorite ox, the black one with brown stripes, comes in from the field, calling softly. He knows Tjikuume has gone. Now it is his time.

Tate helps uncles take the life from black ox with brown stripes. They cannot use a knife. No blood must spill when we're mourning. But once the ox is dead, they use a knife to cut the skin away from the meat and bone. Tjikuume was an important man, so some uncles say many oxen must be killed for his feast. Uncle Horere says too many cattle died during the sickness. There aren't enough cattle for a huge feast. Uncles agree to kill four more oxen.

Uncles wrap Tjikuume in the skin of the black ox and lift him to their shoulders. Tate asks Tjikuume where he wants to be buried. Uncles wait for an answer. If he isn't buried right, the family will be cursed.

"There," Uncle Horere points toward a thorn tree growing by the kraal. Uncles dig a big hole under the tree. They put Tjikuume in the hole and cover his body with dirt. They put the horns of the slaughtered oxen on the tree that marks Tjikuume's grave.

Tate goes home with Ramata and Karemarama. But Mama and I stay with Tjikuu for many days. Mama says women are at birth and at death. It is our part in the circle of life.

Lots of people come to tell Tjikuu stories about Tjikuume. They tell about good things and bad things Tjikuume did. I ask Mama why.

"It gives balance to his life," she says. "And it helps clean our sadness."

Mama Uiiue, the sister of Tjikuume, tells a story about when her brother was a boy like Ramata. "He was teasing me," she says. "Our tjikuu told him if he didn't stop, she would beat him with a switch. He didn't believe her, so he kept teasing me. 'I told you,' Tjikuu said quietly." Mama Uiiue talks like her tjikuu.

We laugh.

"When Tjikuu went to get a switch, my brother ran away so he wouldn't get beaten. He ran and ran and ran until he could run no more. Then he walked and walked and walked. He stopped only when he thought Tjikuu would never come that far," Mama Uiiue says. "But Tjikuu was a strong, stubborn woman. She walked half the day, switch in hand, until she caught up with him. Without saying a word, she beat him. Then she went home. After the beating, brother was too tired to run. He was even too tired to walk so he spent the night out on the veld with all the wild animals. He came home the next day. And he never disobeyed Tjikuu again."

I laugh again with Mama and the others. It's hard to think of Tjikuume as a boy. He was always an old man to me.

When the mourning time ends, our family goes to the tree by Tjikuume's grave. Uncle Horere sprinkles us with water and uses a tree leaf to wash the sadness from us.

Mama says we are ready to go home. We will not take sadness with us.

TUAEKUA EHI

I am playing storyteller with some cousins when I see Tuaekua Ehi and ask her to play. She is the best storyteller in the village. "I can't," she says. "I must go with Tjikuu."

Later, I ask Mama why Tuaekua Ehi went away.

"It's time for her to become a woman," she tells me. "Her tjikuu is teaching her the way of being a grown woman."

"What are they doing?"

Mama smiles. "You will learn when it's your time."

Three days later, a strange young woman walks into our village. She wears a long skindress, a headdress, many bangles, and ankle and wrist cuffs.

"What clan do you belong to?" I ask her.

"You don't recognize me?" The young woman laughs shyly.

I look very closely. The voice is Tuaekua Ehi. But this is a woman, not a girl. Is this some kind of trick? "Who are you?" I ask.

"It's me. Tuaekua Ehi."

"You sound like Tuaekua Ehi. But you don't look like her," I say.

She laughs again. "It's just the clothes, Jahohora."

"No," I say. "You're not Tuaekua Ehi."

"Yes, I am. I've just grown up."

"In three days?"

Ramata and the other cousins come over. They tease Tuaekua Ehi. Then they ask her to race. She is very fast. The boys always try to beat her. But they can't.

Tuaekua Ehi shakes her head. "I can't race anymore," she says.

"Why not?" Ramata asks.

"That's for children. I'm no longer a child."

That night, all the family gathers at the holy fire. Tate tells the ancestors Tuaekua Ehi has become a woman.

A few days later, Tuaekua Ehi comes to visit Mama and me to tell us she's getting married. She's been promised for many years. Now she's a woman, so the day of her marriage has been set. The whole village is excited. I'm happy, but I'm also sad. When Tuaekua Ehi gets married, she will move to the village of Vijanda, her husband.

"You will still get to see her," Mama tells me.

"Not every day," I say. Vijanda lives in Tjikuu's village. He is a cousin from Mama's clan.

At last, the day is here. Vijanda's family comes to our village. They build small huts of branches behind Tuaekua Ehi's house. That's where they'll stay until the marriage is done. Uncle Kozondanda gives Vijanda's family a cow to kill for food.

Just before the sun sleeps, both families meet at the kraal for okuhitisa ongombe, the ceremony of take cow in kraal. Strange cows are in the kraal; they belong to Vijanda's family.

Tuaekua Ehi is led to the kraal. Her head is covered with a goat skin so she can't see. One at a time, young men lift her covering and say mean things about her. Everyone laughs.

"That's the biggest nose I've seen until now," one of the men says as he lifts the veil.

"That's not funny," I whisper to Mama. "And it's not true. Tuaekua Ehi doesn't have a big nose."

Mama smiles. "Those men are Vijanda's age mates. They must protect Tuaekua Ehi," she says. "They insult her so she will know who to go to if she needs help."

"Why would she want help from someone who says mean things about her?" I ask.

"They are only saying those things so she will remember who they are. A woman never forgets the face of a man who insults her," Mama says.

After the last age mate has his say, the goat skin is lowered once again so Tuaekua Ehi can't see. She is led into the kraal and told to gently hit one of the cows. We all laugh as she stumbles and feels her way toward the cows. They call out softly and back away from her. Finally, she touches a cow – the red one with a stripe on its face. That cow now belongs to her.

When the sun wakes the next morning, the families come together again. Oruramua, the meat from cow's mouth, is taken to Vijanda. He kisses it. It is then given to Tuaekua Ehi for her to kiss. "Why do they do that?" I ask Mama.

"It shows that they are now tied together as husband and wife," she says.

After oruramua, Mama makes Karemarama and me rest. "But I'm not sleepy," I tell her.

"We will have lots of singing and dancing later," she says. "You need to rest."

I lie down, but I don't sleep. I'm too excited. This is the first marriage I remember.

In the afternoon, we all meet at the house of Uncle Kozondanda. He gives orunde to Vijanda's family. They give him the same piece of meat from one of their cows. Vijanda's clan sits on the ground on one side; our clan sits on the other. Each clan chooses its best singers and dancers. They try to outdo each other. All afternoon and long after the sun sleeps, they sing traditional outjina and dance omuhiva. I think my clan is the best. Then I remember Vijanda is a cousin, too. Both sides are my family. I watch Uapiruka dance for Vijanda's family. He is very good. He sees me watching and smiles. I clap and cheer. He is the best dancer, I think. Soon, we are all singing and dancing and laughing together. Until now, I have never had so much fun.

I am tired when the party is over. But I have trouble going
to sleep. My feet hurt from dancing and I keep thinking about
Uapiruka smiling at me.

Before the sun wakes the next morning, Tate calls the village
to the holy fire.

"It is time to tell Tuaekua Ehi goodbye," Mama says as she
makes me get up.

I stumble sleepily into the morning twilight and take my
place at the fire. Vijanda's clan is told to take their wife. Elders
from both families give Vijanda and Tuaekua Ehi advice on being
a good husband and wife. Tate tells them to find balance in their
lives. "But if you can't find peace, come get me," he says. Both
families laugh.

Tate turns to the holy fire to tell the ancestors that Tuaekua
Ehi is married and is leaving her family. "Do not look for her
here anymore," he says. "She is going to the village of Vijanda."
He names Vijanda's ancestors so our ancestors know where to
find her.

Tuaekua Ehi hugs me before she leaves with Vijanda's family.
"Come see me soon, little cousin," she tells me. "I will miss you."

I'm quiet. I don't want her to leave. I go into the house so I
don't see her walk away from the village.

Mama finds me there later. "What's wrong, Jahohora?" she
asks.

"I miss Tuaekua Ehi."

Mama laughs. "She's only been gone a little bit."

"What do you think she's doing?" I ask.

"It's almost time for the ondjova."

"What is that?"

"It's when Tuaekua Ehi is introduced to Vijanda's ancestors
at his family's holy fire. She will eat sheep meat with Vijanda.
And when they're done, they'll bury what's left in a secret place."

I wrinkle my face. "Why do they do that?"

"If any animals eat what's left, Tuaekua Ehi or Vijanda might
die."

I look at Mama to see if she's teasing. There's no smile on her
face. "I hope they bury it deep in the ground. I don't want bad to
come to Tuaekua Ehi," I say.

TJIKUU

Karemarama and I stay with Tjikuu while Tate and Mama arrange a marriage for Ramata. Tate has already gone to the girl's family. But now Mama must join him to settle it.

"Will Ramata have one wife?" I ask as I help Tjikuu gather wild berries.

Tjikuu sighs. "One is enough for now. A man with many wives and children must have many cattle. After the sickness, Herero cattle are few. It is hard to have more than one wife today."

"One wife is good," I say. "Mama is Tate's only wife."

"Your tate is a healer. He likes peace." Tjikuu chuckles as she moves to the next bush. "When I was a girl, most Herero men had several wives and lots of children. Then the Missionary came. He said it is evil to have more than one wife. So the Herero who followed Missionary had to choose one wife to stay with. They left their other wives with no husband and no father for their children."

Tjikuu shakes her head as she continues picking berries. "I don't understand white people. The German farmers and soldiers have one wife, but they take many women. Then they leave those women when their bellies get big with babies and go back to their wives. That is evil."

We pick berries in silence. My thoughts run in many paths – from the strangeness of white people to my future marriage. "Tjikuu, when will Tate and Mama arrange my marriage?" I ask.

"It won't be long," she says. "But they have to wait for a boy's family to come to them."

"I hope he's nice and that I'll be his only wife."

Tjikuu shrugs. "You will do all right. After all, you come from the big house of Omukuatjivi, your father is an important healer, and you are his only daughter."

As we take berries back to Tjikuu's house, she softly sings an old song: "When you get in trouble where you are, go to the eagle." Tjikuu often sings this song when she's working.

"Tjikuu, what does that mean?" I ask. "How can an eagle help me?"

She stops singing and laughs. "The eagle is your mother, your aunt, your girl cousins – the eagle is any woman. Maybe even a white woman. When you have trouble, go to another woman. She will understand. And she can help you."

"Why shouldn't I go to a man?" I ask. I think of Tate and his wisdom.

I can't read Tjikuu's face as she looks deep into my eyes. She shrugs. "Men will always be men."

When we get back to Tjikuu's village, I go to see Tuaekua Ehi. Her belly is big. I smile at her shyly.

She pats her belly and smiles back. "I missed you, Jahohora," she says. "How is your family?"

I tell her Tate and Mama are arranging Ramata's marriage.

"Have they made a match for you yet?" she asks.

I shake my head.

"I'm surprised," she says. "Your mama's brothers have lots of sons."

I swallow. Until today, I hadn't thought about my marriage. "Do you like being a wife?" I ask Tuaekua Ehi.

She shrugs. "We are women. We get married so men have a place to live and we have a father for our children." We both laugh. It's an old joke.

"Vijanda is a good husband. And he will be a good father." Tuaekua Ehi pauses. "I do miss my parents. And I miss playing with you." She looks down at her belly. "But I will have my own child to play with soon."

That night, I sit outside Tjikuu's house and look up at the sky. The stars shine like many cow eyes in firelight. As I gaze deep into the sky, I see the colors of the stars – white, yellow, red, and blue – all blazing against the blackness. I jump up and stretch my arms out, trying to reach the stars. I laugh at myself and sit down again.

Tjikuu joins me. She looks up at the stars and frowns. "The rains will be late."

"How can you tell?" I ask.

She points up at a bright red star. "See where that firespot is? That means the rains will come late. If it were over there," she points again, "it would mean the rains won't come at all."

We sit silently, looking at the stars. I move closer to her. "Tjikuu, where does the sky begin?" I ask.

"The sky is like life," she says. "There is no beginning or end. It is." She hums quietly.

"It makes me feel small," I say after awhile.

She chuckles. "When you look at the sky and the veld, we are small. But we are all part of the circle of life. Yesterday, these stars," she points to the brightest lights in the sky, "all shone down on the ancestors. Now they're shining on us. Tomorrow, they will shine on your children."

* * * * *

Karemarama wakes me early the next morning. He wants to play. I go outside with him. "Race you," he says, running toward the veld.

"That's not fair," I call after him. "You cheat — just like Ramata!" I run after him and quickly pass him. He may have long legs, but they're not as long as mine.

"Jahohora!" I turn to see who's calling my name.

It's Uapiruka. I slow down so he can catch up. "I heard you were visiting Tjikuu," he says.

"Yes. Mama and Tate are arranging Ramata's marriage." I laugh shyly. I've never been shy around Uapiruka before.

"I know. Mama's been talking about my marriage."

"Has it already been arranged?" I don't like the thought of Uapiruka getting married.

"No. But I heard Mama telling Tate that it's time to settle it," he says.

We walk back toward the village. Karemarama throws a rock ahead of us and then runs to pick it up. He tosses it again.

"And you?" Uapiruka asks me. "Have you been promised?"

"Not yet."

Uapiruka smiles at me. "What if they arrange for us to marry?"

I feel warm inside. I want to say I'd like that. Instead, I run toward Tjikuu's house. "I'll beat you," I call over my shoulder.

Uapiruka laughs as he runs after me.

The next day, Mama comes to Tjikuu's house. "It's settled," she says. "Ramata will marry Ngambui when she's old enough."

Tjikuu smiles and nods her head. "It's a good match."

"Ngambui? She's younger than me," I say. Ngambui is the daughter of Tate's oldest sister.

"Yes," Mama says, "but she will be a good wife for Ramata."

"Where's Tate?" Karemarama asks.

"He had to go see the chief after we arranged the marriage," Mama says. She sighs. Tate has become an important adviser to the chief so he's gone a lot. Mama's proud of Tate. But she misses him when he's not home. Life is out of balance when he's gone, she says.

Everyone respects Tate now. Even the white people. They know Tate is a man of peace. And his words carry wisdom and healing.

As we leave Tjikuu's village, I see Uapiruka walking with his father. I smile at him.

"Goodbye, Jahohora," he calls to me. "See you soon. And you too, Karemarama."

Uncle Horere looks at me. Then he turns to Mama. He asks about Tate.

"He's with the chief," she says.

"When will he be back?" Uncle asks.

"In a few weeks."

Uncle nods.

THE GAME

I walk to the kraal with Mama. It's time to milk the cows. Mama pushes me in the back. "Is your mama dead?" she asks. It's her usual saying when I don't stand tall.

I put my shoulders back and hold my head high. I notice I'm nearly as tall as Mama.

She sees, too. "You'll be a woman soon," she says. "Then someday you'll have your own daughter."

"And you'll be a tjikuu," I tease.

Mama smiles.

I stop teasing. "When Ramata gets married, where will he and Ngambui live?"

"They'll make a house here – close to Tate and me," she says.

"Will I get to live here, too?"

"You will go to your husband's village. Like Tuaekua Ehi did when she married Vijanda. Like I did when I married your tate. And like Tjikuu did when she married Tjikuume."

"But what if I want to stay here? Close to you and Tate?"

Mama pats my hand. "It's the way of women," she says. "They live with their husband's clan."

"That's not fair," I say. "I don't want to get married if I have to leave you and Tate."

"It will be different when you're older," she says. "Then you'll be ready to have your own house."

Tate comes home a few days later. He and Mama talk in low tones so I can't hear their words. They both have worry on their faces all day. In the evening, Tate sits by the holy fire as the sun sinks toward its sleep. I see his mouth moving, but no words come out. I know he's talking to the ancestors. He looks very tired.

Mama sees me watching him. "Jahohora," she calls. "Come help me finish grinding the maize before it gets too dark to see."

As we mash the maize between two big stones, Mama is quiet. Usually, she sings a praise song while we grind.

Tate is talking with his brothers by the fire when I go into the hut to sleep. Their shadows dance against the flames as they lean toward each other and gesture. I can hear their voices, but I can't hear their words. They sound upset – as if they're arguing. Their voices weave in and out of my thoughts as I doze off, mixing with my dreams.

I wake up when Tate comes in. He and Mama talk quietly. Again, I can't hear most of the words. But I do hear enough to know the white people have done something. Since the white people live far from us, what they do doesn't matter to me. I yawn and roll over on the herb-scented skin, finding sleep once more. This time, it's a sleep without grownup whispers.

Mama is quiet the next day when we milk the cows. She has no songs, no stories, no smile. I ask her a question, but her ears are closed. Her bangles clang loudly in the silence.

"Uri naua?" I ask her.

Mama looks at me, but her eyes don't see me.

"Mama, uri naua?" I ask again, a little louder.

Mama sighs. This time she sees me. She tries to smile. "I'm all right," she says.

I can tell she's not. I watch her move through the day as if she's not there. I have never seen Mama like this. I don't like it.

As the sun begins its goodbye to the day, Mama and I cook in silence. Tate sits just as silently by the holy fire. I think he's talking to the ancestors again. Suddenly, he laughs. It's a strange sound. Tate hasn't laughed for many days.

Mama looks over at him. "What's wrong?" she asks.

"Look," he says, pointing to the veld behind our house.

I look where he's pointing, but I don't see anything. Then something – or someone – moves toward our hut.

"I think we're about to have visitors," Tate says. He sounds more like himself.

I look again. Now I can make out a few people. "It's a strange time to visit," I mumble.

"That depends on why they're coming," Tate says. He gives Mama a funny smile. Because of Tate's talk with the uncles and Mama, I think the visitors might be white men. But when the people stop close to the house, I see they are Herero. I recognize them. One is Uncle Horere. The others are older cousins and a few of the other uncles from Mama's clan.

"Why did they stop behind our house? What are they waiting for?" I ask Mama.

"The sun," she says.

I look toward the far-off mountains where the sun is sending out the last light of the day. Just as it is about to slip behind the mountains, Uncle and the men with him drop to the ground. Moving on their knees, they approach Tate.

"Let's go inside," Mama tells me. She smiles at Tate. She looks happy again.

I want to stay outside, but I follow Mama into the house. I'm surprised when she stands just inside. She motions for me to stand on the other side of the opening.

"What's going on?" Karemarama asks. He's been playing in the hut.

"Shhhh," Mama tells him.

I peek outside. I listen hard to hear Tate's words.

He greets the visitors. "What brings you here?" he asks.

"We came to ask for one of your female sheep so we can put it together with one of ours and they can live together," Uncle Horere says, still kneeling.

"I hear you," Tate says very seriously.

Mama covers her laughter.

"What are they talking about?" I whisper. "We don't have sheep – only goats and cows."

Mama pulls me away from the opening. "They don't want a sheep," she says. "They want you."

"Me? I don't want to live with one of Uncle's sheep."

Mama laughs again. "They're asking for you to be Uapiruka's bride."

My eyes get big. I swallow. "Why don't they just say that instead of asking about sheep?" My face feels hot, but happiness fills me.

"They're men," Mama says. "They have to play their games."

"So what did Tate's answer mean?"

"Nothing yet."

I must look sad, because Mama says, "That's the way they play the game. He can't say yes the first time."

Tate calls to Mama and me to bring food for our visitors. The men sit around the holy fire as we serve them. I feel their eyes watching me as I give meat to Uncle Horere. Uncle smiles at me. The others laugh.

The men talk by the fire until late in the night. Mama sends Karemarama and me to bed.

"Are they staying here all night?" I ask.

"They'll sleep behind the hut," she tells me. "But they'll be gone before you get up in the morning."

She's right. When I go to milk the cows in the morning, I look toward the veld behind the hut. There's no sign of Uncle Horere and the others.

The next few days Karemarama teases me. "J'hora's a sheep," he says. "An' she's going to live with sheep."

"Mama, make him stop," I say.

Mama just smiles.

"Baa-aa-aa," Karemarama teases.

"That's enough," Mama finally tells him. But she's still smiling. It's good to see her smile again.

When Ramata comes home from tending the cattle, Karemarama is the first to tell him about Uncle Horere's visit. I wait for Ramata to tease me, too. But he doesn't.

"Uapiruka?" he asks. "I like him. And he will be a good husband. He's the eldest son of the eldest uncle – and he has a lot of uncles to inherit from. He will be a good father for all my nephews."

"What if I have daughters?" I ask.

"You must have sons to inherit all my wealth," Ramata teases. "But you'll also need to have lots of daughters to marry the sons Karemarama and I will have."

"I'm not getting married," Karemarama says.

Ramata and I laugh. "That's not your choice," Ramata tells him.

Our days follow their old routine, except Tate goes to see the chief again. With Tate gone so much, Ramata has to spend more time with the cattle in the fields. Tate used to share the work with him.

"When will Uncle Horere come again?" I ask Mama more than once. "Do you think Tate scared him away?"

She laughs. "Give him time," she says. "He'll want to make sure Tate is going to be home."

Sure enough, a few evenings after Tate returns, I see a small group of men approaching the back of our hut. Once again, they drop to their knees as the sun goes to sleep behind the mountains. And once again, Tate sends me inside the house with Mama.

I stand close to the doorway so I can hear them talk. This time Uncle Horere asks for one of Tate's female goats to live with his goat. Great. Now I'm a goat.

"Baa-aa-aa," Karemarama says as he crawls toward me with his head down as if he's going to ram me.

Mama laughs and hushes him. We don't hear Tate's answer.

I'm sleeping when Tate comes in late that night, but I wake up when I hear Mama's voice.

"What did you tell my brother?" she asks.

"I said, 'I heard you.'"

Mama laughs softly. "You're making him come back again?"

"Jahohora is my only daughter," Tate says. "She's worth coming back for. And I want to have my fun."

Mama is silent for a long time. I think she and Tate have gone to sleep. I'm thinking about being Uapiruka's wife when I hear Mama's voice again. "Do you think this is the right time to promise her? We don't know what's going to happen." Once again, the happiness is gone from Mama's voice. Instead, there's fear. But what is she afraid of?

"From the time the Germans first came to Hereroland until now, we have not known what tomorrow will bring," Tate says.

His words come slowly and quietly, like he's trying to calm Mama. "All we know for sure is that the sun will rise in the morning. And the ancestors will be here with us. We must live as we always have. But we must be ready for tomorrow. We can sleep better knowing our daughter is promised to a good man who will take care of her. The ancestors are smiling on her."

Mama smiles more the next few days. But her eyes don't smile. They are sad, even though Tate stays at home. I catch her looking off into the distance as if she's waiting for something or someone to come across the veld. I think she's waiting for Uncle Horere. Maybe she's sad because he hasn't come back yet.

A few days later, Uncle Horere returns for the third time. From inside the house, I hear him once again asking for a female goat.

Tate nods. "You can return home. I will let you know when it's time for Okukomba," he says.

I see a big smile spread across Uncle Horere's face as he sits by the fire with Tate.

"Okukomba? What does cleaning have to do with marriage?" I whisper to Mama as we stand close to the doorway.

Mama spreads her hands. "It's part of the game," she says. "It means the marriage is almost arranged. But for now, we've got hungry men to feed."

* * * * *

The sun beats down on me, making beads of sweat shine on my arms. I work hard as I tan a new goat skin. I stretch and look up at the sky to see if I have time to finish the skin before the sun sleeps. The sun is already beginning its day-end ritual. I bend over the skin again. I should be able to get it done before dark. I am so busy with my work that I don't notice the people coming across the veld until Mama says something to Tate. I look up to see Uapiruka's tate and mama coming toward us on their knees. Several other people, including some of my aunties, are with them.

"Go in the house, Jahohora," Tate tells me.

I wait for Mama to join me. But this time, she stays outside with him.

Again, I hear Uncle Horere ask for a female goat to live with his goats.

"It is fine," Tate says. Uncle and Auntie stand up. They smile big smiles.

"We will tell you when the wedding will be," Tate says.

Uncle Horere and the other men sit with Tate. I help the women cook a small feast. As I give Uncle Horere food, I realize that soon I will be living in his village. The thought makes me sad. I will have to leave Tate and Mama. And Ramata and Karemarama. But I'm also happy. Tjikuu lives in Uncle's village. Tuaekua Ehi lives there, too. And so does Uapiruka.

Our visitors sleep behind our house that night. They will leave before the sun greets the morning. But I don't think about tomorrow. I'm enjoying tonight. It is a clear night. The full moon and the stars make it almost as light as day. As I look up at the sky, I'm reminded of what Tjikuu said about the stars shining down on my children. They will be the children of Uapiruka and me. I smile. And thank the ancestors.

I sing as I help Mama milk the cows the next morning.

"You sound happy," she says.

I nod. "When will the marriage be?" I ask her.

"It wasn't that long ago that you said you never wanted to leave Tate and me," she says, "but now you're in a hurry to go."

"No, Mama. That's not what I mean."

"I know." She smiles sadly. "The marriage will come after you become a woman."

"When will that be?" I ask.

"It's different for every girl." She looks at me from the tips of my feet to the top of my head. Her eyes focus on my bare breasts that are starting to stick out a little. "It will probably be a few more seasons."

We finish with the cows and the mixing of the omaere. "I'm glad you're going to marry someone you like," Mama tells me. "You and Uapiruka will balance each other. Just like Tate and I do. Uapiruka is a good man. He's slow to anger. That will be important tomorrow."

"What do you mean, Mama? What are you so worried about?" I ask.

Mama sighs deeply and walks back toward our hut without answering me.

STORM CLOUDS

The wind wakes me up. It whistles as it swirls around our hut. And then I hear the thunder. Echoing through the veld, getting louder as it approaches our village. The rain, when it comes, crashes against the ground. I snuggle against my cow skin, happy that I'm inside where I'm dry and protected from the wind. Then I remember the holy fire. It's not rainy season, so we didn't think to protect the fire. If it goes out, we can't start it again. Only Tate can do that. And he's with the chief. The ancestors will think we've forgotten them.

I hurry out into the darkness. I see no light from the fire. The wind and rain beat against my body as I hurry to the fire circle. Lightning crackles across the sky. In the bright flash, I think I see a thin whisper of smoke swirling away with the wind. It's too late to weave branches into a protecting shield. But maybe the fire is alive enough to carry into the house.

More lightning streaks the sky. I see Mama standing in the opening of the hut. I think she's calling to me, but I can't hear her over the thunder and roaring wind.

Using my short skin skirt to protect my hands, I grab a piece of wood from the fire. I feel the heat rising from it as I bend over it to protect it from the wind and rain. I carefully, but quickly, carry it into the hut and lay it on top of a few pieces of dry wood Mama has set in the middle of our hut. I lean down to blow on the wood, hoping the wood will fan into flames. Mama gently pulls me back.

"The holy fire must start itself," she tells me.

"What if it doesn't?" I ask. I think back over the seasons. As far back as I can remember. But I can't think of one time the holy fire went out.

"It's a sign," Mama says quietly.

"Of what?"

"It means something is wrong with the family." Mama turns away from me. "Leave it be."

The next morning, I rise before the sun. Mama is sitting beside the wood in our hut, staring at the charred branch from the holy fire. There is no flame. No smoke. Just the faint smell of burnt wood. I step into the morning twilight, hoping that the fire outside is still burning. The rain has stopped, and the thirsty ground is already dry. I hold my hand low over the blackened branches and ashes. A few small coals still glow with a little heat. I lay small pieces of dry wood and grass on the coals. Maybe they will catch.

I look up. Mama is standing behind me, watching the fire. "Let's give it time to start," she says. Her voice sounds funny. It's flat. Without hope. I follow her as she heads toward the kraal to milk the cows.

After the cows are milked, we walk slowly back toward the fire. I think I see a tail of smoke curling upwards. But there is nothing. The coals are black and gray. And the splinters of wood and grass I had placed on the embers are cold to the touch. I cry. It's my job to keep the fire going. And I let it die. "I'm sorry, Mama."

"It's not your fault," she says. "Something is wrong." She catches her breath and sits on the ground, shaking her head. Fear is in her voice.

I remember her days of silence. The days without laughter or smiles. Of her hushed, worried talks with Tate. There's something she's not telling me. Maybe the bad luck is already here. I think of Tate. Of Ramata and Karemarama. Are they in danger? Or is it someone else in Tate's clan?

Mama is still sitting by the dead fire when Uncle Kozondanda walks by. He sees the fire is out and stops. "What happened?" he asks. I hear the worry in his voice.

"The storm," Mama says quietly.

"It is not a good sign. Especially now." He looks down at the ground. "When will Mutihu be home?" Tate is the only one who can start the fire again.

"Soon, I hope." Mama sighs.

For the next several days, Mama keeps Karemarama and me close to her. I often see her looking across the veld. She's waiting for Tate and Ramata. I know she's afraid for them. Aunties and uncles also are afraid. The holy fire is for the whole family. When it goes out, it's a bad sign for everyone.

* * * * *

I'm helping Mama cook when I see Tate coming across the veld. "Mama, it's Tate!" I call.

She looks up. She has no smile. But her face is lighter – as if a big load of rocks has been taken from her back.

Tate raises his hand to greet us. He seems tired. As he reaches the clearing in front of our hut, he stops by the holy fire. His mouth drops open. He sits down quickly. "How?" he asks.

"A thunderstorm put it out," Mama says.

"A storm? When?" He nods slowly when Mama tells him. "Is everyone all right?" Tate sounds worried.

"Ramata and some of your brothers are still with the cattle. Everyone else is here."

"Good," Tate says.

As soon as the sun goes to sleep, Tate starts the holy fire again. He's still talking with the ancestors and his brothers when I lie down for the night. I'm almost asleep when I hear him say the Germans have pushed Samuel Maharero into fighting them. Maharero is a Herero chief. The white people made him chief of all Herero. But Zeraua is still our chief.

I yawn and close my eyes. Maharero lives far from here. What he does has nothing to do with us. I roll over on my side and go to sleep.

Over the next few days, Tate and uncles talk about nothing except Maharero's war. Even though the fighting is far from us, the news has traveled throughout Hereroland. The white people are scared that their Herero neighbors will attack them. Chief Zeraua has told the white people many times that he wants only peace, but they don't believe him. Some of them are rounding up their Herero neighbors and putting them in fenced kraals, like cattle, to keep them from attacking. Other white people are killing Herero.

Although our chief has not joined the war and is asking his men to keep the peace, a few uncles want to join Maharero. "The white people will use this war to turn on all of us," one uncle says to the others who just want their families and cattle to be safe.

Tate tries to keep them calm. "Maharero has ordered that no Herero is to hurt German women and children. And he's given his protection to the missionaries," Tate says. "Surely the Germans will do the same. They will not harm our wives and children. And they know I am a peacemaker. If you, my brothers, show you will not make war, they will leave us alone.

"No white people have settled near us, so we should be safe." Tate looks at each of his brothers. "For now, we will keep the cattle close to our village. And we will all stay in the village, so the Germans don't mistake us for Maharero's men."

A few uncles and cousins go to the fields to get the cattle and the men who are watching them. I'm happy that Ramata is coming home. I would never tell him, but I miss his teasing. And ever since the storm put out the holy fire, I've been worried that I might not see him again.

Kov

PAPA

"I'll see you tomorrow, Kov!" Christof hollers as he heads out into the wintry afternoon.

"Kov, Kov," Papa mimics when the door shuts behind my friend. He picks up one of the tin soldiers I've painted and examines it critically. "Your name is Yaakov. It's a good name for a Jew. And it's the name your Mama and I gave you."

"But Papa, I prefer Kov. I think it's a better name for a German who happens to be Jewish." I know better than to provoke Papa, but sometimes I can't help myself.

"We are Jews who happen to live in Germany," he insists. "Be content with what God made you. You can't be both a German and a Jew. They will never forget you're a Jew."

"And you will never let me be a German," I say, a bit too mockingly.

He shakes his head sadly. "It's not worth the price, Yaakov."

The faraway look in his eyes signals the conversation is over. I know that look. I know where he has gone. To that moment, back in 1819, when his grandfather was beaten to death by a peasant mob during the Hep Hep Riots in Frankfurt. It was long before Papa was born, but the telling of it is so etched in his mind he might as well have lived it. For Papa, it was a wrong never righted, a memory never to be forgotten. It is a moment, he says, that sums up both the German character and the essence of being a Jew in Germany.

I look at Papa's rigid, frail body, prematurely aged by a world he can't forgive. And I promise myself that the tragic events that have defined my family's past won't dictate my future. But I have to admit Papa is right, at least partially. There are some Germans who passionately believe Jews don't belong in Germany – even if our families have been here for nearly a thousand years.

These notions have been around for generations. But ever since Fritsch published his manual on anti-Semitism a few years ago, the hate is growing – even here in Fürth, which has long been a refuge for Jews. I see it in the hooded stares at the market and hear it in the not-so-quiet whispers at school. I try to ignore them and focus instead on the Jews who have made a name for themselves as doctors, scientists, and even politicians. Papa says most of them are no longer Jews. Some of them might agree with him. But there are those who, even though they have converted, have not forgotten their roots.

Why else would Ritter von Epenstein ask Papa to make a special toy for his godson's birthday? With his wealth, he could have commissioned any of the famous Nüremburg spielwarenmachers to craft the little tin figures of the German officials who were the first to govern South West Africa. Instead, he came to Fürth to see Papa. Of course, Papa's handmade toys are a work of art. And everyone knows it.

Even though we can use the money, Papa isn't happy about doing business with the Jewish doctor's son who has bought himself a title and traded in his faith. Papa says you can't trust people who turn their backs on who they are.

I've heard stories – and whispers – about the ritter ever since he bought the ruins of Burg Veldenstein two years ago. But I'd never met him until he swept into our shop the other day. Physically, he's not a tall man, but his presence overwhelmed the workspace, making it seem even smaller than it is. And when Papa hesitated to accept the commission, Epenstein insisted in a formal but charming manner. He's obviously used to getting his way. He handed Papa some photographs of Reichskommissar Göring surrounded by African Herero for Papa to use as a guide.

Intrigued by this man who used to be a Jew and is now every inch a German noble, I ignored Papa's disapproving frown and volunteered to deliver the figures to Epenstein's castle when they're finished. With a nod in my direction, the ritter donned his hat and stepped briskly out into the cold winter air.

* * * * *

"Kov!"

I turn to see Christof grinning at me just as he throws a snowball in my direction. I duck as it whizzes inches above my head.

"Good timing." He laughs as he runs to catch up with me. "Hey, what are you doing tomorrow? We're all going skating on the river. You've got to come along."

Christof is my only friend who isn't Jewish. While I like doing things with him, I'm not comfortable with his friends. They don't make much of an effort to hide their dislike of me.

"I can't," I tell him, glad that I've got an excuse.

"Tell me you don't have to work tomorrow," he groans. "It's a school holiday."

"I'm not working in the shop. I have to make a special delivery."

"All day?"

I nod.

"Where are you going that it's taking you the whole day?"

"I'm taking the train to Burg Veldenstein." I try to keep the smugness out of my voice.

"The old ruins?" Christof's gray eyes open wide. He loves history and all things military. If the stories are true, the fortress is brimming with both.

"I'm not sure the castle is still considered a ruin," I tell him. "Ritter von Epenstein is restoring it."

"You've got to take me with you." Christof's face is lit with excitement. "This is going to be so much more fun than skating with Georg and Jan!"

BURG VELDENSTEIN

I like traveling with Christof. He knows more about the history and landmarks of the Bavarian countryside than I could have imagined. I don't know where he gets it; we sure haven't learned it at school. While I enjoy his conversation and the way he punctuates it with laughter, I also enjoy being silent with him. Christof is the only person I know whom I can be quiet around.

As the train rolls past the neat German farms spreading out from the winding Pegnitz River, I'm comfortably lost in my meandering thoughts. With Papa, I would be searching for some prattle to cover what would be an awkward silence. It's odd how Papa and I – who have lived, worked, and worshipped side by side – have so little in common. I know Papa finds it equally unsettling. The generational divide between his parents and him was merely a measure of age. But the many decades that separate us are uncrossable rifts in place, time, and culture. Mama was able to bridge those differences. When she died, I lost my connection to Papa.

"Neuhaus Village." The conductor's call cuts off any further thoughts. I glance out the window at the white stone houses with their red-tiled roofs that push up from the river to the foot of a steep cliff crowned by a medieval walled fortress.

Christof nudges me, pointing to the center of the fortress wall where an old stone tower crumbles down the hillside, its loose rocks threatening the village below. "Burg Veldenstein," he says quietly, trying not to sound like a tourist. "That must be the tower where they kept the gun powder. It exploded when it was hit by lightning about 200 years ago."

"It looks like Epenstein still has a lot of work to do," I respond, just as quietly. The buildings of the old fortress are built into its stone walls, which look like ragged outgrowths of the granite mountainside.

After getting directions from the stationmaster, we walk up the narrow cobbled roads of the market town, past the brewery and an old Catholic church, veering toward the castle ruins. A large stone portal announces the entrance to the castle grounds. A coat of arms, emblazoned in rock above the archway, speaks to the history of the place. Christof studies it for a minute or two. "That's Prince Bishop Henneberg's crest," he says.

"How do you know this stuff?" I ask.

He shakes his head and gives his funny smile. "I like the trivia of history. You never know when it will come in handy in a conversation – or on one of Herr Buchner's tests."

I laugh, remembering the perfect scores Christof got on Buchner's exams last year and the medal he won for being the outstanding student in German history.

Christof squints to read the worn script on the seal: "Master Erhart has built the walls, towers, and doors. God and the heavenly hosts will protect it. Amen."

"That's ironic, given the lightning strike," I say a bit sarcastically.

"Well, it did withstand a lot of attacks," Christof murmurs.

"Yes, but the one that toppled it came from heaven itself," I remind him.

"Aided by the gun powder stored inside," he says dryly.

As we enter from the outer wall, we are silenced by the incessant noise of the renovations, which had been a muffled thudding down in the village. Roofers, carpenters, and masons scramble along the wooden scaffolding that encases large sections of the inner walls and towers. We walk up a long, winding drive, pausing to watch as a master stonecutter carefully fits a freshly hewn rock into a gaping hole. I whistle softly. "At this pace, it will take a century to restore the fortress."

The drive curves with the edge of the granite cliff. A young boy jumps down from the wall, trying to block our passage. "Halt!" he orders with the authority of a commanding officer.

Startled, I size him up, taking in the cut-down Hussar dress uniform that's still too big for him. The blue wool is dressed up with gold shoulder boards and tin oak leaves on the stiff collar. The boy's pale blue eyes gaze steadily at us from under the brim of a soldier's hat kept in place only by his ears. His hand rests on the hilt of a wooden sword thrust into a leather belt that's tied, its brass buckle dangling against his thigh.

Trying not to laugh, Christof and I click our heels and salute in what we imagine to be perfect military form.

"State your business," the boy commands.

I step forward, holding out the package I've been carrying. "A delivery for Ritter von Epenstein."

He reaches to take it. "I shall deliver it to the Generalfeldmarschall."

Realizing this boy may be Epenstein's godson, I tuck the package securely under my arm and shake my head. "My orders are to deliver it to the Generalfeldmarschall himself – and only to him."

"Very well. Follow me." The boy does an about-face and marches toward a staircase that cuts up the hillside to the residence of the fortress. Resisting the urge to mimic his march, we fall in line behind him.

The boy leads us into the main hall. "Wait here," he orders us. He turns and marches down the long corridor, his steps repeating off the stone floor.

While we wait, Christof and I take in the medieval armor and the timeworn tapestries hanging on the old walls. I walk over to a suit of armor guarding a massive doorway, measuring myself against the hollow metal. "Whoever wore this must have been a child," I whisper to Christof, trying to keep my voice from echoing.

Christof shakes his head. "Funny how we always think of knights as being larger than life. But the truth is, most of them were smaller. We're actually getting bigger, you know – survival of the fittest and all that."

Before I can reply, I hear two sets of footsteps. Looking down the hall, I see a servant, dressed in medieval garb, hurrying in front of the portly ritter. Stopping in front of us, the servant bows and, with a flourish, announces the master of the castle.

As the servant steps out of the way, I feel as if I should bow. It somehow seems fitting in this fortress, and I am, after all, merely a delivery boy. Watching Christof from the corner of my eye, I take my cue from him and make an awkward half bow.

Epenstein acknowledges us with a nod of his dark head. "I see you have met General Göring, my godson," he says with a smile.

"Yes, sir. He seems like quite a boy. I am sure he will appreciate these tin soldiers." I hand him the package.

Box in hand, he leads us into a drawing room off the grand hall and shuts the door. Placing the package on a wooden table near a window, he carefully unties the twine securing it and opens the lid. One by one, he pulls the pieces out, holding them to the light so he can inspect them. "Ahhh. These are superb. Your father is truly an artist." He sets the pieces upright on the table.

"May I?" Christof hadn't seen the soldiers before Papa and I boxed them.

Epenstein waves him over. "These are not your typical tin soldiers. They're based on people I met and served with in German South West Africa."

"You were a soldier in Africa, sir?" Christof can't keep the excitement out of his voice.

"I was an army surgeon. That's how I met Reichskommissar Göring and his lovely wife. The Chancellor sent him there to establish our colony."

"Did you see any action, sir?" Christof asks.

"Not really. I mostly took care of the few German officers who had been sent there – and the missionaries and other settlers. Africa was...."

A knock on the door interrupts him. Epenstein pulls a gold watch from his vest pocket and glances at it. "You'll have to excuse me. I have an appointment with Herr Groeschel to discuss rebuilding the tower." He carefully replaces the tin figures in the box and then hands me a few marks. "Thank you for delivering them. You both will have to come back again when I can give you a proper tour of the castle."

That was the first of many visits to the old fortress. Sometimes Christof comes with me. Sometimes I go alone. Papa doesn't say much, but I know he doesn't approve. He thinks the ritter is a bad influence.

People do talk about Epenstein – behind his back, of course. They whisper that he converted to Catholicism just so he could marry the daughter of a wealthy banker. And now that he's a widower, they say he's carrying on with Frau Göring, right under her husband's nose. In fact, they say, Albert, the youngest Göring boy, is actually Epenstein's son. I've met Albert, and I have to admit that the brown-eyed, dark-haired child looks more like the lord of the manor than he does any of the Görings. But it's Hermann Göring – not Albert – who calls the wealthy doctor "Papa." And Epenstein favors Hermann over all the others.

But these are not the things I talk about at Burg Veldenstein. When Christof is there, Epenstein tells us stories about his time in Africa. And he shows us photos – of him with his foot on a large leopard he had killed, of half-naked Herero with their cherished cattle, of Rhenish missionaries who gave up the comforts of home to try to bring German civilization to the heathen.

On the rare occasions when Reichskommissar Göring is sober, he joins in the conversation, embellishing the doctor's stories with political philosophy. He drones on about the mistake Chancellor Bismarck made in not sending troops to reinforce Germany's claim on South West Africa from the very beginning. "It is a mistake we will live to regret," he says, stamping his cane on the stone floor for added emphasis.

Seeing that Göring is in a talkative mood, Christof and I prod him to tell us about his time in the German colony. The old man leans against the wall, closing his eyes to the world around him.

His head slumps forward and a low hum that could be a snore escapes his lips.

Thinking the beer has taken him off, I clear my throat and turn to Epenstein. Our host smiles indulgently and puts his finger to his lips. After a few minutes of silence, Göring opens his watery blue eyes and stares through me. "Where was I? Oh, yes, South West Africa. What a God-forsaken country that is. The natives are constantly fighting each other. And for what? A stretch of desert and some scrawny cows. Ah, the cows. They are the meaning of life – and life itself – for the Herero and the Nama."

The old officer shifts on his wooden seat. "If only I had been given some troops. It could have been a prosperous colony by now – well, at least one that was paying its own way."

"When were you there, sir?" Christof asks.

"In the beginning. Bismarck sent me in 1885 to secure treaties and send a message to the English to stay out of our colony. Me, along with Chancellor Luis Nels and Police Chief Hugo Goldammer. I ask you, what good is a barrister in a country with no law? Or a sergeant-major with no soldiers to command?" Göring looks up at Epenstein. "And, of course, there was the good doctor. I don't know what Frau Göring would have done without him."

Christof and I try not to smirk at the old man's naivete. Epenstein himself steps in. "I attended the birth of Olga, her second child. It was a difficult delivery with none of the conveniences Frau Göring would have had here at home. She is a courageous woman."

Ignoring the interruption, Göring continues his story. "My first task was to get a treaty with Maharero, the paramount Herero chief. So early that October, we all headed to Okahandja to negotiate a treaty with the chief, but when we got there, he refused to see us. He was too busy preparing for a meeting with the Witboois."

"The Whiteboys?" Christof asks, struggling with the pronunciation.

Göring sips from the stein that is always close by. "Hendrik Witbooi was the chief of the Nama and the arch enemy of the Herero chief. The two were always fighting over land and cattle." He twirls his long, bushy moustache.

"Maharero had reason to be concerned about Witbooi, despite the treaty they supposedly had at the time. Witbooi was a wily character. Saw himself as some sort of prophet or avenging angel," Göring continues. "You could always spot his men by the white kerchiefs they tied around their brimmed hats.

"While we were waiting in Okahandja for the Herero chiefs to meet with us, Witbooi and some of his men arrived in Osona, a nearby cattle outpost, to talk with Maharero about the two of them joining forces to stand up to us and the English. But their precious cattle came between them." He closes his eyes and appears to drift off.

"What do you mean, sir?" I ask, somewhat loudly.

Göring starts. "What's that?"

"What happened with the cattle?"

He takes a long draught from the stein, looking a bit confused. Epenstein leans forward and touches the older man's shoulder. "You were telling them about Maharero's meeting with Witbooi before you got the treaty."

"The treaty? Oh yes." Göring pauses to gather his thoughts. "You see, the Herero never go anywhere without their cattle. So both chiefs and their men brought their herds to the meeting place. While Maharero and Witbooi were negotiating, some of the men argued about watering the cattle. The next thing you know, they were shooting at each other...."

"Shooting?" Christof interrupts. "They have guns?"

Göring laughs. "Of course they have guns. This is the nineteenth century – even in Africa."

"But how did they get guns?"

"We sell them guns. English and German traders, that is," Epenstein inserts dryly. "They give them the guns in exchange for land and access to trade routes."

Ignoring the interruption, Göring resumes his story. "The fight became quite a skirmish. Two of Witbooi's sons were killed, and the old rascal ran off to lick his wounds. Maharero brought all of his wounded men back to Okahandja."

"Which gave the Kommissar the opportunity he needed," Epenstein interjects. "He pushed up his sleeves and set to work bandaging the wounded until late into the night with no thought to his own comfort. I had no idea he was so skilled in medicine."

Göring beams with modest pride. "I was not the only one," he says. "We all did what needed to be done that night. Anyway, it showed the chief that we were his friends. And his run-in with the Witboois convinced him that having German protection might not be a bad idea, so he was finally willing to talk about a treaty."

"Do you speak African then?" Christof asks in surprise.

Göring laughs. "I can speak some Herero now, but not much back then. The old chief spoke some Deutsch, but the missionaries did most of the translating. It took three days for us to get our treaty." He leans his head against the wall, once again lost in his memories.

After a few moments, he takes another drink and continues. "I confess, I had my reservations about the negotiations." He shakes his head. "Most of the other Herero chiefs had left after the fight, so Maharero was on his own in negotiating the treaty. He wanted to wait for the rest of his chiefs to return. I saw the wisdom in that, but the missionaries insisted he didn't need all his advisers. As the paramount chief, they said, Maharero had the right to sign a treaty that affected the whole country. I think they were afraid he might change his mind.

"So he signed it, along with the few minor chiefs who were still there. We celebrated by firing some rockets and hanging German flags from Maharero's brick house. It was quite the little celebration." Göring smiles, enjoying the memory. "I'll never forget the sight of our white flags with their black crosses and imperial eagles flying in that African village. It was proof that we were at last a world power and that the German Empire would soon rival that of the English."

"But what did the treaty do?" Christof asks.

Göring laughs. "Not much. It promised the Herero protection against their enemies. But how much protection could three German officers give them?" He rubs his forehead thoughtfully. "What it really protected was our claim to the territory. It was like putting a fence on paper, telling the English in Cape Town to stay out. It also gave Germans the right to claim land in South West Africa and settle on it."

The old man takes a long drink from his stein, stretches out, and promptly falls asleep.

Epenstein nods to us. "Perhaps we should walk in the garden," he says quietly, "and leave Heinrich to enjoy his dreams."

A PRIVATE AUDIENCE

The next time I visit Burg Veldenstein, I'm alone. Christof would have come with me, had I asked him, but there are things I need to discuss with the ritter. Things Christof wouldn't understand. Things I can't talk about with Papa.

Now that I'm having what amounts to a private audience with Epenstein in his trophy room, I'm at a loss for words. I feel like an awkward boy trying to make conversation with the headmaster.

"You wish to speak with me?" The doctor looks at me patiently.

"Yes, sir." I hesitate before blurting out, "I have so many questions I want to ask you, but I'm not sure how to ask them. I don't want to offend you."

Epenstein quirks an eyebrow. "Well, I suppose you could just ask your questions. If I'm offended, I'll tell you. Otherwise, I'll try to answer. How's that?"

"Very well, sir." I look down at the floor, trying to find a focus. "You know that I'm a Jew."

"Yes, I'm aware of that."

"Well, I've heard that your family is Jewish and that you converted. Would you mind me asking why? It's not that I want to convert. It's just that. . . ." I trail off, not knowing quite how to voice my thoughts.

Epenstein nods understandingly. "You want to be German."

"Yes." I smile with relief.

"To my way of thinking, being Jewish is how you choose to serve God. Being German is how you choose to serve the Fatherland." He pauses so we both can mull his words. "I know there are Germans and Jews who wouldn't agree with that. But it's easier today than it was when I was your age."

"Is that why you converted?" I ask.

"It probably is what started me thinking. But it's not the reason. Faith isn't a matter of convenience – no matter what anyone tells you." He absently spins an antique globe sitting on the richly carved desk between us. "I've always had a lot of curiosity about this world and the next, so I've studied a number of religions. I became a Catholic because I believed the teachings of the church."

Epenstein chuckles softly. "Kov, if my conversion was to become more German, I would have become a Lutheran. It is, after all, a German church."

"So, do you feel German?"

"I feel like a man who lives in Germany, who has served his country, and is proud of the opportunities his country has given him. If Germany were attacked, I would be among the first to defend the Fatherland – even if it meant my life. So yes, I guess I do feel German." He looks at me thoughtfully. "But I think the question you're really asking is whether others see me as German."

I nod.

"That's more difficult to answer. Since I also have Burg Mauterndorf in Austria, some may think my loyalties are divided." He strokes his goatee thoughtfully and then looks at me shrewdly. "What do you think? I'm sure you've heard plenty of stories about me."

I smile sheepishly. "I think you're German. And the Görings obviously see you as a fellow countryman."

"Ah, but you're my friends. I know there are many people in both Austria and Germany who will never view me as anything but an opportunistic Jew who somehow took something that rightfully should be theirs. Some of them are my neighbors and the people I do business with. Others will never know me except by name and rumors."

Epenstein pauses to choose his words. "The older I get, the more I realize that what other people think about me has little to do with who I am. All of us – Jews, Catholics, Lutherans, even the godless – will always be seen by others through their personal spectacles of perception. Any heroic deeds we accomplish will be filtered and interpreted by their assumptions." He sighs heavily. "We can't change other people, and we can't force them to see us the way we would like to be seen."

He nods his head toward the door. "Take my friend Heinrich. You couldn't ask for a better man – or a better German. He was a brilliant, well-connected public servant who sacrificed his life, his family, and his reputation for his country, serving wherever the Chancellor sent him. But look at him now. His only comfort is his stein."

He leans back in his chair and turns slightly so he can look out the window at the men repairing his castle. "When I first met Heinrich in South West Africa, he was a man with the promise of a bright future. But he was sent on a fool's mission that was doomed to fail."

"I thought he got the treaty."

"Yes, he did. And for a short time, he was seen as a bit of a hero. But the politicians back home still hadn't committed to supporting a colony in Africa, so Bismarck refused to send the troops needed to provide the protection the treaty promised. It didn't take long for Maharero and the other chiefs to realize Heinrich lacked the power and the resources to keep up his side of the bargain. He had a few big guns but little else. Those were not pleasant times to be a German official in South West Africa." He pauses, lost in the faraway places of his memories.

"What happened?" I ask.

"After negotiating the treaty with Maharero, Heinrich set about getting all the other Herero chiefs to sign it. It took some work, but Heinrich was good at diplomacy. Well, diplomacy as we know it, that is." Epenstein chuckles. "His next step was to get a protection treaty with Witbooi. But the old warrior was a far different man than Maharero. He thought he was called by God to deliver his people from the strangers in their land. To prove it, he constantly made raids on the tribes that signed the treaties. With no troops, Heinrich was powerless to stop him.

"With each raid, Witbooi became bolder – and the other chiefs more desperate. Seeking the protection the treaty promised him, Maharero and many of his people moved with their cattle to Otjimbingwe where we had established the German administration. One night, in his most brazen move yet, Witbooi and his allies slipped into Otjimbingwe and stole our horses and raided Maharero's cattle. With no horses and no troops, Heinrich couldn't give chase. And the Herero chief lost all confidence in our ability to protect his people and cattle.

"The chief summoned Heinrich and the missionaries to his house. After declaring the treaty void, he ordered the German officials and the missionaries to get out of his country. There was nothing Heinrich could do but gather his family and trek

across the desert to Walvis Bay to wait for orders from Bismarck."
Epenstein turns away from the window to face me. "It was the
beginning of the end for Heinrich."

"What do you mean?"

"When Heinrich was sent to South West Africa, he was well
respected and had a bright future in the diplomatic corp. But
when the newspapers in Germany got word of the treaty failure,
they blamed it all on him. Calling the Herero ignorant heathen
who just needed a firm hand to lead them into civilization,
they portrayed Heinrich as a weak, bumbling fool who had no
business leading a colony.

"Despite the public humiliation, Heinrich remained committed to the treaties he had signed. So when Bismarck sent him
back to South West Africa a few years later, he worked diligently
to get the treaty with Maharero reinstated."

"He obviously succeeded," I say.

"Yes and no," Epenstein responds. "A lot had happened in the
colony during Heinrich's absence. More troops, led by Captain
Curt von Francois, had been sent there to maintain the peace.
But Francois and his brother Hugo were more interested in
lining their pockets than brokering peace between the tribes.
They used their fort in Tsaobis to control the trade routes and
build up their own cattle herds. They were hard taskmasters to
any native who challenged their authority.

"When Heinrich returned in 1890, the Francois brothers
made a big deal of escorting him, with a camel caravan and
most of the military troops in the colony, to Maharero's house in
Okahandja. Once again, the old chief was preparing for an attack
by Witbooi. Surrounded on all sides by the troops, Heinrich, in
all sincerity, offered Maharero German protection in exchange
for a treaty opening up more land for settlement. The chief, out
of desperation, accepted."

Epenstein lights his pipe and takes a long draw on it before
continuing. "It didn't take Heinrich long to realize the Francois
brothers had no intention of upholding our side of the treaty. All
they were after was more land. Seeing he had been played for a
fool, he left Africa for good and requested another post."

"What happened then?"

"Shortly after Heinrich left, Witbooi attacked the Herero
cattle posts. When Maharero appealed to Captain von Francois

for protection, he was told the German troops couldn't get involved in native affairs. Witbooi attacked the Herero again a few months later. This time, German soldiers had coffee with him during a lull in the fighting. And he herded the stolen cattle right by the German fort in Tsaobis, trading with the Francois brothers while he was there. Maharero, who had trusted Heinrich, died a broken man. As for Heinrich, he was sent to Haiti, stripped of his pride, his reputation, and his self-respect."

Epenstein leans forward. "All Heinrich has ever done was serve his country. But you see, being a good German can come at a high price – perhaps too high. Only you can decide if it's worth it. As for me, I go on with my life, living it as I see fit. To hell with what everyone else thinks."

"No disrespect, sir, but you're at a point in your life where you can get by with that attitude. I'm just starting out." I hesitate before plunging on. "You say it's getting easier to be a Jew in Germany, but I don't see it – not with Fritsch's new handbook on anti-Semitism and the Dreyfus affair in France."

My host nods in agreement. "And don't forget Wilhelm Marr. He's still being quoted." He looks down his nose and mimics the author of modern anti-Semitism in pompous, self-righteous tones: "'Even the most honorable Jew is under the inescapable influence of his blood, carrier of a semitic morality, totally opposed to Germanic values, aimed at the destruction and burial of German values and traditions.'"

We laugh, but the only humor we find in Marr's words is how off the mark they are.

"Sir, I know the best I can hope for is to be considered a 'German of the Jewish faith,' but I have no idea where to begin," I say. "What would you suggest?"

Epenstein narrows his eyes shrewdly. "You must serve your country."

"But how?" I ask. "Since I have no family connections, politics is out of the question. And it's almost impossible for Jews to join the army. The few who do – " I shudder. "I've heard the stories."

He nods. "Yes, but there is a way in. You could become a doctor. The army desperately needs good doctors, so it couldn't care less whether they're Christians or Jews."

"A doctor," I murmur. "I could do that. Mama always wanted me to be a doctor or a rabbi – she said I should devote my life to healing people's souls or their bodies."

"That's a worthy ambition," he says with a smile. "Give it some thought. And if you decide that's what you want, I can get you into the medical school at Würzburg and then arrange a military post for you."

"Thank you, sir." I stand up to leave.

"Save your gratitude," Epenstein says. "Who knows? Someday, you may be cursing me for this."

THE RABBI

When I get home, Papa and the rabbi are waiting for me. I quickly retrieve my yarmulke from my coat pocket and discreetly put it on my head. Papa clears his throat disapprovingly.

"What is it?" I demand, even though I know what's coming.

"Yaakov," Papa says under his breath, "show some respect. Your mama and I raised you better than that."

"I'm sorry, Papa," I say meekly as I take off my overcoat. I nod to the rabbi. "Good evening, Rabbi."

The rabbi embraces me, kissing me on both cheeks in the old custom. "Yaakov, where is the little boy I used to bounce on my knee? You have become a full-grown man overnight." He smiles at me through his thick, gray whiskers.

"Sit, sit," Papa says, flitting around like a nervous old woman.

I wait for the rabbi to settle back onto the worn sofa before I sit in Mama's old rocker.

"We have missed you in synagogue," the rabbi tells me.

"Let me get some tea." Papa slips away into the kitchen.

"I have missed going," I reply honestly. "I've been so busy studying for the Abitur."

At the mention of the comprehensive exam that comes at the end of high school, the rabbi smiles understandingly. "And what will you do after you graduate?"

"I'm preparing to go into medicine. The world can never have too many doctors."

"Ach, that is good." The rabbi strokes his beard. "We can always use another doctor at our Jewish hospital. Your papa must be very proud of you."

"I haven't told him yet," I confess. "I know he would like for me to continue as a spielwarenmacher. But with all the new mechanism, I could never compete with Bing and the other big toy companies."

The rabbi nods. "I think your papa would like having a doctor in the family."

Papa walks into the room bearing a heavy tray laden with Mama's tea service and a plate of kugel. "What would I like?" he asks as he carefully places the tray on a nearby table. I notice his hand shakes slightly as he pours the tea.

"Yaakov was just telling me he wants to be a doctor." The rabbi winks at me. "You must be happy."

"What?" Papa quickly covers his surprise. "Oh, yes, yes." He looks at me questioningly. "His mama would have liked that – a doctor in the family. But if he's serious about this, he will have to study harder and stop all his socializing."

The rabbi turns to me. "Your papa tells me you have struck up a friendship with Ritter von Epenstein."

"Yes, I have. He's offered to help me get into the medical school at the University of Würzburg."

"On what condition?" Papa asks. "The doctor is not known for his charity – except to the Göring family."

I bristle at Papa's uncustomary sarcasm. "That's not true. The doctor is a good man. And there are no conditions." I look down, knowing I'm not being totally truthful. Papa wouldn't be happy if he knew I planned to use medical school as my door into the military. He would see it as a personal betrayal, me helping people who wish we didn't exist.

The rabbi breaks the awkward silence that followed my outburst. "Be that as it may, Yaakov, you would do well to keep some distance from the ritter. Any man who would turn his back on God would do far worse to a friend. It is for that reason that King David warned us not to walk with ungodly men."

I know better than to argue with the rabbi in front of Papa. But I make a mental note: "He's not ungodly. He just worships God differently."

The rabbi changes the subject. "Würzburg. That is where they've come up with a way to take photographs inside the body. Röntgen rays – that's what they call it." He smiles broadly. "It is a good choice for you. And you will be close enough to come home occasionally, especially for the High Holy Days."

Papa offers the rabbi more tea before turning to me. "Yaakov, you will make a wonderful doctor. I'm proud of you. But you must understand that Würzburg is nothing like Fürth."

"I know that, Papa. Fürth is just a village..."

The rabbi interrupts me. "That's not what he means, Yaakov. For centuries, Fürth has welcomed our people. It has been a refuge for us, and we have grown strong here. We have become a community – with our many synagogues, our own hospital, schools, theater, and all of our stores. Yes, there are people here who barely tolerate us, but they leave us alone."

"It's not the same in Würzburg," Papa says. "They have a history of murdering Jews or banning them from the city."

"It's not like that now?" My response is both a question and a statement.

The rabbi laughs rather hollowly. "They haven't killed any Jews in Würzburg for a few hundred years. But you know, for us, that's like yesterday." He sips his tea. "No, Yaakov, you will be physically safe there, but I'm afraid your faith will be tested. You will need to get back into the habit of going to synagogue and studying the Talmud. You should go to the Hauptsynagoge there. Rabbi Bamberger follows in the steps of his father."

"Ahhh, the Würzburg Rav," Papa murmurs. "Now he was a Talmudic scholar. May he rest in peace."

The rabbi nods in agreement. "Unfortunately, Seligmann was the last of his kind. No one can fill his shoes, but his son Nathan is a scholar in his own right and is much loved in Würzburg."

The rabbi sets his teacup down and stands to go. "Speaking of synagogue, I expect to see you every Sabbath until you leave for university. And when you go, you remember your prayers, young man."

I smile and nod.

Papa hands the rabbi his overcoat. "Will you give Yaakov a blessing? He will need high marks on the Abitur to get into medical school."

"Of course." The rabbi turns toward me and prays solemnly: *"Baruch atah Adonai Eloheinu Melech Haolam, shenatan me-ichachmato l'vasar vadam."*

ON MY OWN

True to his word, Epenstein made sure I was accepted into the medical school at the University of Würzburg. For the first time in my life, I am away from home, from my friends – from Papa. I'm excited about the future, but I'm also afraid. The city, with its Catholic history visibly etched into the town's structure, can be intimidating for a Jew. Its Christian fervor is evident in the statues lining Old Main Bridge. The four-spired cathedral that has stood for nearly a thousand years. The bigger-than-life sculpture of the Prince Bishop of Würzburg looking up at the 13th-century Marienberg fortress standing guard over the vineyards and red-roofed houses and shops clustered along both sides of the bend in the river.

Ever since I was a child, I've heard the stories of the Jewish massacres in Würzburg. I know they happened hundreds of years ago, yet I can't help but wonder if a young Jewish man will be welcome in this city today. I remind myself that I am a man preparing to serve the Fatherland. I force myself to stand a little taller, to look the Germans walking toward me in the eye, to smile confidently – even though I feel no confidence.

As soon as classes start, I have little time to worry about my place in the city, or in the growing German empire, for that matter. My head is too full of the marvels of modern medicine. With awe, I walk by Professor Röntgen's laboratory at the university. I have seen the images from his rays, which look through the skin and muscles to the skeletal structure of the body. On occasion, I see the professor himself. Like many of the other faculty, he and his family live in apartments above the physics classrooms and laboratories.

Of course, Röntgen rays – he calls them X-rays – are not the only discoveries revolutionizing the study and practice of medicine. The lecture halls are filled with the bacteriology work of Louis Pasteur, Robert Koch, Paul Ehrlich, and Ferdinand Cohn. The fact that some of these scientists are Jewish gives me greater hope for the future. The more we can contribute to the intellectual advancement of our country, the more our work will be recognized and we will be proudly embraced as German citizens.

In my spare time – what little I have – I often pass by the
impressive Juliusspital and stroll through its botanical gardens,
wondering if I'll ever treat the sick in this centuries-old hospital.
Then I remember my goal. I'm going to be an army doctor. No
fancy hospitals with beautiful gardens for me. I'll be caring for
the soldiers who are offering their lives for the Fatherland –
young men like Christof who represent the best of Germany.

On the weekends and rare days of no classes, I get together
with my new friends for quiet walks through the public gardens,
scientific discussions over a glass of the local wine, and rowdy
political and philosophical debates in each other's rented rooms.
My friends, for the most part, are Jews, but few of them are
religious, which makes it hard for me to keep my promise to Papa
and the rabbi.

I've walked by the Hauptsynagoge several times, but I've yet
to attend services. It's difficult to force myself to go to synagogue
when my friends are planning study sessions and outings in
the countryside. I keep telling myself I'll go next week. But
something always comes up, and I put it off again. One of these
days.

* * * * *

At last I've done it. I've gone to synagogue. Actually, I go
quite often now. Not because of my promise to Papa, but because
of Hanna. I met Hanna at the university; she's the cousin of one
of my friends. But unlike Emil, Hanna's quite devout.

I know it sounds silly, but the moment I met Hanna, I loved
her. She's so much like Mama – gentle, patient, wise beyond her
years. Hanna makes me want to be a better man, and a better
Jew. Because of Hanna, I say my prayers daily, I read Torah, and
I go to synagogue regularly. I even wear my yarmulke in classes
and around town. My friends tease me, but I don't care. I love
Hanna. And, miraculously, she loves me.

Today, Hanna talks my friends and me into going to a
memorbuch service at synagogue. I confess, I have some reservations. Although most Jewish communities haven't read their
memorbuchs for years, I've heard about them – long lists of local
Jewish martyrs dating back to the First Crusade, along with
prominent members of the community who have died over the

centuries. Some of the books have thousands of names. I'm concerned about the time the service will take. My studies are piling up and I have several exams in the next few weeks.

The custom was for each community to read the names in its memorbuch in a special ceremony twice a year – on the ninth of Av in remembrance of the two destructions of Jerusalem and on the Shabbat before Shavuot, the anniversary of the massacres that took place in the First Crusade. The reading gave the martyrs back their names and ensured they wouldn't be forgotten by God. When Jewish communities were forced out of a town, they would take their memorbuchs with them, grafting their memories and their ancestors into their new homes.

Papa often mentions the Frankfurt memorbuch, sometimes reciting whole passages from it. He refers to the people of the book as if they're old friends. When I was a boy, it took me awhile to realize that Papa had never met Rabbenu Gershom, "the Light of the Exile" and one of the names in the Frankfurt memorbuch. I learned later that this great Talmudist was the first entry in most memorbuchs.

Gershom lived nearly a thousand years before Papa was born, yet Papa talks about him as if they were boyhood friends. I swear, even if I should live to be 100, I will never understand Papa's obsession with the past. Yes, it's important to know where one comes from, but I think it's much healthier to live for the hope of tomorrow than to be mired in memories that can't be undone. Papa can have the past. I will look to the future – with Hanna.

THE MEMORBUCH

As usual, the sound of the shofar stirs me as it resonates throughout the synagogue. I have never understood how a simple ram's horn can produce such beautiful, haunting music. Closing my eyes, I hear it echoing through history, calling the faithful to prayer, the nation of Israel to repentance, and our great warriors to battle.

Despite the solemnity of the service, I can't help but chuckle under my breath. I'm thinking like Papa! Then it hits me. The purpose of tradition. It ties us irrevocably to the past and to our ancestors. But at the same time, it reaches forward, connecting us to the future and to our descendants – so long

as they remember and honor the traditions. It's a cycle that
holds us together as a people. I savor the thought, vowing to be
more understanding of Papa and to honor my Jewish traditions
no matter how German I become.

As the echoes of the last notes of the shofar fade, the
congregation sits down, and the reader approaches the bimah
with the Scroll of Esther. He carefully lays the scroll on the
stand and unties the satin cord that binds it. As he chants
the familiar story of the Jewish girl who became queen and
her victory over the murderous Haman, the congregation grows
raucous, shaking fists and booing and yelling whenever Haman's
name is mentioned. Again, it's tradition. The story of Purim
– of triumph at the moment of defeat. A story that happened
thousands of years ago, but for us, it is recent history.

When the reading is finished, the scroll is carefully rolled and
tied. The cantor comes to the bimah, carrying a huge leather-
bound book with hundreds of handwritten pages. A reverent
silence falls upon the congregation as the cantor carefully opens
the worn memorbuch. *"Mi she-Berakh,"* he intones as he chants
the familiar Hebrew blessing. *"May He who blessed the souls
of our fathers Abraham, Isaac, and Jacob bless the souls of ..."*
And then he chants the list of names and dates, beginning with
the Würzburg victims of the First Crusade and continuing to the
Second Crusade. "Isak ben Moses – murdered 1147. Isak ben
Eljakim – brother of Hiskia ben Eljakim, martyr 1147. Mose –
murdered together with his wife Belet 1147 ... "

The names of the rest of the victims of the Second Crusade,
along with those of long-deceased rabbis and scholars, continue
in a monotonous hum. One catches my attention: "Isak ben
Ascher haLevi – Born 1200. Broken on the wheel, 1221. Disciple
of Eliëser ben Joel haLevi." Twenty-one – my age. And just
because he was a Jew, he was condemned to one of the most
painful, gruesome deaths ever imagined. Could my faith stand
up to that test?

The cantor is now chanting about the 900 Würzburg Jews
who were killed in the Rindfleisch pogroms in 1298 – "the
ten sons and daughters of Menachem ben Natronai Kobelin;
Chamlin ben Ephraim – murdered with his family; David ben
Meir – murdered with his family; Elia ben Samuel – murdered
with his wife and son; Ephraim ben Abraham – together with

his family drowned to death in the mikveh; Isak ben Natan – murdered with his family; Jechiel ben Ephraim – murdered with his family; Josef ben Nathan – murdered with his family; Meir ben Elasar haDarschan – murdered; Simon ben Jakob haLev – slain in his home." The list seems endless.

Finally, we reach the Black Death persecutions when the Würzburg Jews were accused of poisoning the town well. "Asriel ben Eliëser – author of a section in Midrasch Schoftim. Died in the persecution year 1349. David haKohen – murdered. Goldknauf – murdered. Simon ben Levi – last rabbi of the Jewish community in 1349. Voluntarily chose death in the flames." The names give way to numbers in the families who, like ben Levi, chose to set fire to their homes and die at their own hands rather than face the tortures of the Würzburg mob. The names and numbers continue – disturbing, and yet numbing, in their quantity.

The cantor continues with name after name, but the stories of horrific persecutions end. Yes, there are reminders of the bans and exiles of Würzburg Jews, but for the most part, the lists now are memorials to the rabbis, Talmudic scholars, and other notable Jews of more recent times. Of course, "recent" is relative for us.

I silently pray my own Yizkor for my family members – my grandparents, my sister who died in infancy, and Mama. Having lived simply as Jews, they carried no prominent name or accomplished deeds for others to remember, but their memory lives within me. "Yizkor E-lohim," I pray for Mama. "Nishmat imi morati, Elise bat Eliyahu, shehol'chah l'olamah, ba-avur sheb'li neder etayn tz'dakah ba-adah. May her soul be bound in the Bond of Life, together with the souls of Abraham, Isaac, and Jacob; Sarah, Rebecca, Rachel, and Leah."

When Shabbat ends the next evening, Hanna and I meet with some of our friends who had attended the reading of the memorbuch. We all are more reflective than usual. The reading hit each of us in different ways, but it definitely affected us. After a few glasses of wine, the quietness wears off and our contemplation takes voice.

"It was a beautiful service," Hanna says. "I don't understand why we have stopped the tradition."

"Because it's dangerous," Emil retorts. "It binds us to a past that makes us fear and hate our German brothers. If we're truly to become German, we must forget about the wrongs that happened hundreds of years ago and focus on tomorrow."

"But if we forget the past, we could be lulled into a false sense of safety," Yosl argues. He's the Zionist in the group. "Anti-Semitism seems to go in cycles here. All it takes is one financial downturn, one failed war, or another Wilhelm Marr to make us the scapegoats for all that's wrong with Germany."

"But we're entering the twentieth century," Hanna says. "We're all more civilized now. Even the Germans."

"Are we?" Yosl asks scoffingly. "It was less than eighty years ago when a couple of students at our university touched off the Hep Hep riots. Just because one professor spoke in support of Jewish rights."

Emil starts to protest, but Yosl cuts him off. "You want something more recent? Have you forgotten that, only a few years ago, the good Germans elected nineteen deputies to the Reichstag because of their anti-Semitic views? And the League for Anti-Semitism is growing." Yosl shakes his head. "Germany will never be our Fatherland."

"What do you think, Kov?" Hanna squeezes my hand.

I hesitate, choosing my words carefully. "While I'm not as pessimistic as you, Yosl, I realize a lot of Germans hate us."

Emil and Dovet start to interrupt me, but I hold up my hand. "How many German friends do you have?" I ask them.

"A few," Dovet says.

"Where are they? We're with you all the time, and we've never met them. Why?"

"That's not a fair question," Emil chimes in. "We all come from religious families, right?"

"So what are you saying? That you can only become German if you give up your faith? You want to become a Mendelssohn?" Yosl shakes his head. "That's too high a price for me."

"No, you didn't let me finish," Emil says. "I simply meant we all grew up in Jewish neighborhoods, went to Jewish schools, and had Jewish friends. If we want the Germans to accept us, we have to let them get to know us. People only fear what they don't know." Point made, he sits back in his chair.

"I don't think it's as simple as that," I say. "Yes, I grew up in a Jewish neighborhood, but I went to a German school. And I have one German friend to show for it. Christof is like a brother to me, and even though he tried to get the other boys to do things with us, he never succeeded. They always looked at me with suspicion."

"So are you becoming a Zionist?" Tsirl asks.

"Hardly," I smile at her. "I haven't given up on the Fatherland." I playfully punch Yosl in the arm. "But I don't think the Germans are ever going to accept us unless we prove ourselves to them. We have to make them see that we love this country, that we are proud to be German."

"And how are you going to do that?" Lazi has been sitting almost detached from the rest of us.

I swallow and look down at the table. I haven't discussed my plan with Hanna yet, and to bring it up now – like this – doesn't seem fair to her.

Lazi laughs at my silence. "Well?"

I clear my throat. There's no way out. I look into the distance – anywhere but at Hanna. "I plan to serve in the army as a doctor," I say quietly.

"How are you going to pull that off?" Lazi asks. "The Kaiser said a man who isn't a good Christian can't, under any circumstances, accomplish what's required of a German soldier."

I nod. "Yes, I remember. It caused quite a stir in the papers. And a number of them pointed out the bravery of Jewish soldiers serving in the army. I'll be going in as a doctor, not a soldier."

"You've got to be joking," Yosl says. "How can you even think of putting on a German uniform? That's not just forgetting the past – that's turning your back on everything we've suffered. You might as well reach your hand back in time and add to the torture of our ancestors."

I ignore Yosl. Instead, I look into Hanna's eyes. I see surprise and confusion. I take her hand, knowing that I must convince her of my reasons – right now, right here – if we're to have a future. It doesn't matter what the others think. Only what she thinks.

"I'm doing this because of the past. But I'm also doing this for the future – for my future and for the future of my children. We can't forget our history, but we can't let it hold us frozen in time. We must learn from it and then move forward."

I can't read Hanna's eyes. But she doesn't pull her hand away, which I interpret as a good sign.

IN THE GARDEN

Taking advantage of the beautiful spring weather, Hanna and I stroll, hand in hand, through the botanical gardens at Juliusspital. We seem comfortable in our silence, but I know we both are thinking of the conversation last night, waiting for the other to speak. She brings it up first. "You're serious about being an army doctor?"

"Yes. It's why I came to school here."

"What does your father think?" Hanna met Papa during a university holiday. As I thought he would, he loved her the moment he met her.

I kick at a pebble on the path. "I haven't told him yet."

"And what about me?" she asks quietly. "How do I fit into your plans?" She stops and gently grasps my arm.

As I look into her eyes, I can feel her love washing over me. I don't want to hurt her, but even she can't disrupt my plans. "Hanna, this was my dream long before I met you. It's something I have to do."

"I understand, Kov. But is there room in your dream for me? I need to know."

I brush her blonde hair back from her eyes. "I love you more than life itself. But this is my dream, my plan. I can't expect you to share it. Life as the wife of an army doctor isn't easy. But being the wife of a Jewish army doctor would be worse. We could be separated for years at a time – or have to live far from here, where there are no synagogues and no other Jews. And we wouldn't always be welcome, with either the Germans or our own people. I love you too much to ask you to shoulder that life with me."

"But what if I want to?" she whispers, looking down as the toe of her shoe digs into the path.

I tilt her head up, peering intently into her eyes. "You deserve so much more. You deserve a husband who can be with you, who makes you his priority. I won't be able to do that. Is that really the kind of marriage you want?"

Hanna laughs up at me. "If that's your idea of a marriage proposal, I accept."

I gulp. "Are you sure?"

"Of course I'm sure. You're not getting out of this one," she says playfully. She puts her arm through mine and leads me over to a bench. "I realize it won't be an easy life. But you should know by now that life is rarely easy for us Jews."

We sit quietly, letting the reality of our sudden betrothal sink in. Again, Hanna is the first to break the silence. "Have you heard the history of this place?"

"Of the hospital?"

"The gardens. Back in the winter of 1147, the body of a man was found in the river. Blaming the local Jews for his death, the good folk of Würzburg turned him into a martyr." She pauses. I remain silent, waiting for her to connect this story to us.

"Meanwhile, the Crusaders, egged on by the rabble from the nearby villages, saw they didn't have to wait for the Holy Land to kill some Jews. They attacked the Jews living here in Würzburg, murdering twenty-two people. One young woman was dragged to the cathedral where they tried to force her to be baptized. When she refused, they beat her, burned her, and left her for dead." Hanna's voice breaks.

I wipe a stray tear from her cheek, still wondering where her story is going.

"After the mob left, an old Christian widow found the woman and saw that she was still alive, although barely. The widow took the woman to her house, hid her, and nursed her back to health. Other Jews survived the massacre by hiding in the homes of friendly Christians and seeking refuge in the bishop's fortress. Saddened by the slaughter, the bishop ordered that all the mutilated bodies of the Jewish martyrs be sanctified with holy oil and buried in his garden. In this garden. Later, he sold the garden to what was left of the Jewish community to be used as a cemetery."

Surprised, I look around, searching for some remnant of a cemetery. Hanna smiles. "You won't find it," she says as if reading my thoughts. "Hundreds of years later when the Jews were banished from Würzburg, Bishop Julius confiscated the cemetery, erasing its history. It eventually became a medicinal garden, producing the herbs used to treat the people in the hospital that was named for him."

I know I will never feel the same about this garden rooted in the bones of my people. "It's a sad story, but...."

"What's the point?" Hanna finishes my question. "The point is that this tragic history is marked with acts of kindness. Yes, some Germans ruthlessly murdered Jews simply because they could. But others risked the senseless anger of their countrymen to do what was right. It all came down to a choice – a choice each person had to make for himself. And some of them, many of them, chose to do good."

Hanna gestures toward a flowerbed ablaze in colorful blooms. "So out of all this suffering, all the sadness – all the hatred – beauty and goodness triumph. Like Queen Esther standing up to Haman. So life will be for us."

I impulsively kiss her – a lingering, gentle kiss sealing our betrothal. "I love you, Hanna Heitzfeld," I whisper.

As we leave the garden, I look back, overwhelmed by a sense of peace and the knowledge that we have added to the history of this place.

THE DAY OF RECKONING

With graduation only a few months off and Epenstein arranging for my commission as an army doctor, the day I've been dreading has arrived. I must tell Papa about my plans. I've rehearsed this conversation so many times that I have it memorized, but I still feel like Daniel facing the lion's den.

As I enter the apartment above Papa's shop, I'm shocked by how frail he has become. The old stooped man who welcomes me is but a remnant of the father of my boyhood. The doctor in me wants to examine him, but I know he'd never permit it. Trying to mask the shock that I'm sure is apparent on my face, I grasp Papa's thin veined hand and lead him over to the threadbare sofa. He leans on me heavily as he lowers himself onto the cushions.

"How are you doing, Papa? Have you seen Dr. Goldstein lately?"

"Dr. Goldstein! What does he know?" Papa waves his hand feebly. "All he does is give me some new tonic and tell me not to work so hard. I have too much to do to waste my time listening to him."

I make a mental note to check in with Dr. Goldstein but decide it's better to drop the subject with Papa. "So how is business?" I ask politely.

"The demand for hand-painted tin soldiers isn't what it used to be," he says ruefully. "And these hands," he holds up his trembling hands, "are not as steady as they used to be. But I get by, and I should have enough work to keep me busy until I die."

"Papa...."

He lays his hand on my knee. "We cannot pretend, Yaakov. We both know I'm not getting any younger. That's why you need to hurry up and marry that Hanna of yours. I want to hold my grandson before I die."

I swallow hard. This conversation is not at all what I had rehearsed. Oh well. I take a deep breath and plunge in. "About that...."

He lifts his hand from my knee. "You have broken it off with her! She is such a good girl – and so right for you. Just like your mama, may she rest in peace."

"Hanna and I are getting married, but we will be moving to Hamburg."

"Hamburg? The Jewish hospital here is not good enough for you?"

"It's not the hospital. I am to be posted at Hamburg as an army doctor."

Papa looks as if all the life has been beaten out of him. "An army doctor?" he whispers hoarsely.

"Yes, Papa. It's something I have to do."

He pulls away from me. "This is what comes of your friendship with gentiles."

"That's not fair, Papa. Christof is my only friend who isn't Jewish. And, yes, he is now an army officer. But my decision has nothing to do with him."

"Christof is a German," Papa says. "It's his duty to serve the Kaiser."

"But we are Germans, too."

"We are Jews. Our duty is to One higher."

"Yes, Papa. But we also have a duty to our homeland."

Papa sighs heavily. "We may live here, but it can never be our home."

"Times have changed."

"Oh, so times have changed," he mimics me. "Yes, our young men are now allowed to offer their youth, their very lives to prove they are as loyal to the Fatherland as any German. But for what? You tell me," his gnarled finger points at me, "how many Jews have been recognized for that sacrifice? How many have been made an officer or awarded a medal? Not one."

"But, Papa ... the Talmud was not written in a day. We cannot expect Germans to lay aside hundreds of years of hatred overnight. It takes time. And we must be willing to take the first steps, to offer a sacrifice."

Papa looks heavenward, spreading his arms in helplessness. "Our story is nothing but sacrifice. And now my only son wants to lay his life on the altar. I am no Abraham."

I grasp Papa's worn hands and look directly into his watery eyes. "It's not as if I'm going off to war in China. I will have a comfortable billet in Hamburg, and I will spend my days checking recruits and tending to minor ailments. Hanna and I will visit you often. Or perhaps you can come live with us."

Papa shakes his head. "No, I will never live near a German army base. Besides, I have my work."

I laugh gently. "Perhaps you will change your mind when you have a grandson to spoil."

THE CHUPPAH

Today Hanna becomes my wife. I lie in bed thinking about the events of the day and the momentous vow I'm about to make. I have no doubts about Hanna, but once again I wonder if I'm being fair to her. I can only imagine the sacrifices she will have to make being married to an army doctor. I know her parents, like Papa, are not happy with my enlistment.

Papa comes into the room we're sharing at Hanna's uncle's house. At least, I think it's an uncle. She has such a large family that I lose track of how each one is related.

"This is not the day to be lazing around," Papa tells me. He's already dressed in his best clothes.

I stretch and leisurely get out of bed. Papa fusses about me, making sure I wash and dress properly. I stand in front of an old mirror, adjusting the white kittel over my dark suit.

Papa looks over my shoulder. "Your mother, may she rest in peace, would be so proud. Her son, the doctor, about to be married to a wonderful young woman."

"I wish Mama were here," I whisper hoarsely, trying not to tear up.

Papa awkwardly pats my shoulder. "She would love Hanna." He brushes an imaginary hair from my arm. "You know what to do?" he asks offhandedly.

"At the ceremony or tonight?"

Papa blushes. "Both."

I smile. "Yes, Papa. I have been to a number of my friends' weddings, and I have discussed the ceremony with the rabbi. And about the other" – I grin at Papa – "I'm a doctor. I know how things work."

"Being a husband is not just about how things work," he says gently. "Up to now, you have basically had to think only of yourself. But from this day forward, every decision you make will affect another life. It's a big responsibility, Yaakov. And there will be times when it will weigh heavy upon your shoulders."

"So what advice would you give me?"

He seems taken back by my question as I've never been one to ask for advice, especially from him. After a brief hesitation, he responds, "Love her and take care of her, even when you don't feel like it. After God, she and your family come first – before country, before job, before your personal ambitions. Remember that and He will bless your marriage."

I nod, knowing that Papa thinks I have already placed country before Hanna. Maybe I have, at least temporarily. But I'm serving in the army to make the future easier for her and our children.

"Enough talk," Papa says brusquely.

We walk to the nearby synagogue where Hanna's father and the rabbi meet us for the signing of the ketubah. I glance over the beautifully wrought marriage contract, which spells out my financial commitment to Hanna, and sign my name with a flourish. Once the witnesses sign the contract, the rabbi, Papa, and Papa Heitzfeld lead me to the room where Hanna and her mother are waiting for the badekan ceremony. All the male guests follow, forming quite the procession.

As we enter the room, the older men step out of the way so I can have a clear view of my bride. I gulp when I see her, in a white gown, sitting regally on a chair in the middle of the room. She has never looked more beautiful. She could be Queen Esther, but the heart she has captured is not that of a king.

Hanna looks up shyly, blushing at the jokes of her brothers and cousins. But when her hazel eyes meet mine, they sparkle with love and excitement. Again, I'm humbled that such a wonderful woman would agree to be my wife.

The rabbi speaks, pulling me back to a ritual rooted thousands of years ago in the deception of Jacob. I nod, affirming that, indeed, this is the woman I want to marry. As I step forward, Hanna's mother hands me the wedding veil. My bride laughs up at me as I clumsily arrange the fine lace over her face.

The preliminaries over, it's time for the ceremony. Papa escorts me down the aisle toward the chuppah, where the rabbi and Emil, my best man, wait. I glance at Papa as his grip tightens on my arm; tears are rolling down his face. I know he's thinking of Mama, who should be here walking down the aisle with us. Trying not to tear up myself, I squeeze Papa's arm against my side and smile at all the friends and family gathered for my wedding.

Standing with Papa and Emil, I turn to watch as Hanna's sister comes down the aisle to join us. At last, it's Hanna's turn. My heart skips a few beats as my bride, swathed in the lace veil, is escorted by her parents. Hanna stops a little shy of the chuppah, waiting for her parents to take their place under the canopy. Then she turns toward me and, alone, takes the last three steps, symbolizing that she is marrying me of her own free will.

After the rabbi reads the marriage contract in Hebrew, I place a plain gold ring on Hanna's finger. "Behold, thou art consecrated to me with this ring, according to the law of Moses and Israel," I recite after the rabbi.

Emil puts a wine glass, wrapped in a white linen cloth, on the floor by my right foot. I stomp on the glass as hard as I can. As the glass shatters, shouts of mazel tov! ring through the synagogue.

* * * * *

I wake up early the next morning, surprised to feel someone snuggling up against me. Then I remember. I'm married. I smile and drift back to sleep.

IN THE ARMY

Hanna and I soon settle into our new home in Hamburg. For me, adjusting to married life has been easier than adjusting to army life. While to my face, everyone at the army hospital is cordial enough, I often sense underlying tensions and resentment. I try to ignore it and go about my rounds with a forced smile and false cheerfulness. Fortunately, I know what I'm talking about when it comes to medicine. I graduated at the top of my class, and I make a point to read up on all the new advances being made. The other doctors frequently have to ask for my opinion, albeit grudgingly.

I'm learning to balance my knowledge with humility as no German wants to be outdone by a Jew. A few of the doctors and nurses would rather be wrong, and let their patients die, than ask or take my advice. These are the people who make it difficult for me, complaining to my commanding officers and subtly encouraging the patients to ignore or question my instructions. Dealing with complaints and criticism is becoming a way of life for me.

Thus, when I hear a commanding voice call "Herr Doctor" as I'm treating a soldier with a lung ailment, I expect to hear yet another complaint. I turn around to see a young officer approaching me. There is something familiar about him, but I don't recognize him.

He laughs when I salute. "I never dreamed I'd live to see a salute coming from you, Kov."

"Christof! I didn't know you in that uniform." I look my friend up and down. "The past few years have been good to you."

"And to you." He playfully punches my shoulder. "It's good to see you again."

I invite Christof to the house to meet Hanna and catch up on old times. A few nurses look up curiously. Ignoring them, he accepts without hesitation.

When Christof comes home with me the next night, Hanna meets us at the door. "You didn't tell me she was so beautiful," he says sincerely. "Tell me, Hanna, how did he trick you into marrying him?"

We laugh and sit down for an evening of conversation and Hanna's good cooking.

After Christof leaves, Hanna turns to me with a big smile. "I like him," she says. "I can see why you two are such good friends."

"He's the closest thing I have to a brother."

We clean up and head to bed. Just as I think Hanna has dozed off, she murmurs, "Why can't the others be like Christof? Germany would be a much nicer place."

"That's what I'm working for, my love." I kiss her gently on the forehead.

After that, Christof becomes a regular at our house, and he stops in often at the army hospital. It may be just my imagination, but it seems like the rest of the staff is treating me better because of him. But there are still complaints. And there are still soldiers who refuse to be treated by a Jewish doctor. I finally discuss the problem with Christof at a beer garden close to the hospital.

"I know it's hard for you, Kov. And I admire what you're trying to do. But you knew going in that it wouldn't be easy." He looks around the hall and then leans toward me. "As for why so many of my countrymen are this way, I have no idea. I can't even make excuses. All I know is that these feelings about Jews date back before the Crusades. I guess it's part of the German psyche to hate Jews. That doesn't make it right, but it seems to be true."

"So why aren't you infected with this hatred?"

He laughs at my medical metaphor. "It's how I was raised. And I was fortunate enough to grow up with a nice Jewish boy who became my best and most loyal friend." He drinks from his stein. "You know I'm not the only German who feels this way."

"You're the only one I know. But you give me hope," I raise my stein in a mock toast. "That doesn't make things any easier at the hospital though."

Christof leans back in his chair. "Perhaps you should put in for a transfer to the navy. While you'd still run into some of the same old prejudices, you're more likely to be left alone there. It's something to think about."

IN WAITING

With a sense of wonder, I pat Hanna's burgeoning belly and feel my child kick against the pressure. Hanna puts her hand over mine and smiles.

"I love you so much," I whisper.

She snuggles against my shoulder. "I love you too, Dr. Wolf."

I'd like to think this is how our life will be forever, but I know it can't be. Ever since the newspapers reported that the Herero in South West Africa had risen up and murdered hundreds of German settlers and their families, I've been waiting for my transfer to the navy and my new orders. We'll be sending naval forces to help quell the uprising, which means surgeons will be needed. The deserts of Africa are not a sought-after posting for well-bred, ambitious medical doctors, which means I'm likely to be sent. If only I could wait till our child is born.

"Have you heard yet whether you'll have to go?" Hanna looks up at me with the glint of tears in her eyes.

I'll never understand how she can read my mind so easily. I shake my head, wanting to talk about it and yet wanting to talk about something – anything – else. "I'll know soon." I stroke her long blonde hair. "But if I have to go, it won't be a lengthy separation. A few tribesmen armed with knives and old guns will be no match for our artillery."

She settles back against my shoulder. "Do you ever regret your decision to join the military?" she asks.

"No." I lean my chin gently on her head. "If I'm sent to Africa, I'll regret being away from you, but I won't regret my service to the Fatherland."

"Even the way they treat you?"

I've tried not to tell Hanna about the offensive comments, the vulgar gestures, and the hateful slurs that have been aimed at me by officers, soldiers, and some of the other doctors, but I can't hide my feelings of isolation from her entirely. She knows me too well. She also suspects that it's no coincidence that I'm routinely assigned to Friday night and Saturday rounds so I can't go to synagogue.

"My service is not for them," I murmur. "It's for you, for Papa, for our children, and for all the Jews who call Germany home. And if that means I must endure some bullying or be separated from my family, so be it."

THE BLESSING

I have my orders to go to South West Africa. But first, I'm to be sent to the Baltic naval base at Kiel. In the few weeks we have left together, Hanna and I are trying to make every moment last a lifetime. It's not that I'm afraid of being killed in battle. I'm sure the uprising will be over before I get there. And even if it's not, I won't be on the front lines. No, what worries me are all the other things that could happen – a shipwreck, malaria, or Hanna dying in childbirth. I try not to think of that last possibility, but the thought is never far from my mind.

We've decided Hanna will stay with Papa while I'm gone, if it's all right with him. I'm sure she'd be more comfortable with her parents in Würzburg – what with the baby coming – but Papa needs someone to look after him, and the Heitzfelds' house is already crowded with extended family.

When we arrive at Papa's, his gaunt face lights up, especially when he sees me hoisting Hanna's trunk. "You're coming home?" His calloused hand pats my cheek.

"Yes and no," I say, lowering the trunk to the floor. "I'm being sent out of the country, and I wondered if Hanna could stay with you while I'm gone."

"Of course. My daughter is always welcome. Although I doubt I will be much use when the little one arrives." He motions for Hanna to sit down, fussing about her as he tries to make her comfortable.

"We've made arrangements for that."

"And what about you? You should be here when your child is born." He looks up at me narrowly.

"I know, Papa. We can discuss this after I get Hanna settled in." I pick up the trunk and carry it into my old room.

I take my time putting Hanna's things into the wooden cupboard. The hardest part is putting away the baby clothes and blankets she has made. They're so tiny. And I know our child will have long outgrown them before I get to see him, or her. I have to remind myself, once again, that I'm doing the right thing, that my service to the Fatherland will earn our children the respect of their fellow countrymen.

I gaze out the bedroom window, absently noting all the things that have changed and stayed the same, as I listen to the pleasant hum of Hanna and Papa talking. The conversation breaks off as Papa coughs, a dry hacking sound that echoes through the small apartment.

He's still doubled over coughing when I reach the living room. Hanna offers him a glass of water, but he waves it away. He sinks onto the couch. I kneel beside him, waiting for him to regain his breath.

"How long have you had this cough?" I finally ask in my best bedside manner.

"A few months." His voice is raspy, and his breathing ragged.

"What does Dr. Goldstein say about it?"

"What does he know?" Papa says evasively.

As I kneel there looking up at the feeble old man Papa has become, I sense that this will be my last visit with him. Feeling the tears welling in my eyes, I pat his knee awkwardly. I wish I could just once tell him how much I love him, but the barrier that's always been between us holds me back.

Assured that Papa is all right, Hanna excuses herself on the pretense that she needs to rest. But as she leaves the room, she gives me a look, one that says she expects me to talk with Papa about Africa. I swallow hard and walk over to the front window where I can look out at the narrow street lined with Jewish shops. Keeping my back toward Papa, I try to be nonchalant. "You've heard about the uprising in South West Africa?"

"Yes, I've read about it in the papers." His voice is steadier now. "Terrible mess."

I remain silent, giving him time to make the connection.

"That's where you're going? To Africa?"

"Yes, Papa." I turn to look at him. "And I would like your blessing."

"My blessing?" He sits in astounded silence for a few minutes before continuing. "My blessing to kill strangers who have never harmed you? My blessing to die in a land that is not ours? My blessing to break my heart?" Silent sobs shake his frail body as he stares down at the worn rug for moments of eternity.

When he finally looks up at me, his usual weary dignity has dissolved into raw anguish. "Son, from the day you were born, you became my life – my future."

Surprised by Papa's open expression of his feelings for me, I sit next to him, embracing him. "My going to Africa doesn't change that. I'm going as a doctor, not as a soldier. I will be healing people, not killing them." I speak softly. "I will come back. I promise."

Ignoring my words, Papa rushes on, "All your life, you had only to ask me for something, and it was yours. But this request, Yaakov, I cannot honor. I cannot give you my blessing to fight a war that should not be fought."

"But, Papa . . . ."

Shaking his head, Papa puts his trembling finger to his lips. The discussion is over.

SAYING GOODBYE

Before leaving for Kiel, I visit with Ritter von Epenstein. As I get off the train at Neuhaus, I glance up at Burg Veldenstein standing guard over the village and am amazed at the progress that's been made. No longer a ruin, the old castle looks as solid as the day it was first built. I quicken my pace, eager to see the restoration up close.

"Dr. Wolf!" I hear as I reach the courtyard of the fortress. I turn just as Epenstein emerges from the woods, followed by an adolescent carrying a brace of fowl. I wave and wait for my host to catch up with me.

A servant runs out to take Epenstein's rifle and relieve the boy of the game. The ritter turns toward me. "Ah, Kov, my friend. It is good to see you." He embraces me. "It looks like military life agrees with you." He pats his hunting companion on the back, nudging him forward. "You remember my godson Hermann?"

"You've grown." I shake hands with the boy as he sizes me up with his ice blue eyes.

"Yes, Hermann is quite the young man," Epenstein says. "He's going to leave his mark on this world. You just wait and see."

Hermann seems to take the comments in stride, accepting them as fact rather than flattery.

"So you're off to Africa?" Epenstein leads me into the fortress.

"Yes, sir. I'll be in Kiel for a few weeks, and then I'm heading to South West Africa as part of the Marine Expeditionskorps."

"Who's your commanding officer?"

"Major von Glasenapp. Do you know him, sir?"

Epenstein shakes his head. "Only by reputation. But what I have heard is good. He served the country well in China, and the men who served under him truly love him."

As we enter the house, my host points out all the changes that have been made since my last visit. The renovations are both artistic and practical. I'm suitably impressed.

Over lunch, Epenstein prepares me for the journey to Africa. "You've never been on a ship, have you?" he asks me.

"No, sir."

"Do you get sick when you travel by train?"

I smile sheepishly. "Sometimes, especially if I'm looking out the window and we're going fast. I get over it though by fixing my eyes on something steady."

He chuckles. "You're going to get so seasick, especially if you hit rough seas. When the seas are churning, there's nothing steady to rest your eyes upon."

"I wouldn't get seasick, Papa," young Hermann pipes up, giving me a withering look from across the table.

"You have a hardy constitution, my boy. But even you might be a bit queasy the first time you're on a ship." Epenstein looks over at me and laughs. "You should see your face. You're green already and you have yet to set sail! There's no reason to worry. All the first-timers will be sick, too. The only difference is that you'll be expected to take care of them."

He sips his wine before continuing. "The key to conquering seasickness is learning the rhythm of the waves. Once you have mastered that rhythm, you'll be fine. I also suggest you take some ropes to tie yourself in bed, in case you run into a storm."

Seeing my expression, he laughs again. "You should have mostly smooth sailing this time of year. Just never take the sea for granted. Even in relatively calm waters, the difference between the trough of a wave and its peak can be several meters. If you're standing at the bow or the stern of the ship and you're not hanging on to something, you can go flying into the air when the ship descends. And when you land on that hard deck, it hurts.

"I remember this one young sailor who loved to 'soar,' as he called it, despite the broken bones he suffered when landing. One calm afternoon, he was playing at the stern of the ship with some of his mates. As the boat descended into the trough, he flew at least six meters into the air. But this time, he didn't land on the deck. Instead, he crashed into the ocean. He was never seen again."

"But how could he disappear like that, sir?" I ask, half wondering if Epenstein is joking.

"Consider that, in all likelihood, only his shoulders and head were above the water. And he was surrounded by an endless sea of two-meter waves that made him virtually invisible to everyone on the boat." He pauses as he butters a slab of bread. "I'm not trying to scare you. I just want you to be careful. If that sailor could disappear in the middle of the afternoon, in smooth seas with a boatload of people watching, imagine what could happen at night or in a storm."

Epenstein takes a few bites. "It should take you about three weeks to get there – provided you have calm seas. And with the Habicht already on its way, the rebellion could be over before you arrive."

I nod. The newspapers are full of reports of the gunboat being redirected from Cape Town to quell the uprising.

"If I were in charge of the army, the fighting would have been over the week it started," Hermann says matter-of-factly. "And all those murderous natives would have been executed."

Epenstein winks at me as he tousles Hermann's hair. "Sounds like we have the wrong general in command!"

He excuses Hermann to run an errand. As soon as we're alone, Epenstein takes on a more serious demeanor. "You're a good, kind man, Yaakov. I hope you will find it within yourself to forgive me one day."

"Whatever for? You've done nothing but help me, sir."

He smiles sadly and shakes his head. "I'm afraid that I have done you a huge disservice by getting you a military posting." He looks down at the table. "This isn't going to be an easy war. The Herero have every reason to rise up against us; they're fighting for their homes and their freedom. But there are those Germans who will not be satisfied with a quick victory. They will want nothing less than the total destruction of the Herero people."

He raises his hand when I start to interrupt. "Yes, you're going as a doctor. But you're also a marine. You may be ordered to do things that you know are wrong. And you will have to follow those orders. May God have mercy on your soul."

* * * * *

The next morning, I wake up early and roll over so I can watch Hanna sleep. Her large belly rises and falls beneath the blue quilt Mama made for me years ago. The hint of a smile tugs at the corners of her mouth. Her long eyelashes flutter against her pale cheeks. She is so peaceful and content. This is how I'll remember her when I'm in Africa.

Her eyes blink open, and a shy smile plays over her face. I lean down to kiss her forehead. "It's early," I whisper. "Don't get up yet."

"Where are you going?" she asks as I kick the covers off.

"I have to say goodbye to Mama."

Dressed in my suit, I walk to the Jewish cemetery at the edge of town. It's been a while since I've visited Mama's grave. As I reach the graveyard, I pick up a pebble and pocket it. Then I do the ritual cleansing, washing my hands at the pump provided for that purpose. Entering the gate, I recite the customary blessing: "Blessed are You, the Lord our God, King of the universe, Who fashioned you in justice, nourished and sustained you in justice. Who knows your total count in justice, and Who in the future will revive and keep you alive in justice. Blessed are You, the Lord, Who resurrects the dead."

Thinking of what Epenstein told me yesterday, I find new comfort in the ancient words. I ponder their meaning before continuing with the proper passages from Isaiah and the Psalms: "Your dead will live again; my corpses will arise. Awake and sing, dwellers of dust! For the dew of light is Your dew, and the earth will give forth the dead. And He is merciful, atones for sin and does not destroy, frequently turns away His anger and does not arouse all His wrath."

Being careful not to step on any graves, I walk over to the granite, tablet-shaped stone marking Mama's resting place. The tombstone is covered with the pebbles Papa has left on his many visits. Seeing how often he's been here, I am ashamed of my long absence. Placing my left hand on the headstone, I trace the etched menorah and Hebrew lettering with my right: *"Here lies Elise bat Eliyahu. May her soul be bound in the bundle of life."*

I begin the prayers for Mama, but the words seem to apply to me as much as to her: *"And the Lord will always guide you, and satisfy your soul in scorched places, and resurrect your bones. And you will be like a watered garden, and like a spring of waters that never fail. From you will rebuild the ancient ruins; the generations-old foundations you will re-establish. They will call you 'the repairer of the breach, the restorer of the ways of civilization.' Rest in peace until the coming of the Consoler Who will proclaim peace."*

After reciting the Psalms, I tell Mama about Hanna, the baby, and my concerns about Papa, asking her to intercede for them. "Tomorrow, I'm leaving for Kiel, and from there, I will be going to South West Africa. I know I'm hurting Papa deeply; I wish you were here to explain it to him. You could make him understand why I have to do this."

I choke back a tear. "No matter how far away I go, you will always be in my thoughts. Mama, I miss you so much."

Before leaving the grave, I pledge my charity and finish the memorial prayer: *"May her repose be in paradise. May the Lord of Mercy shelter her under the cover of His wings forever and bind in the bond of life her soul. The Lord is her heritage. May she rest in peace on her resting place."* I take the pebble out of my pocket and put it alongside all those left by Papa. At the gate of the cemetery, I ritually cleanse myself of death.

I spend the rest of the day with Hanna and Papa, trying to act like it's just another day while at the same time engraving every glance, every word, every lingering touch into my memory. Hanna hovers near me, tending to my needs. I should be the one taking care of her instead of traipsing off across the world.

She laughs at me as, once again, I review the arrangements we've made for the baby. "Stop worrying about me," she says. "The baby and I will both be fine. You just promise me you'll take care of yourself. Our baby needs his father."

I reach over to kiss her cheek. "What did I ever do to deserve you?" I murmur.

"Nothing," Papa grumbles.

"I know that, Papa. No one has to tell me," I say agreeably. Today is not a day to argue. It's a time to store up memories – of Hanna laughing, her hazel eyes twinkling in the candlelight; of Papa chanting his prayers, his fingers stroking the tzitzit of his prayer shawl as his voice rises and falls with the Hebrew syllables. I cling to every moment, wanting each one to last forever. But I can't ignore the ticking of the mantle clock, counting off the few hours I have left with my family.

All too soon, it's time to go. With tears in my eyes, I hold Hanna one last time. Then I turn to Papa. He embraces me in his awkward way. "I love you, Papa," I whisper almost inaudibly into his grizzled beard.

His hold tightens. "I cannot give you my blessing, son," he murmurs with a sob in his voice, "but you will be in my prayers."

Hiding my tears, I bend down to pick up my rucksack. As I step out the door, I can no longer hold back my emotions. When I reach the street, I look back. Hanna and Papa stand, arm in arm, tears streaming down their cheeks, watching me from the window. I wave sadly and resolutely turn toward the train station.

I have never felt more alone.

BOOK 2

Jahohora

WORDS OF WAR

Tate stays home now, but Mama is still sad. I see her glance across the veld several times a day. She is afraid. I don't know why. We are all safe. The white people leave us alone. They haven't come to our village since the cattle sickness. Besides, Tate and uncles are here to protect us.

After my work is done, I play with my cousins. We take turns racing. I am the fastest now, so the others want to try to beat me. I'm far ahead of all the others when Mama calls after me, "Don't leave the village."

My cousins stop. I pretend I don't hear. I'm tired of staying in the little circle of huts. I run into the veld, but I can still see my house. I slow to a walk, listening to the birds singing to each other. I smile. It feels good to leave the quiet sadness of the village. I stop when the birdsong quickly turns to a loud screeching of warning cries. I look out across the veld. In the distance, I see a dust cloud rising from the ground. Horses. Someone is coming toward me. I turn around and run as fast as I can back to the village.

"Mama ... Tate!" I shout as I gulp for breath. "Someone ... is ... coming ... on horses."

Tate tells all the women and children to go to their huts. Uncles get their weapons. Most of them have kirris or knives. A few have boom sticks. Tate doesn't need clubs or boom sticks. He has words. He says words, even the softest ones, are louder than boom sticks, harder than clubs, and sharper than knives. And they have more power. Tate and uncles gather by the holy fire and wait for the visitors.

Two Herero men ride into the village. They are headmen sent by the chief. It's been many days since anyone has come to our village or left it, so we don't know what's happening in other parts of Hereroland. As uncles and Tate talk with the headmen, Mama stands close to the doorway of our hut, listening. I want to stand by her. She shakes her head and tells me to play with Karemarama.

Tate and uncles talk with the headmen for a long time. I hear their voices rise and fall, but their words are a mumble. I watch Mama's face. She is very worried. And angry. She looks like she wants to cry and shout – all at once. She turns her face when she sees me watching her. I can still see her hands making hard fists.

"J'hora, tell me a story," Karemarama demands. "Tell me about first day."

"Not now," I say.

"Then I'll tell you the story."

I only half listen as he tells how Njambi Karunga called Mukuru and Kamangarunga, the first Herero tate and mama, out of the omumborombonga tree into the darkness of the first day.

"Then Njambi Karunga called the first ancestors of all the tribes and all the animals out of the tree. But he didn't call the tate and mama of white people from the tree," he says. "Njambi Karunga told the tate and mama of the white people they had to live in the tree until now. Njambi didn't want white people to come to Hereroland."

I laugh. "That's not what happened."

Karemarama sticks his bottom lip out. "It's what should have happened," he says. "Do you think we can make white people go back into the omumborombonga tree?"

I shake my head. "It's too late to chase the white cattle from the holy fire," I say, remembering Tjikuu's praise song. "They are too many."

The hut grows darker. I look up. Tate is standing in the opening, blocking the sunlight. He asks Mama to cook some food for the headmen. It's been a long time since they've eaten, and they have many other villages to visit.

It's almost twilight when the headmen leave. Tate calls all the uncles and aunties to the holy fire. We have important things to discuss with the ancestors, he says. Like always, Tate takes water in his mouth and spits on the youngest children. He doesn't spit on me. I'm old enough now to drink from the gourd myself.

After naming everyone who's at the fire, Tate tells the ancestors the words the headmen brought. Our chief and his counselors keep promising peace to the Germans. The chief even wrote a letter to the German governor. But more soldiers have come to the chief's village. They built a fort in the mission compound and filled it with the big guns that make lightning and thunder. White settlers from the farms have gone to the fort, seeking safety. They bring stories of Herero murdering women and children. The chief tells the missionaries the stories aren't true.

But the German soldiers and settlers don't listen. They're afraid of the Herero, so they're getting ready for war.

A few Herero stole some cattle and broke into a trader's store. The chief made them give everything back to the white people, Tate says. Then a Herero who didn't listen to the chief killed an English trader. The chief sent his men to bring the man to Otjimbingwe for trial. But the Germans still didn't trust the chief. Now a German boat has come to Swakopmund. The soldiers from the boat are making war on the Herero. They put chains around the necks of many Herero. Even the women and children. And the tjikuumes and tjikuus. They send them to live in a big boat that got stuck on the sands of Swakopmund, far from their homes in Hereroland. They're not allowed to leave the boat. Many of them get sick and die.

The news gets worse. When the soldiers from the boat came to Karibib, they beat some Herero and forced them to tell lies about how their friends and family killed German settlers. The soldiers tied ropes around the necks of the men who had been accused of murder. They tied the other end of the ropes to tree branches spreading high above the earth. They left the men hanging from the trees as food for the vultures. Then the soldiers began killing everyone who lived in Karibib. One boy escaped and ran all the way to Otjimbingwe to warn the chief that the soldiers were coming to his village. The soldiers are coming now. And in every village along the way, the soldiers are killing Herero. Young and old, men and women.

Tate shakes his head sadly. "This is not the way to make war," he says. "When the Witboois make war on the Herero, they take our cattle and shoot only our warriors who fight against them. Once they have what they want, they go home."

"The Germans will never go home," Uncle Kozondanda says. "They want the land itself."

Tate nods. "It's not safe for us to stay here. If the soldiers come, they won't care that we are peaceful." Tate turns to the holy fire and asks the ancestors what we should do. He pauses, listening to their answer. Then he faces us again.

"The ancestors say we must leave this village and go to the Okavaka Mountains," he tells us. "We will be safe there until this ends. We will be far from the Germans, so they won't mistake us for warriors."

Some uncles don't want to hide. "We're not old men who can't defend themselves," they say. "Hiding is for women and children. If the Germans bring war to us, we must fight like Herero warriors."

Tate nods. But he's sad. "The ancestors said some of you would join Maharero." He's quiet while he thinks. "You must take some of the family cattle. When the Germans and Maharero put down their weapons, you will bring the cattle back to the village."

The uncles talk about who will join Maharero and who will go with Tate to the Okavaka. Tate says the soldiers are two days' journey from our village. We must all leave the next night when there will be no moon. The moonless sky will help hide us.

What about Tjikuu? I wonder. And Tuaekua Ehi? And Uapiruka? Where will they go? Mama Uajoroka asks the question for me. She is Tuaekua Ehi's mama.

Tate says we will stop in their village on our way to the mountains.

The next day, Tate and Ramata go with uncles to divide the cattle and goats. Mama and I pack food for our journey. Mama tries to smile. She tells Karemarama that we're going on a big adventure. It will be like when we go with Tate to take the cattle to the high country. But we'll go even higher into the Okavaka this time.

He's excited. "Will we see lions? And leopards?" he asks.

"I hope not," Mama says.

That afternoon, Mama makes us lie down to sleep.

"But I'm not tired," I say.

"You must sleep," Mama says. "We will walk all night tonight, so you need to rest now." She lies down too.

I try and try to sleep, but my eyes aren't heavy. I'm too excited, and worried, about going to the mountains. Walking at night across the veld can be dangerous. Even without soldiers. There are snakes. And hungry animals. And what about tomorrow? What happens then?

Just as my eyes close, Mama wakes us up. Tate and Ramata are back. We must get ready to leave. We eat a quick meal. As the sun sinks toward the distant mountains, we meet all the uncles and aunties by the holy fire. Tate tells the ancestors where each of us is going so they'll know where to find us. Then he takes a piece of charred wood from the fire. He will use it to start a new holy fire when we get to the mountains. Tate also picks up the branch of the sacred omumborombonga tree and puts it in his pack. He turns away from the holy fire.

"Aren't you going to put it out?" I ask.

"It must die on its own," he says. "We cannot put out what we don't start."

The last light of the sun is fading when we're ready to leave. Aunties and cousins cry as they say goodbye. Uncles quietly herd the cattle and goats. Most of the clan is going to join Maharero in the land where the sun wakes the day. They go first, driving the cattle before them. The rest of us watch silently as they disappear into the veld.

When our small group leaves the village, I turn to look back. Darkness grows about the empty huts and kraal. The only sign of life is the tail of smoke that rises from the holy fire. It's as if the ancestors are waving us on our way. It makes me want to cry. Mama sees me looking back. She puts her arm around my shoulders and pulls me close. "It's all right," she says. "We'll all be back together soon."

We walk quietly across the veld. I walk with Tate, who leads the way. "How do you know which way to go?" I ask. "There's no sun to guide you."

Tate points to five stars shining brightly in the white sky path we call the omukuangu. "The Otjikoroise Tjovaeve shows us the way at night," he says.

I look up at the stars. Four of them are very bright. But the reddish one is much smaller and dimmer. "How do you read them?"

Tate uses his finger to draw a line between the top and bottom stars. "Wherever the Otjikoroise Tjovaeve is in the sky, those two stars will always point toward home," he says. His finger moves to the bright star just above the small red one. "That star points to where the sun wakes."

There's no moon tonight. Tate says that's good because it makes it easier to follow the stars. They don't have to fight with the light of the moon.

As we walk, I'm frightened by the many noises that fill the night. I can make out the growl of the brown hyena, the whistle of the duiker, the bark of wild dogs. These are all sounds I heard in the distance in the village. But out here on the veld, they're much closer. I remind myself that Tate and Uncle Kozondanda will keep us safe. I shut my ears to the wild sounds, listening instead to the gentle, familiar lowing of the cattle. It calms me.

We finally come to Tjikuu's village. It seems much farther at night. When we get near the village, Tate calls like a bird, so we won't surprise anyone. It's a sign mama's brothers recognize. One of them calls back and comes out to meet us. He talks quietly with Tate. They have heard about the soldiers. Some uncles and cousins have already joined Maharero. The few who remain gather in the center of the village. Tjikuu is there. And Tuaekua Ehi and Vijanda with Karikuta, their baby boy.

I hold my arms out to Karikuta. He kicks his feet and laughs as Tuaekua Ehi hands him to me. "Where is Uapiruka?" I whisper to Tuaekua Ehi.

"His family is joining Maharero," she tells me.

Tate says we can't stay long. We must get to the mountains as soon as possible. Tuaekua Ehi and Vijanda want to come with us. A few of the others do, too. They quickly gather whatever they can carry.

Mama asks Tjikuu to come. But Tjikuu shakes her head. "I'm too old for the mountains," she says. "I will stay here in the village with my sisters."

"But you will have no one to protect you," Mama says. "All the men are leaving."

"We will be safe," Tjikuu tells her. "The white people have no reason to fear a few harmless old women."

Mama nods and smiles. But I know she is worried about Tjikuu. "Please come with us, Tjikuu," I say.

"Climbing mountains is for the young." She gives me a long hug. "When we meet next, you'll be a grown woman."

I laugh, but her words make me sad. Tears wet my eyes.

At last, we're ready to go again. I walk with Tuaekua Ehi and her mama, Uajoroka. We take turns carrying the baby, being careful not to stumble on rocks or shrubs. The night grows long, and I'm very tired. I want to lie down and sleep, but I keep walking. Except for the soft jingle of the women's beads and bangles, we move silently over the earth – as our ancestors did before us. It's the old way of the Herero – to move from place to place so our cattle have fresh grazing. But since the white people took our land, we have had to stay mostly in one place.

The darkness lightens as the sun prepares for a new day. Tate leads us to a waterhole. I hadn't realized how thirsty I was until the cool water runs down my throat. We water the animals and fill our waterskins for later in the day. Mama Uajoroka lies down on the ground. "This is a good place to rest," she says.

"We must go a little further before we can stop for the day," Tate tells her. "We can't stay by the waterhole. It would be too dangerous. The soldiers may come here to drink and water their horses."

Mama Uajoroka sighs as she gets slowly to her feet. We fall in line again, following Tate as he leads us closer to the mountains, to a place white people don't come. Here, we will sleep for the day, hidden by the tall grass of the veld and protected by the shade of a few trees.

I'm so tired I don't mind the prickliness of the grass or the unevenness of the ground. I just want to lie down. Then I see Mama set off toward the milk cows with a gourd. The cows don't care that we've been walking all night. They want to be milked. I know Mama is just as tired as I am. I look down at the ground and yawn. I want only to sleep right now. But Mama needs my help. She smiles wearily when I join her. Aunties also help. The milking goes much faster since we don't have as many cows. But we still have enough milk to make omaere for everyone.

The milking done, I lie down near Mama. Sleep comes instantly. But in my dreams, I'm still walking. It's a journey with no end. The sun beats down on me, setting me on fire with its heat. I raise my hand against its brightness. There's no blocking it. I stumble as I move forward, forcing myself to take another step. And then another. And another. I realize I'm alone. I look for Mama and Tate. For Ramata, Karemarama, and Tuaekua Ehi. They are nowhere. But I'm not afraid. I feel nothing. I'm too tired and too hot to feel. I can only walk, even though my legs are like heavy rocks. I stir in my sleep and begin another dream. Again, I'm walking. And I'm alone. The dream repeats itself as I slip in and out of sleep, tossing in the heat of the afternoon sun.

A fly buzzes in my ear, breaking the stream of my dreams. I open my eyes, shielding them from the sun with my hand. Tuaekua Ehi is feeding Karikuta. A few others are moving about quietly. But most of the group are still sleeping. I see Ramata sitting on the edge of our makeshift camp. He looks out across the veld. I walk over to him, being careful not to step on Mama or Karemarama.

"What are you doing here, Ramata?" I whisper from behind him. "Can't you sleep?"

He spins around and looks at me. "Don't come up behind me like that. You startled me."

"Why are you sitting here?" I ask again. "Have you slept at all?"

He yawns. "It's my turn to watch," he says. "I slept while Tate and the others watched."

"What are you watching?" I look out over the veld. Other than our cattle and goats grazing nearby, I don't see anything except a herd of wildebeest and some dark clouds rolling together where the mountains touch the sky.

"I'm making sure no white people come. Especially soldiers," he says.

"What would you do if you saw a soldier? You have no boom stick." I laugh softly.

"Neither does Tate. And he watches."

"But what would you do if soldiers were coming?" I ask.

"I'd wake everyone up so we could hide."

"It would be hard to hide the cattle," I say.

"I guess the soldiers would take them. And then they'd look for us." Ramata slumps down.

"Let's hope they don't come this way." I look again across the veld. The clouds are piling on top of each other as they race toward us. "It's going to storm," I say. "We should wake the others so they can hide from the rain."

We get everyone up. They gather their things quickly. I help Tuaekua Ehi with the baby. We all move beneath a clump of trees. They'll give us some protection from the wind and the rain the clouds will bring.

As the clouds roll in, the wind hits first, stinging us with the sand it blows against us. Tuaekua Ehi and I bend over Karikuta, using our bodies to break the wind. The tall grass dances wildly, while the trees bow low, scratching us with their thorny branches. Then the rain comes, like a broad river rushing from the sky. The thirsty veld drinks what it can and lets the rest of the water run off into the river beds formed when our ancestors walked the earth.

The rain ends as quickly as it began. Wet but not soaked through, we leave the shelter of the trees to let the sun dry us off. Karemarama runs to a nearby termite hill. "Mama!" he shouts. "We need a fire."

Mama turns to Tate. He looks out over the veld and then nods his head slowly. The young cousins chatter happily. We're going to have roasted termites! It's a rare treat we get only after a rain. Mama gets a calabash and the two flint stones she uses to start a fire. As she and I walk toward the termite hill, I keep my eyes on the ground, looking for a dry hollow branch. I find one and then pull handfuls of grass. Even though it's just rained, the grass is already dry.

Karemarama is closing off the holes of the tall termite hill.

"Be careful," Mama calls. "Look for snakes first."

He backs off and checks for snakes at the base of the hill. Snakes like termites as much as we do. Especially puff adders. They hide in the shade of the termite house. While most snakes usually slither away, adders will bite. And their bite can be deadly.

"No snakes," Karemarama says as we join him. I help him close off the rest of the holes, except the main opening at the bottom of the termite hill. I have to close the openings at the top. He isn't tall enough to reach them without knocking down the hill.

Mama takes the hollow branch I found and fills it with the dry grass. She puts it in front of the main opening. Then she strikes the flint stones against each other, causing a spark that lights the grass. As it begins to burn, Karemarama and I quickly get more grass to build the fire.

We hold the big calabash close to the fire so we can catch the winged termites that try to escape the heat. They swarm out all at once – right into our calabash. Mama covers the calabash with a skin so none of the termites can escape.

By time we get back to the camp, the aunties have made a fire and are ready to roast the insects. Mama carefully releases the termites into a hot pan. As the termites roast, an auntie gently tosses them into the air so their thin wings fall off and float away. The now-wingless termites drop back into the pan. While termites taste good, their wings don't. One time I ate a termite that still had its wings. They stuck to the top of my mouth. I had to pull hard to get them out.

The cousins laugh while we eat the roasted termites. Even Tate and Mama are smiling. That evening as we wait for the sun to sleep, the aunties tell funny stories. This is a big adventure, I think happily as I play with Karikuta.

THE OKAVAKA MOUNTAINS

After a few nights of walking, we reach a waterhole near the base of the Okavaka just as the sun wakes up. The rock face of the mountain, glowing in the early light of the sun, seems to grow almost straight up out of the veld. I drink my fill of water and then put my head back so I can see the flat top of the mountain. My head is so far back it hurts my neck. How will we ever get up there? If we had wings like a bird, it would be easy. But we have cows and goats and babies and young children.

Mama Uajoroka says out loud what I'm thinking.

Tate grins. "You're right," he says. "We can't go up this side. We will have to go around to where the mountain rises more slowly from the earth. It will be an easier path, but it can still be dangerous, especially now in the rainy season. We will have to climb it while the sun is awake."

Mama Uajoroka moans. "I won't go any further until I get some sleep," she says. "We've been walking all night."

Tate nods his head. "We're all tired," he says. "We'll rest here most of today. This waterhole is not one the Germans will find.

But just before the sun sets, we must find the path. We'll camp there tonight."

We milk the cows and finish watering the animals before lying down in a bit of shade. Ramata says he will take the first watch.

Knowing that we're near the end of our trek makes it hard to sleep, especially in the late summer heat. I roll over on the stony ground, trying to hide my eyes from the bright light of the sun. But there's no hiding. And the rocks push against my side. I sit up and look around. Everyone but Ramata is sleeping. I wish I could sleep. I quietly sweep the rocks from the ground so I have a smooth place. Exhausted, I lie down again. This time, my eyes close.

It seems like I've just gone to sleep when Mama wakes me. It's time to eat.

"I don't want to get up," I say. "I'm still tired."

"Everyone else has been awake for a while," Mama says. "You've got to get up."

We eat and rest a little longer before setting out again. The sun is low in the sky, making it cooler. I want to run so I can get there faster. I'm tired of all the walking. But Tate sets the same slow pace we've traveled the past few nights. I know it's so everyone can keep together. Still, the sooner we get to the path, the sooner I can sleep again.

We keep walking long after the sun is gone from the sky. Tate leads us to where the mountain rises slowly from the veld. It's like a huge dark shadow that hides the moon. Tate's been here many times. He knows the easiest way to the top. But the path is hard to find in the dark. Finally, he tells us to rest while he looks for the path.

I sit on the ground with my back against a rock. Tuaekua Ehi wants to talk. I'm too tired. Her voice becomes a soft hum as my eyes close.

I'm in that place between sleep and wake when Tate returns. I hear him say we can stay here until morning. He has found the path. It's close by. Tuaekua Ehi gently shakes me. "Jahohora," she says, "you need to lie down so you can sleep better."

I open my eyes and stretch. I almost hit Tuaekua Ehi. "Sorry," I say sleepily. I kneel and look for a place without rocks.

"Over here." Tuaekua Ehi leads me to a spot close to where Vijanda lies with the baby. She lies down. "There's room for you here. It's a good place to sleep."

I curl up on the ground and sleep.

The next morning, we are all rested and ready to begin the climb up the mountain. Tate tells us it will be a harder walk today, but we must keep going. We have to reach the top before dark.

Tate leads out, and the women and children follow. Ramata, Vijanda, Uncle Kozondanda, and the other men walk behind, herding the animals. Once again, I walk with Tuaekua Ehi and Mama Uajoroka so I can help with Karikuta. Tate quickly finds what he says is the path. It's not really a path. It's just one of the many places the water runs down from the mountain after a rain. But today, it's dry.

At first, the ground rises gently so walking is easy. It's a good thing. The sun is already hot and uncomfortable. Especially since we're used to walking in the coolness of the night. Tate stops a few times so the aunties can rest. He teases them about not being able to keep up. "This is the easy part," he says. "Just wait till we get to where the mountain really rises. By then, you'll be walking with your hands and feet."

"Not me," Mama Uajoroka says. "If it gets that steep, you'll have to carry me up the mountain, Mutihu." Mama and the other aunties laugh.

"You'd break my back," Tate says. "You'll have to get your own husband to carry you."

Uncle Kozondanda grabs his back as if it's broken. He makes a funny face. We all laugh again.

Tate grins and picks up his pack. "Now you keep up, Uajoroka," he says as he starts walking.

The path slowly becomes steeper. I watch my feet so I can step over the many rocks that washed down with the rains. I hear Mama Uajoroka breathing heavily behind me. I look back at her. She is using her hands to balance herself and grab onto the nearby bushes. "You need a walking stick," I tell her.

She doesn't have the breath to answer.

The sun is high in the sky when we come to a small grassy valley. Tate says we will stay here until it's cooler. I stretch out in the grass. My feet are happy to have a rest. Tate talks quietly with his brothers and Ramata. I hear him telling them that we must leave the cattle here. This is the last grass before the rocks of the mountains begin, and the cattle won't be able to make the steep climb. Ramata and one of the uncles will stay with them while the rest of us go on. Tate and Vijanda will come back once we're all settled. Then the men will take turns staying with the cattle.

"How much farther is it?" Mama asks as Tate lies down beside her.

"We have a big walk yet," he answers. "The hardest climb is ahead of us."

"How will we milk the cows if they're down here and we're all the way up there?" Mama looks up toward the top of the mountain.

"You don't want to come down here and milk them every day?" Tate laughs. "Are you getting lazy?"

Mama gives Tate her stop-joking look. "I guess you men could learn to milk them."

"We'll have to let them go dry." Tate isn't teasing now. "Even if we milked them, it would be too hard to carry the omaere to the top."

We start walking again. The path quickly rises to a steep climb. Rocks fall down on me as the people in front push forward. I slow down, putting more space between us. I try not to kick rocks down on the people behind me. I glance back. Mama Uajoroka is crawling on her hands and knees. Tate is right. We couldn't carry jars of omaere up this path every day.

The climb is hard. We have to stop often to rest. I look up. The top of the mountain doesn't seem to be getting any closer. "We must go faster," Tate says. "We have to reach the top before the sun sleeps. There's no other place to camp."

Mama Uajoroka moans. But she doesn't argue. No one wants to be on this path in the dark. It's too steep and rocky. And at night, it would be a good resting place for snakes. We try to walk faster, but Mama Uajoroka and some of the children can't keep up. And Tuaekua Ehi is having trouble carrying the baby. "Let me take him," Vijanda says. Tuaekua Ehi nods. She looks very tired.

"Hurry," Tate says. "We must race the sun."

The sun almost wins. The last rays of the day are sinking behind the earth as we reach the top of the mountain. It's a broad rocky plain that looks out over the desert. Up here, there are few trees to block the wind that sweeps over us, chilling us as the darkness spreads. Tate finds a spot that's a bit protected and calls us to him. This will be the holy fire.

As he lays out the fire circle, I help my cousins gather a few pieces of wood and some of the scraggly grass that has managed to grow through the rock of the mountaintop. We put it in the fire circle, along with the charred wood Tate brought from the holy fire back in the village. He lays the sacred branch of the omumborombonga tree nearby. Using Mama's firestones and a hollow tube with dry grasses, Tate sparks the fire. We crouch around so the wind doesn't kill the sparks before they light the grasses and then the wood.

The wood is dry, so it catches quickly. I am happy for its heat. I warm my front and then turn around so the flames can warm my back. I sit down next to Mama. Tate drinks from his waterskin and spits on Karikuta. Everyone else is big enough to drink from the skin. Tate calls to the ancestors and names everyone sitting around the fire. "We have done as you told us to," he says. "We thank you for our safe journey." He then tells the ancestors where they can find the rest of the family. He asks them to bring all of us good luck.

Tonight, we lie on the ground of our new home, huddling close to the fire and each other to keep warm. No dreams come to me. I'm too tired for dreams.

In the morning, we begin building our new village around the holy fire. Tate, Vijanda, and the uncles explore the area, looking for water, food, and places to hide. The rest of us scramble over the mountaintop, gathering branches and stripping the bark from trees. We use the bark to tie the branches into temporary round houses, like the ones our ancestors used when they moved their great herds of cattle across the veld. The huts will not keep out all the wind, but they will be better than nothing. And they will give us some protection from the rain and the heat of the sun.

It takes us most of the day to make the houses. By time we're through, my belly is growling with hunger. But there's no omaere, no grain, nothing. "What are we going to eat?" I ask Mama.

Tate laughs. "All you ever think about is food," he says. "Well, you're not going to starve up here." He points to the cooking fire. Mama Uajoroka is roasting a few plucked birds.

I smile. "Where did those come from?" I ask.

"The men hunted while the rest of you made the houses. We will have lots to eat here. There are plenty of uintjes, wild berries, birds, and animals. The ancestors are good to us," Tate says.

"What about water?" Mama asks. "I don't see any water-holes."

Tate nods. "The nearest ones are at the base of the mountain. But this is the rainy season. We will use our calabashes to catch water. And the ground itself will hold water for us." He points to several dark spots in the rocks where rain collects.

Tate's answer doesn't make Mama happy. "What happens when the rains end?" she asks.

Tate laughs and shakes his head. "You're always one to worry, Tutejuva. We'll be back home by then."

"And if we're not. . . ?"

Tate pats her back. "If we're not, we will go down the mountain to get more water when we need it."

Mama says nothing more. It is time to eat the birds Mama Uajoroka has roasted.

Our days quickly take on a new rhythm. In many ways, it's like being back home in the village. Except there are fewer of us. And Tate doesn't go visit the chief. Instead, he takes turns watching the cattle with Ramata, Vijanda, Uncle Kozondanda, and the other uncles. The men also hunt, using their knives, sharpened sticks, and stones to kill small animals and birds. I help Mama and the women gather berries and dig for uintjes.

When I'm not working, I help take care of Karikuta or play with Karemarama and the younger cousins. I teach them how to play stone echo and to build little houses of stones. And we race. All over the mountaintop. Mama Uajoroka keeps reminding us to watch out for snakes. I see their tracks, but I don't see them.

In the evenings, we play storyteller. Mama, Tuaekua Ehi, and aunties often join in, telling us stories about when they were children or about our ancestors. When Tate isn't with the cattle, he tells stories too. I like his stories the best. They're always funny. He tells about jokes he played on Uncle Kozondanda when they were boys.

"My brother Kozondanda is a brave man," Tate says with a big grin. "The only thing he's afraid of is snakes. It doesn't matter if it's poisonous like an adder or a black mamba or if it's a harmless house snake." Tate hisses like a snake. "If it's a snake, Kozondanda will run from it, screaming like a little girl."

Mama Uajoroka nods her head. "He makes me check the house for snakes every night," she says.

Tate laughs. "You can blame me for that. When Kozondanda was a little boy, I made a pile of leaves and dung and convinced him that it was a very poisonous snake. I told him the snake liked to play dead until it could trick someone into stepping on it. It was a very patient snake. It could lie there motionless, just waiting for him to come near. It could wait until he was a grown man, if it had to. But if he ever got close enough, the snake would rise up and sink its huge fangs into his leg."

Tate makes his fingers like fangs and pushes them into Karemarama's leg. Karemarama screams. The other cousins laugh.

Tate continues his story. "I told Kozondanda he would fall to the ground dead before he felt the pain of the bite, because the snake was so poisonous."

"Did Uncle Kozondanda believe you?" Karemarama asks.

"Yes, he did," Tate says. "He wouldn't go anywhere near that pile of leaves and dung. Then one day, Mama asked him to bring her something that was by the pile. 'No,' he said, 'the snake will kill me.' 'What snake?' Mama demanded."

We all laugh as Tate makes funny voices for his mama and Uncle Kozondanda.

"'That snake right there.' Kozondanda pointed at the leaves. 'What are you talking about?' Mama asked. She walked right over to the pile of leaves.

"'Mama, don't!' Kozondanda shouted. 'The snake will get you!' Mama jumped on the pile of leaves as hard as she could. Kozondanda screamed and covered his eyes as dirt and leaves flew all over the place. 'See,' Mama said, 'there's no snake.'"

Tate pauses. But no one interrupts. We want to hear the rest of his story. "By this time, Kozondanda is shaking and crying like a baby. He looked so funny that I started laughing. I couldn't help myself. Mama turned around and looked at me. 'What did you tell your brother?' she asked me. 'Nothing,' I said. But I was never very good at lying to Mama. 'Mutihu,' she said, 'I want the truth.' So I told her what I had done."

"Did she spank you?" Karemarama asks.

Tate shakes his head. "My mama was a gentle person. She never hit us. She scolded me though. But all the while she was scolding me, I saw laughter in her eyes. And ever since then, Kozondanda has been scared of anything that looks like a snake."

The next morning, the clouds roll in, threatening us with rain. We quickly weave branches together to shield the holy fire. We finish just as the winds blow across the mountain. Our huts shake in the wind as if they want to fly away. Then the rains come, pouring through the branches of the hut and getting us all wet. Just as suddenly as the storm came, it lifts off the mountain and spreads out over the valley.

I sit on a rock at the edge of the mountain, watching the shadows of the storm clouds dance over the veld below. Small streams of water rush down the steep mountainside, carving their way into the rock. They flow together at the bottom, flooding a dry riverbed with life.

"Stop that!" I hear Mama shouting. I turn around. Karemarama and the other boys are splashing in a pool of water. "Get out of there right now," Mama says. "That's our drinking water."

The other boys hang their heads as they climb out of the pool. But Karemarama laughs as he drips water all over the rocks.

"You're just like your tate," Mama says. I smile at the laughter in her voice. It's a nice sound. Almost as nice as when she sings. But it's been many yesterdays since I heard Mama sing.

THE SURPRISE

I help Mama tan a skin Tate brought up the mountain the last time he came home. One of the cows was attacked by a leopard. Tate and Vijanda chased the leopard away before it could drag the cow off. But the cow was so badly hurt they had to kill it. We now have fresh meat and a skin.

Mama and I work all day to make the skin soft. While we work, I ask Mama when we'll get to go home. "I miss Tjikuu," I say. "And Uapiruka and all my other cousins."

"I miss everyone, too," she says. "It shouldn't be long now."

She sings softly. I look up, surprised. "I like it when you sing," I tell her. "Especially the baby songs."

"You remember those?" she asks.

I nod my head and tell her about the time I snuck across the veld to the baby house when Karemarama was born. "Even though I couldn't see you, it made me happy to hear you sing."

Mama smiles. "I used to love to sing. But it's not the same now." She looks sad, like a cloud has covered her face. "Someday you'll understand."

"I know ... when I'm a woman," I say. "Why does everything have to wait until I'm a woman? I'm smart. Tate says so. I can understand just as much as Ramata. And everyone treats him like a man. I want to be treated like a woman."

"You're right, Jahohora. You are very smart. I think you could survive in the desert on your own if you had to. But don't be in a hurry to grow up. You don't really want all those worries right now."

"What's there to worry about, Mama? A few snakes? A leopard? Karemarama getting our drinking water dirty?"

Mama smiles. And sighs. "You'll understand when...."

"I'm a woman." I make a face.

We work in silence. The sadness deepens in Mama's face. I wish she were singing again. I wish I hadn't said anything to make her sad.

Mama shoos me away from the hut the next day. I know she has work to do, but she doesn't want my help. She tells me to play with my cousins.

"I'm not a child," I tell her. "I don't want to play with little kids."

"Then go talk to Tuaekua Ehi and help her with Karikuta," Mama says.

I walk slowly to the little house Tuaekua Ehi shares with Vijanda. I don't want Mama to be angry with me. I want her to smile and sing again. But I don't know how to make her happy.

Tuaekua Ehi is sitting outside watching the baby crawl around on an old goat skin. "He's getting big," I say. "He'll be walking soon."

Tuaekua Ehi smiles at me. "He's growing too fast," she says. "Sometimes I wish I were still a girl and could race with you and the other cousins. I know I could still beat you."

"I wouldn't be so sure," I say. "I've gotten a lot faster."

We sit quietly, watching Karikuta play. There are so many questions I want to ask Tuaekua Ehi. Questions about being a woman. About being a wife and mother. I'm sure she would answer my questions, but I don't know how to put them into words. "Is it hard being a woman?" I ask at last.

"Hard?" Tuaekua Ehi laughs. "I wouldn't say it's hard. It's just what we become when we grow up. But it's not always as fun. And there's more to worry about."

"That's what Mama says." I tell her about my talk with Mama and how I made her upset.

"I don't think your mama is angry with you, Jahohora. But I know she's worried – about you and Karemarama and Ramata."

"Why? What does she have to worry about?"

"All mamas worry about their children. It's part of being a mother," Tuaekua Ehi says. "We don't want our children to get sick or hurt. We don't want them to be sad. We want them to live long lives filled with happiness and children of their own."

"But worrying won't change anything."

Tuaekua Ehi laughs. "You're right. But we can't help it. We're mamas." She pauses. "You know, it's not just you and your brothers your mama is worried about. She also is worried about her mama. I don't know what I would do if my mama had stayed in the village."

"Is Tjikuu in danger?" I ask quietly.

"I hope not," she says, just as quietly. "My tjikuu is there with her."

I feel badly for not worrying about Tjikuu and her sisters. And for not understanding Mama's sadness. I promise myself I will do better.

Mama shoos me out of the house the next few days. I don't want to make her sadder, so I don't say anything. Instead, I talk with Tuaekua Ehi and play with Karemarama and the younger cousins. All they want to do is beat me in races. We run and run and run. But none of them is fast enough to beat me, even when they cheat.

I'm sitting on the ground resting when I see Tuaekua Ehi and Mama Uajoroka go into our hut. I want to go to, but Karemarama insists that I have to race again and again and again.

By time I go to our hut, I'm so worn out that all I want to do is lie down. But Mama meets me at the opening. "You can't come in right now," she says.

"But, Mama, I'm tired."

"Tate should be home soon. Stay outside and wait for him," she tells me.

I'm surprised. I didn't think Tate would be back for several days. I sit beside the holy fire and wait. And I wonder what Mama, Mama Uajoroka, and Tuaekua Ehi are talking about that I can't hear. I can't wait until I'm a woman and I can be part of the grownup conversations.

My eyes close. I don't hear Tate until he's standing beside me. I open my eyes to see him smiling down at me. "Today is a special day," he says.

"Why?" I ask.

"You'll see."

Just then Mama, Mama Uajoroka, and Tuaekua Ehi come out of our hut. They're each holding something, and they all have big smiles on their faces. I think they have something for Tate. But they come over to me instead.

"You've been wanting to be a woman so much, Jahohora, we're giving you a taste of what it is to be one." Mama holds out beaded wrist and ankle cuffs. She bends down to tie the cuffs on my ankles.

I hold my arms out so she can tie the wrist cuffs. "They're beautiful, Mama. Is this why I couldn't come in the house?"

"I wanted it to be a surprise," she says. "Mama Uajoroka and Tuaekua Ehi helped me with the beading. You helped, too."

"I did?"

"This is the skin you helped me tan."

I touch the smooth soft leather and finger the beading. The cuffs are beautiful.

Mama Uajoroka steps forward. She holds out a long skin-dress. Mama helps her tie it around my waist. I take a few steps. The ankle cuffs make me walk flat-footed and slow, like a proud

Herero woman. The long skirt swishes around my legs. I feel graceful and all grown up. Mama smiles at me. Her eyes are wet.

"That's not all," Tuaekua Ehi says. She takes off some of her chest bangles and tries to put them over my head. "Bend down. You're too tall."

I bend my knees to make myself shorter. I laugh as Tuaekua Ehi puts the bangles around my neck. They feel heavy against my bare chest. Then she places a tall beaded headdress on my head. I move my head as I stand up tall. The beads jangle softly.

Mama and Mama Uajoroka bring out another surprise for me. They've cooked some of the cow meat. It's like a feast. We all eat and eat until we're full. The cow meat tastes good after all the birds and rabbits we've eaten.

When we're done eating, Mama tells me to walk around more. "See how it feels to be a woman," she says.

I walk slowly around the mountaintop, enjoying this taste of my future. Karemarama stares at me. "Let's race," he says. "I could beat you now. You couldn't run fast in that."

"You're right," I say. "That's why Herero women don't race. We don't like losing."

Tate and the women laugh. "You've already figured out one of the most important things about being a woman," Mama says. "You'll be quite a wife for Uapiruka when the time comes."

I walk in the grownup clothes a while longer. Then Mama says I must take off the headdress and the chest bangles. I give the bangles back to Tuaekua Ehi. Mama helps me remove the headdress. "You will have your own bangles soon," she says. "We'll put the headdress away until you're fully a woman. But from now on, you can wear the long skindress and the ankle and wrist cuffs. They'll help you learn to move like a Herero woman."

After the others have gone to sleep, Mama sits with me by the fire. "Did you like your surprise?" she asks me.

"Oh yes, Mama. Thank you." I give her a big hug.

"You know, Jahohora, in many ways you are already a woman. You do a woman's work. And you think like a woman. I sometimes forget that – because your body isn't a woman's body yet."

"When will that happen?" I've asked the question before, but Mama's never given me a real answer. I hope tonight she will.

"When you begin to bleed," she tells me.

"But I bleed now. See?" I point to a scratch on my arm.

She smiles at me. "This is a different kind of bleeding. It comes from between your legs. You'll know when it happens."

"Is that what happened when Tuaekua Ehi went away with her tjikuu and came back in the long skirt?"

"Yes," Mama says. "Her tjikuu showed her what to do about the bleeding and told her why it was important."

"Will Tjikuu show me what to do when my body is ready?" I ask quietly.

Mama looks at the fire. I don't think she heard me. I start to ask the question again, but she stands up. "I'm tired," she says. "I need to get some sleep."

I stay outside a little longer, thinking about Mama's surprise. I walk slowly to the edge of the mountain. I like the feel of the long skirt against my legs. Happiness fills me as I look up at the stars. I am growing up. But even better is that Mama understands.

"Not sleepy?"

I jump when Tate asks the question. I didn't hear him come out. We stand quietly looking out over the veld, each of us filled with our own thoughts.

I break the silence. "Look, Tate, there's the Otjikoroise Tjovaeve." I point to the five stars.

"Do you remember how to follow them?" he asks.

I make a line between the top and bottom stars. "Is that the way home?"

He nods. "Now, where does the sun wake?"

I point to the bright star on the right.

"Very good," Tate says.

An odd star catches my eye. It shines just above a far-off mountain. But instead of shining steady, it blinks. I close my eyes and look again. It's gone. I look around the valley spread out below me. I see another star blinking in the distance. But it's close to the ground where no stars live.

"Tate, what's that strange star?" I point it out to him. Just then, the star on the mountain begins to blink again. "There's another one," I say.

Tate walks closer to the edge of the mountaintop. He watches the blinking stars. "Those aren't stars," he says softly.

"What are they?" I ask.

"It's how the German soldiers talk to each other over long distances."

"They talk with stars?"

Tate laughs. It's not a happy laugh. "They use lamps. In the darkness of the night, the light can be seen across the veld."

"What are lamps?" The only light I know that's not in the sky comes from fire.

Tate tries to explain. "They put a small fire in a square jar that you can see through on two sides. The other sides are shiny, so they make the light of the fire look brighter."

I wonder if he's teasing me. Jars aren't square. And the only jar I can see through is one with holes in it. Maybe that's what he means. The light must shine through the holes. "But how do they talk with light?" I ask. "You need words to talk."

"They make words with the light," Tate says. "See how it blinks? Some blinks are short. Others are long. Each blink is a different word."

"What are they saying?" Tate knows the strange words of the white people. So he must know their light words.

"I wish I knew," he says. "I was with the chief when the German soldiers showed us how the lamps worked. They didn't tell us the words, though. Their light words are different from the words they talk." We sit down and continue our watch. The lights blink a few more times. Then they go dark. I yawn.

"You should go in so you can sleep," Tate says.

"Are you coming?"

He stretches. "I will in a little while."

I get up early the next morning. I am quiet as I go outside. I don't want to wake anyone. I shiver in the early morning chill. I see Tate sitting on the edge of the mountaintop. It's where he was last night when I left him. He's still looking out over the valley. He seems tired and very worried.

"Have you been out here all night?" I ask him as I sit next to him.

He nods quietly. "It wasn't a night for sleep." He doesn't look at me. His eyes watch over the valley. "There it is again," he says, more to himself than to me.

"The lights are still blinking?"

Tate points to the far-off mountain where I saw the blinking light last night. I see another blink of light, but this one is different. I have to look harder to see it.

"They can't use the lamps in the day," Tate says. "So they use the sun to make words."

"How do they do that?"

"You know how you can see yourself in the river during rainy season?"

I nod.

"That's a reflection. The Germans use something shiny they call a mirror to reflect the sunlight the same way they use the lamps at night," he says.

We sit in silence, watching the lights. I think about Tjikuu and Uapiruka and all my other cousins and aunties and uncles. I miss them. I miss home.

"Tate, when can we go home?"

He turns and looks at me. "I don't know," he says sadly. "I had hoped we would be home by the end of the rainy season."

"The rainy season ended many days ago," I remind him.

He nods. "I don't think it's safe to go home yet." He pauses. "Show me again which way is home."

"That way." I point behind us.

"Good. Do you remember how to get down the mountain?"

"Yes. The path is over there." I point at the break in the rocks that leads to the path.

"There are other ways down the mountain. Some of them are too steep. They're only for the rains and for wild animals. But I've found a few that are easier to walk." He shows me where the different paths begin. "If you ever take any of these paths, you must watch for snakes and leopards. And you must look closely or you will lose the path."

He looks back to the veld in front of us. He points out the Waterberg and the other mountains. He shows me where to find waterholes. "There's Hamakari," he says, pointing toward an area near the Waterberg. He names other Herero villages that are scattered across the veld.

"Maharero and the Herero who are with him are out there." Tate points across the veld toward the Waterberg and where the sun wakes.

"What's beyond there?" I ask.

"The Omaheke," he says. "It's a place of death. There's little water. And the sun burns anyone who walks there."

"Where is the land of the white people?"

Tate points to where the sun sleeps at night. "Beyond those mountains is a big river. It is so big that you can't see the other side. The Germans come from a land beyond the river."

I look to see if he's teasing. There's no smile on his face. "If they have a land on the other side of the river, why do they want our land?" I ask.

Tate shrugs. "Maybe their land is too poor for cattle." He looks at the mountains and out over the veld. "The land Njambi Karunga gave the Herero is a beautiful place. Maybe the Germans like it better than their land."

"J'hora!" Karemarama hollers. He's standing near our hut with some of the cousins. "Mama says you're supposed to help us get berries."

I look at Tate. I want to stay here talking with him. He smiles and pats my hand. "You'd better do what Mama says."

I decide to try one of the new paths Tate showed me. We've picked all the berries on the mountaintop and along the closest part of the main path. Maybe there will be more berries in the other places.

"Be careful," Tate calls. "And don't go too far. Stay within shouting distance."

The path I choose is steep. And it's a little hard to see at times. We soon find an area with lots of berries. We look around for snakes before we begin picking. We eat the first berries we pick. When we're full, we pick as many as we can carry back up the mountain. Climbing is harder in my long skirt and ankle cuffs. But they protect my legs from bramble bushes. And I can carry more berries in my skirt.

The sun is high in the sky when we reach the top of the mountain. I'm hot and tired. After we take the berries to Mama and the aunties, I sit under the shade of a tree to rest. I see Tate still sitting at the mountain edge, watching the light blink from mountain to veld to mountain. Mama tries to get him to come and eat. But he refuses.

"You can watch with a full belly better than you can with an empty one," Mama tells him. She takes him some of the meat left over from last night.

He eats it. But he doesn't seem to notice what he's eating.

When the sun goes to sleep, Tate leaves the mountain edge to sit with the ancestors at the holy fire. He talks to them quietly. Then he goes back to the mountain edge to continue his watch in the darkness. I stand beside him for a while. The lights are blinking again. I wonder about the lights. But I wonder more about Tate. Why is he so worried?

Mama joins us. But she isn't interested in the lights. She's worried about Tate. "You must sleep tonight," she tells him. "You need to be strong. Those lights are going to blink whether you're standing here or not. And watching them isn't going to help you know what they're saying."

Tate nods and turns to me. "Jahohora, make sure Kare-marama is sleeping. It's time for you to sleep, too. Mama and I will be in soon."

I leave them standing there in the darkness whispering to each other.

I'm tired, but I can't sleep. I lie on the skin, waiting for Mama and Tate. Mama comes in without Tate. My eyes close before Tate comes.

Even though Tate went to sleep late, he gets up early the next morning. I hear him go outside. I get up and join him. The first rays of the sun streak the sky with ochre-colored paths of light that grow as the sun climbs over the mountains that lead to the Omaheke. I watch as the morning light chases away the shadows of night. Tate and I sit on the edge of the mountain. I look for the blinking lights.

"It's too early," Tate says. "The sun has to be higher in the sky before the soldiers can catch its light."

"What's that?" I ask, pointing to large tails of black smoke rising from many places across the veld.

"Those are Herero villages," Tate says.

"They must have big holy fires to make all that smoke."

Tate shakes his head. "It's the wrong color. That smoke isn't from a holy fire."

We sit in silence. I wonder about the smoke and the blinking lights. Suddenly Tate stands. I start to speak, but he motions for me to be quiet.

"Do you hear that?" he asks.

I listen. But it's strangely quiet. Not even the birds are singing. Then I hear it – a small thunder coming from the direction of the sun. And then another. And another. The thunder rolls on top of itself and echoes through the mountains. But it's like no thunder I've heard before. It's too short. And too fast. And there are no clouds or lightning in the sky.

I look up at Tate questioningly.

"It's begun," he mumbles.

"What is it?" I ask.

"Those are boom sticks – German guns. They're shooting."

I've seen my uncles' boom sticks. But I've never heard them shoot. I stare across the veld, trying to see what's going on. "Where are they?"

Tate points toward Hamakari and the Waterberg. "It sounds like they're fighting over there. But it is too far for us to see anything."

All morning, we listen to the booming thunder. Then, as the sun climbs higher in the sky, I see a bright fire flare up across the veld. Like lightning, it's gone as quickly as it came. But it leaves a small cloud of smoke that hugs the earth before disappearing into the sky. A loud thunder shakes the ground. Karemarama and the cousins run to us to see what's happening. Mama and the aunties follow.

Another fire flares up and the ground shakes again with thunder. The cousins are excited. They want more "lightning and boom." But Tate, Mama, and the aunties look worried.

"What is that?" Mama whispers.

"That's the Germans' big guns," Tate says. "They're so big that they have wheels, and oxen have to pull them. Two men are needed to fire each gun. One man feeds it bullets that are this big" – he holds his hands apart to show us the size – "and the other man puts fire to it to make it shoot."

"I wish I could see that," Karemarama says. "What does it do?"

Tate looks at Mama. She shakes her head. "It puts big holes in the ground. And it can knock down trees and make mountains into piles of rocks," Tate says.

As the sun reaches the top of its journey through the sky, the lightning and booms come faster – one after the other and sometimes on top of each other. I see a big cloud of black smoke rising above the flames of lightning. I imagine a smoke-filled valley covered with holes and broken trees. I'm glad I'm not there.

At last the lightning stops and the booms fall silent. Once again, I hear the small thunder of the boom sticks. They're still sounding in the distance when Tate sits with the ancestors that evening. Tate has a long, quiet talk with the ancestors. He's still talking with them when I go to sleep.

I wake up when I hear Mama and Tate talking late in the night. I lie still so they won't know I'm awake.

"We can't stay here much longer," Mama says quietly. "The water is almost gone. And it's a long time before the rainy season comes again."

"It's too dangerous to go home," Tate whispers. "Especially after today. I'm afraid this is just the beginning."

"But we're not fighting. They have no reason to hurt us," Mama says.

"To the Germans, one Herero is like another. They don't know that we want peace," Tate reminds her.

"It's not just the water," Mama says. "We're also running out of food. We've picked all the berries up here and dug up all the uintjes. And you and your brothers have hunted most of the rabbits. All we have left are our cattle. And they're not giving milk."

They are quiet. I think they've gone to sleep. Then Tate speaks again. "We'll wait a few days, and then we'll go down to the waterhole at the bottom of the mountain. The women can look for berries and roots while the men fill the waterskins."

"What about the children?" Mama asks.

"Ramata will stay with the cattle. The rest of the children will remain here with Uajoroka. That way she won't have to climb the mountain again." Tate laughs as he mimics Mama Uajoroka huffing and puffing as she came up the mountain.

"Shush," Mama tells him. She isn't laughing. "You'll wake Jahohora and Karemarama."

THE WATER TRIP

Once again, Tate is sitting at the edge of the mountain when I get up. I must have been tired because I didn't hear him leave the hut. I sit beside him, listening to the morning sounds. The birds are singing, and there's no rumble of boom sticks. "Is it over?" I ask.

"I don't know," he says. "It's quiet today. But I think you should keep the children close to the huts. Don't go searching for berries down the mountain."

We walk back to the huts where the women are watching the children play. Tate repeats his warning. "Karemarama, do you hear me?" he calls to my brother, who's running off to play stone echo. "You keep those long legs close to the huts. And no hiding. Stay where Mama or Jahohora can see you."

Karemarama throws a stone on the ground and turns around. He isn't happy. He hates to be with women all day.

"But what about food?" Mama Uajoroka asks. "We were going to look for more berries. We could all stay together."

Tate shakes his head. "We'll have to make do with what we have. And drink as little water as possible. We must make it last a few more days."

Uncle Kozondanda and Ramata come up the mountain before the sun rises too high in the sky. Tate takes them to the mountain edge. I start to follow, but Mama calls me back. I watch the men talk. Tate is telling them about the blinking lights and the lightning and booms. Uncle Kozondanda and Ramata are nodding their heads. Then Uncle Kozondanda talks. Tate looks worried. And sad.

Their talk over, the men join us again. It's Tate's turn to help watch the cattle. Uncle Kozondanda and Ramata will stay here. Tate tells me goodbye. "I'll be back in a few days," he promises.

The next few days are very long. My belly is hungry, but there's nothing to eat. My mouth feels like I've eaten dirt. And my throat sticks together. We stay inside so the sun doesn't make us thirstier. No one talks much, so I tell myself stories. I can hear Karikuta cry. His cry is weak and raspy because he's hungry. Tuaekua Ehi can't make good milk when she doesn't eat.

When the sun goes down, we sit outside. Mama Uajoroka holds Karikuta. She sings to him, trying to stop his crying. Mama silently gives the last of the berries to the children and Tuaekua Ehi. Mama doesn't keep any berries for herself, and she doesn't give any to the other women or me. Tuaekua Ehi tries to share her berries with us, but we won't take them. "You must eat them so you can feed my grandson," Mama Uajoroka says.

Even though my belly begs for food, I'm happy. Mama is treating me like a woman. Herero women always put the children first.

The next day we wake to a surprise. Uncle Kozondanda and Ramata had set traps during the night. Now we have three rock rabbits to eat. It's like a feast as we fill our bellies for the first time in days. But we're still thirsty. The water is gone.

Uncle Kozondanda shows us how to dig up roots that hold water. We chew on the roots, squeezing the water out. I dig up a lot of roots before my thirst is gone.

"It's better to get the roots at night," Uncle Kozondanda says. "They hold more water then. That's why so many animals eat at night."

It's early the next morning when Tate returns. He calls us to the holy fire as the sun begins to peep over the distant mountains. "The guns have been quiet for many days," he says. "It should be safe for us to go down the mountain to get water and food."

Karemarama lets out a loud whoop. He wants to explore.

"Not you, son," Tate says. "Only the men and women will go. Mama Uajoroka will stay here with the children. And you will do what she tells you to." Tate looks right at Karemarama.

We laugh.

"Now I want all of you children to listen closely to what I say." Tate looks at each of the cousins and then at me. "You heard the boom sticks. You know what they sound like?"

We all nod.

"If you hear a boom stick close by the mountain, you must run as fast as you can from here." Tate looks at Mama Uajoroka and the smallest children. "If you can't run, you must hide. And you must be very, very quiet so no one finds you. Whether you run or hide, you must do it alone. It's easier for the soldiers to find you if you're together. Do you understand?"

Again, we all nod.

"When can we stop hiding?" I ask.

"You must be very still and wait a long time after the boom sticks are silent. Listen to make sure there are no voices or footsteps. Listen to the animals and birds. You know the warning cries they make. When you're sure it's safe, leave this place. Make sure you leave no tracks. And remember, you must go alone."

Tate makes us repeat what we must do. Then he looks at the men and women. "You're to do the same if you hear the guns."

"But where should we run?" Mama asks. "Back to our village?"

"No," Tate says. He stares at the ground. "There's no village to go back to. It's been burned."

There's silence. No one looks at each other. Mama Uajoroka is the first to speak. "How do you know?"

Uncle Kozondanda kicks at a rock. He's not happy. "The last time I was with the cattle, I went to the waterhole," he says. "I met a Herero who was wandering in the veld. He told me the German soldiers burned all the villages back that way."

"What about my mother and aunties?" Mama whispers.

No one answers.

Mama wipes tears from her eyes. She puts her arms around Karemarama and me and holds us close. "So if we must run, where do we run?" she asks again.

"To Maharero," Tate says. He points to where the sun starts the day. "There's no other place. You must find the uncles and aunties who are with him." Tate turns to the holy fire and tells the ancestors what we're doing. He asks them to keep all of us safe.

I help Mama and the aunties gather the waterskins and calabashes. "Am I coming with you, Mama?"

"No, I want you to stay with the children."

"But I'm almost a woman," I say.

"I know. That's why I want you to stay here. Mama Uajoroka will need another woman to help with the children. Tuaekua Ehi will stay here, too, so she can take care of Karikuta."

We all walk with Mama and Tate and the others to where the path begins.

"How long will you be gone?" Karemarama asks Tate.

"If we're not back in three days, you'll have to leave the mountain to look for food and water. But don't take this path. Go to the waterhole on the other side of the mountain," Tate says. "Then run to Maharero. Look for the rest of our family."

"What about you?   Will you go to Maharero, too?" Kare-marama asks.

Mama and Tate look at each other. It's a look I can't read.

"We'll find each other," Tate says. Then he turns to Ramata. "I know you'll be watching the cattle. If you hear the boom sticks, leave the cattle and run. The ancestors will understand." I don't like Tate's words. They fill me with fear.

It's my turn. "Don't forget to keep the holy fire burning," Tate says as he hugs me. I nod and hug Mama. I don't want to let her go. But if I'm to be treated like a woman, I must act like one. I hold back my tears as I watch Mama and Tate disappear down the path with my aunties and uncles.

I play games with the children so I won't think about Mama and Tate. I know they'll be safe. Tate said so. But all day long, I worry. That evening as I put more wood on the holy fire, I wonder if they've reached the waterhole yet.

Mama Uajoroka and Tuaekua Ehi join me at the fire after the children are asleep. Mama Uajoroka must see the worry on my face. "They'll be back soon," she tells me. "And then we'll have plenty to eat and drink again."

Karikuta cries. He is trying to drink from Tuaekua Ehi, but she doesn't have enough milk to fill him. Auntie takes him from his mother and rocks him in her arms. I see for the first time how skinny he is.

"He doesn't look well," I blurt out.

"He isn't," Tuaekua Ehi says. She looks down at the ground. "I haven't had good milk for a long time. And I can't get him to eat anything else. He's got the teeth for it, but when I put food in his mouth, he just spits it out."

"It's not your fault." Mama Uajoroka pats her daughter's arm. "Look how skinny you are. Eating berries and uintjes with a bit of rabbit or bird now and then may take the hunger away, but it doesn't help you make milk for a baby. You need fresh milk and omaere."

I look closely at Tuaekua Ehi. I'm surprised I haven't noticed before how thin she's become. "We've got to make you fat again," I tell her. "Tate will know what to do when he gets back."

Tuaekua Ehi smiles weakly at me.

I yawn. "I'd better go to sleep," I say. "I'm getting up early so I can hunt for berries. I think I know where I can find some."

Mama Uajoroka nods. "We'll need food for the children tomorrow."

I go into our hut. It seems empty with only Karemarama and me. Karemarama rolls over. "Are you asleep?" I ask softly.

"Not quite," he mumbles.

"I'm going berry hunting in the morning. Do you want to come with me?"

"That's women's work," he says.

"You like picking berries," I remind him.

"I like eating berries."

I lie awake trying to think of something to keep Karemarama busy tomorrow. I don't want him troubling Mama Uajoroka. "Karemarama?"

"Hmmm?"

"Do you know how to make the traps Ramata and Uncle Kozondanda used to catch the rabbits?"

"Of course I do," he says.

"Instead of berry picking, you need to make some of those traps tomorrow. We're going to need more food before Mama and Tate get back."

"All right." He rolls over again. "Can I go to sleep now?"

I get up early the next morning to put more wood on the holy fire. Tuaekua Ehi and a few of the cousins are waiting for me. "We're going with you," Tuaekua Ehi says.

"You can't," I tell them. "The path is too steep." I look at the younger cousins. "Your legs are too short for the climb."

"Mine aren't," Tuaekua Ehi says.

"But you're not strong enough. You must stay here and rest. Karikuta needs a strong mama."

She starts to argue. I shake my head. "Come with me to the path. You can see how steep it is. And you'll know where I've gone so you can watch for me."

Tuaekua Ehi and I walk arm-in-arm around the edge of the mountaintop – just like we did when we were little girls. But there are no giggles or shrieks of childish laughter. Only silence.

I unhook my arm when I see the path I plan to take. Tuaekua Ehi looks down and shakes her head. The path is very steep and covered with loose rocks. "Be careful," she tells me as I start to climb down it. "There are probably snakes."

"I shouldn't have to go too far." I look up at her and smile. Her face is the last thing I see before I disappear over the mountainside. I walk slowly, looking both ways for berry bushes and glancing down at the ground for snakes. I have to go a little farther than I had planned, but at last I find bushes loaded with fruit.

I start to eat a few berries. But then I remember that Tuaekua Ehi, Mama Uajoroka, and the others are just as hungry as I am. I will eat when they do. I pick and pick and pick until the sun is high in the sky. My hands and arms are stained with juice and the skin pouches I brought are filled with berries. I tie the pouches around my neck and begin the steep climb to the top of the mountain.

The thunder of boom sticks and screams echo against the mountain. I drop to the ground, clinging to the mountainside. I quickly look for a hiding place. I crawl to a long narrow crack between two rocks. I hide the pouches of berries in a pile of rocks on the ground. Then I squeeze into the narrow crack and wait. The rocks shade me, but it is still hot. I want water. I want to sit. I want to check on the others. But I stand still, hidden between the rocks.

I think I hear footsteps, then more thunder and screams. Some seem to come from below, others from above. They're all around me. I hear rocks falling. And distant thuds, like something falling on the boulders.

I wait and wait. I hear the birds and the buzzing of flies. But nothing else. I wait some more.

The sun is sinking behind the mountain when I step out of my hiding place. I stretch. My feet and legs hurt from standing still so long. I look around, but I don't see anything.

It's too dark to find my way off the mountain. I must wait until morning. I sit close to my hiding place and eat my fill of berries. I think sadly about the others. Of Karikuta's hungry cry. Of Tuaekua Ehi's growing weakness.All I can do is hope Karemarama caught a rabbit. Hope they're all right. Hope Mama and Tate will make it back up the mountain.

Hope. It's all I have.

Before the darkness settles, I find a rock ledge. I pick up a stick and poke it under the ledge to check for snakes. Knowing it's safe, I crawl under the ledge to sleep. I will need my rest.

Tomorrow, I must run to Maharero like Tate said. I must find Uapiruka and Uncle Horere and all the others who joined Maharero. And I must do it alone.

Kov

IN KIEL

Once in Kiel, I throw myself into my work, trying to stave off my loneliness and forget my worries about Hanna and Papa. We've all been given our assignments, so there's a lot to do. The few doctors with family connections or years of distinguished service will work out of the main German hospital in Windhük. As part of Major von Glasenapp's first and fourth seebatallions, I'll be one of eight surgeons with the Marine Infantry Company. We've been assigned to mobile field hospitals, which are basically glorified ox carts. Even a few weeks in South West Africa will not be easy under these conditions.

In between gathering supplies for the field hospital, I have to attend training sessions taught by a weathered old German who has literally operated on the front lines of battle under heavy artillery fire. In reviewing standard field procedures, he's rather dismissive of what we'll face – a few broken bones, perhaps some cuts and contusions, and mild cases of dehydration and dysentery. Like many of the officers, he thinks the skirmish will be over before we get there. He refuses to call it a war as war implies we're facing an enemy somewhat our equal.

"It's good that it's not a real war," he tells us derisively. "You upstarts would never make it. You have been spoiled by city hospitals, and you're so afraid of germs. If you were in a real battle, you would know there's a lot more to fear than invisible bugs."

In addition to preparing for my billet, I have to examine the naval troops who have volunteered to serve as infantry in South West Africa to make sure they're fit for the tropics. Most of them are country boys eager to see a little more of the world. I'd be as excited as they are if it didn't mean leaving my family.

I sometimes have to hide a smile when I see these fresh-faced boys marching along the streets in their high yellow boots and blue woolen tunics. It's easy to spot the ones heading to Africa. They swagger about town, greeting everyone and bowing to each other with an exaggerated solemnity not shared by the ones who'll be staying here at home. To hear them talk, I'd think these boys were seasoned sailors who have been around the world a time or two.

A sense of celebration fills the town as we prepare to leave. Generally, the citizens keep to themselves, but now they're stopping all of us, even me, to congratulate us on our upcoming adventure. Those who have retired from the sea regale us with their tales of heroism and danger. Others wish us a safe journey. It's a camaraderie built on patriotism and the vicarious prospects of facing the unknown.

Tonight I'm to take the train, with all the Kiel volunteers, to the North Sea naval base at Wilhelmshaven for the first leg of our travels. Many of the troops are reuniting with family for one last outing. All along Holsten Street, the young sailors are surrounded by parents, brothers and sisters, wives, or sweethearts. Walking by myself, I feel conspicuous – and very much alone.

I duck into a restaurant for a good meal, but I realize my mistake as soon as I enter. The place is crowded with families and young couples, clinging to their last hours together. I sit in a corner, trying to look nonchalant as I eat my sauerkraut and roast beef. I can't help but eavesdrop on some of the conversations – mothers worrying about the dangers of war and malaria, young children asking about the wild animals, and fathers trying to be experts on the situation in Africa. "Not much of an enemy," one father says. "Just a bunch of naked savages using spears and clubs."

Recalling Kommissar Göring's stories, I smile at the naiveté and wonder how brave these brash boys will be when they're facing Herero warriors with guns. It's one thing to shoot, from a distance, people armed only with clubs, but I would think it's a whole lot different when they're shooting back. It's a sobering thought, as I may have to operate on some of these boys. If the rebellion hasn't been put down by time we arrive, I may have far more than a few contusions and malaria to deal with.

My thoughts drift off in scattered directions as bits of over-heard conversations lead them one way and then another. There are promises to write every day. Admonitions to keep well. A mother praying for her son. A sweetheart vowing to wait for a sailor's return. A child clamoring for souvenirs. "I'll bring you something," a sailor promises his young brother. "Perhaps a horn or some ornament worn by one of those savages. And what would you like, Father?"

"How about one of their skulls?" the father responds.

I cringe, glad that I've finished eating and can leave the restaurant.

It's dark by time I reach the barracks. Ignoring the music and laughter spilling from the enlisted men's quarters, I head to the solitude of my room. I sit down on the bed, feeling sorry for myself. Just then, a young clerk enters my open door. "You have a telegram, sir," he says, clicking his heels together. He hands me the message, waiting for me to read it.

"Mazel tov. Son born. All well. Papa," I read quietly to myself.

"Would you like to send a reply, sir?" the clerk asks.

It takes a minute for the abbreviated message to make sense. When it does, I smile – a big, goofy smile that I'm sure makes me look like an idiot. "I have a son," I say simply.

"Congratulations, sir. Is there a response?"

I quickly jot a brief message – "Give my love to Hanna. Kiss my son for me. Here's to our future. Yaakov" – and hand it to the clerk along with a few marks.

After he leaves, I close the door and look at the telegram again, letting the words sink in.

I have a son! I'm a father! All the loneliness and self-pity of the past few hours vanish in the shadow of this miracle. Hanna and I have had many discussions about our children, about this baby. But none of those talks prepared me for the emotions that sweep over me at the thought of my son. Is this how Papa felt when I was born? I feel guilty, knowing how little I understood or respected that love – until this moment.

I pour myself a small glass of wine and make a solitary toast to my son. "L'chaim, my son. May you be a king among men."

I picture Hanna lying in my boyhood bed, cradling our son. I can see the love and pride shining from her eyes. I wish so badly I could be there, enjoying this moment with her, holding our son, laughing as Papa fusses over his first grandchild. Instead, I have to settle for being grateful from afar.

If I were home, I'd go to the synagogue with Papa to say the Birkat HaGomel on Hanna's behalf, offering thanks for her deliverance from the dangers of childbirth. But I don't even have time to go to the synagogue here. God will understand. I place my yarmulke on my head and wrap my tallis about my shoulders. I look toward heaven. *"Baruch atah Adonai Eloheinu Melech Haolom, hagomel lechayavim tovos shegemalani tov."*

Shivering in the wintry cold, I gather with the battalion at midnight. Accompanied by a brass band, we march through Kiel on our way to the train station. All the families crowd around us, cheering and yelling, offering to carry our bags and weapons. Along the way, we're greeted by citizens pouring out of their houses to wave at us or toss flowers. I look around, bemused by the hundreds of people flanking us. What would it be like if they thought we were going to a real war?

By time we reach the station, the city square is swarming with people. An old man who has worn the Iron Cross for three decades speaks a few words about bravery and duty to the Fatherland. Caught up in the fervor of patriotism, we all cheer. "We will fight honorably," Major von Glasenapp promises the crowd. "And if it must be, we will die for the honor of Germany." The cheers go up again – raucous, solemn, naïve.

The crowd lingers, still calling out, as we file onto the train. The last thing I see as we pull out of the station is a sea of German faces and waving hands.

UNDER WAY

I try to sleep, but all I can manage is fitful dozing broken by the occasional jerking of the train and scattered conversation among the marines. Half-formed dreams of the baby and Hanna vie with wide-awake thoughts of what the day will bring. I make mental notes of the supplies I must check. And I think a letter to Hanna. And one to Papa.

Several hours later, and very much in need of sleep, I arrive in Wilhelmshaven. Too tired to go into town with the others, I head toward the port to make sure all the medical supplies are properly loaded on our ship. Accustomed to the naval base at Kiel, I'm surprised at the activity and immensity of the base here. Tucked against the Jade Bay and protected by a series of locks and fortifications, Wilhelmshaven is literally the womb of Kaiser Wilhelm's new naval fleet. On my way to the floating docks, I walk past the massive Kaiserliche Marine Werft. The blocks-long brick buildings make up one of three shipyards charged with building thirty-eight new battleships over the next fifteen years.

When the Kaiser announced his shipbuilding plan a few years ago, all of Germany praised his vision, but many were skeptical about the ambitious time frame. I had my doubts, but not now. Seeing the workers bustling about, hearing the clanging and banging of steel parts being shaped and fitted together, I'm convinced the fleet will be built on time. At last the Fatherland will have a navy superior to that of the English! Germany will rule the seas! With that heart-felt burst of patriotism, I walk a little taller as I head toward the docks and the SMS Darmstadt, the battleship that will be my home for the next few weeks.

The port is so big and so crowded with ships that I have to ask for directions. A young dockhand points me toward a big steamer with twin stacks flanked by towering masts. I whistle beneath my breath; it's the biggest ship I've ever seen.

As I get closer, I take in its intricate details – the ornate scrollwork on the elegantly pointed bow, the giant guns jutting out from a turret. I'm dwarfed by its shadow as I walk along the quay.

I show my papers to a guard, who studies them carefully before waving me on board. With a sense of eager anticipation, I walk up the long narrow flight of steps onto the ship. I'm met by a sailor, who leads me down the main passageway to the infirmary. After checking the inventory of medical supplies against the manifest, I sign off on it and head to the medical staff quarters next door.

I stow my gear in the compartment beneath the mattress of my bunk and settle down for some alone time. Alone. That's a pretty common state for me. Even when I'm surrounded by marines, I'm alone. Papa and Epenstein were right – wearing this uniform may make me feel more German but it hasn't changed how Germans see me. At least, not yet.

At the thought of Papa, I pull the telegram from my breast pocket and carefully unfold it. As I read the message again, I chuckle over Papa's frugality. I can picture him at the telegraph office, counting the words and crossing out any he deemed unnecessary.

Again and again, I read the telegram. Holding the paper and reading the words "Son born" make my firstborn real. It's proof that I'm a father. I close my eyes, trying to picture him, to hear his baby cries and gurgles. Does he have Hanna's heavily fringed hazel eyes? Or my black ones? Blonde hair or dark hair? Or any hair?

I'm missing out on so much – my son's introduction to the world, Hanna's first days as a mother, and Papa finally becoming a grandfather. For him, this child is the promise that his family will go on, that he and Mama and all of our ancestors will not be forgotten. Although he had difficulty being a father, I know he will be a great grandpa.

I pull out my writing paper and pen. "My beloved Hanna," I write. "Thank you – for our son, for your love, and for your faith in me. Although I cannot physically be with you, I am there, always, in spirit. I miss you so much. I am impatient to begin this journey so I can return all the more quickly to you. When I return, I promise to never leave your side again, my love."

Writing to Papa is a bit harder. I have so much I want to say to him, but I don't want to sound like a sentimental old woman. There are things I must write because I fear he won't live to hear them from my lips. "Dear Papa," I pause, twirling the pen in my fingers, leaving an ink smudge on the paper. Then the words spill out: "From one father to another, thank you. Thank you for the lessons you taught me, for the opportunities you gave me, and for the care you are now giving to Hanna and the baby. We have had our differences over the years, but I never doubted your love for me, and I have always loved you. I know it was difficult for you when Mama died. It can't be easy raising a child by yourself when the love of your life is gone. I pray I will never have to face such sorrow. If I'm a good father, it is because of the example you have set."

Hearing voices in the passageway, I glance at my pocket watch. It's almost boarding time. If we don't make it out of the port by noon, we'll have to wait until the next high tide washes in at midnight. I quickly finish my letters and find a clerk who will post them for me. Despite the bitter cold winds blowing from the sea, I stand on the deck overlooking the quay teeming with sailors and crowds of well-wishers. The marines line up, two abreast, and attempt to march up the steps onto the boat. From my perch above them, they look like little boys playing soldier. God help us all, I pray silently.

The engines throb to life, and we stand at the rail, watching the slip of water between the ship and the quay grow larger as we creep toward the locks. Even though I have no one to see me off, I join the others in waving and shouting until the well-wishers on the dock become specks on the horizon. Then I turn toward the locks, curious about how they work. I wish Christof were here. He'd be able to explain it all.

Christof.... I haven't seen him since I left Hamburg. I might even enjoy this trip if he were traveling with me; it would be so much easier to have a friend on board. But he's with the army. The marines, with the help of the soldiers already in the colony, are expected to put down the uprising on their own. So even though Christof is never one to miss an adventure, it looks like he'll have to sit this one out. Oh, the stories I'll have to tell him when I return!

I pull my coat collar up over my ears. The wind, wet with the icy sea, bites at my face as we leave the relative shelter of the port. Although it's midday, the sky is the iron gray of twilight, mirroring the winter grayness of the bay. I shiver and decide it's time to head down to the relative warmth of my berth.

The other surgeons and I quietly arrange our possessions in the tiny cabin that we're to share. I can hear the laughter coming from the large quarters down below where all the marines are housed. While I appreciate the dignity of the medical staff, right now I could use some of the camaraderie of military life.

I join the other surgeons and some of the officers for dinner, but other than a bit of small talk, I have little to contribute to the conversation. I'm content to sit back and listen as the grizzled old hands share their war stories. A few were in China during the Boxer Rebellion and another had helped General von Trotha quell native uprisings in German East Africa. They try to outdo each other with their tales of brutality and bravery. A captain, one who had been with the general, gets particularly gruesome as he laughs about the public hanging of Abushiri, who had led a revolt against the German colonial authorities in an effort to reclaim the East African colony. In the commander's reckoning, Abushiri, an Arab half-breed, was hardly human –

not only because of his race, but because he dared to oppose the Fatherland.

I don't join the laughter. I discreetly look around the table. Apparently, I'm the only one who's troubled by this callous dismissal of a fellow human being. As soon as I can politely do so, I excuse myself and head back to my berth.

But I'm too disturbed to sleep. I bundle into my heavy woolen coat, cap, and gloves and head for the fresh air of the deck. Although the sea is relatively calm, I remember Epenstein's words of caution and hold tightly to the railing as I come out on the deck. I fumble in the darkness with only the faint yellowish glow of the ship lights reflecting off the water to guide me. Hearing voices, I strain to make out where the men are so I can avoid them. I've had enough company tonight. I need to be alone with my thoughts.

As my eyes adjust, I realize it's not as dark as I had thought. The daytime clouds have cleared, giving way to a night sky dazzling with bright points of starlight. And the horizon is dotted with specks of motionless light – perhaps from lighthouses or a few ships. I stand at the rail, watching as those distant lights grow fainter and fainter. The steady hum of the ship's engines and the lapping of the dark waves lull me into a melancholy that overwhelms me when, for the first time, I fully sense the distance separating me from my family. And I know that distance will only grow in the weeks ahead.

Roll call comes too early the next day. Bundling into my warm coat, I join all the marines and officers on deck for what is to become our morning ritual. Winter dawn on the North Sea is, at best, a murky twilight. Today, it's hard to determine where the endless gray sky gives way to the endless gray ocean. It's only our first day on the open sea and already I'm dreading the monotony that's to come.

The men, however, are in high spirits as they drink in the novelty of being at sea. Their laughter grows louder as our tropical khaki uniforms, complete with cork helmets, are handed out. The marines make quite a show of putting on their great pot-shaped helmets before we all head to our quarters to try on the rest of the uniform and fasten on the buttons and appropriate insignia. My insignia, that of the surgeon, is a serpent wrapped around a pole – the healing stave of Moses. What irony, I think, as I affix it above the top stripe of the sleeve. The military, with its deep anti-Semitism, embracing a symbol that's so Judaic.

The buttons attached, I carefully fold my new uniform, fingering the thin linen fabric. It's hard to believe there's any place on earth right now where I could wear this uniform and not freeze to death. It serves as yet another reminder that I'm heading off to a strange new world where nothing will resemble home.

Late in the afternoon, I force myself to join some of the others at the bow. If I'm going to be on a ship with these men for several weeks, I might as well try to get to know them. Unlike at the base, officers and marines mingle more freely, discussing everything from hometown reminiscences to astronomy and maritime history. A few of the young volunteers pepper me with questions about scurvy, sea sickness, and other common ailments of the sea. The conversation quickly turns to advances being made in medicine, and I'm pleasantly surprised that they're not all the country rubes I had supposed them to be. Scattered among the tradesmen and farmers are teachers and even a few lawyers. Perhaps this voyage won't be as bad as I had thought.

My hours of leisure end the next day as we approach the English Channel. A lieutenant fetches me to look after one of the marines who's sick in his bunk. After tending to the young man, I join the lieutenant on deck as we pass by the steep chalk cliffs of the English coast. We lean against the starboard rail, watching the tiny fishing boats, with their gray and black sails, rocking on the waves.

"Have you met any Englanders?" I ask the lieutenant, who has been to sea several times.

He nods.

"What are they really like?" Most of us in Germany consider the English our rivals – inferior ones, whose day of greatness is being eclipsed by our ingenuity and know-how.

The lieutenant raises his voice so I can hear him over the wind and the waves. "I've come across English sailors in every port I've visited. And like most seamen, I'd have to say I admire them. They're decent, respectable people. Despite what you hear back home, England is truly the first nation of the earth."

"How so?"

"As a people, they're distinguished, wise, brave, united, and wealthy. Then you take us Germans. Yes, we're brave. We've always been a brave people. And we're slowly acquiring the riches England enjoys. But whether we can distinguish ourselves or acquire wisdom and unity remains to be seen." He blows on his hands and rubs them together to get them warm.

"Germany hasn't been united very long. Many of us still think of ourselves as Bavarians or Prussians rather than Germans," he continues. "And we're experiencing a lot of growing pains as we try to figure out who we want to be as a nation. Having a big naval fleet and fancy uniforms are just trappings. What's more important is having the wisdom to use those trappings wisely and build a culture embraced by all Germans. Then and only then will we be a distinguished people."

I think about the lieutenant's words as I go back to the infirmary. Is there room in his vision for Jews? Is that what he meant by unity? Or does he see unity coming only as a result of ridding the country of "outsiders"? I wish I could ask him such questions.

Right now, I have other things to deal with. Although our ship isn't rolling like the fishing boats in the channel, I'm beginning to feel a bit queasy. When I reach the infirmary, I see I'm not alone. I force myself to straighten up and tend to the young men experiencing their first bout of seasickness.

"That wasn't so bad," I tell myself as the last man leaves the infirmary.

But then the next bout hits as we pass out of the Channel and sail down the coast of Spain. I'm standing by my cot when suddenly the floor pushes up diagonally under my feet. I grab onto the bunk, struggling to keep my footing as supplies crash around me. From down below, I can hear the sailors shouting. The ship creaks loudly as the bulkheads shift. The other side of the ship thrusts up, tossing me against the door. I panic, convinced the ship is breaking apart. But then I remember Epenstein's stories and force myself to calm down. "We've hit rough seas. This is what it feels like. Stay in control," I tell myself.

Just as my nerves calm down, I begin to feel like I did when Christof and I snuck one of his father's expensive cigars. My head is too heavy to hold up and my stomach rises in my throat.

I break into a cold sweat as I retch my way to the bunk. I fall onto the bed, clinging to it to keep from being tossed off. I'm drowning in motion. But there's no lifeline of calm. Trapped in the middle of the ocean, the ship is my world. There's nowhere I can go that's not affected by the upheavals of this wretched sea.

I take little comfort in knowing that some of the other surgeons and most of the marines are probably feeling the same way. The only reason the men aren't banging down our door is that they can't walk far enough to get to the infirmary. I feel guilty that I'm not tending to them, but I know I couldn't manage the passageway in this state. Besides, there's not much that can be done for seasickness.

Thinking I might be able to sleep it off, I scramble for the rope Epenstein advised me to bring and tie myself into bed so I won't be thrown out by the rollicking waves. My sleep is almost delirious as the motion of the sea merges with disjointed dreams of home. I toss and turn, thankful the rope is securing me. Having emptied my stomach, I at last drift into a dull, heavy sleep.

When I wake, it's nearly morning, and the sea is a bit smoother. We're no longer climbing up mountains of waves only to plunge into deep troughs, but the ship still rocks on the waves like a cork bobbing in the water. Only now, there's a rhythm to it. If I can just match it. . . .

I untie the rope and gingerly sit up, trying not to focus on anything. Having mastered the sit, I try for a stand. It takes a few attempts, but at last I'm on both feet, standing more or less erect. I manage to get dressed before I have to sit down again, doubling over from the stench lingering from last night. One of the other surgeons groans as he vomits violently. I've got to get out of this confined space.

On my feet again, I match my steps to the rocking of the ship and lean heavily on the heaving walls and rails as I make my way to the deck. Clinging tightly to the railing with both hands, I gulp in the fresh morning air. I force myself not to focus on the huge roiling waves, but to look upwards at the gray sky instead. Although it's still chilly, the bite is gone from the wind and there's a promise of sunshine on the eastern horizon.

Feeling better, I look around and see I'm not alone on the deck. Scattered about the rails are miserable-looking fellows, too ill to be embarrassed by their lack of stamina. I hope I don't look as bad as they do. I take another deep breath and head down to tend to the sick.

SHIPBOARD ROUTINE

It's been eight days since we left Kiel, but it feels like a lifetime. As soon as the seas calmed, we established a daily routine. Every morning, we have shooting practice at the stern where a target has been secured to a beam. The marines are getting used to their new rifles, and the officers take aim with their pistols. The other surgeons and I are not excused from the drill. "You never know what you're going to encounter," the lieutenant tells me.

I'm not a great shot. I can hit the target, but I'm rarely dead on. Still, I enjoy the camaraderie as the men brag about their guns and exploits. The new volunteers tell about their hunting adventures while the old-timers reminisce about glorious days of battle. Other than at mess, the social divisions that separated us in Germany have slipped away on the boat. Here, in this small world, we all have our jobs to do, and no one seems to care how we worship God or where our families came from.

In the afternoon, we sit on the deck, basking in the warmth of the sun as we sail south. I've put away my woolen coat, but I have yet to swap my standard uniform for the tropical one. The men spend this time cleaning their guns or washing and mending their clothes, singing and whistling as they work. When I have free time, I write letters to Hanna and Papa and generally read through my medical books, honing up on everything I'll need to know in the field. I won't have time to look anything up when the bullets are flying.

In the evenings, one group plays skat constantly, paying no attention to the passing of a ship, a beautiful sunset, or the occasional school of flying fish. The rest of us sit in a circle, telling stories of home and discussing the future. I usually just listen, unless they talk about Africa. Then I sometimes share some of Epenstein's stories.

The biggest worry is that the skirmish will end before we get there, and we'll be given orders to go home without ever stepping on the shores of the Dark Continent. It would be a shame to have come all this way and then be deprived of that great adventure.

For most of the men, it's a very real fear. After all, how can a few natives armed with primitive weapons hold out much longer against German troops? I tell them the Herero have guns, but they brush it aside. Such talk frightens some of the younger volunteers, who sit there quietly, their eyes glowing big in the twilight. The farther from home we sail the more they realize this isn't a lark they signed up for. I temper my comments, not wanting to scare them more. But I wonder if this is a disservice. These boys need to know what they might be facing so they can be prepared.

As the talk winds down tonight, the sailors head below deck, where some of them are putting together a makeshift band comprised of flutes, drums, clappers, and a comb. But I stay out a little longer, enjoying the quiet peacefulness as I think about home. It has been eight days since my son was born. He would have been circumcised today.

I can almost hear the mohel blessing my son and giving him the name Hanna and I agreed upon: *"Our God, and the God of our fathers, preserve this child for his father and mother, and his name in Israel shall be called David ben Yaakov.... Give thanks to God for He is good, for His kindness is eternal. May this small infant David grow and become great. As you have come into the Covenant of Abraham, so may you come into Torah, into marriage and into good deeds."*

David is now part of the Covenant that binds our family through the generations to Abraham. I should have been there to give my blessing. Tears roll down my cheeks as I think of all I'm missing. How can I ever make this up to my son? To Hanna? Or for that matter, to myself?

I look out over the dark ocean in the direction of home, longing to be with Hanna and David. From down below come the sad strains of *Nach der Heimat möcht' ich wieder*. How fitting. I softly hum along on the familiar ode to home. Right now, Germany seems so far away, so unreachable. And then I notice the phosphorescence gleaming in the moonlight, like stars on the water, forming a glittering path pointing home. I wipe away the tears and whisper my blessing to David, my son: *"Zeh hakatan gadol yihye. Mazel tov!"*

* * * * *

The novelty of being at sea has quickly worn off. Every day I follow the same routine, meet the same people, feel the same constant throbbing of the ship's engines, and see the same heaving gray waves stretching endlessly in all directions. Occasionally, we pass another ship. When we do, we greet it with a frantic waving of hands and a volley of shouts and cheers. It's as if we're starving for human contact beyond the confines of our boat, for a reminder that we're not alone on this vast ocean.

To keep my spirits up, I follow our progress on the chart hanging in the companionway that shows the landmasses out of sight to the east. According to the chart, we're passing the entrance to the Strait of Gibraltar, but the only differences we notice are an increase in the number of ships we see and a shift in climate as we leave Europe and head for northern Africa. The heat from the sun makes our woolen uniforms unbearable, so we begin wearing the tropical khakis we were given all those days ago when we were freezing on the North Sea.

As we head further south, the monotony grows – until we're informed at roll call that we'll be making a port call in Portuguese Madeira. We're like schoolboys being told of an unexpected holiday. After everyone quiets down, the lieutenant reminds us of what's expected of German sailors. "I know you will want to get souvenirs, but don't buy everything you see," he cautions. "You don't have room for a lot of things. And remember, not everything you see will be genuine. Don't be taken in by fake gems and great-sounding offers. And one more thing – watch how you drink the wine."

Everyone laughs, and a few men, known for their drinking, are singled out for good-natured teasing. The rest of the day, our chores seem lighter and the mood merrier as we all keep an eye on the southern horizon for our first glimpse of the island.

I'm on the deck early the next day when a young sailor calls out excitedly, "There it is!" Sure enough, there on the distant horizon, the sheer rock walls of Madeira rise up, like a mirage, out of the ocean desert. The word spreads quickly throughout the ship, and soon, all the young volunteers are crowding on deck, eager to take in every aspect of the foreign coast as it draws closer and closer.

As the ship sails around the island to the southern port of Funchal, I take in the volcanic outcroppings and the dense jungle crowning the rocky peaks. After the winter gray of the north, the island is a feast of color. Even the ocean around it has put off its drabness for ribbons of blue in shades I never would have imagined. How I wish Hanna were here to enjoy this with me.

At first glance, the southern side is as rocky as the rest of the island, but then the craggy heights break open to reveal a bay that seems to spill out from a city flowing from the jungle-crested peaks above it. The red-tiled roofs and gleaming white walls of the houses form a mosaic with bright fields of flowers. There is much ooohing and aahing as we each point excitedly to everything that catches our eye.

Sharp whistles and shouts from down below pull my attention from the city opening up in front of me. Small boats laden with fruits and vegetables approach us. Olive-skinned men, dressed in colorful clothing, shout to us, waving baskets of produce. I smile and wave, but I'm not interested in their wares. I'm saving my money for the markets in the city.

That afternoon, I wait my turn to descend the long rope ladder let over the side of the ship to a big rowboat below. Once on shore, I'm dazzled by the sights and smells of the island. Vendors call to me, holding up colorful silk shawls and blouses. Others invite me to sample their food or the wine that makes the island famous.

My comrades break into groups of twos and threes, but once again I'm alone. This time, I don't mind. I'd rather explore the city at my own pace. I walk up a steep street lined with four- and five-story buildings, admiring the iron balconies and Portuguese architecture and enjoying the feel of solid ground beneath my feet. A side street takes me into an area of steeply gabled houses, painted in bright reds and blues, their pitched roofs covered in a tightly woven thatch. Because of the European influences, everything is at once familiar and yet exotic. I drink it all in – the heavy aroma of the tropical flowers, the dark-eyed women wrapped in their colorful shawls, the pealing church bells, the sun glinting off the turquoise water of the sea, the men swaggering about with bright scarves tied about their waists. Having seen little but gray for the past several weeks, I'm almost blinded by the festival of color.

Overwhelmed, I head back to the markets to buy a few postcards to send to Papa and Hanna. I want to get a silk scarf for Hanna, but they all seem too bold for her liking. After much searching, I find one in soft, muted colors that will complement her pale skin. For Papa, I buy a bottle of the famous wine – and hope he lives long enough to drink it.

The afternoon ends too quickly, and I fall in line with the rest of the men heading back to the Darmstadt, each of us clutching our treasures and the impressions of this island paradise.

A few days later, I'm standing by the rail in the dawn mist, waiting with some of the marines for the morning drill, when one of the men points out a strange cloud hovering motionless above the water. It's unlike any cloud I've seen – snow white with a glistening sheen.

One of the other men laughs. "That's no cloud," he says. "That's the peak of Teneriffe."

We watch in awe as the mist unfolds, revealing the ancient volcano rising out of Spain's Canary Islands. It looks as if some great giant heaved boulder upon boulder to create this towering peak. But the most amazing feature is the eternal cap of snow that doesn't melt, even under the scorching sun of Africa. As we glide by the stony base of the island, I remember Epenstein telling me about the peak and the dog-worshippers of old who are responsible for the islands' name. Wishing we could visit this island, I think of all the countries that lie beyond it in northern Africa and of all the sights they hold. Sights I'll never see. For the first time in my life, I fully realize the world is much bigger than the Fatherland.

I'm reminded of that again a few days later when, according to the navigational chart, we're passing by Cape Verde. I stand on the deck peering toward the east where the island should be, but nothing interrupts the expanse of ocean.

Soon after passing the Canary Islands, I get my first glimpse of Africa as we approach the Liberian coast where we will take on laborers who will help unload the ship when we get to Swakopmund in South West Africa. Again, I join the other men lining the deck to feast on the visual wonders of the land. It's exactly how Epenstein had described it – the grass huts, slender palm trees, and lush forests of mangrove trees crowding the narrow beach.

Tearing myself away from the sight of land, I head back to my quarters to get the stack of postcards I've written to Papa and Hanna before the mailboat goes to shore. I take a minute to jot one last note about my first impressions of Africa. Suddenly, I hear such a clamor and shouting that I rush back to the deck to see what's going on. Our ship is surrounded by canoes carrying black men of all ages – our Kroo-boys. Within minutes, the men swarm over the sides of the boat; the pots and bundles they have tied to them bang against the metal sides of the Darmstadt in a percussive rhythm. I stare in astonishment at these new bare-chested arrivals who smile their greetings as they straighten their bundles. I've never seen a black person before, outside a photograph. And now I'm surrounded by nearly 100 of them – old men with their toothless grins, muscular men in their prime, and young boys shyly returning our stares. They're all laughing and joking in a language that sounds oddly familiar.

The headman takes out a cloth and dries himself off before shaking hands with the lieutenant, who greets him in English. After a few words, the headman nods and the Kroo-boys run across the deck to vanish into the hold below. "Those heathen speak English?" one of the marines asks incredulously.

"Of course they do," the lieutenant replies. "The Kroo are master seamen when it comes to navigating the rough waters along the coast. They've been helping the British for more than a century. Now all the European ships use them."

The days return to the old routine as we continue our journey ever southward, except the drills become more frequent and target practice more meaningful. As we approach the equator, some of the older men tease the country boys about being on the lookout for the line in the water that marks the equator so they have time to find something to hang onto as we head downhill.

By now, the heat is intolerable, even with our tropical uniforms. The worst part is trying to sleep at night. I stay on deck until I'm ready to drop, but then I toss and turn in my stifling quarters, longing for just a breath of winter wind. The Kroo-boys sometimes join the rest of us on deck, but they stick to themselves, squatting around their pots of food and joking with each other in a mixture of English and their tribal language. They don't seem to mind the heat that has the rest of us sweating through our clothes. Of course, they're not wearing as much clothing as we are.

When I hear the men complaining about how hot it is, I wonder how they're going to hold up in the deserts of South West Africa if they're forced to march with all their gear. Seeing how well the Kroo handle the heat, I think the Herero could have an advantage over us. They're used to the climate and the terrain, but it will all be foreign to us. Sunstroke and dehydration could win half the battle for them.

SWAKOPMUND

After another few days at sea, we finally get the news we've been waiting for – we will reach Swakopmund in South West Africa today. I help pack up the medical supplies and get my gear in order before joining the others in a vigil on deck. Eager to end our long voyage, we try to peer through the deep fog shrouding the coastline. It begins to lift at about noon, revealing several German ships on the horizon. But still no sign of the great city of Swakopmund. Having explored Funchal and glimpsed Monrovia in Liberia, we're sure that the German port will be no less their equal.

As the fog recedes, we see an endless ridge of sand rising up behind the ships, but still no sign of a town. "Perhaps it's just a sand bar that protects the city," one sailor muses as he wipes the sweat from his forehead.

"Or maybe it keeps the lions and palm trees from getting wet," another one jokes.

The midday sun burns off the rest of the fog, becoming more unbearable as we approach the coast. It's only February, but on this side of the equator, we're in the intense heat of summer. Shielding my eyes from the bright sunlight reflecting off the sand, I finally see Swakopmund – a few wooden houses, a makeshift barracks, the imperial flag flying above some sort of government building, and a squat round lighthouse, all surrounded by an ocean of sand.

The joking stops as the men take in the foreboding landscape. This is the great German colony? This is what we're supposed to offer our lives for? "To think we came so far for a country like this," one man says, putting words to my thoughts.

"The rest of it can't be like this," a corporal muses. "After all, this is part of Germany."

A gloom, born of the harsh landscape and the looming reality of war, settles on the ship as we wait to disembark. It's been a long journey, and the destination is not what we'd imagined. I should have been prepared for this, given all the stories Epenstein and Göring had told me. But they had been here twenty years ago. I had thought that surely in two decades we would have brought civilization to the land. Isn't that the purpose of colonies?

The uneasiness grows as we continue to await our orders. For hours, our signalmen exchange frantic flag messages with the nearby gunboat Habicht. Several of the marines try to interpret the signals, and rumors spread quickly: "The revolt is over. We're heading home tomorrow."

"No, it's only just beginning. This is going to be a long, drawn-out campaign."

I think most of us hope the first rumor is true. We've already had enough of the heat, and there's nothing enticing about the looks of this country.

I head to my sweltering quarters again that night, not knowing what tomorrow will bring. As we rock in a heavy swell, sleep doesn't come easy. And when it does, my dreams are torn with strange images and unfamiliar sounds.

We get our orders early in the morning. We're disembarking.

It's easier said than done. It's just past dawn, but already the sun is beating down, and the sea is rough. We line up on deck with all of our combat gear strapped on our bodies. The men closest to the rail look squeamish as they approach the rope ladder to make the descent to a flatboat rising and sinking on the treacherous waves. They have to time their jump from the ladder to the boat while it's on a crest or they could end up dropping more than seven meters or, worse yet, missing the flatboat entirely.

Clambering down the rope ladders in rough seas is always tricky. But today, we have to do it with our knapsacks and blankets strapped to our backs, guns on our shoulders, cartridge belt with dangling water bottle cinched about our waists, and bread bag and flask hanging from another strap. I watch as, one by one, the men clumsily make the descent. There are a few close calls, but no real mishaps, as the first thirty men fill the flatboat, which is then towed to shore by a tugboat.

At last, it's my turn. Shifting my knapsack and adjusting the bundles of medical supplies tied about me, I waddle to the rail and look down. The boat, nearly full, flounders in the waves, violently hitting the side of the ship and then jerking away. "I can't do this," I think. Panic nearly paralyzes me when Epenstein's horror story of the young sailor lost at sea flashes through my mind. I calm myself. If all the other men can do it, I can too. Praying that I won't be the first casualty, I carefully lower myself over the rail, feeling for the top rung with my foot. Rung by rung, I cautiously descend, training my eyes on anything but the churning waves below. As I near the bottom, I finally look down, trying to find the flatboat. I see nothing but the waves crashing violently against each other. "Jump!" an officer shouts from somewhere beneath me. All the hours of drills kick in as I automatically obey the command. I let go of the rope ladder – and fall.

I land in a heap against one of the marines. Just as I try to pull myself off of him, the boat plunges into a trough, throwing me against him again. Someone gives me a hand to help me steady myself in the rocking boat. "Good job, Doctor," a voice says. I move quickly to avoid being knocked over by the next man falling into the boat.

When we can squeeze no one else in, the boat is fastened to the tugboat for the rough ride over the crashing surf. The boat pounds against the waves, plunging into troughs so deep that I can't see the Wörmann steamer grounded nearby. Then, just as suddenly, it rises to the top of a watery precipice only to fling downward again. With every heave, the boat shudders as if it's about to break apart. It takes on so much water that I'm soaked to the skin. Several of the men, overcome with seasickness, lie in the bottom of the boat; others pray for our safety. A few Catholics discreetly cross themselves as they whisper their "Hail Marys."

At last, we emerge from the torrent into smooth water that carries us to the sandy beach. As we wait for the rest of the men to join us, we take a few minutes to calm our nerves and reassemble our baggage. Squinting against the summer sun that reflects off everything as if it were a metallic surface, I watch in wonder as the Kroo-boys maneuver lighters, a type of flatboat loaded with our heavy artillery and horses, through the turbulent surf.

"Welcome to the Mole," a Schutztruppe captain calls out as he walks toward us.

"The Mole?" the lieutenant asks.

"That's what the locals call it. It was supposed to be a manmade harbor, but the ocean has other ideas." The captain points to a large sandbar that threatens to choke off access to the pier. "The ocean controls everything around here. See the lighthouse over there? That's the second one since I came here. The first one was washed out by a giant wave. This is a tough land, but it grows on you if you have the grit to handle it."

"What's with the steamer?" The lieutenant nods toward the grounded *Gertrud Wörmann*.

"She wrecked last year," the captain says. "It's a wonder more ships aren't lost, what with this cursed surf. But it's not a total waste. The Wörmann line is using the *Gertrud* as an internment camp for Herero laborers and prisoners here in Swakopmund. By keeping them locked up on the ship when they're not working, we can make sure they don't go home to join the uprising."

Everything has been unloaded, and now the real work begins. We make a semblance of marching through the deep hot sand, weighed down by our waterlogged gear, as the heat of the sun literally sizzles off our wet uniforms. We had expected to be greeted with a parade, with throngs of German settlers thanking us for coming to their rescue. Instead, we're met with silence and a sense of desolation. If this is an omen, I think it doesn't bode well for us.

Trudging in rhythm to the pounding surf, we pass a few wooden houses that look as if they're losing the battle with the encroaching sands. Two pelicans, each nearly as big as a small man, spread their pink-tinged gray wings and strut for a minute before resuming their feather grooming. As we pass another house, I see a weathered man standing in the shadow of the verandah. There's no welcome on his face – only a weary indifference.

A semblance of a town begins to appear as we march onward. Much of it seems to be under construction. Several strong black men – Herero, I'm guessing – do the heavy lifting under an armed German overseer. They're building a tower on the elaborate Wörmann headquarters. And more work is being done on the statehouse that sprawls beneath the lighthouse. I'm surprised to see a modern hospital and the elegant two-floor headquarters for the Eastern and South African Telegraph Company. Despite my first impressions, I rather like this frontier town and its optimistic outlook.

At last, we reach the start of the Otavi Mining and Railway narrow-gauge line that stretches east across the desert to Windhük, the colonial capital. Although the rail line is still under construction, the tracks already look old and rusted. We take turns going into the makeshift station to brew some coffee for the long train ride. Nearby, I see the beginning of what looks like a grand station.

We wait quietly for our train, blinded by the sun's relentless glare and sobered by the reality that our trek is far from over. At this moment, I would willingly travel all the way across the ocean in that flimsy flatboat, tossing in the most violent waves, if it meant I could be home with my family instead of in this harsh land.

ACROSS THE DESERT

I hear the train before I see it, an old rattletrap coughing and sputtering its way toward us, hissing with steam. I stare in disbelief as it creeps along. Seven tiny engines, looking as if they came out of some tinker's shed, pull an endless string of open wooden boxes on wheels – boxes we're supposed to ride in with no protection from the sun. Perched precariously on the 610-mm track, the train seems more of a toy than a reliable mode of transportation across the Namib Desert. We count off and are herded into the gondolas, as the boxes are called, while the Krooboys load all the artillery, horses, and supplies into some of the rail cars.

Shouldering my way to the side of the small gondola the medical staff is to ride in, I rest my arms on the chest-high wooden wall so I can gaze out at the strange land we're passing through. With several puffs and a lot of rattling, the train jerks forward. And just as we had in the flatboats, we fall against each other and then steady ourselves for the long haul to the interior of the colony.

Hour after hour, the train climbs slowly upward through an endless expanse of rust-colored dunes, rising like giant waves from the desert floor. At first, I'm intrigued by the wind-blown lines in the dunes, their ragged crests, the cloud shadows spilling over the sands. But the scenery quickly becomes monotonous in the unbearable heat. I take a slow sip from my water flask, swirling the wetness slowly around my mouth, letting a little seep over my lips to cool them from the burning sun.

Another surgeon cautions some of the men in the next car who are gulping their water. "You need to make it last," he says. "Who knows when we will get more."

Some nod and put their flasks away, but others shrug and continue drinking.

After a few hours, the train rattles to a stop. We're told to get out and stretch our legs and take care of any necessities. One of the men takes a swig of the coffee brewed in Swakopmund. "Puh!" he spits it out, making a horrid face. "It's soured!" He tosses the rest of his coffee onto the ground. A few others sip from their coffee with the same results. The rest of us reluctantly spill our coffee into the sand, where it quickly evaporates, leaving only dark stains.

The break is over too soon. This time when we pile back into the gondolas, I sit with my back against the wall and my legs tucked under me. But soon, my legs grow numb and I'm forced to stand once again.

Late in the afternoon, the train creaks to a stop with much hissing and sputtering. The narrow track in front of us rises steeply as the land continues its ascent. One of the engineers hops down and motions for us to get out of the cars. The long train can't make it up the steep grade, so we have to disassemble the cars and rearrange them into three shorter trains. That means carrying each car to its new position.

Amidst a bit of muttered grumbling, the men stack their gear out of the way and shuffle back through the hot sand to do the heavy lifting. I'm pushed aside when I step up to help move the car I've been riding in. "We don't need an injured doctor," the lieutenant barks at me. "What good would you be then?"

As the marines strain to carry the wooden cars to their newly assigned places on the track, I help unload the medical supplies from the freight cars and then reload them when the gondolas are realigned. A few of the other surgeons, who are resting in the sand, glare at me. They finally get up to help stack the medical gear back in the cars. We're told we'll have to walk as the engines can't pull our weight up the incline. We stand back as the first train tries to inch forward. It soon becomes obvious that we have to add some manpower to the horsepower of the engines. The marines get behind the engines and cars and push as the train creeps up the track. Again, I'm not permitted to help, so I trudge slowly up the sandy hill with the rest of the surgeons and some of the officers.

At last, all the cars and engines are reassembled into one long train again. We're not really at the top, but the grade levels out enough for the train to continue on its own steam and in one long line. The men, covered in sweat and sand, flop exhaustedly into the cars. A marine in the next gondola drains the last few drops from his water bottle. Noticing his sun-cracked lips and labored breathing, I offer him a drink from my canteen.

As the sun sinks toward the horizon, we finally reach the top of our ascent. I look back at the way we've come. The narrow track stretches downward, a thin thread in the rusty sands that flow toward the ocean, which is little more than a blue speck on the distant horizon. It's hard to believe that just this morning I was in a ship on that ocean. I swallow, tasting nothing but sand and wishing I had even a drop of the soured coffee I had so thoughtlessly tossed.

"Look at that!" one of the men hoarsely exclaims.

I turn to look toward the front of the train. Huge, wild mountains of naked rock jut out of the sand, row upon row, forming what appears to be an impenetrable barrier that stretches as far as the eye can see. The closest mountains glint steely gray in the setting sun, while the more distant ones rise up like shrouded specters on the horizon. A sudden chill comes over me as the train begins winding through the rocks towering ominously over us. A deep foreboding settles over me. It's as if these mountains are telling us to go home. Hoping to shake off the uneasiness, I peer into the twilight to make out the alien landscape.

A bone-chilling cold descends quickly in the high desert. We wrap our white woolen blankets tightly about us and huddle together to keep warm. We ride in silence through the dark mountains cutting into the star-speckled sky, each lost in thoughts of home and the strangeness of this land. We've been told to have our guns loaded and ready – an unwelcome reminder that this is more than just an uncomfortable trek through the wilderness. It's another night with little sleep.

The sun rises early, and with it comes the heat of the day. There's no stopping as we continue through the mountain rifts. It's too dangerous, we're told, and besides, there's no water for hundreds of kilometers. "You had better get used to it," the lieutenant tells us. "We've got three more days before we roll into Windhük."

"Three more days!" a few of the men grumble.

There's little talking as we creak along the tracks – our throats are too dry to speak. Listlessly, I drain the last few drops from my canteen well before noon. Oh well, we'll be stopping soon, I figure. The next station has to have water.

It's a little after noon when we finally roll into a station so the engines can refill their water tanks. I join the others crowding around the water troughs. In their thirst, the men closest to the water cup their hands for a quick drink. Almost simultaneously, they spit it out in disgust. "It's full of salt!" one of them sputters in a raspy voice.

For now, I must satisfy myself with a bit of boiled rice. The half-cooked grains dull the hunger pangs a bit, but they do nothing for my thirst. I think ahead to the long afternoon with no water. I'm going to have to do a better job of rationing if I'm to survive.

I doze off and on through the afternoon, trying to ignore the dryness burning my throat and the cracking of my lips. But even in my fitful dreams, I find no relief as the relentless motion of the train and the scorching rays of the sun penetrate my subconscious. I'm searching for Hanna, calling out to her to bring me some water. But she's nowhere to be found. Someone jostles against me, and I wearily open my eyes to the sun's glare.

Coming out of my stupor, I look around and see that the landscape has changed again. The dark mountains are behind us, and now we're rolling across a wide plain with patches of tall dry grass interspersed with thorny brambles. We're told it's called a veld. A herd of antelope grazes on the grass, ignoring the rattling of the train. One of the officers shoots his gun. The animals spring into the air, running and jumping swiftly across the veld. The officer laughs. "That's why they're called springbok," he says.

As we progress across the plain, the thorn bushes become so dense they form a thicket in places. Not for the first time, I marvel at the stamina, and stubbornness, of the men who laid the rail track across this inhospitable country. And again, I question why we would want this as a colony.

Here and there, isolated mounds of rock interrupt the savannah, and strange cones – I'm told they're termite hills – pop up out of the scraggly grass like half-finished sculptures of sand. In the distance, herds of giraffe and deer-like animals chase across the veld. Suddenly, Heston, one of the men in the next gondola, grabs his gun and takes aim at a black figure squatting a few meters away. We laugh when we see it's a baboon.

"I thought it was a Herero," he says.

We become more cheerful as we approach what looks like a farm of sorts. But the laughter quickly gives way to silence when we get close enough to see it's only what's left of a farm. The train stops, but we don't get out. Instead, we soberly take in our first sight of the rebellion. The small house has been burned; its tin roof pulled off. Bits and pieces of broken furniture litter the ground around the charred ruins. I spot a mound of white stones on the edge of what used to be a garden. A makeshift wooden cross marks the grave, bearing the words: "Fallen by the hand of the murderer."

A few scruffy Germans, who identify themselves as sailors from the Habicht, step out of the rubble to report to our officers. Their uniforms are so dirty and stained brown that it's nearly impossible to tell they're marine uniforms. One of the men, recognizing a friend from home, stops at the gondola next to mine. "Karl, how did you ever talk them into taking a flat foot like you?"

"Dieter?" Karl asks incredulously. "I didn't recognize you under all that dirt and hair."

Dieter nods solemnly, stroking a matted beard. "We stained our uniforms with coffee and tobacco so the Herero couldn't spot us so easily from a distance. I haven't been out of these clothes for three weeks. No bath. No shave. And a lot of hard work." He glances toward the grave.

"But everything is about over, right?"

Dieter attempts a hollow laugh. "Hardly," he says. "We've had some heavy losses, and I'm sure there will be a lot more before this thing ends."

"Losses? You mean ... deaths?" a young volunteer asks nervously.

"This is not a game, boy," Dieter says flatly. "Germans are dying. We've lost several men in the last week."

"But ... how?" The boy swallows hard. I recognize him as one of the young ones who was always bragging about how the Germans would wipe out the Herero in a matter of days.

"The Herero have guns. Good ones that they got from us. They shoot well. And this God-damned country is taking its toll, too." Dieter looks at Karl as the train starts to lurch forward. "I hope you return to your mother."

Further on, we stop at a large station where we're to bed down for the night. After getting our fill of water and eating a little more rice, we head to the corrugated iron barracks. A few young marines worry about lions attacking in the night. They're quickly hushed by the jeering that follows. While everyone else stretches out on the ground for a good night's sleep, I tend to a man whose face is so blistered with sunburn he can barely see. Exhausted, I finally get to rest. Using my knapsack as a pillow and wrapped in my blanket, I lie on the hard ground and immediately drop into a deep sleep.

I wake before dawn to whispered voices. "What if I don't make it?" a youthful voice asks.

"You'll get home. Don't worry about it," another man responds.

I drift off again, but this time it's an uneasy sleep.

We board the train again at noon to continue our trek through the savannah. The land seems more fertile, the long yellow grass more plentiful. Herds of strange animals and an occasional tree or bush disrupts the flatness. And there are more farms, all of them destroyed, with heaps of rocks marking fresh graves.

We stop at another station for the night. This one is even bigger, and it's been fortified. The windows have been walled up into slits just wide enough for a gun barrel; all the provisions have been hauled into two stout buildings under heavy guard. Sitting in the walled courtyard, we finally get a real meal, our first since we left the ship. Pea soup never tasted so good!

WINDHÜK

We arrive in Windhük the next afternoon. It's a relief to leave the crowded gondola behind, even if it means marching through the hot sun and sand to the Alte Feste, a white fort at the top of a high hill. Weighed down by my knapsack, which seems much heavier than when I started out four days ago, I waste little effort glancing around at the meager town. All I can think about is water and clean clothes.

As soon as we reach the walled fort, the men break rank and run toward the faucets in the middle of the courtyard, laughing and shouting and stripping off their filthy clothes as they go. I head toward the hospital unit to bathe in private. I don't need to remind everyone of my circumcision.

Clean at last, I tour the fort hospital with the other surgeons, getting a better idea of the conditions I'm about to face. Lieutenant Reiniger, the surgeon in charge at Windhük, paints a grim picture. The brutality of the enemy, coupled with the severity of the climate, is resulting in an unexpected number of casualties. And our medical supplies are barely adequate.

"Politicians!" Reiniger mutters. "They're all about waging war over a pitiful scrap of desert, so they'll spend a small fortune on guns and ammunition. But just try to get money for medicines and surgical supplies." He waves his hand toward the half-empty medicine closet.

"It's even worse for the mobile field units," he says, giving us a pitying look. "Have you seen one yet?"

"Only in pictures, sir," I say.

He laughs dryly. "Come on. I'll show you the real thing." He leads us out into the fortified courtyard.

I'm surprised at the variety of people I see. The home guards – dressed in brown velvet coats, trousers, riding boots, and soft gray hats – patrol the grounds. Some of them are wounded or sick; the healthier ones will serve as our guides, Reiniger explains. These are German settlers, called out as militiamen. Most of them have been in South West Africa for years. Some of them stayed after their army service ended, many of the younger ones were born here.

A group of women, Herero prisoners, are washing clothes for the soldiers. Some of the women are fully clothed in long cotton dresses, the others, covered from head to foot in some kind of reddish paste, are in what must be their traditional dress. Leather aprons hang from their waist in both the front and back. Except for an assortment of beads, their chests are bare. A few of them wear tall, three-pointed leather headdresses, adorned with iron beads, which add to their stature. Beaded hide bands or copper rings encase their wrists and ankles. Altogether, their dress is both regal and curious.

Heston and a few of his friends mill around the younger women, flirting with them in signs, low Deutsch, and broken English. The women try to ignore the unwelcome advances. The older women, their faces wrinkled from years in the elements, sit passively, smoking short pipes.

"They're at your service," Reiniger says, with a nod toward the women. "I know you've been on the boat for nearly a month. And it could be quite awhile before you see another female."

Embarrassed by his implication, I look at a group of bearded Boers, crouching in the shade of one of the corner towers. The sun-beaten, leathered men are to serve as our wagoners. Reiniger leads us out the broad doors of Alte Feste toward a long line of sturdy, four-wheeled Cape wagons, covered with linen hoods, waiting on the dirt road just below the fort. "Over here," he says, pointing to one of the smaller wagons.

"This is a mobile field hospital," he adds. He lifts a flap to show us the cramped space inside. I climb in, stooping to keep my head from hitting the rounded canvas hood. Reiniger recites the inventory, opening the chest of supplies that sits in the center of the wagon and showing us the folding operating table. He demonstrates how to extend the flaps on all sides of the wagon to provide some shelter for the sick and wounded.

"It's medicine at its roughest," he tells us. "But the lessons you learn will be invaluable when you return to the luxury of a hospital back home. That is, if you survive."

In the evening, we're divided into companies and given our marching orders. I'm introduced to Arnold, a quiet orderly who looks like he's hardly old enough to shave. Since no surgeons are in the field yet and the need for emergency medical care is growing, Arnold and I are part of the medical staff assigned to the company that's leaving first thing tomorrow; the others will follow in a few days. The plan is for the various units to form a giant arc around the Herero so they can't escape into the neighboring territory, which is controlled by the English.

Before turning in, I add another letter to the stack I have ready to post to Hanna and Papa and take them all to the fort dispatch. The young clerk smiles at me as I hand him the pile of letters.

"You must be with the division heading out tomorrow," he says casually.

I nod.

"These will be the last you'll be sending in quite awhile then. Good luck, sir. From what I hear, you'll be needing it." He salutes me.

As I lie on the ground that night, I try to shut my mind to what tomorrow may bring, but I can't stop the echo of Reiniger's and the young clerk's words. What if I don't survive? What if I never get to meet my son? Or hold Hanna again? What if this desert becomes my grave?

BOOK 3

Jahohora

ALONE ON THE MOUNTAIN

I wake up early the next morning. My body hurts all over. But I can't remember why. I stare up at the rock ledge just above my head. Where am I? Then it all comes back to me. The screams. The thundering of the boom sticks. The hiding place in the crack between the rocks. It wasn't a bad dream. It really happened.

I lie there quietly, listening to the sounds of the day waking up. I hear the birdsong and the skitter of a rabbit. But there are no people sounds. No baby cries. No children laughing. No footsteps. No clang, clang from Mama Uajoroka's bangles.

I slide out from under the ledge. I start to open a pouch of berries. No, I should save these. I go back to the bushes and pick my fill of fresh berries as I think about what I must do. I know Tate said to run far from here if we heard the thunder of the boom sticks. But I want to go to the mountaintop to make sure everyone is all right. I don't want Tuaekua Ehi and the others to go hungry just because I was too scared to bring them food.

I pick a few more berries and then search for the path to the top of the mountain. It's so steep I must crawl on my hands and knees. It isn't easy with the pouches of berries hanging from my neck. About halfway up, I stop to rest. I'm about to start again when I hear footsteps. And voices speaking strange words. They come from above.

I press myself against the rocky side of the mountain. I must think quickly. I can't go to the top. And the path I'm on is too close to the one Tate and Mama took. I must find another way down. I remember a path Tate showed me on the steepest side of the mountain. Only the rains and wild animals go that way, he told me. Today, I must be a wild animal. But first I must get to that path. It's on the other side of the mountain.

I look at the rocks on either side of me. The paths all run down the mountain, not around it. I must make my own way. It isn't going to be easy. I hug the mountain, scrambling over the rocks to the left of me. I try to move quietly. But my foot hits a loose rock, sending it tumbling down the mountainside. I hear a shout from above. I lie against the mountain, barely breathing. Two voices on the mountaintop make strange words. A boom stick thunders. Something whistles over my head. It hits a rock below me. And breaks the rock. If it can break a rock, what could it do to me? I don't move. I wait and wait, trying to make myself unseeable. A fly buzzes in my ear. I want to shoo it away. Or shake my head. But I force myself to lie still against the mountain.

The voices are quiet. There are no footsteps coming down the path. I begin climbing again – to the left and downward. This time, I'm more careful. I move my left foot slowly, making sure I don't hit any loose rocks. I reach out with my left hand, grabbing onto a rock ledge. Then I move the other side of my body. One step at a time, one handhold at a time, I slowly slide around the mountain. The rocks cut my hands and feet. The sun burns my back. I try not to think about the pain or the heat. The hunger in my belly. Or the thirst in my mouth. I don't let myself think about Tate and Mama. Or the rest of my family. I must get off this mountain. That is the only thought I can have.

The sun is sinking toward the earth when I reach the path on the other side of the mountain. It's not much of a path. And it's very steep. Too steep to walk down. Especially in the dark. I look around for somewhere to hide during the night. But there is no place I can lie down. No place where I won't fall if I sleep. My belly is shouting with hunger. My hands and feet are bleeding. I'm so tired I can barely move. But I have no choice. I must keep going. At least a little farther.

I crawl down the path, my back to the ground. I'm thankful for the moon and the light it gives. But I wish it had some of the heat of the sun. It's cold. A cold that burns through me. I shiver. And keep moving. I go slowly, feeling my way with my bruised hands and feet. My foot touches a pile of loose rocks and sends them down the mountain. The sound echoes in the darkness. I lie still against the mountain, holding tightly to the rocky ground as I wait for the boom stick to thunder again. I hear only the bark of the wild dogs and the whistle of the duiker.

I'm about to move on when I see a shadow crouching by a rock. It's the wrong kind of shadow for a man. Without thinking, I move my leg. I feel my skin skirt brush against it. And I remember. It's the skin from the cow the leopard killed. On this mountain. I stare at the shadow. It could be a leopard.

I take a long, quiet breath. I lie as still as a rock. I watch the shadow, waiting for it to move. But it remains crouched. My heart beats loud and fast. I must stay calm. And I must be patient. I wait and wait and wait. I don't take my eyes off the leopard-shadow. It doesn't move. Not even a muscle twitch.

The moon slips behind a thin cloud. Suddenly, the leopard-shadow moves toward me. I shut my eyes. I don't want to see my death. But nothing happens. I slowly open my eyes. The cloud has passed over the moon. And the shadow is back in its place. I stop myself from laughing as I begin crawling down the path again, past the shadow of a "crouching" rock.

I'm so happy the shadow is a rock and not a leopard that I move too quickly. In the half light of the moon, I don't see that the path drops from beneath me. Suddenly, my feet slide into air. I try to grab onto the mountain with my hands. But I can find no handhold in the loose dirt and the rock smoothed by the rains. As I fall, I bend my head forward, covering it with my arms.

I land in a small grassy clearing. Every part of me hurts. But the pain tells me I'm still alive. I lie on the ground, staring up at the steep ledge from where I fell. It's as high above me as a tree. I'm happy it wasn't higher. I move my legs and arms. I make myself stand up and take a few steps. Nothing is broken. But I'm too sore to walk much farther.

Even though I haven't eaten all day, I don't think about food. I just want to lie down and sleep. Maybe then the pain will go away. And I can wake up from this bad dream. I see a hiding place under a rock ledge. I walk over to it. Slowly. I bend down to check for snakes. The pain makes me want to cry. I put the skin string of one of my pouches in my mouth and bite down to keep from crying out as I crawl under the ledge. I lie there, listening to dry branches snapping in the cold night air as I wait for sleep to find me.

A loud cry wakes me. I quickly sit up, hitting my head on the rock. I try to ignore the pain as I lie back down. My body hurts all over, but I make myself crawl out from under the ledge. It's still dark. I open my ears and listen hard, hoping to hear the cry again. All I hear are the night sounds I have known since childhood. Then it comes again, softly echoing against the mountain. *Karikuta!* is my first thought. Remembering the strange voices I heard this morning, I stop myself from shouting the name.

The cry echoes once more. It's not Karikuta. It's a brown hyena. I crawl back under the ledge. I wipe the tears from my eyes.

When I wake again, it's morning. I lie under the ledge, listening to the sounds of the mountain. My belly growls for food. I slowly crawl out and look around. The rock walls of the mountain rise steeply behind me. In front of me is the small clearing. The path, cut long ago by the rains, slopes gently downward through bunches of yellow grass.

Sitting with my back against the mountain, I take my fill of the berries I picked two days ago. They're smashed together in my skin pouches. But they're food. And the juice wets my throat.

With my belly a little happier, I explore the clearing. I move slowly. My feet and legs are too sore to walk fast. Seeing no signs of man, I become a little braver as I search for food. I dig up roots to chew on for water and find more berries to fill my pouches. I crawl to the edge of the clearing and look down. The path is wider and not so steep. And the bottom of the mountain is closer than I had thought. I will rest in the clearing today. When the sun sleeps, I will leave the mountain. Maybe then I will feel better.

As soon as darkness falls, I follow the path down the last part of the mountain. It's not as steep as the top part of the path. It would be an easy walk if I didn't have so much pain. Because the path is more even, I don't have to think about where I put my feet. So all the thoughts – all the questions – I've put away for the past few days fill my mind. And a loneliness so big it makes me want to cry.

But I keep walking. As I come to the bottom of the mountain, I listen for people voices. All I hear are the animals of the night. Keeping in the shadow of the mountain, I walk into the veld. I'm scared walking alone in the darkness. Not of the animals I hear. But of the things I don't see. Of what I don't know. I shake my head. I can't let myself be frightened. Even though I'm alone. I must think about finding water. The roots helped, but I need much more water than they hold. My mouth tastes like sand. I look to the stars for direction. I find the Otjikoroise Tjovaeve and look for the bright star above the dim one. The one Tate told me to follow to where the sun wakes. I start toward the first waterhole he pointed out to me. It shouldn't be too far.

A giant tree grows out of the morning twilight. Its dead limbs stretch high above the earth. What looks like the skin of a huge ox covers many of the branches. When I get closer, I see that it's not a skin. It's many, many bird nests woven together. As I walk by the tree, the weavers sing loudly.

"Shhhhh," I tell them. I look around, hoping no one hears the birds' warning. A movement in the tree catches my eye. A big, black snake moves slowly from the nest. It hisses, moving its head back and forth. I move away as quickly as I can.

A little farther, I see the trees that grow by the waterhole. I must reach the water before the sun fully rises. I wish I could run. But I'm too tired. And my body is too sore. I walk slowly forward. I see something move near the waterhole. I hide behind a tree and listen. At first I hear only the tree branches creaking. Then a low moan rises softly. I know that sound. It's the cry of a cow. There's another sound, even softer. I open my ears and listen hard. A woman sings. She sings the song Mama sang to Karemarama when he was a baby. She is Herero.

I'm so happy to meet another Herero, I want to run to the woman. But I hold back, walking slowly from behind the tree. I stop quickly. A black cow lies on its side, its legs sticking stiffly out. It moans again. Its nose twitches as it takes its last breath.

Beyond the cow lie many Herero. At first, I think they're sleeping. I look closer. A young woman stares open-eyed into the sky. Dark sticky blood covers her big belly. A man lies nearby. His face is to the ground – as if he fell. His back is red with blood. The bodies of Herero men and women, of children and tjikuus lie next to the carcasses of goats and cattle. The smell of death makes my belly rise to my mouth. I'm going to be sick.

Trying not to see the bodies, I look for the woman I heard singing. She's sitting near the waterhole. She rocks gently. Back and forth. Back and forth. I move toward her, trying to walk around the dead people and animals lying in my path. Tears blind my eyes. I wipe them away. I don't want to look down. But I must if I don't want to walk on the bodies. My bare foot touches a body. I want to scream. I cry quietly.

I stand near the woman who sings. She holds a baby to her breast, trying to get him to eat. "Mama," I call to her softly.

She looks toward me. But her eyes don't see me. They look through me as if I'm not there. Maybe I'm not. Maybe this is another bad dream. I wish it were. But it's too real. I sit next to the woman. I wonder at the stillness of the baby. I watch him closely. He is dead.

"Mama," I tell the woman, "the life has left your baby."

She doesn't hear me. She continues to sit there, rocking her dead baby and singing to him.

There's nothing I can do for her. I turn from the woman and go to the waterhole. The smell of death is so strong I pinch my nose closed. I look into the waterhole and vomit. The waterhole is filled with dead goats and cows and dogs. There's no water to drink. I hear a cry from overhead. I look up. Hooded vultures circle high in the sky. They've found their next meal.

Forgetting my pain, I run from the waterhole. I must get as far from this place of death as I can. I run and run and run. I run until I can run no farther. But everywhere I see death. The dead horses of soldiers. Dead oxen and goats. And dead Herero surrounded by everything they had in life – clothing, gourds, and kirris.

I drop to the ground, too tired to move. My eyes close. I see Mama and Tate lying on the ground. Their blood flows together, making a tiny river that runs across the veld. I see Tuaekua Ehi holding Karikuta to her empty breast. He cries no more. I see Tjikuu and Karemarama and Ramata staring up at the sun with eyes that do not blink.

The heat of the sun wakes me. I crouch and look around. I see no path in the tall yellow grass. No sign of lions or other animals. It's good, I think. No white people will find me here. I lie back in the grass. I try to forget all the bodies I've seen. But there's nothing else to think about – except the emptiness of my belly and the dryness of my mouth. Keeping low in the grass, I open my pouches and eat the last few smashed berries. I chew on a root. It's too dry to give me water. My belly is still hungry. My mouth still thirsty. I lie back down, hoping to find sleep. It's my only escape.

THE KUDU

I lie still, my eyes closed, listening for the sound that woke me. There it is again. A low humming – like a man trying to sing a song without words. What if it's a soldier? I open my ears and listen hard. A smile spreads on my face. That's no man. It's a kudu! I crouch like an animal and look across the veld toward the brush. I see nothing but trees and bushes. Then the kudu moves his dark head. I see his long twisted horns. He's standing in the brush at the edge of the grassland.

I crawl slowly toward him so I don't scare him. He watches me as he chews a mouthful of grass. When I get close, the kudu turns and walks into the brush. I stand up and follow him. It's almost evening. He'll be looking for food and water.

The kudu hums as he walks. He stops every little bit to graze on grass or leaves. After grazing, he turns to look at me, to make sure I'm still here. Then he hums and moves on. He stops again and raises his horned head to smell the leaves of a fat bush. He turns and grunts at me. He's found a berry bush. Keeping out of the way of his horns, I pick my share of berries, eating as I pick and then filling a pouch. When we've both had enough, the kudu moves on. This time he leads me to a small waterhole. I crouch in some brush as he drinks. Now it's my turn. I make myself drink the water slowly, lapping it from my hands. My thirst gone, I fill the rest of my pouches with water.

The kudu grunts. I look up. He's watching me from the brush. He lowers his head and paws at the earth. He looks up at me one more time. Then he turns around and disappears into the gray twilight. I run to where I last saw him and stare into the dense brush. I can see no kudu. But I hear him running through the trees. He is a long way off.

I sit down on the ground. I look at the kudu's hoof prints in the dirt. The tips of uintjes push up where he had pawed. I dig and dig until I have several of the wild onions to add to the berries in my pouch. I smile. I know the kudu was a gift from the ancestors.

The sun sleeps. I must start walking. I look up to find the stars that will guide me to Maharero and my family. I move cautiously through the brush, watching for animals that might think I'd make a good meal. I talk quietly to myself. I hope my voice is loud enough to scare off the animals but soft enough not to be heard by any soldiers who might be nearby. I hear the wild dogs bark in the distance. I bark back. I hear the hyenas cry. I try to make the same sound. I laugh at myself. It keeps me from being lonely.

The next few days, I follow the rhythm of the animals. Walking at night. Sleeping in the day. I set my own pace. Stopping when I need to rest. Eating a few berries and uintjes when I'm hungry. And sipping a little water when I'm thirsty. I search for fresh food and water just before the sun wakes and right after it sleeps. I watch the giraffes run across the veld, their long necks swaying to give them balance. I see a baboon sitting on a log. His black eyes stare at me as if he's trying to figure out what I am. I see the wildebeest grazing in the grasslands. The kudu hiding in the brush. But I see no man. Not even a sign of one. It's just me and the animals. I feel like I'm the only person in Hereroland.

It's early morning when I come to a village. Or what's left of it. The huts look like the blackened bones of a cow that's been stripped of its hide and meat. The smell of dead fire fills my nose. I go to where the holy fire once burned. Its ashes are cold. I glance around and see an old man and woman leaning on each other in death. Dried blood covers what's left of their heads. Vultures peck at them, each one claiming a part of their bodies.

Once again, I'm sick. But I don't run away this time. I pick up a burnt piece of wood and wave it at the vultures. "Shoo!" I scream at them. A few of them fly into the low branches of a nearby acacia tree. The others continue their feast.

"Shoo! Shoo!" I scream again. This time I hit the birds with the wood. Not hard. Just enough to make them fly into the trees.

"Mama! Mama!" they cry at me.

I shake the wood at them and then gather branches to cover the bodies of the old man and woman. It's not much of a grave. But it should protect them from the vultures.

The sun rises in the sky. I need a safe place to sleep. I could stay by the village. The soldiers won't come back. They've already burned it. What do they have to come back for? I find a soft spot under an acacia tree and lie down. Sleep doesn't come quickly. I have too many questions. I wonder where the ancestors of the village have gone. Their fire is out. The old man was probably the keeper of the fire. With him dead, how will the ancestors know where to find the rest of the clan?

And what about my ancestors? They sent me the kudu, but I didn't thank them. I had no holy fire. Will they think I've forgotten them? I don't need any more bad luck. And how will they know where to find me tomorrow and the next tomorrow? They knew I was on the mountain with Tate and the others. But if Tate didn't come back to the fire, he couldn't tell them what had happened. I feel very, very sad. I've lost my family and my ancestors. I don't want to lose who I am.

The sun is low in the sky when I wake up. I shiver in the winter cold and reach for my water pouch. It's frozen. I can't drink until it thaws. I glance at the burned huts. Maybe not everything is ashes. I go into a hut that's not burned as badly as the others. I dig in the ashes, looking for anything I can use. I find a sharp cutting stone and two fire-starting rocks. I put the fire rocks in my half-empty berry pouch. I carry the cutting stone outside where there's more light. Using the sharp stone, I shape one end of a branch into a sharp point. When I've finished with it, I put the cutting stone in the pouch with the fire rocks.

I pick up my new spear and set off. Maybe I will have meat tonight. The thought makes my belly growl. I haven't eaten anything but berries and uintjes since Uncle Kozondanda and Ramata trapped the rabbits on the mountain. That was many yesterdays ago.

INTO THE DESERT

I go from one village to the next, finding nothing but bones and ashes. The nights are colder and the water scarcer. I shiver as I walk in the darkness. I wish I could start a fire so I could get warm. And to cook the small birds and rabbits I kill with my little spear. But a fire might bring the soldiers. I've seen what they do to Herero. I've followed their path from one burned-out village to the next. I can't let them bring death to me. I must find the rest of my family like Tate said. So I shiver in the cold. And I eat my meat uncooked.

I don't like the cold. But I'd rather freeze than be thirsty. Yet I'm thirsty all the time. As the veld turns to desert, the waterholes become fewer and fewer. Most of the ones I find are dry. And the others are filled with carcasses. I try digging new holes. I find a little water. It's not enough. So I look for roots.

But soon, there are no roots. No waterholes. No villages. No veld. Just the desert. The sand gets deeper, making it harder to walk. The air stinks of smoke and rotting cow dung and death. All along the way are the ashes of campfires, pieces of clothing, skins, feathers, bangles, even a few headdresses. And the bodies of oxen, goats, and Herero. I pick up a tanned cow skin and drag it behind me. It will keep me warm at night.

By day, I find no shade. The sun beats down on me, setting me on fire with its heat. I raise my hand against its brightness. There's no blocking it. The ground burns my feet. I spread the skin out so I can lie down. I feel the hot sand even through the skin. My throat sticks together as if I had swallowed a termite wing. It hurts to breathe. Big flies get in my eyes, my nose, and my mouth. I can't shoo them away. I have to pick them out. Sleep refuses to come. I lie motionless. Seeing nothing. Hearing nothing. Waiting for nightfall or death. Whichever finds me first.

In the twilight, I hunt for food. But there are few rabbits and birds in the desert. And no berries. I'm so hungry I become like a vulture, using my sharp stone to cut pieces of spoiled meat from the dead cows and goats along the path. And when there's no meat on the carcasses, I chew on the bones. At least it feels like I'm eating something.

At night, I stumble as I move forward in the cold, forcing myself to take another step. And then another. And another. In the distance, I see the glow of fire. At first, I think it's the soldiers. Then I look behind me. Bright stars blink at each other from the mountains. The soldiers are talking. They're behind me. Somehow I got between them and Maharero. Yesterday, that would have made me happy. Today I feel nothing. I'm too tired to feel or to think. I can only walk. Even though my legs are like heavy rocks that I must drag slowly through the sand.

I trip over something. I put my hands down to break my fall. They touch a face with no life. Once, I would have screamed. Not now. I've seen too many bodies to be frightened by death. It is my life.

It's day once again. I see a few bodies covered with brambles near a clump of bushes. As I walk by, I look down. Some are waiting for death. For others, the wait is over. I move toward the bushes, hoping for shade and maybe a little water. There's a waterhole. But it's almost dry. I take what I can get – about a handful of water – and sip it slowly. When it's gone, I scoop up the wet sand at the bottom of the hole and squeeze what little water it holds into my mouth.

I want to lie down in the bushes. They will shade me from the sun. An old tjikuu is already lying there. I crawl in beside her.

"Child, save yourself," she whispers in a dry, cracking voice. "Run as far from here as you can."

"I have been running, Tjikuu. All night. But I must sleep now so I can run again tonight," I tell her.

I lie beside her, feeling her breath on my neck. For the first time since I left the mountain, I'm not alone. I sleep well.

The night cold wakes me. I start to roll over to pull the cow skin up over me. Then I remember the tjikuu. I feel her bony arm next to my back, but there's no breath on my neck. I sit up slowly. I don't want to wake her. I turn to look down at her. She doesn't move. She is sleeping her final sleep.

And so I move on. I walk past the stiff bodies of cattle, goats, and dogs. Their bellies are big with death. I walk around the bodies of many dead or dying Herero. They are so skinny they seem like shadows on the ground. The hyenas look up from their twilight meals to stare at me curiously before returning to their feast. Above me, the pink-faced vultures circle.

As I walk, the tjikuu's words "save yourself" repeat over and over in my head. Why? I ask. My family is gone. My ancestors are lost. And my people are dying. Why should I save myself? Why should I live when everyone else is dying? I don't want to be alone any more.

For the first time, I think about my death. I don't want to die out in the open where the vultures and hyenas can feast on me. No. When I can't walk any farther, I will gather brambles and dig a hole. Then I will climb into the hole and cover myself with the thorny branches. And wait for death.

That's good, I tell myself. But what if death comes to me when I'm sleeping? I won't be able to dig a hole. I think on that a little while. I'm very weak. I've had little food or water for many days. I could go to sleep and not wake up – just like the tjikuu. From now on, I must only sleep under a bush. Or cover myself with brambles before I sleep.

A fire glows in the darkness. I want to run to its warmth. My teeth chatter. And I shiver. But I walk slowly, hiding in the shadows. Even though the soldiers are talking with their star-lights behind me, some could be sitting around the fire. As I get closer, I hear voices. Women's voices. Then words. Herero words. I walk faster, but I'm still careful.

I'm close enough now to see the faces of the voices. Two tjikuus huddle over the small flame. I know I should keep walking. The soldiers aren't that far behind me. But I'm shivering with cold, and the fire promises warmth. "Tjikuu," I call softly as I step out of the shadows.

The women look up, startled. Their faces soften when I come closer. "You must warm yourself, child," the oldest one says to me.

I rub my hands together over the fire. When my front is warmed, I turn my back. The heat spreads from my legs up to my shoulders. It almost burns me. But I'm still cold on the inside where the fire's warmth can't reach. I sit down next to the women.

"What are you doing out here by yourself?" the older one asks. She gives me a small gourd filled with water.

I drink before I answer her. "I'm looking for my family."

"Who's your family?"

"I'm Jahohora, daughter of Mutihu and Tutejuva of the Omukuatjivi clan."

"Of the big house or the small house?"

"The big house," I say. I tell them what happened on the mountain. "Now I must find the rest of my family like Tate said."

"They were with Maharero?" the quiet one asks.

"Yes," I say. "Have you seen them?"

The women are quiet as they look into the fire. The older one sighs. "You weren't at the Waterberg?"

I shake my head.

She tells me the soldiers pushed all the Herero, and all their cattle and everything they had, into the valley beneath the Waterberg. "All night long, we saw the soldiers' stars flashing from mountain to mountain," she says. "Early the next morning, the boom sticks roared. And then came the lightning and boom of the big guns. Our men fought back – the ones who had boom sticks. They gave their lives to keep the soldiers from killing all of us in the Waterberg." Her voice cracks. "As soon as darkness fell, we gathered our things and ran toward the morning sun. The soldiers have been chasing us until now."

"Where are the others?" I ask.

"So many have died," the younger one whispers.

"Maharero and those who live are still running – deep into the Omaheke. It's what the soldiers want," the first woman says. "Karikondua" – she nods her head toward the other woman – "and I can go no farther. We will die here."

"If Maharero is in the Omaheke, that's where I'll go," I say. "I must find my family."

The older woman shakes her head. Her eyes, shining in the firelight, look into mine. "This is the Omaheke. The beginning of it. If you keep going, you won't find your family. You'll only chase ghosts – and a slow death. You must go back to Hereroland. You can't live in the desert."

"But the soldiers...."

"You can escape them. If you're careful. And alone."

I shake my head. I don't want to be alone anymore.

"Child, you must listen to me," the old woman says. "You have to save yourself. For your family. And for our people. Someone must live to tell our story."

The sound of horses and wagons echoes in the night. There are lots of them. "The soldiers," Karikondua says quietly. "You must run, child. Quickly."

"What about you, Tjikuu?"

"We're too old to run any more. We'll sit here by the fire and wait for death," the older woman says. She sees the look on my face. "We have lived too many days. But you're young. You must live. Hurry!"

The horses are getting closer. I run toward the desert. I stop when I hear the short thunder of a boom stick. I can't run further. The soldiers might see me. I must hide. I look around, but all I see are shadows on the ground. Lots of them. The moon shines through the clouds. It shows me the shadows are bodies. Herero bodies. A few move. Most of them lie still. I wonder if any of them are Uncle Horere or Uapiruka. Even with the moonlight, it's too dark to see faces.

There are no hiding places. So I lie among the bodies. If the soldiers come, maybe they'll think I'm dead. I see the glow of the soldiers' fires. I wish I could feel their heat. I pull the cow skin over my body. But my teeth still chatter in the cold. I move close to a mama, hoping she'll help me get warm. But her body is cold. The smell of death fills my nose. I slowly move away from her. I turn over. I'm face to face with the cold body of a Herero man.

I roll onto my back and try to think of things so I won't sleep. The fires from the soldiers' camp will keep some of the wild animals away. But the smell of death may give them courage. I don't want to become food for a hyena or wild dog while I'm sleeping. That would be a bad way to die.

I stare up at the stars. They make me think of Tjikuu. And the night she told me the stars would someday shine down on my children. She was so sure. It was the circle of life, she said. Now that circle is broken. I want to cry. But I have no tears.

I think about what the women by the fire told me. If what they said is true, my uncles, aunties, and cousins who joined Maharero are either dead or running toward the slow death of the desert. I wish I were with them. If I'm going to die, I want to die with my family. But if I die here, at least I will be with other Herero.

I watch the last stars fade as the first light of the new day pushes the darkness away. I can see many, many Herero lying on the ground. There are more than I thought. More than I've seen before, living or dead.

I look toward the soldiers' camp. They're still sleeping in their little cloth houses. I should run. But I'm too tired and too weak. I slowly pull a bramble bush over my body. Its thorns catch on the cow skin that covers me. I push the skin off. It's getting too hot anyway. A horse whinnies in the soldiers' kraal. I feel eyes watching me. I lie still.

All is quiet again. I slowly pull another branch up over my head. I turn my face so the thorns don't scratch my eyes. Once I'm covered, I lie still. The soldiers are waking. I listen to their strange words as they take down their houses. I smell food cooking. My belly growls. It's been many yesterdays since I've eaten.

I hear footsteps coming toward me. My heart beats fast. A soldier stands above me. I close my eyes so he won't see the life in me. I lie still as death, even when I feel his pee trickling down on me. It makes me sick. I want to scream at him. But I'm quiet as his dirt spills on me.

When he's done, he doesn't go away. I peek through my eyelashes. I watch him bend down over the dead Herero woman next to me. He takes her chest bangles and puts them in his pants. He makes a strange noise. Like the wind blowing through the trees.

I hear several soldiers walking nearby. I see one take the headdress from another woman. Then he takes the bangles from her arms. One of the soldiers calls to the others. He bends over a young Herero woman. She still has life. He pulls down his pants and lies on her. He laughs as he jerks his body forward. His laughter sounds like a hyena screaming. The others make the same sound as they watch him. He stands and pulls up his pants. One by one, the other soldiers lie on the woman. When the last one is done, they smile at each other. One of them picks up his boom stick. It has a spear on it. He pushes the spear into the woman's belly. The soldiers laugh as they go back to their camp.

I close my eyes and try not to breathe as they walk by me. I hear the horses in the distance. The other soldiers are getting ready to leave. I breathe slowly. I'm safe. But now there are other footsteps. Coming toward me. They stop at my side. A skinny soldier stands above me. The hair on his face is long and matted. His dark eyes stare at me. I know he sees me. I lie very, very still and keep my eyes almost shut. I want him to think I'm dead. He bends down and pushes something under the bramble branch. I see a snake wrapped around a tree branch on his shirt.

The soldier starts to stand up. He stops and slowly pulls a small boom stick from a pouch tied around his belly. He knows. I close my eyes tightly. And wait for death. My eyes blink open when I hear the thunder of the boom stick. That's when I see it – a black mamba close to my hand. It falls backward and dies. The soldier must be a snake hunter. That's why he wears a snake on his shirt. He protects the other soldiers from snakes. I'm glad he was here to protect me.

I'm no longer afraid of him. I stare up through the brambles into his dark eyes. They are kind but full of sadness. It's as if he has lived too many yesterdays. But he's not an old man. Not like Tjikuume was. He's not even as old as Tate.

As the snake hunter turns from me, he whispers. I slowly look around to see who he's talking to. No one's there. His voice rises and falls like Tate's when he talks to the ancestors at the holy fire. I open my ears to hear the soldier's words as he walks away. I don't know them, but they make me want to live. I wish the soldier would come back. That he would talk to me. And walk with me through the desert. That he would protect me from snakes. Even though he's a soldier and a white man, I know I'd be safe with him.

But he's gone. And I'm lying here alone among the dead, waiting for the soldiers to leave this place. I hear the crack of whips and the drivers shouting at the oxen as the wagons move out. They roll over the bodies of the Herero. I listen until the wagons sound like thunder rumbling in the distance. I lie there longer until the only sound is the buzzing of a fly and the flapping of vulture wings. I slowly lift the brambles off me. I sit up and rub sand all over my body. I want to clean the first soldier's dirt from me.

Feeling a little cleaner, I look around for what the snake hunter left. I find a small jar. It is square. And I can see through it – like the jar Tate told me about. I open it and smell. It's filled with water. I take a few slow sips and close it. The snake hunter also left a little bundle. I pick it up and look at it closely. I have never seen anything like it. It's tied, but not with a piece of skin or tree bark or even grass. And the wrapping is smooth and white. It tears easily when I open it. Inside are pieces of meat and flat bread. I eat a little of the meat. I smell the bread. Then I take a few small bites. It doesn't taste like anything I've eaten before. But it's food. And it's more than I've seen for many, many days. It's almost like a feast. And it will keep me alive.

My belly isn't full. I want to eat all the food. But I bundle up most of it. I must keep it for tomorrow and the next tomorrow. I don't know when I'll find more food. I tie the skin string from one of my pouches to the bottle and hang it from my neck. I pretend it's like Mama's chest bangles.

I usually sleep in the day, but I can't sleep today. Too many thoughts fill my head. I think about the snake hunter who gave me the food. About what the tjikuus told me by the fire last night. About my family. Maybe some of them are here among the dead. I get up and look at the faces of the bodies that cover the ground.

I look and look and look. I see babies and children. Mamas and tates. Tjikuumes and tjikuus. But no one I know.

The sun is high in the sky. It makes the desert very hot. I start to drink from the jar. I remember the water the tjikuus gave me last night. There is a waterhole here. And maybe the soldiers left some food. I walk slowly to the place of the soldiers' camp. Thin tails of smoke still rise from their fires. I find the waterhole. It's dry. The soldiers and their horses and oxen have taken it all. I dig a new hole close by. A little water bubbles up. I drink some and put what I can in the jar and one of my pouches.

I hunt for food in the empty camp. I find a few pieces of meat and flat bread scattered on the ground. I pick them up and brush the sand away. They will feed me for a few more days. I put them with the food the snake hunter gave me. I also find a soldier's shirt. It doesn't smell good, but it will help keep me warm at night.

At the edge of the camp, I see the fire where I sat with the tjikuus last night. The fire still smokes. The two women lie beside it. They no longer wait for death. It has found them. I want to bury them. But I'm not strong enough to dig a hole and put their bodies in it. Instead, I find several brambles to pull over them. The thorns cut into my fingers. I don't care. This is something I must do.

Darkness comes. I'm too tired to walk. I haven't slept in two days. I think about staying here in the camp. The soldiers won't be back. But the hyenas will feast tonight, now that the fires have burned out. No, I must walk. It isn't safe to sleep at night with the dead.

The darkness brings the cold. I put on the soldier's shirt. It's big enough for three more Jahohoras. I wrap it around me and tie it in place. Then I put the cow skin around me like a cape. I'm a little warmer.

I stand at the edge of the soldiers' camp, thinking about which way to go. The desert and death are all that wait for me if I follow the soldiers chasing after Maharero. But if I go back the way I came, there might be more soldiers. I look up at the night sky. I find the Otjikoroise Tjovaeve. I make a line from the top star to the bottom star. I will go that way.

As I leave the camp, I think about all the Herero who died here. There's no one to bury them. To mourn for them. To tell their ancestors where they are. There's no one who knows their names. I shake my head. I'm very sad. But there's nothing I can do for them. If I don't want to become food for the vultures and hyenas, I must leave this place.

I walk through the night. Shivering in the cold wind that stings my face. Stumbling with sleepiness. Thinking about home with no family. My eyes close. I feel myself falling. But it's like I'm falling in a dream.

I wake up with my face in the dirt. What am I doing here? I remember the soldiers' camp. The tjikuus sitting by the fire. The snake hunter saving my life. But I don't remember where I am or how I got here. I stand and look at the sky. There's my star. I walk toward it. I stumble again. I make myself keep walking. Walking. Walking. I quietly sing the praise songs Tjikuu and Mama taught me. Singing helps me stay awake. But it makes me sad. It makes me think of Tjikuu and Mama. I wonder where they are. I wonder if I'll ever see them again.

At last, the sun wakes. I can sleep safely. I find a good hiding place. If soldiers come by here, they won't see me. But the vultures might come. I gather a few thorny branches and then sit under a ledge while I drink a little water and eat a small piece of meat. At last, I sleep. A sleep without dreams.

It's dark when I wake. I'm cold and still very tired. But I must walk. I try not to think about how cold I am. Or how hungry and thirsty. Instead, I think about what I should do. I must stay far, far away from the soldiers. I also must stay away from the farms and villages of the white people. If they find me, they might give me to the soldiers. And somehow, I must get back to my home.

I don't think about what I'll do when I get there.

SURVIVAL

I sit down to rest. I want to sleep, but I must leave the desert before my food and water are gone. There'll be plenty of food in the veld. But there's little in the desert. I do find a few waterholes. They're very far apart. And they're all dry. I see the holes that others have dug around them. They're dry. I don't try to dig new holes. They would be dry, too. And I'm too weak and tired to dig for nothing.

Instead, I look for food. I make a trap for mice, but I don't catch any. I look at the cows and goats that have died along the way. The vultures, hyenas, and wild dogs have already feasted on them. All that's left is bones and hide. I cut the skin from a big goat using the sharp stone I found many yesterdays ago in the burned hut. I scrape little pieces of meat from the hide. It's old and stringy. I chew and chew. It's like chewing on skin. But it's food.

I hold the water pouch to my lips. I need something to help me swallow the tough meat. The pouch is empty. I was sure there was still water in it. I look at it closely. I see a small hole. I drop it on the ground and take a small sip of water from the jar tied around my neck. I will need another pouch. This jar is too small to hold much water. I use the cutting stone to turn part of the goat skin into a pouch. It takes me all day. I'm so tired, I have to rest a lot. But at last, the pouch is done. It's very stiff. But it will have to do. I tie it with a long, skinny piece of skin and put it around my neck.

After working all day, I'm too tired to walk tonight. I hurt all over. Especially my hands. I hold them up to my face. They're covered with cuts and blood. They also are very skinny. I hadn't seen that before. They look like skin stretched over bone. And my fingers are like the thinnest branches on a bramble bush. Am I that skinny all over? I put my hands around my belly. My fingers almost touch. I sit down and stretch out my legs. They are just as skinny. I need to fatten up. I've got to find food.

Over the next few days, I get weaker and weaker. Too weak to walk very far. So I walk as long as I can. Then I rest. It takes me longer to reach the veld than I thought it would. By eating only a little food and drinking a few sips of water each day, I make what I have last until I come to the edge of the grassland.

I'm very sad when I look out over the veld. I thought it would be easy to find berries and roots and rabbits. But there's no tall yellow grass. No green bushes. No birds flying in the sky.

Instead, the veld is black from fire. There will be few berries and uintjes. And even fewer birds and rabbits. I keep walking. At least the veld will have more waterholes than the desert.

But I soon find many of the waterholes are dry. I see wagon marks in the dirt and the ground pawed bare by hundreds of animals. Soldiers came this way. The waterholes had enough water for some Herero. They didn't have enough for all the Herero and the soldiers and all their horses and oxen.

Other waterholes have been poisoned with death. I shrug my shoulders and walk to the next hole. I've had very little to eat or drink for so many yesterdays that I don't feel hungry or thirsty anymore. But I know I must find food and water. I look up at the sky. I see no clouds. There will be more food and water when the rainy season comes. If I can live that long.

I walk alongside the ruts made by the soldiers' wagons. They dig deep into the earth. I follow them to where the soldiers camped. I look for scraps of food. I dig in the ashes of the campfires and find a few bones with a bit of old meat. I'm surprised the wild dogs or hyenas haven't picked them clean. Then I remember. They have plenty to eat. They don't need to gnaw on dry old bones. I chew the meat off the bones and look for more food. I pick up a small piece of bread. It's hard. Like a rock. I try to eat it. But it's too hard to chew. I try to suck on it to soften it. My mouth is too dry. I put the bread in my pouch. Maybe I can eat it when I find water.

I check the waterhole at the camp. It looks dry. I drop a small rock into the hole and listen. There's no splash. Just a thud when the rock hits the bottom. I scratch at the dirt with my fingers, trying to make a new hole. The sun beats down on me. I feel like I'm on fire. Every part of me burns. My head hurts – like someone is using it for a drum.

I hear someone breathing very loudly. I'm too tired and weak to be scared. I look around. No one is here but me. I close my mouth. The breathing stops. I open my mouth. The loud breathing starts again. It's my breath that's loud. I try to laugh. But no laughter comes out.

I want to lie down. Right here. With the sun burning me. But I know I can't. Not yet. If I do, I may never wake up. I have to get water before it's too late. I find a stick and use it to help me dig. I dig and dig and dig. No water fills the hole. I dig some more. I'm about to give up when I see the dirt at the bottom of the hole is darker. I dig a little deeper. At last, a trickle of water covers the dirt. I cup it to my mouth, drinking more dirt than water. I dig again. I find enough water to fill the jar the snake hunter gave me.

I hear a noise in the distance. I look up. A cloud of dust rises on the veld. Riders! Coming toward me. I run to a clump of trees. But it's too close to the waterhole. And the riders will stop to drink. Water is hard to find right now. The thunder of the riders comes closer. It sounds like wagons. Lots of them. I have to get farther away. I run as fast as I can, keeping low to the ground. There is no grass to hide me. It's all been burned.

I hear the wagons stop. I lie on the ground, listening to the soldiers shouting strange words at each other. I see a bramble bush in front of me. I slither toward it like a snake. I cover my face and body with the cow skin so the thorns don't cut me as I crawl into the bush. A very bad smell hits my nose. It makes me sick. I peek out from under the skin. Something that looks a little like a body is in the bush. Most of the skin has rotted away, leaving mostly bones. I want to scream. To run away. To wake up from this bad dream. Instead, I cover my eyes and lie down next to the body.

I lie there all night. I watch the smoke from the soldiers' campfires and listen to the clang of pots as they cook. But the stink of the rotting body is all I can smell. My belly rises to my mouth. And my head pounds. I close my eyes. Maybe sleep will chase the stink away.

I'm back on the mountain. My pouches are filled with berries for Tuaekua Ehi, Mama Uajoroka and all the others. I'm happy that they will have food. Tuaekua Ehi will get stronger. And she'll have more milk, so Karikuta won't cry. I take the berries to the little clearing between the huts. I turn in slow circles, looking for my auntie, brother, and cousins. But no one is there. "Mama Uajoroka!" I call out.

My voice echoes back at me. "Tuaekua Ehi! Karemarama!" I shout.

Again, echoes are my only answer. I sit by the holy fire and watch the thin tail of smoke climb toward the sky. The smoke bends toward me. It splits in two and circles me. I hear voices calling to me from far, far away. They're the voices of Mama and Tate. Of Tjikuu and Ramata and Karemarama. Of all my uncles and aunties and cousins.

"Where are you?" I ask them.

"We're with the ancestors," Mama tells me.

I have to listen hard to hear her words. "Wait for me. I'll come with you," I say.

"No," Tate tells me. "You can't. You must build our house again. Or we'll all be forgotten."

"But I miss you. And I don't want to be alone."

"You're not alone, Jahohora," he says. "You'll never be alone."

The voices fade. The smoke disappears. The holy fire is just a heap of cold ashes. I look around the clearing again. I see what remains of a body. I look closer. It's Tuaekua Ehi. Her face has been pecked by the vultures. In her arms are the bones of Karikuta. I scream and run away. The berries spill all over the ground.

I wake up, shivering in the cold. Hoping I didn't scream out loud. The noise of a boom stick cracks in the darkness. I hear soldiers shouting. A few walk into the veld. They wave branches of fire. I lie very, very still as two come toward me.

"Puh!" one of them says. I don't understand the rest of his words. But I think the smell of the rotting body is making him sick. The soldiers start to turn away. One of them stops to touch his torch to the ground. I'm scared. They're trying to burn the place. I don't want to get trapped by a fire.

I don't need to be scared. The flames don't spread. This part of the veld has already been burned. There's no dry grass to make the fire run.

I lie in the bramble bush long after the soldiers leave the next day. I want to get away from the bad smell. But I must wait until I know it's safe. The sun is high in the sky when I walk slowly across the veld toward the camp. I dig in the ashes of the soldiers' campfires and look closely at the ground, searching for scraps of food. All I find is a jar that I can see through. It has something in it. But it's not water. I put it to my nose. It doesn't smell good. I take a small drink. It burns all the way down my throat. I quickly take a sip of water from my water jar. I swish it around in my mouth, trying to get rid of the awful taste.

I walk away from the camp, looking for food. I dig in the ground until I find several uintjes. Even though they were buried in the dirt, they were burned by the flames that blackened the veld. I eat them anyway. I look for roots that hold water. I find a few. Most of them were burned, too.

So I live. Hiding. Walking. Sleeping. Scratching at the dirt to find food. And waiting for the rainy season to bring life to the veld.

RAIN

The sound of thunder wakes me. I think it's a boom stick. I lie very, very still. I hear it again. A deep rumble that drums over the veld, echoing against the distant mountains. A flash of light cuts the sky. And the thunder rolls again. I look up into the early morning twilight. Dark clouds roll over each other as they race across the sky. I relax. There are no boom sticks. No soldiers. Just the rains.

I look around for a better hiding place. This spot is in a small valley. Even a little rain could flood it. Big drops of water hit my face as I run to some bushes growing where the ground rises. I stick out my tongue, trying to catch a few. I cover myself with the cow skin and crawl under the bushes.

Howling like a wild dog, the wind spits sand. The bushes dancing above me protect me from the sting. But their branches scratch against my face. I tuck my head under the skin and listen as the rain hits the earth. It splashes down hard. The sound of it beating against the dry ground makes me sleepy.

When I wake up, the rain has stopped. As I crawl out from under the bushes, they drop water on me. It feels good. I jump in a small puddle and laugh. I feel like a child again. My laughter stops when I remember Karemarama and my cousins splashing in the puddle on the mountaintop. I can hear Mama shouting at them to stop. The memory makes me sad.

I walk to the edge of the rise and look across the veld. A small river flows over the place where I slept last night. It's good that I moved. I turn in a slow circle, looking for waterholes and people. I see a few waterholes. But there's no sign of people. No tails of smoke curling into the sky. No clouds of dust racing across the earth. Nothing. I'm alone in the veld. I feel safe. And sad. Since I left the desert, I've seen too many Herero who are dead or dying. But I've met no one who's living. There have to be others. I can't be the only one.

I look up at the sky again. A big, dark cloud moves quickly over the earth. I watch it come toward me, waiting for its rain.

As it gets closer, the cloud gets bigger and bigger, spreading its blackness across the sky. A loud humming thunders around me. It's not a storm cloud. It's a swarm of locusts!

I crouch by some rocks and pull the cow skin around me to protect me from the swarm. I watch as the locusts drop to the ground. Their silver wings – as long as my finger – shine in the sunlight. They're beautiful. But terrible. Wherever they land, there will be no food.

As quickly as they came, the locusts take to the sky and move on. I look out across the veld again. The locusts have eaten everything that lived. I'll have to go on to the next waterhole to find food. I plant in my head the path I'll take. I walk to the little river in the valley and drink my fill of water for the first time in many days. Then I fill my jar and pouches.

I wish I didn't have to leave. There's plenty of water here. And I'm so tired and weak. If only I could find some food, then I could stay here for a few days. That way I could rest and build my strength. Maybe something survived the locusts. I set a few traps. There might not be any berries or uintjes. But maybe tomorrow I'll have meat.

As soon as the sun wakes, I check my traps. The first two are empty. The last one has a rabbit. It's a skinny rabbit. But it's a rabbit. I use my cutting stone to sharpen a branch into a new little spear to kill the rabbit. I'm sorry I have to kill it. I've seen too much death. But I need its meat so I can live.

After I skin the animal, there's little meat left. The rabbit was as skinny as I am. I want to cook the meat. But even though I didn't see anyone in the veld, I'm afraid to make a fire. Someone could see it. So I chew the raw meat until nothing is left but bones. With my belly almost full, I rest awhile. And then set the traps again.

For the next few days, I feel like I'm feasting. I drink lots of water and eat several skinny rabbits and birds. When I'm not eating and drinking, I sleep. I stay in the valley until the dry ground swallows the river. Then I begin walking toward the next waterhole where the sun sleeps at night.

More rains come. The black veld turns green. Bright flowers grow among the long yellow grass. White flowers cover the thorn bushes. Long-stemmed yellow and purple flowers cling to the tall trees. I breathe deeply, smelling the spring sweetness. It's easy to find berries and uintjes and roots again. There are lots and lots of rabbits and birds. And the waterholes are filled with fresh water. I have everything I need. Except my family. When I get lonely, I talk to myself. I tell the stories Mama and Tjikuu told me. I must remember them. Someday I will tell them to my children. I think about Uapiruka. What if I can't find him? Who will be the tate of my children then?

I want to go home to see if any of my family is there. But I'm afraid to go back. What if the white people have taken our land? I feel safe in this part of the veld. No white people live here. It's too close to the desert. Since I have enough food and water, I stay several days near each waterhole before I walk to the next one. Every time I stop, I build a small hut of branches. I make it look like it's part of the bushes. In the day, I check my traps and gather berries, uintjes, and roots. When I walk at night, I go slowly, using the moon to light my path. I don't want to step on Herero bones hidden in the grass. There's new life in the veld, but it's growing over the dead.

The sun is waking when I come to the next waterhole. Even though I've seen no one for a long, long time, I always stop before I reach a new waterhole. This time, I quietly climb a tree so I can look over the area. I see a small tail of smoke. My heart beats loudly. I hear voices. They're using Herero words! I look closely. A Herero man and woman sit by the fire. Don't they know how dangerous that is? Even when I know I'm alone in the veld, I eat my meat raw. A fire would show soldiers where I am.

I slowly climb down from the tree and walk toward the fire. The man and woman don't see me until I'm almost by them. The man looks up first. He picks up his kirri. We stare at each other. Both of them are so skinny they look almost like the bones I've seen lying on the ground. They are cooking a bird on the fire. It smells good.

The woman calls to me. She asks who I am.

"I'm Jahohora, daughter of Mutihu and Tutejuva of the Omukuatjivi clan."

"Of the big house or the small house?" the man asks.

"The big house," I say. "Do you know my family?"

They shake their heads and tell me their names and clan. "Have you seen our son?" the woman asks. She seems very sad. "We lost him when we went into the Omaheke with Maharero."

"I've seen many dead Herero," I say. "I haven't met anyone living until now." I tell them what happened on the mountain. "Since then I've been alone. I walked to the Omaheke to find my family. But the soldiers were already there."

We sit in silence. When the bird is cooked, the woman gives me a piece.

I shake my head. The bird is small. And the man and woman look like they need the food more than I do. I've been eating well since the rains came. I open one of my pouches and give them some berries and uintjes. They eat them quickly. I wish I had something more I could give them.

After they've eaten, the man and woman tell me how the soldiers pushed them deeper and deeper into the desert. To a place where there were no waterholes. They were the lucky ones. Many, many Herero died. And many more were taken by the soldiers. The prisoners were treated badly. The soldiers gave them little food or water and forced the women and girls to lie with them.

One day, the big German chief made all the soldiers line up. He dragged the Herero prisoners out in front of them. The chief slowly rode his horse between the soldiers and the Herero. Then he turned toward the prisoners and told them that Hereroland now belonged to the white people. And because the Herero murdered and stole from the white people and because they cut off the ears and noses of wounded soldiers, all the Herero people must leave German land.

"But it's our land!" I say. "It's the land of our ancestors. It's the land Njambi Karunga gave to us. The white people took it from us. And they killed many, many Herero."

The man nods his head. "The white people have big guns, so they are stronger than the Herero. They can take what they want. Some Herero had boom sticks, but most of us only had our kirris." He looks at his club. "They aren't any good against an enemy who's afraid to fight you hand to hand."

His wife tells the rest of the story. "The big chief told the prisoners that if the Herero did not leave this land, he would force them out with the big gun that makes the ground shake and the thunder boom. Every Herero found in the German land – with or without a gun, with or without cattle – would be shot. The soldiers would take no more prisoners. Not even women and children. They would all be forced back into the desert or they would be shot." The woman pauses.

"What happened to the prisoners, Mama?" I ask.

She looks like she hurts. "When the sun woke the next day, the soldiers took all the men prisoners and tied ropes around their necks and hung them. They made the others watch. Then they told the women and children they must run to Maharero and tell him what the big chief had said. The soldiers shot their boom sticks into the air to make the Herero run."

I shake my head. I can't believe anyone would do those things.

"Only a few of the women made it to where Maharero and the rest of us were camped," the man says. "The others died in the desert."

"What did Maharero do?" I ask.

"He didn't want to leave the land of his fathers. But there weren't enough of us to fight the soldiers. He said he would try to cross the desert into Bechuanaland. The Germans haven't taken that land. Those who were strong enough said they would go with him. I don't know if they made it to Bechuanaland." He looks at his wife. "We knew we couldn't walk that far with no water."

"How did you get past the soldiers?" I ask. "It was easy for me. I was behind them. But they were between you and the veld."

The man smiles sadly. "The Omaheke is a big place. Too big for even the German soldiers."

"Did others come back?" I ask. I think about my family. Maybe some of them are walking toward the veld.

The woman pats my hand. "If we came out of the desert, I'm sure others will make it, too."

The sun is high in the sky. I need to sleep if I'm going to walk tonight. I fill my water jar and pouches. And then I tell the man and woman goodbye. They ask me to stay. I'd like to. It's nice to talk to someone. To not be alone. But I remember Tate saying we must run and hide alone. It's easier for the soldiers to find groups of people than it is for them to find one young Herero girl.

"I must go on alone." I smile at the man and woman as I leave. I walk toward the next waterhole, looking for a hiding place so I can sleep.

SURVIVORS

As I walk that night, I think about turning around and going back. Not to where the man and woman were. But toward the desert. Maybe I'll meet more Herero coming out of the Omaheke. Maybe I'll find Uncle Horere and Uapiruka and the rest of my family. The thought makes me smile. Then I think about what the man said. The Omaheke is a big place. The path I took is not the only way out. They could come on many other paths. No, I will go on to the next waterhole. Maybe I will meet more Herero there. Maybe they will know where my family is.

I reach the waterhole before the sun wakes. But I don't go to it. I want to make sure it's safe. I lie back in the tall grass and stare up at the sky. I watch the stars blink out and the darkness turn gray. I see the first pink light of the sun stretching across the sky. I sit up slowly and look toward the waterhole. No one is there. I walk to the hole. It has lots of water. I look at the ground around the hole. No one has been here for many days. I glance all around. I see several trees on a small hill a way from the waterhole. That's where I'll stay.

After I rest, I make my camp, weaving branches together into a small hut under the trees. I lay my cow skin on the dirt floor. I smile. It's almost like home. I go back to the waterhole and look up toward the trees. I can't see the hut. That's good.

The next few days, I explore my new home. I find the best berry bushes and look for roots and uintjes. I see good places to set many traps. Soon, I have plenty of food. But I keep gathering more. I'll need it. The rainy season is over. When I'm not hunting for food, I sit in my hut and watch to see if anyone is coming toward the waterhole.

But I'm not watching when they do come. I've been checking my traps and am on my way back to the little hut. I look down toward the waterhole. Three people are sitting there. I crouch in the tall grass, hoping they didn't see me. I peep over the grass. I can't tell who they are. I sit in the grass, waiting for them to leave. But they lie down to sleep. I crawl slowly to my hut. I worry about the people by the waterhole. Are they Herero? Or are they soldiers? It's hard to know from this far away. I wait and wait for them to wake.

The sun is about to sleep when I see smoke rising. They've started a fire. I hear women's voices. They're speaking Herero. I feel safer now. But I'm careful as I walk toward the waterhole. I call out to the women as I get close. They look scared at first. But they relax when they see me. They are very skinny, just like the man and woman who had escaped the desert. And their eyes are deep in their face. It's hard to look at them. But it's hard not to. They look dead. But they're still breathing. And moving. And talking.

I join them at the fire. I tell them my name and clan and ask if they've seen my family. They shake their heads. They've lost family, too. They ask if I've seen them. It's my turn to shake my head.

I look at the fire. Nothing is cooking on it. "Have you eaten?" I ask.

They stare at me. Their eyes seem dead. They were in the desert too long.

"I'll get you food," I tell them. "But you should put the fire out. It isn't safe. Soldiers might see it."

Instead of getting food from my hut, I pick more berries and dig for uintjes. I don't want anyone to see where I'm staying. It's safer that way. I put the food in my skirt and carry it back to the waterhole. The fire is out. Two of the women are sleeping. The third one, Mama Uaporimana, is waiting for me. I give her some of the food. She grabs it out of my hand and puts it in her mouth. She is very hungry. I sit beside her while she eats. I look at her closely. Her skin is cracked and bleeding. Sores cover her mouth. She looks very old. But I don't think she is.

When she's done eating, Mama Uaporimana tries to smile at me. The sores on her mouth bleed. She begins to cry, but she has no tears.

"What's wrong, Mama?" I ask. I don't know what else to say or do.

She rocks back and forth. "My baby," she says.

"Where's your baby?" I glance around, looking for a child.

"I left him."

"You left him? Where?"

"In the Waterberg," she whispers. She stares off into the distance.

I wait for Mama Uaporimana to tell me what happened. But she's silent.

She's still sitting there looking across the veld when the other women wake. After they eat, I take the strongest woman to the berry bushes so she can help me get more food. I ask her what happened to Mama Uaporimana's baby.

"She was one of them – one of the mamas who gave milk to our warriors," the woman says quietly.

"What do you mean?" I ask.

"You weren't at the Waterberg?" She stops picking berries and looks at me.

I shake my head.

"The ancestors were good to you." She looks into the distance. There is much pain on her face. "Maharero and his men had stopped fighting. But the soldiers wouldn't stop. They went from village to village, killing our people. We had to run. We took our cattle and went to the Waterberg with Maharero, hoping the soldiers would leave us alone. But there were too many of us. The waterholes went dry and there wasn't enough food. We were slowly starving. Then the soldiers came after us. The only way out was toward the Omaheke." The woman pauses to eat a handful of berries.

"To give the rest of us time to escape, Maharero and all the men with boom sticks prepared to fight," she said. "But some of the men were too weak to fight. They had gone too long without food or water. To give them strength, several mothers with babies gave what milk they had to the men. Mama Uaporimana was one of them. She didn't have enough milk then for her baby. He and the other babies died so the rest of us could live."

I shake my head. I have no words to say what I feel.

Later, I help the women trap a rabbit. Even though it's not cooked, they eat it quickly. I wonder if their bellies will ever be full again. If the pain will ever leave their faces.

The women stay by the waterhole a few more days. I know it's not safe, but I stay with them. I like not being alone. When they get ready to leave, they ask me to come with them. They're going back to their village near Hamakari. If any of their family escapes, that's where they'll go. I think about going with them. The soldiers have already taken what they want from Hamakari.

They have no need to go back there, the women tell me. It will be safe.

"But what about the words of their big chief?" I ask. "He said no Herero can live in the white people's land. The white people say all of Hereroland belongs to them now."

One of the women laughs. It's not a happy sound. "Hereroland is a big place. Too big for the white people. Land is not like a headdress or a long skirt that belongs to one woman. Land is a gift from Njambi Karunga. No one can own it."

I sigh. "You're right, Mama. But the white people don't think like us. They don't understand."

The women leave when the sun sleeps. I don't go with them. "I must find my own family," I tell them. "My village is a long, long way from Hamakari."

I watch the women until the twilight swallows them. I'm sad. And I worry about them. The rest and food has helped them. But they're still weak. Especially Mama Uaporimana. Life has not come back to her eyes. Her soul is dying.

I go back to my little hut on the hill. It's very quiet. Too quiet. I talk softly to myself and sing songs. It breaks the quiet, but not the loneliness. It's hard to sleep. I think about the women. About my family. About home.

The sun is high in the sky when I wake. I feel sad. But I don't know why. Then I remember. Mama Uaporimana and her friends are gone. I will have no one to talk to today. No one to pick berries with. I look around for something to do. If I'm busy, I won't think about everyone I've lost. I've explored most of the places close to the waterhole. Maybe I'll go farther today.

I hang my pouches around my neck. I don't want to leave them in the hut – someone might come. Then I head off toward a pile of big rocks in the distance. I walk slowly. I'm in no hurry. I watch a young giraffe stretch its neck, trying to reach the leaves in a high tree. Its mother eats nearby. She reaches the leaves easily. I make up a song about the giraffes. I sing it softly as I walk. I stop suddenly as a warthog crosses my path. He's very fat, so he takes his time moving out of my way. I walk all morning, but the pile of rocks doesn't seem to be getting any closer. Every little bit, I turn to make sure no one is coming behind me. The sun is very hot. But I don't care. I'm used to it by now.

At last, I reach the rocks. They look like they were thrown together by a giant. The pile is much taller than it seemed from my hut. I look for snakes before sitting down in the shade of one of the rocks. I drink from the jar the snake hunter gave me. I wish he was here. This would be a good place for snakes to hide. He could protect me. Then I wouldn't have to worry about snakes. I could worry about everything else.

I climb up to the top rock. It isn't easy. It takes me all afternoon. When I stand at the top of the pile, I turn in a slow circle. I can see to the end of the earth everywhere I look. The veld spreads out before me. Way, way off in the distance – where the sky meets the ground – are the Okavaka Mountains where I hid with my family. When I look the other way, I see the beginning of the Omaheke. In between, the veld lies empty and silent. It makes me sad. I don't know what I thought I'd see. But it wasn't this emptiness. There has to be someone out there somewhere.

I climb down the rocks. The sun is preparing to sleep when I reach the veld. I will sleep here tonight. Tomorrow I'll go back to the hut for a few more days. If no one comes, I'll find my way home.

I lie on the ground, looking up at the stars. I see the Otjikoroise Tjovaeve. It's very bright tonight. I smile. It's like an old friend. My smile goes away when I see the other stars in the milky omukuangu. A firespot shines bright red. Tjikuu said firespots in that part of the sky mean the next rainy season will be dry. That's not good. It'll be hard to find food and water. One more thing to worry about.

I watch the firespot until my eyes close in sleep. It's a bad sleep. The stars blink out of the sky, leaving it so dark I can't see my hand in front of my face. I want to run, but I can't. If I move, I might fall off the rocks or run into a soldier or a snake. I open my ears and listen hard. I hear nothing but my heart. It beats so loudly it sounds like thunder. I slowly walk forward, feeling in front of me with my hands. There's nothing to feel. I'm hungry and thirsty. But I can't find any food or water in the dark. I'm very, very scared. I don't know where I am. Or where I'm going. Or where I've come from.

I wake up. I'm covered with sweat. But the night is cold. I shiver and pull my cow skin around me. I still shiver. I look up at the stars to make sure they're shining in the sky. Then I close my eyes. The dream comes back. It's scarier than before. I wake up and tell myself stories so I won't sleep again. As soon as the sun begins to wake, I pick up my things and walk back toward the waterhole.

I'm very hungry when I get back to my hut. I sit in its shade, eating berries. I need to set my traps. I'm too tired. I'll do it tomorrow. I lie down, but I'm afraid to close my eyes. I don't want to dream again.

I walk down to the waterhole as the sun shines it last light of the day. I take long drinks and then fill my jar and pouches. Even though I'm staying near the waterhole, I must always have plenty of water with me. If soldiers come, I'll have to leave quickly. I'm putting the pouches around my neck when a shadow falls across me. I look up in surprise. A Herero man stands on the other side of the water. He seems just as surprised to see me. I look at him closely.

He wears a soldier's shirt that's too big for his skinny body. He drags his kirri behind him. It's thicker than he is. A small breeze could blow him over.

"You need to sit down, Uncle," I tell him. I hand him a water pouch to drink from. He's too weak to get his own water.

He tries to smile at me. He can hardly open his mouth.

"I'll be right back," I say. I go to my hut to get some uintjes and berries for him. I don't care if he sees where my hut is.

When I return, he's lying on the ground. His eyes are closed. I don't know if he's sleeping or dead. I watch him closely. I see his chest move a little with each breath. Good. I won't have to bury him. I put the berries and uintjes next to him. Even though I'm tired, I must set my traps tonight. He needs more than berries to eat.

I check on the man the next morning. He's still sleeping. He hasn't eaten the food I left for him. He must be very, very, very tired. I go to my traps. A rabbit is in one of them. Good. I kill it and skin it. I think about starting a fire to cook it. No, I decide. If any soldiers came, they would kill the man. He's not strong enough to run and hide.

I take care of the man for several days. As soon as he's able to move, I help him get to a good hiding place. It's not safe to lie in the open by the waterhole. He smiles at me. It's not much of a smile. But it's a smile. I bring him food and water every day. And I fill a few of my pouches with berries and roots. The veld is starting to dry up. Food will be hard to find soon.

At last, the man is able to sit up and drink without me holding the water pouch for him. He talks softly. His voice is just a whisper. He asks my name.

"I'm Jahohora, the daughter of Mutihu and Tutejuva of the Omukuatjivi clan."

"Mutihu? The healer?" he asks.

"Yes," I say in surprise.

"He's a great healer. And a good man." The man smiles at me.

I see that his bottom teeth are gone and his top ones are pointed – just like Tate's.

"I can see that you're his daughter. You are a healer, too."

His words make me feel good. And sad. "How do you know Tate?"

"I'm Ikuaterua. We're age mates," he says. His voice is almost gone.

I want to ask him lots of questions about Tate and my family. He's too weak and tired. "You must rest, Uncle. We'll talk later." I help him lie down. His eyes close quickly.

We do talk. A little bit more every day. Ikuaterua knows my family, but he hasn't seen them. He says he was only one of thousands of Herero who went into the Omaheke with Maharero. He didn't see who all was there. And too many died along the way.

I don't know "thousands." He tries to tell me. "It's like the stars in the sky," he says.

I nod. That's a lot. I'm sure not all the stars know each other either.

As soon as Ikuaterua is strong enough, he wants to leave. "This waterhole is too close to the desert," he tells me. "You should leave, too. The soldiers are hunting Herero all around here. They don't want us to leave the desert. They want us to die there."

"I've been here many days," I say. "I haven't seen soldiers."

"They'll come," he warns me. "And what they do to Herero girls is very bad. They just kill the men, but they force the girls and women to lie with them. Then they kill them."

I remember what the soldiers did to the woman near their camp the day I met the snake hunter. I don't want that to happen to me. "Where should I go?" I ask him.

Ikuaterua shakes his head. "No place is really safe. But it's safer the farther you get from the Omaheke."

"Can I come with you, Uncle?"

Again, he shakes his head. "You're safer alone. You can hide better." He looks sadly across the veld. "I escaped the desert with five others. We found an old Cape wagon in the bush a few days' walk from the Omaheke. We thought we were safe. That all the soldiers were still in the desert, chasing Maharero and the others. It was very cold that night, so we started a fire by the wagon. We sat around it – talking and eating scraps of food we found in the wagon."

Ikuaterua pauses. His thoughts bring pain to his face. His voice is very soft when he talks again. "I heard a strange noise and looked up. Five soldiers were creeping up on us. I shouted a warning. But the soldiers started shooting. I escaped into the bushes. My friends were all killed." He looks over at me. I see tears in his eyes. "I've been running ever since."

I can't sleep tonight. I know Ikuaterua is leaving in the morning. I'm sad. Taking care of him has filled my days. Now they will be empty again. I think about what he told me. Maybe it's time to leave this place. I don't want soldiers to find me. I'll leave tomorrow night. I feel safer walking at night.

I tell Ikuaterua goodbye when the sun wakes. Just before he goes, he thanks me. "You saved my life, Jahohora," he says. "I will never forget you. Mutihu must be very proud of you."

I watch him walk away – toward where the sun sleeps at night. "*Mukuru ngakare punaove*," I call after him. It's my wish for him. He turns to wave. I try not to cry. It's very, very hard.

BECOMING A WOMAN

As the sun rises in the sky, I try to sleep. I must rest today if I'm to walk tonight. I'm a little sad about going. I've been here so long, it's like leaving home. I roll over and shut my eyes. I have to stop thinking. I've got to sleep.

At last, it's dark. I fill my jar and water pouches one more time at the waterhole. I stand and look up at the sky, searching

for the Otjikoroise Tjovaeve. There it is. I follow it away from the
waterhole. I'm in no hurry. I have no place to go. Just a place to
get away from.

Once again, I live like the animals. Walking at night.
Sleeping in the day. Gathering food and water at twilight.
But now, I see more signs of people. Fresh hoof prints by the
waterholes. Fires that aren't quite cold. Bones picked clean of
meat. Dust clouds across the veld.

I must be very careful. I try to walk far from the paths cut by
the soldiers' wagons. When I come to a waterhole, I lie low in the
grass, watching to make sure no one is there before I go to get
water. And when I need to sleep, I find hiding places away from
the waterholes.

Sometimes I see other people. But they don't see me. I
watch quietly as soldiers ride past me on their horses. Several
Herero walk in a line between the soldiers. They're very skinny.
And they walk funny. Almost like they're falling, but catching
themselves before they do. Then I see why. They're tied together
with heavy metal ropes about their necks and wrists. If one
stumbles, the others do, too. The first Herero is tied to the saddle
of a soldier's horse. The soldiers stop to drink at the waterhole.
They let their horses drink. But they don't let the Herero.

After they rest, the soldiers move on. They go in the direction
I'm heading. They're probably going to Windhük. It's a big, big
village far from my home. I've never been there. But I heard
Tate talk about it. Windhük is in Hereroland. But it is the white
people's biggest village.

I stay in my hiding place long after the soldiers leave the
waterhole. I come out only when it's dark. I quickly get some
water and then go back to my place in the bushes. I'll rest
tonight. I want the soldiers to get far from here before I start
walking again. I don't want to catch up with them.

I wake up suddenly. Sharp pains circle my belly and back. It's
like someone is squeezing me. I have never felt this pain before.
It scares me. I wish Tate were here. He would know what to do
to make the pain go away. I think about what he'd do. He'd feel
my head to see if it's hot. I touch it. It's not. He would look at my
eyes and mouth. I can't do that. And he'd ask what I've eaten.
Raw meat and berries. It's all I've eaten for many yesterdays. It
didn't make me sick before. Why should it now?

Maybe someone cursed me. Who would do that? Ikuaterua is the last person who saw me. And that was many, many yesterdays ago. Ikuaterua wouldn't curse me.

Maybe the ancestors are angry because they think I've forgotten them. But they don't know where I am.

Maybe I'm dying. I've never died before. This could be how it feels. I lie there thinking about death. I don't want to die. But if I have to, I want to go to the ancestors. How will I find them? I need Tate to show me the way.

The pain comes again. Harder this time. I push against my belly. That helps a little. Maybe it would feel better if I get up. I stand up slowly. Something drips down my leg. I look down at the ground. There's a little pool of blood. That scares me. Is that from me? I've never bled like that. I must be dying. I lie back down to keep the blood from coming out of me. To slow the final sleep. I cry. I want Mama. And Tjikuu. I don't want to die by myself.

I think of all the things I'm going to miss. Little things, like running across the veld. Looking up at the stars in the sky. Drinking cool water on a hot day. And I think about the big things. I'll never marry Uapiruka. I'll never become a woman.

I start laughing. I'm not dying. I'm becoming a woman. Mama said I'd be a woman when I started bleeding between my legs. I'm a woman today. I hug the thought to me. I'm happy. I'm also very sad. I need Mama and Tjikuu to tell me what to do. I have so many questions. I know they have the answers. But they're not here to give them to me. I must learn this on my own.

My biggest worry is the bleeding. How do I stop it? I don't want blood running down my legs. It makes me feel dirty. And the smell of it could bring wild animals. I don't want to be dinner for a lion or a leopard. I gather some large leaves and tie them between my legs with a long thin piece I cut from the cow skin. I go down to the waterhole and wash the blood from my legs. The pains still squeeze my belly. But I feel much better.

I sit on a rock, letting the sun warm my body. The veld looks different now that I'm a woman. Life is different. I'm no longer a girl. I think about when Tuaekua Ehi came back to the village when she became a woman. She was so different I didn't know who she was. Would my cousins know me? Karemarama would tease me. And he'd want to race just so he could finally beat me.

If I were home right now, I'd be getting ready to marry Uapiruka. But I can't think about that. I can't think about everything I've lost. I must think about now. About staying away from the soldiers. About gathering more food before the veld dries up. About staying alive.

It gets harder and harder to find food and water. Even though it's the rainy season, no rain comes. The waterholes are drying up. And the berries are gone. It's been too long since the earth had water. And it's been too long since I had much to eat or drink. I dig in the dry ground for roots and set my traps. Too often, the traps are empty. When I do find food, I eat only a little so I'll have something for tomorrow. And when I find water, I take small sips. It's like being in the desert again. My lips crack. My mouth sticks together. And it hurts to swallow. I walk only a little way each night. I'm too weak to walk further.

My pouches and cow skin become too heavy to carry. But I don't want to leave anything. I need the skin to keep me warm at night and to protect me from stinging sand when the wind blows. And I need the pouches to carry food and water. When I can find any.

It's almost twilight. I see dust clouds rolling across the veld. Riders. They're coming this way. I have to get away from this waterhole. All the others in the area have dried up. Whoever is coming will stop here. I quickly fill my jar and pouches and start walking.

The pouches hang heavy on my neck. I wrap the cow skin around me. It will be cold soon. I walk and walk and walk. Until I can't take another step. I'm so tired that my eyes close before I drop to the ground.

When I wake, the moon shines big and round in the sky. It's so bright it covers the light of the stars. I can't find the Otjikoroise Tjovaeve. I rub my eyes so I can see better. I still can't find my guiding stars. I don't know which way to go. I don't want to go back the way I came. Soldiers are there. I look around. I can't remember how I got here. I stare at the ground, trying to see my footprints in the dust. The moonlight may be bright, but it's not enough to show my path. I sit down by some bushes. I'll have to stay here until the sun wakes.

I shiver in the cold. I reach for my cow skin. It's gone. I look all around, but I can't find it. I remember wrapping it around me when I started walking. It must have fallen off somewhere along the path. I was so tired I didn't feel it fall. I'm wearing the soldier's shirt. But it doesn't keep the cold out anymore. It's been cut by too many thorns. I sit with my knees up to my chest. I wrap my skinny arms around my skinny legs, trying to keep warm. It feels like bone hitting bone.

I'm too cold to sleep. And I'm too worried. How close are the soldiers? I look up at the moon. It's still high in the sky. I couldn't have walked very far. I hope it's far enough. I don't like walking in the day. It's too easy for someone to see me. But I'll have to walk at first light. I must get some place safer.

As soon as the sun begins to lighten the sky, I know which way to go. I pick up my pouches and begin walking. My water pouch is very heavy. I try to take a small sip of water. I can't. The water is frozen. I hang the pouch about my neck. It makes me very cold. I try not to think about it. I must take it with me. I don't know when I'll find more water. And later today, the sun will be hot again.

Sure enough, it gets hot. Very hot. I almost wish the water was ice again. The cold would feel good against my burning skin. I stop on a small rise and look out over the veld. I see no dust clouds. Good. I can rest. I sit in the shade of a camelthorn tree. I take a small drink from my pouch. The water is hot. It does little to wash away the dryness in my mouth. My belly wants food. But I don't have any. I lie down. Sleep will help me forget my hunger. That is my hope.

Voices wake me. I lie very still, listening. It's a Herero man and woman. They're close to me. But they don't see me. I quietly roll over so I can see them. Both of them are very skinny. The man has something shiny around his neck. It catches the sunlight and makes it brighter.

"Where are we going?" the woman asks him. "Our village is gone. Our family's gone. No place is safe. We can't just wander in the veld."

"Why not? That's what out ancestors did," he says quietly. I have to open my ears and listen hard to hear him.

"But they had cattle to give them omaere. We have nothing," his wife reminds him.

"We had cattle. The white people took them. We'll take them back." The man pulls at the shiny thing around his neck.

"It will be easier to find us if we have cows," she says.

"So they'll kill us. It's better then dying slowly of hunger."

"They could send us to a death camp." She almost whispers.

"I escaped from there once," the man says. "If they catch me again, they'll have to kill me. I'm not going back to the camp."

I stretch my legs a little bit. They hit some dry seed pods. The man jumps at the sound and looks over toward my tree. "Who's there?" he calls. His voice is weak. He picks up his kirri. "Come out here where I can see you."

I stand up and slowly walk toward the man and woman.

"Are you alone?" the man asks.

I nod my head.

He lowers the kirri. "Who are you?" he asks.

"I'm Jahohora, the daughter of Mutihu, the healer, and Tutejuva. From the big house of the Omukuatjivi clan. Do you know my family?"

The woman smiles at me. But she shakes her head. "What are you doing out here by yourself?" she asks me.

I tell her my story. The man looks at me in surprise. "You've been in the veld for two years? By yourself?" he asks me.

I shrug my shoulders. I don't know "years." "I've been by myself a long, long time," I say.

"Where are you going?" his wife asks.

"To my village. I must find my family."

She looks at me sadly. "There's no village for you to go back to. There are no more Herero villages. The soldiers burned them all."

"So where do the Herero live?" I ask.

"We hide in the veld. Or we die in the white people's camps," the man says. He touches the shiny thing around his neck. "There's nothing else for the Herero."

"I thought the big chief of the white people said all Herero had to leave the land or they would be killed," I say.

The man laughs. It's not a happy sound. "There aren't many of us left, so the soldiers no longer kill us with their guns. And they've stopped pushing us into the desert to die. Now they send us to their camps," he tells me.

"What are these camps?" I ask.

"They're places they send us to die," he says. "In Windhük, Swakopmund, and Lüderitz."

I know of Windhük, but I've never heard Swakopmund or Lüderitz. "Where are those places, Uncle?"

"They are far from Hereroland – by the big river that you can't see across. The camps are very, very bad places. Soldiers are there. They make the Herero work until they die. Every day – from before the sun wakes until long after it sleeps. It's hard work. Pulling heavy wagons. Moving big rocks in the icy water of the big river to form new land. Carrying iron bars into the desert to make a path for the white people. Even the women and children must do this work. And there's no food. Only a handful of uncooked rice." The man's face fills with pain. "If the Herero don't work hard enough or fast enough, the soldiers beat them to death and leave their bodies for the vultures. Or they make other Herero throw them into the big river for the fish. Many, many, many Herero die every day in the camps."

"It's harder for the women and girls," the woman says. "The soldiers lie with them at night. And then they have to work all day – even if they carry a soldier's baby."

"What happens to the men?" I ask.

The woman looks at her husband to see if he's going to answer. He does. "The soldiers still kill the chiefs and any men they say made war on the white people. They buy the other ones. Or send them to the camps to die with the women. The men don't live long in the camps. If they do anything to make a soldier angry, they are hanged. It could be a look, a hand movement, a question – anything. You never know what's going to make a soldier angry."

The man looks across the veld. But his eyes see the camps. "What's worse is that the men in the camps have to watch the soldiers lie with their wives and sisters and daughters. There's nothing they can do to stop it."

I don't want to think about a soldier lying on top of me. I ask another question. "You said the soldiers buy Herero men. How can they buy a person?"

The man looks down at the ground. He's silent. Maybe he didn't hear me. I start to ask the question again. The woman answers. "The soldiers pay some Herero men to find people like us who are starving in the veld. The bought men forget who they are. They forget what it is to be Herero. All they think about is feeding their own bellies. So they tell other Herero of missionary camps where they'll be warm and safe. Where there'll be lots of food and water. And medicine. They say there'll be work so the Herero can earn money to feed their families. They say, 'Bring your families. They will be taken care of.'"

"They'll be taken care of all right," the man says.

The woman ignores him. "The bought men take the Herero to the missionaries. But a few days later, the Herero are sent to the camps where they are made prisoners. There's no food. No warmth. No medicine. Only death."

The man speaks again. "If you don't go with the Herero men who are bought by the soldiers, they'll tie you and force you to go. That's what happened to me. A man I called 'Uncle' since I was a boy put a chain around my neck and gave me to the soldiers. They gave him money for me." His voice is flat. It holds no anger.

"You were at the camp?"

He nods. "That's where I got this." He pulls hard at the shiny thing around his neck. "The soldiers put these on everyone who comes to the camps to show they are Herero prisoners. I can't break it off." He swats at a black fly buzzing around his head. "I was one of the lucky ones. I escaped. But if a soldier sees this" – he pulls again at the shiny thing – "he will hang me. Prisoners aren't supposed to escape. The white people don't want them telling other Herero what the camps are really like."

I look closely at the shiny thing. It has funny lines on it. I look at the woman to see if she has one.

"I wasn't at the camp," she says. "I got away when he was taken. We found each other again after he escaped."

"What are you going to do now?" I ask.

"Starve," the man says. "I'd rather die wandering in the veld than work for a white person." The sun is about to sleep. I need to find food. I tell the man and woman goodbye.

"It's good that you walk alone," the man tells me. "You'll be safer. Just remember – you can't trust anyone. Not even Herero."

His words echo in my head as I walk into the veld.

HERERO HUNTERS

I was careful before. Now I'm even more careful. I have no village to go back to and no family to find. So I walk only when I have to find food and water. The rest of the time, I hide. From the wild animals. From the soldiers. And from the Herero who were bought by the soldiers. Since I don't know who they are, I hide from all Herero.

The hunt for food and water gets harder and harder. The rains refuse to come. More waterholes dry up. And the earth is too thirsty for berries and uintjes. No grass grows to hide the whitened bones of the Herero and their cattle who died many yesterdays ago. I set my traps. The few animals I catch are as skinny as I am. Eating them is like eating bones.

I see more Herero. They are very skinny, too. And they seem to have little life. I watch them from my hiding places. I see the same people over and over again. They wander in small groups. They have no place to go, so they move in big circles over the veld. Some of them make small huts from branches. The weakest ones lie down in the middle of the veld and never get up.

The sun is about to sleep, so I leave my hiding place to hunt for food. It has been too long since I have had more than just a few drops of water and dried-up uintjes. I must find food and water. I stand on a large rock and look over the veld. I see a bunch of trees that are greener than the others. That's a sign of a waterhole. I glance around again. I see no dust clouds or people. It's safe. I slide down from the rock and walk toward the trees.

As I get close, I can almost smell the water. I'm so thirsty, I go to the waterhole without looking around again to make sure it's still safe. I bend over the hole. It still has water. I lower the jar the snake hunter gave me into the hole and fill it up. I take a long slow drink from the jar. The water feels so good going down my throat. I fill the jar up again and then fill my water pouches.

I stand up and turn around to go back to my hiding place. I take one step and stop. Four Herero men stand in front of me. They are bought by the soldiers. I can tell by looking at them. All the other Herero I've seen are like shadows. But these men are well-fed. They must have been hiding. And waiting for someone to come for water.

I back up until I'm standing next to the waterhole. I hold my pouches close to my chest. As if they'll protect me from these men.

The headman asks my name.

"I'm Jahohora ... the daughter of Mutihu ... and Tutejuva,"
I say softly.

"Jahohora?" one of the men asks me.

I look at him closely. I don't know him. But I know his voice.
I think hard, trying to remember him.

"Where are your parents?" the headman asks kindly.

"I don't know," I say. "I lost my family."

"Are you sure you're not hiding them?" he asks. His voice isn't
as kind now. "Who are you getting all that water for?"

"It's for me. I have a lot of walking to do," I tell him. "And the
waterholes are drying up."

He looks at me like he doesn't believe me. "Where are you
going?"

"Nowhere."

"Then why are you walking?" He stands close to me.

"I am keeping away from the soldiers. I know what they do to
Herero girls."

"You do? Then you should know they have camps where they
give Herero lots of food and a hut. You don't have to starve out
here in the veld and worry about dry waterholes." He puts his
hand on my arm. "Come with us and we'll take you to the camps.
And everyone who's with you."

"I told you I'm alone. I don't lie." I pull my arm away from
him and shake my head. "You're not going to get money for me.
I'm not going with you."

The man puts his arm around my shoulders and holds me
tight. "It's for your own good," he says. "You and everyone with
you will die out here. You don't want that."

I stand as tall as I can. And try not to show how scared I am.
"I would rather die out here than with a soldier on top of me."

My fear suddenly goes away. I'm angry now. "You're not
Herero," I tell the man holding me. "You're worse than the white
people." I look at each of the men. "You're cowards who give
Herero a bad name."

The headman tightens his hold on me. But two of the men
lower their eyes. The man with the voice I know looks at the
headman. "Leave her alone."

"We will take her in. And we'll find the others who are with
her," the headman says.

"There are no others," the other man says. "Jahohora has been alone in the desert for two years." He looks at me. I see sadness in his eyes. I know those eyes. It's Ikuaterua!

"How do you know?" the headman asks him.

"She saved my life after I came out of the desert."

"How could she survive in the desert by herself that long? She's just a girl," the headman says.

"She told you. She's the daughter of Mutihu, the healer. He taught her well." Ikuaterua looks at me. "Let her go."

The other two men agree with Ikuaterua. "There are plenty of others," one of them says.

"But the soldiers said we must bring every Herero to the camps," the headman says.

"One girl living alone in the veld isn't a threat to the soldiers. They won't even know she's here," Ikuaterua tells him.

The headman lets me go. "This time," he says. "But if I see you again, I'll take you to the soldiers."

I walk slowly away. My head held high. My back straight. A true Herero woman. Ikuaterua comes after me. "Here, take this." He hands me a small bundle of food. "I'm sorry," he says. Shame fills his face.

"Thank you." I have no other words. I walk away, hoping the gathering darkness will hide my path. Just in case the headman decides to come after me.

I move on. I have to find a new waterhole and a new hiding place. A long way from here. I'm too weak to walk very far. So I stop often. The food Ikuaterua gave me helps. And I have enough water for a few days.

I'm more careful about where I hide and when I walk. I know others are hunting the Herero in the veld. Next time, Ikuaterua won't be there to save me. I need more protection. I think about it as I walk. But I have no answers.

Each day, I eat only a little of the food Ikuaterua gave me. It's soon gone. I look and look in the veld for uintjes or roots. They're hard to find. But I see the medicine plant Tate showed me when the cow sickness came to Hereroland. I remember going into the veld with him to gather it for our cows. I wish Tate were here. He would know where I could find food. He always knew what to do. Like when he stopped me from touching the bad plant that looked a little like the medicine plant. Tate said if I touched it, I would get sores all over my body.

That gives me an idea. If I'm covered with sores, no one will come near me. Not the soldiers. And not the Herero men bought by the soldiers. I try to remember what the bad plant looked like. That was so long ago. I walk around the veld, looking at every plant. At last I find one that might be the bad plant. I tear a leaf off. It stings my hands. It must be the right plant.

I think about what I'm going to do. The plant might make me sick, but it could protect me. I pick more leaves and rub them all over my body. I feel like I'm on fire. I look down at my arms and legs. They're covered with little bumps – like lots and lots of bug bites. I don't want to put the leaves on my face, but I have to. I gently rub them up my neck and then on my cheeks, my chin, and my forehead. I'm careful not to let them touch my eyes. When I'm done, I itch so badly that I want to scratch my skin off. I know I can't. I look for a hiding place. If I can sleep, I won't think about the itching and stinging.

I dream that I'm lying in a hole in the ground. Tiny little bugs crawl all over my legs, eating my skin. I try to kick them off, but the bugs come back. Bigger than they were before. They crawl up my body until they're eating my face. I scream and jump up, happy to be awake. But I can still feel the bugs crawling on me. I look at my arms and legs. It's too dark to see anything. I touch my face. It's covered with sticky pus. I wonder what it looks like.

In the morning, I'm too sick to walk. I pull my water jar up to my lips and try to drink. My lips hurt too much. But I have to drink. I force myself to take a small sip. My hand shakes as I close the jar. I look down at my hand. I can't see it very well. My cheeks are so big they get in the way. I have to look straight down to see my hands. They're covered with big open sores. I look at my legs and belly. The sores are all over my body. Good, I think. No one will want to touch me now.

The pain makes me sleep a lot. Every time I close my eyes, I have the same dream – of bugs crawling on me and eating my skin. One day I wake up and see that the dream is real. Tiny little maggots have crawled inside the sores, making them worse than they were before. I want to dig the maggots out. I can't. There are too many.

I get weaker and weaker. If I want to live, I have to get more food and water. I pull myself up, using a tree branch. It hurts to touch anything. And when I stand, the earth moves as if I'm turning in circles. I almost fall. I grab the tree again to steady myself. I pick up a broken branch to use as a walking stick and walk – very, very slowly – toward a waterhole.

I can't climb a tree or pull myself up on a rock to see if the waterhole is safe. As I come close to the waterhole, I hear the voices of Herero men. I hope the sores are enough to protect me. Leaning on the broken branch, I take the last few steps toward the water. The men look up at me. Their eyes get big when they see me. They back away as I go to the water.

I know the headman. He's the one who tried to take me. I look for Ikuaterua. He isn't there. I fill my water jar and pouches. I hear the men whisper. I can't hear their words. The others wait to see what the headman does. He watches me. But he doesn't come close.

When I have my water, I quietly leave the waterhole. The pouches are almost too heavy. I bend over. The branch keeps me from falling. I take very small steps. I have to stop after each one. I breathe deeply. And then take another step.

I'm a little way from the waterhole when the headman laughs. It's an ugly laugh. "Inaavinuise!" he shouts at me.

The other men laugh. But their laughter is sad.

I don't turn around. It would take too much effort. I need the little strength I have to get back to my hiding place. I'll need to rest there before I can look for food. Each step brings pain. I keep my eyes on my hiding place and make myself keep going. At last, I reach the trees. I cry when I drop to the ground. The tears run into the open sores on my cheeks. They bring more pain.

The pain will go away, I tell myself. But the sores will take many, many tomorrows to heal. That's good. They will protect me. Just like they did today. I think about what the headman called me. Inaavinuise. Mother of maggots. I look at my arms and legs. I can see the maggots nesting in my skin. I am Inaavinuise.

The walk to the waterhole made me very, very tired. Even after I rest, I don't have the strength to look for food. I will do that tomorrow. I will sleep today.

FOUND

The sun is high in the sky when I wake. It beats down through the branches of the trees. Its heat burns through my sores. I should get up and look for food. It's been so long since I've had anything in my belly that I don't feel hunger. But I know I have to eat. I try to stand up. All I can do is sit. I open the jar the snake hunter gave me. I take a long drink and lie back down. I'll look for food later. When it's cooler.

It's still hot when I wake again. I want to go back to sleep. But I'm afraid if I don't get up now, I'll never get up again. I sit. I have to rest before I try to stand. I leave my water pouches under the trees. They're too heavy to carry. The jar that's tied around my neck has enough water for today.

I walk slowly, leaning on the broken branch. It's been many days since I walked far in the veld. The earth is very, very dry. Once again, the veld has more death than life. The bodies of Herero who escaped from the desert lie next to the bones of those who never made it that far. I stop when I see a leopard eating what's left of a cow. My heart beats quickly. I can't run faster than a leopard. I can't run at all. And there's no place to hide. The leopard looks at me. He yawns and goes back to his meal.

I walk on, shaking my head. Even the leopards look at me and say, "What do we need with these bones? We have real food to eat."

At last, I find some berry bushes. I pick the few dry berries that still hang on their branches. They're not enough. I walk a little farther, searching the ground for roots or uintjes. I hear a strange noise. I look up and see dust clouds rolling toward me. It's a Cape wagon. It's very close. It's too late to run or hide. I drop to the ground, hoping no one will see me. But there's no grass to hide in. The wagon stops close to me. A white man jumps down. He walks over and looks at me. He says something. But I don't know his words. He speaks white people talk. He bends down. I back away, hoping my sores will protect me. I don't want him lying on me.

The man smiles and holds his hand out to me. "Mevanga oku kuvatera," he says. His voice is soft and kind as he offers to help me. So are his blue eyes.

I'm scared. I don't want him to touch me. But I can't run away. I look at him closely. Maybe he will help me. Or maybe he'll send me to the death camps. I don't know. I do know I'll die in the veld if I don't take his help. I don't want to die. I want to live. For Mama and Tate. For the tjikuus by the fire. For the ancestors. For all the Herero who have died.

I decide to believe him. I put my hand in his.

Kov

ON THE MARCH

It's still twilight when we leave the fort. The home guards, mounted on shaggy horses, ride out first, their long guns at the ready in leather pouches near their right legs. They're led by Hugo von Francois and Otto Eggers, longtime settlers who have served in the Schutztruppe. Recognizing Francois' name from Göring's and Epenstein's stories, I size up the Prussian captain riding through the shadows to the head of the cavalry. A settler now, he rides with the authority of a man who lets nothing get in his way.

Following the home guard are the officers of the Seebatallion, all riding sturdy horses. The wagons, artillery, and troops fall in behind, forming a train that stretches toward the horizon. Each wagon with its long team of oxen measures at least 50 meters. Black drivers run alongside the oxen calling to them by name and cracking the enormous whips they hold in both hands.

"Wörk! Wörk, Osse!" they call out. A division of marines marches behind each wagon, their guns slung over their shoulders, their waists cinched with heavy cartridge belts.

While a few of the surgeons are mounted, the rest of us ride in the hospital wagons, supposedly because it's safer. It's true that I'm less likely to get hit by a bullet, but I'm not convinced it's such a safe way to travel over the rutted trails. As the heavy wheels grind into the shifting sand, the wagon tilts and groans. Then a wheel climbs up over a rock jutting out of the well-worn ruts. Everything lurches with the imbalance, and I brace myself to keep from tumbling into the chest of supplies.

We're forced to stop occasionally when a wagon wheel slips the rut and sinks too far into soft sand, a harness gets tangled, or an ox collapses in the heat and has to be removed from the team. I welcome the unexpected respite from the constant shifting of the wagon and its stifling confines. As I stretch my legs, I take in the hilly countryside. The deeply carved wagon tracks scarring the sand. Sharp brambles breaking up the patches of tall coarse grass that try to reclaim the trail the wagons have forged. The large birds circling overhead. But after a few minutes in that unbearable sun, I'm more than happy to climb back under the shade of the wagon. I'm amazed that the men are holding up in this heat. But if we don't take a break soon, I fear we'll have some patients to look after.

A few hours later, as the sun reaches its zenith, we come to a shady area that, from the looks of it, had been a prosperous German farm. Now Kapps Farm is a ruin. The once stately brick house has gaping holes where its windows and doors should hang. Its yard is littered with broken furniture, smashed dishes, and scraps of clothing. Dozens of torn, soiled books are strewn about. Some of the men rummage through the debris, trying to make sense of the chaos. Karl picks up what's left of a porcelain doll; its face is a mosaic of flesh-colored shards. Seeing no sign of a grave, I hope the young owner of the doll didn't meet a similar fate.

We eat a somber meal of boiled rice and fill our water casks before stretching out in the shade of the wagons. Several men keep guard, while the rest of us, exhausted by the heat, doze off.

Long before we're ready to hit the trail again, we're given orders to fall in line. At least it's a bit cooler now that the sun is slipping behind us to the western horizon. We push on, the monotony broken only by the cries of a strange bird or the sighting of an antelope.

At last, we come to Owikango where we're told to make camp. Even though it has a name, there's no station here – just a clearing and some meager waterholes. Using the scraggly brush for fuel, the men light campfires throughout the clearing, both for light and warmth. As soon as the sun dips below the horizon, the high veld turns from an oven to an icebox. After warming myself by a fire, I help set up the tent flaps on the hospital wagon. A few of the marines put up the tents for the other officers. Since we're in enemy territory, we form a wagenburg – the supply wagons are drawn up in a large square around the campsite to serve as a makeshift fortification that partially blocks the firelight from hostile eyes and keeps us from being easy targets or prey for wild animals. Fifty meters out, sentry posts are erected at each of the four corners. Constructed of brush, each post houses four men who take turns scanning the darkness for signs of the enemy.

After tending to some of the men who suffered minor injuries
on the long hot march, I turn in, pulling my woolen blanket
tightly around me. But sleep is slow in coming as every strange
noise rifles my imagination. The low, soft cry of a distant animal
grows louder. Is it a lion drawn by the smell of our food? Or
perhaps it's not an animal at all, I think, as I hear a jerky, coarse
howl respond. It could be the Herero, signaling to each other as
they lie in ambush. Feeling a bit foolish, I pull my loaded gun
within easy reach. The cold hard metal fills me with confidence,
and I finally drift off to sleep.

I'm awakened by a rapid volley of gunshots. Still in the stupor
of sleep, I think they're close by. I lie momentarily paralyzed,
both by the cold and fear. I hear more shots and realize they're
coming from outside the camp. I grab my gun and hurry out of
the tent. The whole camp is a wave of shadows, surging toward
the wall of wagons. I hear curses as some of the men stumble in
the darkness.

My curiosity drives me forward, but a hand reaches out to
restrain me. It's Lieutenant Eggers. "Your services may be
needed here, Doctor," he whispers urgently.

I nod and head to the field hospital to prepare for the worst.
By lantern light, the other surgeons and I set up the operating
table and gather the tools we may need for surgery. Then we
wait. The gunfire stops, and an uneasy silence settles over the
clearing.

I join some of the officers who are drinking coffee around a
small campfire. Eggers smiles wearily when he sees me. "No
news yet," he says as he hands me a cup of the bitter brew.

"Three sentries are unaccounted for at Post Three," Captain
von Francois says. "We've sent scouts out, but we won't know
anything until dawn."

The darkness is already giving way to gray so there's no point
in trying to sleep again. I huddle close to the fire, waiting quietly
with the others for the scouts to return. For a moment, the camp
looks like a tableau – the old settlers, in their high boots and shirt
sleeves, lounging about their campfires; the marines, wrapped
in their blankets, holding their hands out to the warmth of the
flames; the Boers, keeping their own counsel near the wagons;
the black drivers, squatting in a corner, joking and laughing.

The scene comes to life as the sky lightens and a medley of exotic birdsong spreads across the veld, welcoming the newborn day. Rays of pink fan out from the east, announcing the sun's return. I look in awe at the stark beauty, trying to absorb the moment, to etch it into my memory. It's a reminder that nature is a force unto itself, oblivious to our struggles.

The mood is broken as the men assigned to the next watch stand up and stretch. They reach for their guns and apprehensively leave the relative security of the wagon walls. A few minutes later, the guards who have stood watch all night return. They look tired and relieved.

Suddenly, a cry rises from near the perimeter. A group of black men are riding toward the camp. As they get closer, I see the white kerchiefs tied around their broad-brimmed hats. Witboois. They must be our scouts. The lead man dismounts, revealing a body draped over the back of his horse. It's one of our marines. When the other Witboois dismount, I see two more bodies. I quickly join the other men pressing around them.

"They've been murdered!" A pale-faced recruit shrieks as the scouts lower the bodies to the ground.

I push my way through the growing crowd. The marines lie on the hard earth, their khaki uniforms darkened with blood, their mouths gaping open, their eyes staring sightlessly at the sun.

"Those are the sentries from Post Three," Eggers confirms as he steps up behind me.

I force myself to look closely at the fallen men. I had tended to two of them on the ship. The other one is Heston, who had been in the gondola next to mine on the train. Even though it's obvious they're dead, I kneel down and check their pulse. I shake my head as I close their eyes. The rest of the men stand silently until the lieutenant motions for a few of them to help Arnold take the bodies to the hospital wagon. I follow along behind. I've seen death before but never at the hands of another man.

The other surgeons and I begin the somber task of preparing the bodies for burial. With water in such short supply, we can't waste it cleaning the dead men, but we examine their wounds and search their pockets for personal belongings that we can send back to their families. I pull a blood-stained letter and a photograph of a young girl from the pocket of the man I'm examining and set them aside. Using as little water as possible, I wash my hands.

Francois strolls over with a few of the other officers. "Well?" he asks us.

"They were shot, sir," the senior surgeon reports. "One was clean through the heart. The other two took a number of bullets."

"Any mutilation?"

"No, sir. Just the bullet wounds."

The captain turns to the other officers. "The scouts found no sign of the enemy around the camp," he says quietly.

"Is it possible they were shot by our own men, sir?" Eggers asks.

"Could be. These are young recruits, and it was their first night in a war zone. Someone probably heard something and panicked. And then," he shrugs, "well, you heard all the shooting."

"What should we tell the men?" another officer asks.

"The truth. The Herero killed these men in cold blood," Francois says. He stomps off.

Late in the afternoon, we gather somberly on a hillside just outside the camp to pay our final respects. The three bodies, wrapped in their white blankets, are laid in a freshly dug communal grave. Some of the men stack stones on top of the grave as protection against wild animals while Francois says the Lord's Prayer. A few friends of the dead men put up rough wooden crosses crudely etched with their names and the date of their deaths. I linger behind, saying my own prayers and laying a stone on the grave. I didn't know these men well, but our shared journey had forged a bond. I stoop down to pick up some sand to scrub the touch of death from my hands.

A somber sobriety hangs over the camp the rest of the day. I don't feel like talking much this evening, so I retire to the hospital wagon soon after dinner. As I straighten my supplies, I see the letter I had pulled from the dead man's pocket. I carefully unfold it and hold it up to the lantern light. "My dearest Anneliese," I read. "I know I promised I would return to you, but God has willed otherwise. While I cannot be at your side, know that my love for you is undying. May it comfort you in your grief.

"Do not mourn for what could have been, my love, but treasure the moments we have shared. Wipe the tears from your beautiful eyes, and smile for me. When we meet again, we will walk the golden streets of Heaven hand in hand."

Tears well in my eyes, and I can read no more. I refold the bloodied letter and set it aside with Anneliese's picture. I should write my own letters to Hanna, David, and Papa – just in case. I get out my writing paper and pen. "My beloved Hanna," I begin, but then I struggle to find the words I want to say. Finally, I put pen to paper and just begin to write:

"We buried our first casualties today – three young men who had their whole lives ahead of them. I barely knew them, so I don't know what dreams died with them. The tragedy is that their deaths were needless. They didn't die as heroes in the heat of battle; we have yet to meet the enemy. Instead, their lives were snuffed out by their comrades, who panicked in the strangeness of this land.

"As I prepared the bodies for burial, I fully understood, for the first time, the reality of what we are doing here. It is one thing to talk about fighting wars and serving the Fatherland when surrounded by family back home. But the doing of it, I'm afraid, may test us all in ways no man should be tested.

"Come what may, I want you to know how much your love sustains me. You are my breath, my life, my past, my future. Without you, I am not. Whether I die in this desert or in your arms at home, you will be my final thought."

Four days later, the sentries let up a cry early in the morning. More troops are coming. I want to climb up on the wagons with the rest of the men to watch the long procession winding toward us, but as a surgeon, I'm expected to show the same restraint as the other officers. I let Arnold do the looking for me.

"It's Major von Glasenapp!" he calls down from his perch on a nearby wagon.

After the new arrivals, including a few more surgeons and orderlies, have rested, the major summons the camp to prepare us for what lies ahead. We are to move to the north around the enemy. It will mean forced marches with fewer and lighter wagons. The campaign will be difficult, the major says, as we'll have smaller rations and limited supplies. Water will be scarce, and what water we find must be boiled before it's used. There will be no water for washing our hands, our clothes, or our eating utensils.

Geier, one of the other surgeons, raises an eyebrow. "I hope that order doesn't apply to us. If we have to do surgery, we have to wash our hands and instruments," he says.

"We'll make do," Velten, a doctor from the Habicht crew who has joined our unit, says sternly. "When water is scarce, we'll use sand. There's plenty of that."

We head out the next morning, about three hundred of us. Again, the old Africans of the home guard lead, followed by our mounted officers. The marines, a few hospital wagons, and several Cape wagons, loaded with light artillery, trail out into a long thin line. Glad to be moving again, the men sing out as they march down the narrow track hedged by the tall, dense brambles with their curved, finger-length thorns.

The singing and early morning jocularity fade as the sun rises in the cloudless sky, beating harshly on man, animal, and sand alike. Fortunately, we have water – for this morning, at least. Even though my eyes and throat are already burning in the heat and dryness, I stretch my water supply, taking small sips only when I have to. I've learned that promised waterholes are often dry or soured.

As the sun reaches its zenith, we stop in a clearing to rest and replenish our water from a nearby river, the Epukiro omuramba. But even though we're in the rainy season, what water had been there has evaporated or soaked into the thirsty earth. One of the old settlers shows us how, and where, to dig holes in search of a trickle of water. I'm elated when a little moisture bubbles up in my hole, until I see it's milky with lime. We make do with what we find, boiling out the impurities. After a short rest, we continue our march deep into the cold night.

And so it is, day after day, week after week, the tortuous monotony of our life as we trek through this inhospitable land. Time loses its relevance. Yes, the sun rises and sets each day, but yesterday, today, and tomorrow blur into one as we continue to march in silence under the merciless sun. I see too many men, their eyes glazed, their minds delirious, in need of good water and nutrition. But there's little I can do. The worst cases are allowed to ride in the hospital wagons until they have strength enough to walk again or they're buried in the brambles.

Occasionally, we get a lull when a scouting party brings in fresh game or, more often, an exhausted ox falls. While it's a grim reminder of the difficulties of our journey, it also means we'll have a little meat with our "soup" that night. Lately, we've had a lot more beef than we had in the first days of our march. It's tough and stringy, but it provides more nourishment than our usual fare of half-cooked rice or plinsen.

My hospital wagon is cramped with weakened men, so I walk or share the driver's narrow perch. Since the Boer who drives the wagon speaks only Afrikaans, my mind wanders freely as we move along. Looking out over the line of weary men and wagons, I think of my ancestors wandering with Moses in the wilderness. For the first time, I understand their discouragement. But at least they had their families with them, I think ruefully.

Late that night, I share some "meat bouillon" with Geier. With the growing number of injured and sick to attend to, I've had little time to get to know him. But tonight, exhausted as we are, neither of us is ready for sleep. Feeling the night chill, I pull my blanket around me and move closer to the small fire. I stare into the flames, looking for meaning in the stories of my ancestors as I try to stave off my constant worries about Papa, Hanna, and David.

"Can you imagine forty years of this?" Geier muses.

I look at him questioningly.

"The Israelites wandering in the wilderness," he says. He puts another stick of wood on the fire, watching the sparks dance skyward.

"I was just thinking about that this afternoon," I said. "Of course, God provided for them."

"And He's providing for us." Geier takes a slow sip of the awful stuff we pretend is coffee. "Just like He used that wilderness experience to teach and instruct the Israelites, He will use this time to build the character of our German troops and to purge our colony of the undesirable races."

He leans forward. In the glow of the firelight, I can see the fierce passion in his eyes.

"The way I see it, this is South West Africa's purgatory, and God is testing us, just as he tested the tribe of Judah, to see if we have what it takes to claim this land. Of course, the Israelites ultimately failed that test. And ever since, they have been condemned to wander the earth, unable to call any land home."

Sharp retorts flood my mind, but I bite my tongue. It would do little good to argue with Geier – or point out the errors of his "facts."

He continues, "If we come through these trials, God will bless the Fatherland, and Germany will claim its rightful place in history among all the great empires."

In the following days, I'm often reminded of Geier's thoughts about this being a form of purgatory as more men fall to sickness and fatigue. Those who can still march are mere specters of the jovial crew I met on the ship. Our uniforms, the same ones we wore when we began this trek, hang loosely in dirty tatters about our gaunt frames. Our weathered faces are covered in scruffy beards. But despite the exhaustion, the lack of water, and the dearth of real food, no one complains. We have our orders. So we march. In silence.

REMNANTS OF LIFE

The wagons creak to a halt, and the troops fall out of line. It's too early for the midday break. Perhaps they've found a good supply of water, I hope. But the word comes slowly back. An abandoned wagon is blocking the trail. Some of the men must clear a path around it so we can move on.

Arnold and I walk up to the deserted wagon – the first sign of humanity we've seen since we began this trek weeks ago. It sits askew on the trail, its canvas cover in shreds. Books and letters are strewn about, but nothing else of value remains. Lieutenant Eggers is sifting through the debris with Karl and a few other men, looking for anything that could prove useful. They pick up some of the books and letters.

"Watch your step!" the lieutenant calls as I start to move toward him.

I look down in time to avoid stepping on a human skull. Eggers picks his way over to where I'm standing, carefully avoiding the trail of gnawed human bones. "Any idea what happened?" I ask.

"Looks like a farmer, or perhaps a trader, trying to escape. Probably had a herd of cattle. See how it's trampled over there?" he points to the ground at the side of the wagon. "This is as far as he got. The wild beasts took care of whatever the Herero left."

The lieutenant motions to Arnold and Karl to gather up the bones. The other men dig a shallow grave and tie a couple of sticks together into a makeshift cross. Karl pulls some brambles over the grave to protect the bones from further desecration.

"Where do you think he came from?" Arnold asks. "We haven't seen a house for weeks."

Karl, obviously exhausted by the extra work, shrugs indifferently. "It doesn't matter. He's dead."

Late the next day, we're going up a hill when our march is interrupted by a sharp shout. Despite the men's physical weakness, their survival instincts kick in. Instantly on the alert, the troops in front of my wagon reach for their guns. I make sure my pistol is readily at hand, even though I know it won't be much use against rifles. Still, I feel safer knowing I'm armed.

One of the home guards rides back to explain what's happening. He points into the bush. "A Herero village," he says quietly. "See the fire?"

Peering through the bush, I watch as some of the marines cautiously enter a handful of domed huts. Made of branches and twigs plastered with cow dung, the huts blend in with the bush, especially in the twilight. It takes a sharp eye to spot them. Near one of the huts, a small fire burns. An elderly Herero man and his wife, who are too feeble to flee, sit beside the fire. Two officers stand guard over the couple while the marines continue to search the other huts.

The home guard nods toward the fire. "That's their 'holy' fire," he says derisively. "They think it's where their ancestors live."

The troops finish searching the huts. "These are the only two," a marine reports to the officers guarding the couple.

"Güt!" one of them barks. He takes a smoking branch from the fire and ignites the couple's house. Following his cue, the marines use the fire to light other branches to torch the rest of the village.

"Your ancestors aren't happy with you," the officer mocks the old man and woman. "See what they have done to your village." He raises his revolver and shoots the woman, point blank, in the head. Her body slumps against her husband, who sits passively on the ground.

"My turn," the other officer says as he shoots the husband. The officers nonchalantly wipe the blood and brains from their guns.

As they start to rejoin the line, one of them turns back. "I want to check something out," he calls to his comrade. Using his bayonet, he lifts the loin cloth from the man's body. He laughs and points at the man's circumcision. "It's just like Hugo said. They're black Jews!"

Knowing that some of the men are watching me for a reaction, I keep my face blank, as if I hadn't heard the vulgar comment. Inside, I'm seething. But I remind myself that these are the attitudes I'm trying to change through my service to the Fatherland. Someday, the hatred will end.

We march on, leaving the stripped bodies for the wild beasts. As I ride along, the scene plays over and over in my mind. I try to justify the shootings, but I can find no excuses to cover such brutality – other than the misery of our never-ending march. Is this really how modern civilized people conduct war?

At camp that night, Geier has nothing but praise for the officers.

I try to keep my face expressionless as I add another branch to the fire. I guess I'm not good at being passive.

"It bothers you?" Geier asks, apparently reading my face. "I would think you of all people would understand the need to purge this land of its inferior races. After all, the Israelites exterminated all the natives when they claimed Israel."

"That was different," I say lamely.

"How?" he demands.

"First, it was thousands of years ago. And had they not done it, those people would have killed them. And, besides, God ordered it."

"My point exactly!" Geier says. "If we don't wipe them out, they'll continue to rise up against us. And it's by divine right that we're ridding South West Africa of these half-humans. As the superior race, we have a duty to conquer this land and people it with hardy German stock."

The conversation ends when Velten comes over with news that the enemy is nearby. We're sure to see action tomorrow or the next day, so we had best get ready. Morale picks up throughout the camp. The sooner we put down this rebellion the sooner we can return to the comforts of home. The men clean their guns and fill their cartridge belts. I help prepare our medical supplies.

Morning dawns to a thunderous sky that rips open, flooding the dry riverbed and making the wagon trail all but impassable. Regardless, the order comes to march. So we pack up our waterlogged gear and fall in line. While the respite from the summer heat is welcome, the struggle to keep the heavy wagons and artillery from being mired in the wet sand or carried away by the violent rush of a flash flood is overwhelming. The officers push us along, saying we must get to higher ground or everything could be swept away. With so few provisions left, we can't afford to lose anything. And we can't risk the enemy getting any of our big guns.

So on we trudge, battling the elements rather than the Herero – the next day, and the day after, and the days after. It's always the same. More oxen falling. More sick men. More wasteland to cross. If this is purgatory, we should all be purified by now.

* * * * *

I'm tending to some of my patients when Sergeant Hansen strolls over. One of the home guard, Hansen is a big man who seems made for wilderness life. If he were given to violence, I could imagine him taking on a Herero or two with his bare hands.

"Doctor, would you have any balm to spare?" he asks in rough low Deutsch. "One of my men cut his hands badly on the brambles."

I nod sympathetically. I'm seeing a lot of men with inflamed hands. The bramble thorns are razor sharp, but the biggest problem is not having water to clean the cuts. "Here you are," I give Hansen a small tin of salve. "I'll come over later to see if there's anything else I can do."

Hansen smiles his appreciation.

After tending to all the men and eating a bit of poorly cooked rice, I head over to Hansen's tent where all the old Africans gather.

"Doctor!" Hansen greets me. "You look exhausted. Sit down." He moves over, making room for me at the fire. The smell of their food is tantalizing. Used to living off the land, the old settlers always seem to eat better than the rest of us, who rely mostly on military rations. Hansen offers me a pancake and a piece of wild game. I know the meat may not be kosher, but at this point I don't care.

After I've eaten, Hansen introduces me to Friedrich, the injured man. I examine his hands in the firelight. The cuts are deep and oozing with pus. He winces when I gently probe one of the wounds. "You've already used the salve?" I ask.

He nods.

"Good. Since we can't keep your hands clean, we need to wrap them." I pull out some cloth strips and deftly bandage Friedrich's hands, giving him what's left of the bandages. "You should change the wrappings at least once a day, but twice would be better. Put more salve on each time. If you need more, come see me."

"Thank you," Friedrich says quietly.

I stay awhile, listening to the old settlers telling about their first years in the colony and all the challenges they endured. Most of their stories are about hunting – lions, rhinos, leopards, even a man-eating crocodile. They also tell of all the native wars and the rinderpest epidemic that wiped out most of the cattle. I look at them with renewed respect. Most of the people I know couldn't have survived such hardships.

When I check on Friedrich the next day, the old Africans are deep in discussion about the cause of the Herero uprising. Curious about their opinions, I listen attentively. "What did we expect?" Daniel, one of the older men, says. "The Herero were farmers with large landholdings. Then we come in to take away their land and their cattle. We force them to work for us. They're a proud race. Of course, they'd rise up in revolt. They're struggling for independence as much as the North Germans were in 1813."

"But how can you justify their cruelty?" Friedrich's brother Gerd asks.

"What cruelty? They spared the women and children, escorting them safely to Windhük," Daniel replies.

"What are you talking about?" I ask incredulously. "The newspapers back home were filled with stories about how they were murdering children and then slaughtering their mothers."

"You believe everything you read? I thought you'd be smarter than that, Doctor. It was all lies. Just a way to sell papers and get the Kaiser and the Reichstag to send troops," Daniel says. "Samuel Maharero, their chief, ordered his men not to harm the missionaries or women and children. We're the ones raping young Herero girls and killing babies and old people. And we're supposed to be the civilized race." Daniel draws on his pipe.

Eggers starts to take offense, but the old man hushes him. "How quickly you forget, Otto. What about that old couple we killed the other day? And remember what happened to the young Herero mother who owed Trader Schuster money? She was publicly flogged with the sjambok – on her bare stomach and between her legs. The beating didn't stop until she was dead. And all the good German citizens watched. Not even the missionaries protested."

"The missionaries." Another man spits. "They're the cause of all this. They came here telling the natives they were our brothers."

"Yes," Daniel continues. "And then we came, and the traders, and the soldiers. And we said, 'You're not our brothers. You're not even our equals. You should feel privileged to be our slaves.'"

"They're not fit to be our brothers. At least, not yet," Francois pipes up. "It's our duty to teach them, to discipline them with a firm, strict hand. With our instruction, they may be ready to become our brothers in a century or two, after they learn what we've already discovered – to dig wells, cultivate crops, build proper houses, and live in peace with their neighbors. We can't treat them as equals until they've learned to be our equal."

"Listen to yourself." Daniel slaps his knee. "Dig wells? They've been digging waterholes in this arid land for centuries. If it weren't for their knowledge, we would never have survived here. And they're building houses, brick ones just like ours. Many of them have become Christians, gone to missionary schools, put out their holy fires, and turned away from ancestor worship. Some of them can read and write in more languages than most Germans. If you ask me, you're just looking for an excuse to justify your actions.

"And this revolt – I think we asked for it," he continues. "We determine the value of a man's worth by the color of his skin, not by his mind or his heart. Even the courts here place the most base German above the noblest of Herero – after we promised them justice and protection in the treaties we signed."

"If that's how you feel, why are you fighting this war?" Francois asks Daniel.

The old man shrugs his shoulders. "I want this to end quickly so we can return to a peaceful co-existence."

"You're a fool if you think that's possible," Francois says. "The Herero can't be trusted. Just look at Samuel Maharero. He's an ungrateful, greedy, treacherous upstart. Why, he wouldn't be chief today if it weren't for German support."

Daniel starts to interrupt him, but Francois ignores him. "I should know. I'm the one who told Samuel the Imperial German government was recognizing him as paramount chief, even though by Herero tradition, he didn't have a claim to his father's inheritance. We made him a powerful, wealthy man. And look at how he repays us."

"You Germans may be good at soldiering and farming, but you know nothing about running a colony," one of the older freight-carriers chimes in, mixing his English and Deutsch.

Francois shakes his head in disgust. "Things were a lot better when my brother and I were in control. But then they sent in the administrators. Look where Governor Leutwein's diplomacy has gotten us. It was his idea to support Samuel."

The old freight-carrier stretches. "The best thing for Germany would be to sell this colony to the English. They know how to manage colonies."

"That will never happen," Friedrich says wearily. "Even if 2,000 German graves have to be dug here, the Kaiser will not give up South West Africa. Germany must have its empire."

"You may be digging those graves this year," the old freight-carrier warns.

MOUNTING LOSSES

A few days later, we make camp in a large clearing with more good water than we've seen in a month. The scouts report back that the enemy is close by, so we fortify the camp more than usual. The marines set up the major's tent under the shade of a big, gnarled camelthorn tree. Once again, the wagons are drawn up in a square around the clearing, and a strong barricade of thorn bushes is erected around the perimeter. Heavily guarded outposts are put at the four corners.

The other surgeons and I leave the setting up of the mobile hospitals to the orderlies while we tend to the growing number of sick men in the camp. "We're almost out of supplies," I note as we check the dwindling inventory.

"The main division should be catching up with us soon," Velten says. "Then we'll have everything we need."

I doubt his optimism. We've been looking for signals from the division for several nights, but we've seen nothing. And its inventories are likely to be as low as ours. Still, it's better to be optimistic in front of the men.

"At least we're going to get a few days' rest. And we'll get to wash up. That will help a lot," I say brightly. "And you're right. The others will likely get here before we have to march again."

But there's little time for the medical staff to rest, given the increasing number of patients. I don't get to relax until late at night. As I lie there on the ground, I look up at the endless sea of stars – some so close I feel as if I could reach out and touch them. I gaze at the Southern Cross and the other constellations that are so different from the ones I saw in Fürth. I'm amazed at the colors bursting over the galaxies, like fireworks frozen in time. I'm reminded of God's promise to Abraham: "I will multiply your seed as the stars of heaven, and all this land that I have spoken of will I give unto your seed, and they shall inherit it forever." I imagine Abraham looking up at a desert sky and pondering that promise. I sleep, somehow comforted by the knowledge that my family is part of that covenant made thousands of years ago in a desert very much like this one.

Morning comes early, and with it, a lot of commotion. All of the home guard and most of our officers are preparing to ride out on a scouting party. They've had reports that a herd of Herero cattle is grazing at Owikokorero. The major intends to capture the herd, which will provide us with meat and milk. And the loss of the cattle would be a blow to the enemy. As the officers saddle their horses and harness oxen to a machine gun and a two-wheeled wagon, the medical staff helps Velten quickly prepare an emergency kit. He's to ride with the cavalry just in case his services are needed.

Riding two abreast, the cavalry heads out of camp on the narrow sandy path. For the rest of us, it's like a school holiday. Throughout the camp, the men strip off their filthy clothes to wash them in trenches lined with waterproof tent cloths. The joking that has been silenced by the long march returns as the naked men play in the water, splashing it on themselves and their comrades.

As soon as the other surgeons and I have washed up, we set the orderlies to boiling big pots of water so we can properly clean our surgical instruments and the injured men. It's an all-day task, but the feeling of clean clothes, clean patients, and clean tools is worth the effort.

After eating a "dinner" of tough rice, I sit by the fire, writing a letter to Hanna. "Who would have thought that such simple things as clean clothes and the hope of a cup of fresh milk could mean so much?" I write. "Living in these harsh conditions has taught me how blessed we are in Germany. I'm glad that you and Papa and little David will never know such hardship."

The sentry shouts, interrupting my writing. A lone rider is coming furiously toward the camp, his horse kicking up a trail of dust that hangs on the air. "It's one of the home guard," Geier says. "But where are the others?"

A few of us grab our medical bags and run to the camp entrance. As I get closer, I recognize the rider. It's Hansen. But this isn't the same confidant man who rode out at dawn. He sways from side to side in his saddle, barely holding on as his horse, lathered in sweat, runs wildly into the camp. As the men help Hansen dismount, they pepper him with questions. "What happened?" "Where are the others?"

Hansen crumples to the ground, too exhausted to speak.

Captain Dannhauer, one of the few marine officers who remained in camp, steps forward to support him, half carrying Hansen to a campfire where he can rest.

"Two more are coming!" the sentry shouts.

Sure enough, two more of the old Africans are riding in, one trailing the other. Their horses are spent, as are the men. They slump in their saddles when they reach the camp. "We lost half the cavalry," one of them gasps, his voice crusted with emotion and the desert dryness.

The questions start anew. "Who was killed?" "Where's the major?" "What happened?" But the riders are too weary to answer.

Hansen, who has had a drink, weakly calls to me, "The cart is coming with wounded officers."

Dannhauer orders the men to strengthen the outposts and sends out a heavily armed expedition, with a few of the doctors, to meet the wounded men. The orderlies gather blankets and stretchers while I prepare for surgery. That means sending some of the convalescing patients, still too sick to return to duty, back to their tents.

Except for the occasional cry of a bird, the camp is silent as we anxiously wait in the gathering twilight for the remnant of the cavalry to return. Finally, in the distance, I hear the cracking of the long whips.

"They're coming!" the sentry shouts.

I peer into the dusk, trying to get a glimpse of the wagon. At last, it emerges from the bush and rumbles into camp, followed by the machine gun. The harness of the oxen is tangled, and blood gushes from a gaping gash in one of the lead oxen. Several wounded officers sit on the chest in the middle of the wagon, and others lie motionless on the sides. But the major, his face pale and his balding head bloodied, stands upright, keeping his balance despite the precarious pitching of the wagon.

The orderlies rush forward with blankets and stretchers. I walk to the rear of the wagon to check on the most serious injuries. Blood streams from the tailboard. One of the surgeons tries to treat the major's head wound, but Glasenapp waves him away. "Tend to the others first," he says. "They need your attention far more than I do."

I help unload the wounded, searching vainly for Velten. The other surgeons and I work late into the night, removing bullets, amputating limbs, and comforting the dying. Whenever we hear another horse enter camp, we send Arnold out to see if it's Velten. But each time, the orderly returns, shaking his head. Our work is somber, the worst I've ever faced. For some of the wounded, there's little we can do given our limited supplies. I think that's the worst part – knowing we could have saved a few limbs, perhaps even a few lives, had we been fully equipped. I complete my last surgery and wash up, grateful that we at least have water.

Hoping to learn more about what happened, I join what's left of the home guard at their fire. Hansen is there, but many of the men I had become familiar with are missing. "Friedrich wanted to come back, but his leg was too shot up," Hansen says. He stares into the fire. "I didn't want to leave him like that. God knows what those devils will do to him."

"He had his gun," Gerd says quietly. "He knew what he had to do."

"Old Daniel was one of the lucky ones," another man says. "He was shot clean through the heart. I doubt he felt a thing."

Someone asks about Lieutenant Eggers. "I didn't see him," Gerd answers.

"He went into cover in the bush as soon as we were attacked. He fell there," Hansen says. "Along with Captain von Francois."

I swallow hard. Of all the men in camp, Eggers was the closest I had to a friend. Since leaving Windhük, he had looked out for me. It's hard to believe he's dead. Just this morning, I watched him ride out with his hat cocked jauntily over his ear. I try to blink away the tears welling in my eyes. I can't cry in front of these stoic settlers who are sitting here dry-eyed despite their heavy losses.

"And the doctor?" I finally ask.

Hansen shakes his head. "He was one of the first to fall. The attack came at both the rear and the front of our line, so we had no warning. The whole thing was a trap, and we rode right into it. We didn't even have a chance to fire the big gun."

"There are a lot of dead considering how few were wounded," I murmur.

"The Herero don't take prisoners. Neither do we," Gerd says. "No one wants to leave a man wounded in such a fight."

We sit in silence, mourning the men who didn't return.

After a few moments, Hansen lifts his cup in a toast. "To the fallen. They all proved themselves. They held their ground, and they faced death with the same courage that they lived life."

A loud boom reverberates through the clearing as balls of red and white fire shoot into the night sky from the signal pistols in the middle of the camp. We stand up and scan the horizon, looking for an answering shot from the main division. But all remains dark.

"They better get here soon," Gerd says. "After what happened today, I'm afraid we're in for a real battle."

As soon as the sun rises, Captain Dannhauer sends a dispatch by heliograph, telling of the attack. I can imagine what he's signaling – "Cavalry attacked at Owikokorero. Seven officers, nineteen men killed. Send help now."

We remain at the camp for several more days, giving the wounded time to heal and hoping the main division will join us. Scouts are sent out daily, but they report no sign of the Herero. The fear is that the tribe, being forced to the east by the other divisions, will come at us en masse to break through into the wilderness. With our dwindling numbers, we're in no position to hold them. We need reinforcements. But there's no sign of them either.

Finally, the drinkable water runs out, and we're forced to march again. Hansen says there are good waterholes ahead, near where our men fell, but the Herero have been guarding them because they need that water for their cattle. As we march, Major von Glasenapp orders foot soldiers to fan out ahead of the main column on either side. The scouts crouch and slink through the dense bushes for long hours. By the end of the day, their hands and arms are cut and swollen from the many thorns embedded in their skin. And with their boots falling apart from the weeks of marching, their feet are blistered stubs of red flesh. I do what I can to ease their pain and recommend they tie their boots together with fresh strips of oxen skin, a trick I picked up from the home guard.

We're marching well into the night when the command comes to halt and push up close together. The wagons are quickly drawn into a tight square. Using the wagons as cover, the troops kneel beside them, guns at the ready. It's a false alarm, and the men are ordered to stack their guns and get their blankets. Guards are posted, but we pass the night without incident.

We reach the new watering place at noon the next day. It's a large field, white with lime. But the water we find in the deep holes is good – and plentiful, at least for a few days. Assured that no Herero are lurking close by, the major orders us to make camp. The other surgeons and I tend to the wounded officers. The constant jostling over the wagon ruts the last few days has not been easy on them. Some of the wounds have broken open and are becoming infected. If only we had more antiseptic. Without it, I'm afraid we may have to amputate a few more limbs.

The camp is quiet the next day as several of the marines and what's left of the home guard go with Hansen to the spot where our men fell, so they can give their remains a proper burial. The rest of us anxiously await their return. We have lost enough men. We don't want to lose any more. I spend the afternoon caring for sick soldiers scattered throughout the camp. When I check in on the wounded officers in the field hospital, I'm alarmed by a black infection spreading up the right arm of a young corporal. I feel his forehead. He's burning with fever.

"Please, Doctor, don't take my arm," the man pleads. "It will get better. Just give me a few days."

"You'll be dead by then."

"I don't care. I don't want to live if I'm not whole." He becomes hysterical.

Geier, who has just come in from his camp rounds, helps me restrain the corporal as Arnold brings us a dose of morphine. As soon as our patient drifts off, Geier looks at the arm. "That has to come off – now."

"I know." I prepare for surgery.

I don't want to be around when the corporal wakes up and finds his arm missing, but it's a duty I can't shirk. I keep busy around the hospital wagon, waiting for him to regain consciousness. I hear him moaning and hurry to his side.

"Doctor, did you ... did you?" he whispers feebly.

"We had no choice." I brush his forehead; it's cooler.

"It wasn't ... your choice ... to make ... you dirty Jew." He turns away from me and closes his eyes.

"Don't take it personally," Geier whispers as I move away from the corporal's cot. "You did what you had to do. And if he lives, he has you to thank."

I turn in that night, weighed down by the life-and-death decisions I've had to make over the past few weeks. As I gaze up at the stars, I realize Passover began at sundown. *"Mah Nishtana HaLeila HaZeh?"* I recite quietly, thinking of all the times over the years that I have asked Papa the ritual question –

Why is tonight different from all other nights? – that begins the recounting of God's deliverance of our people.

I shake my head. Tonight is not different from any other night for me. There is no seder, no Kiddush, no afikoman, no gathering with family. But perhaps the Angel of Death will pass over us tonight. I can only hope – and pray.

* * * * *

We've finally been in one place long enough for mail to catch up with us. Cheers go up as the camel rider comes into camp, his saddlebags stuffed with letters. I wait impatiently for my letters, but once I have them, I'm in no hurry to open them. I hold them close to me, savoring their connection to my loved ones. There are several letters – one from Papa and the rest from Hanna.

I find a place where I can be alone and then arrange the letters by date. I carefully open the first one from Hanna, breathing in the faint scent of my wife. I read slowly, as if fondling every word: "My dearest Kov, It seems like you've been gone forever. But then I look at little David, and realize it's been just a few months. Of course, for him, it's a lifetime.

"How I wish you were home to share in the joy of our son. He looks more like you every day. Papa often comments on some little antic, saying he's just like you. Papa can no longer work, so he sits by David's cradle, watching over him as he sleeps.

"We've received many letters from you, but none since you left Windhük. There is little talk of the campaign in South West Africa and no reports in the papers, so I can only imagine what your life must be like. I pray that this uprising will end soon and God will return you safely to us. There is talk in the Reichstag of recalling the troops. August Bebel has condemned the war, saying the Herero are justified in their fight for liberation. He has refused to budget for more troops or supplies."

I read through the other letters, taking in the routine of my family's lives. It's in such sharp contrast to this alien world I'm in. Oh, to be back there, sharing that life with them! I finally come to the last letter, which is thicker than all the rest. I unfold the parchment covered with Hanna's elegant script to discover a photograph of her holding David. Tears blind me as I stare at the sepia image of my wife and son. My arms ache to cradle my baby,

to embrace Hanna. But all I can do is trace their outline with my
finger. "Is it worth it?" I can hear Papa asking over the distance.
I have to admit, I'm beginning to have my doubts.

Around the campfires that night, we share our news from
home. Many of the men are put off by the talk in the Reichstag.
"Bebel should be tried for treason," one of the lieutenants says.
"By his reasoning, we're the villains. And the deaths of our
comrades were justified."

"Without money for more troops and supplies, he's condemning us to die in this wilderness," another officer observes.

"There's nothing to worry about," the major says. "The
Reichstag will come around, or it will be disbanded. The Kaiser
wants his empire, and Germany will have its day in the sun.
We'll get the support we need."

No one argues with the major. We have too much respect
for him. And, besides, he's got more on the line than any of us.
Delivered with the mail were several issues of the Windhüker
Nachrichten, one of which published an article claiming, "on good
authority," that the major is to be relieved of his command and
court-martialed as soon as reinforcements arrive in the colony.
Blamed for leading "the reckless attack on the Herero" at the
slaughter of Owikokorero, the major, once heralded as a hero, is
now apparently the scapegoat for the prolonged campaign.

Throughout the camp, the men are indignant. After all we've
endured, after all we've sacrificed, this unjust attack on our
beloved leader is too much. With little support from home and
too few men in the field, we've been set up to fail. And when
failure comes, we get the blame.

The scouting party returns later that day with news that the
enemy may be getting ready to break through to the south of
us, threatening our provision line. With still no news from the
main division, the major decides to return to our old camp, which
was easier to fortify. We will wait there for word from the main
division.

It's with heavy hearts that we turn around. Morale is
already low, and no one's looking forward to three more days
of marching. But my biggest worry is water. We had depleted
the potable water at the old camp. The men are already weak
and malnourished. Without a good source of water and fresh

supplies, we'll be in a desperate position. We take as much water as we can from this watering place, knowing it won't last long.

As we fall in line, I'm reminded of our losses. Where once we had a strong cavalry made up of the home guard and officers, we're now led by about twenty men, riding on scrawny horses. The marines are divided into two companies, one of which marches between the little band of cavalry and the cannon. The long line of wagons, each with its team of twenty-four oxen, follows. The second company brings up the rear.

Other than the cracking of the whips, the creaking of the wagons, and the rhythmic cry of "Wörk! Wörk, Osse!" we go in silence. My wagon shifts violently as it drops into a shallow riverbed, which looks as if it's been dry for months. The corporal, who has been delirious ever since I amputated his arm, groans loudly. This isn't going to be an easy march.

When we camp that night, someone remembers that tomorrow is Easter. The reminder does little to cheer the men. Instead, they sit quietly in their private reveries of home. I'm about to turn in when a shout goes up. Signals. On the southwest horizon. Five more rockets explode in flashes of red and white. Help is at last on the way. "I just hope they get here in time," one weary marine mutters.

Before dawn, several of the men build an Easter fire in the middle of the camp. As they gather around the fire to pray and sing a hymn, I check on my patients, preparing them for another day of hard travel. I worry about the corporal. His fever has broken, but he's still delirious. There's nothing I can do for him but watch and wait.

As soon as the sun rises, we break camp, falling in line again behind what's left of the cavalry. Stretching out four kilometers, our line slowly moves down the windy narrow path that cuts through the dense brush. Lulled by the slow motion of the wagon, I doze off, daydreaming of springtime in Germany. Screams of alarm pierce my dreams, jolting me to consciousness. A young man runs by, breathlessly shouting, "The rear is being attacked!" Since the hospital wagons are in the middle of the line, I can see nothing, but I hear gunshots in the distance. An officer rides back, urging us to hurry. There's a clearing up ahead that we can fortify.

Within minutes, we reach the clearing. The hospital wagons are pulled into the camp, while the rest are drawn into a wagenburg. The men take to the ground, using the wagons as cover as they fire at the enemy. The major, surrounded by his officers, stands calmly in the center, watching as some of the men from the rear company, who had been forced into the brush when the shooting started, make it to the safety of the camp. Many of them are wounded. Those who can still shoot are directed to fills gaps in our barricades. The cannon is pulled into position and fired at the enemy; its shells explode into the sandy earth. Wounded marines drag themselves close to the cannon for protection as the enemy pushes ever closer.

The other surgeons and I direct the orderlies to move the injured men from the outer wagons to the center of the clearing where they'll be safer. Then, crouching low, we check the men who have made it in from the bush. The sick and wounded outnumber the marines who are still able to shoot.

I move toward a man who's trying desperately to stanch the bleeding in his arm. From the corner of my eye, I see a Herero, dressed in a uniform of the home guard, pressing in. Without thinking, I raise my pistol and shoot. He falls to the ground with a bullet hole in his head. "Good shooting, Doctor," the marine says. He tries to smile, but it's a feeble effort.

"Shhhhh," I tell him. I have no time to think about what I've just done. "Let me see that arm." It's obvious he's lost a lot of blood. I tie bandages tightly around his upper arm, stopping the flow. "That will have to do for now. I'll have to remove the bullet once this shooting stops."

"Am I going to lose my arm?" he asks.

"I think we can save it – as long as there's no infection," I reassure him. I move on to the next fallen soldier as the artillery fires again, releasing its load of shrapnel into the enemy.

Two hours later, the Herero warriors finally retreat. I scan the clearing filled with injured and dying troops. My work is just beginning. I stand up wearily and look over at Geier, who's tending to a marine's busted leg. He glances up and nods in awareness of all the men who need our attention.

While we take care of the injured, some of the marines scour the bush for any survivors. They bring back thirty-two bodies but no wounded. The dead, some of whom have been mutilated by either the enemy or vultures, are placed in a semicircle under a large camelthorn tree, awaiting burial. Several of the men want to pay their final respects, but Captain Dannhauer turns them away. It's better they be spared this sight, he says. He doesn't want to turn the dead into a spectacle or demoralize the troops.

As the sun sets, the bodies are lowered into a common grave. Twenty men fire over the grave. The old major, as calm and compassionate as ever, speaks of the ultimate sacrifice the fallen troops made for the Fatherland. He reminds the living of the message of Easter, that death has no hold over the righteous. "These men," he says, "have purified their souls through the blood they shed today. They shall reign in Heaven with the saints. But here on earth, they will be remembered as heroes who answered the call of God and country."

I return to the wounded. Some of them are talking softly. Others are delirious or unconscious. A few are gasping their last breaths. I sigh hopelessly, watching as Arnold and the other orderlies feed the men what little food and water we have. There will be more bodies to bury before we leave this place. I'm sure of it.

Exhausted, I stretch out by the fire, staring into the flames while trying to make some sense of the day. I should write to Hanna to assure her I'm all right. With the underwater cable connecting Swakopmund to Europe, I'm sure the papers will soon be filled with sensationalized stories of today's battle. But I'm too tired to think clearly, let alone write. As my eyes grow heavy with sleep, the face of the man I shot looms before me. I killed a man today. I tremble at the memory. "I'm sorry," I tell the man. "But it was either you or me. I have a wife and son back home."

"This is my home," he tells me sadly. "And I have a family, too."

I spread my hands in a helpless gesture.

"This is the land of my fathers," he says. "You're trespassing. No one asked you to come here."

Papa's weary face now dances in the flames. "How can I give you my blessing to kill strangers who have never harmed you?" he asks me. "He was only protecting his home. And what were you fighting for? The foolish hope that someday the 'Fatherland' will embrace you as one of its own? Yaakov, the price is too high if it demands your soul."

I sit up, trying to rid myself of Papa's accusing glare and my own guilt. The fire has died down, and the darkness of night is giving way to the grayness of early morning. It's pointless to try to sleep again. I stand and stretch. With the visions of my dreams still haunting me, I go to check on my patients.

A few didn't survive the night. The corporal is burning with fever again. And Karl, who was shot in the abdomen, is conscious but barely hanging on. If we could stay put another day or two, he might make it. But fearing another attack, the major wants to move on. The dead are buried quickly. As the orderlies load Karl into a hospital wagon already filled with sick and injured men, he attempts a feeble grin. "Beats marching," he says.

I walk alongside the wagon, trying to close my ears to the pain-filled groans when a wheel strikes against a rock and jolts heavily. It's going to be another long, hard day of travel. As we leave the camp, I take one last look at the fresh graves under the thorn tree. How many more will we have to dig as our payment for this scrap of land?

TYPHOID

I check on Karl when we stop at midday. He manages to sip a little of the foul water, but the effort takes most of his strength. The corporal groans nearby in his continuing stupor. And Peter, the young man who was shot in the arm, winces in pain. He refuses to lie down. "I can sit, Doctor. But those men can't," he says, nodding toward the men who are in worse shape than he is.

I look in on the men again when we take another break late in the afternoon. Karl lies motionless, his mouth open and his eyes set. At first glance, I think he's dead, but then I notice the slight rising and sinking of his dirty blanket. He's still breathing, barely. I pat his head and move on.

As I start to examine Peter's wound, he motions toward a dazed man sitting on the wagon chest. "He's been acting really strange, Doctor. He says he can't feel his feet or knees. And he's hot one minute, and the next, he's shivering with cold."

I check the man's pulse, noting the big drops of sweat beading his forehead. "He's the twelfth in seven days," I mumble to myself.

When we finally reach our old campsite that night, I discuss the symptoms I've been seeing with the other surgeons. They've seen the same symptoms. "I think it's typhoid," I tell them. They nod in agreement. "It's to be expected – what with the water the men have been drinking," Geier says. "But there's not much we can do about it without the proper medicine and clean water."

"If it's typhoid, we're in for a long epidemic and a lot of deaths," one of the other surgeons whispers.

We decide to speak to the major about the situation, but otherwise, we'll keep our suspicions to ourselves, at least for a while. There's no sense in spreading panic in the camp.

We work late into the night, caring for the sick and wounded. Since we don't have enough cots for all the sick, the orderlies assemble makeshift mattresses, stuffing folded tent canvases with dried grass. Just as I'm about to leave to get a few hours of sleep, another man limps in, pale as death. He's burning with fever.

"I'll tend to him," the surgeon on duty tells me. "Get some sleep. You can relieve me in a few hours."

I want nothing more than sleep, but I know I must write to Hanna. I scrawl a quick message, assuring her I'm all right. "Please forgive my tardiness in writing. The camp is filled with sick and injured men who need constant attention. Seventeen wounded and fourteen sick, with more succumbing to fever every day. Yet still we march. Although my letters are few, my thoughts are filled with you and home. I wish I had never left. Please tell Papa he was right. He will understand. Give Papa and David a kiss for me. I will sleep tonight dreaming that you're in my arms once again."

When I report to the field hospital in the morning, I learn Karl has died. I look over at his mattress, already filled with another man, and wonder how many more will follow. I push his death from my thoughts as I examine two new patients. They have no pain, but they're exhausted and feverish. Arnold scrambles to make space for them while trying to keep some separation between those who are wounded and those who may have typhus. While the wounded show some spirit, the sick ones lie in apathetic silence, as if they've been stunned.

Every day, more men show signs of the fever. With no more room in the hospital wagons, the major arranges for several canvases to be assembled to form one long tent. The other surgeons and I are so busy caring for our patients, we're oblivious to the daily drills in the rest of the camp or the comings and goings of scouting parties. All we know is that no new provisions have arrived and there's hardly enough water to boil. The most we can do for the sick is make them as comfortable as possible and keep them away from the marines who are still well.

Once again, yesterday mingles with tomorrow as I lose track of time. My days and nights are an endless round of taking care of the ill. There's little time to dream of home or to worry about whether I'll succumb to the fever. By now, many of the wounded also have developed symptoms of typhoid, reducing their chances of survival. When the fever enters its second stage, the news that typhus has hit the camp spreads like wildfire, bringing with it a general malaise that settles over all of us as we mechanically go through the motions of living.

As I head into the hospital tent for evening rounds, I'm almost overcome by the stench of diarrhea. The orderlies try to keep up with the mess, but it's a futile exercise. In the distance, I hear a few men singing *In Strassburg on the Rampart*, a ballad about a young soldier so overcome with longing for the Fatherland that he deserts and pays for it with his life. The last stanza drifts mournfully over the camp:

O King of Heaven, Lord! Take my poor soul away. Take it to you in Heaven. Let it be with you forever, and do not forget me!

Wrapped in melancholy, the camp falls silent. In the distance, the jackals howl, lured by the smell of death.

I finish my rounds the next day by checking on the corporal. He's been unconscious for several days, so I'm surprised when he opens his eyes in a bit of recognition. "Doctor," he whispers weakly, "bury me with my arm."

I start to protest, to reassure him that he'll live. But the look of death in his eyes stops me. It's too late for optimistic lies. His hand grips my arm and then falls back against the cot. Hearing the too-familiar death rattle, I gently close his eyes. I motion to Arnold to take care of the body. We had already buried his arm near another waterhole. Now we must lay the corporal himself to rest.

I sit by the fire tonight, feeling as if I've been touched by too much death. I try to count the number of men we've buried, to remember their names, to picture their faces. But I'm lost in the effort.

We continue to wait for the main division. Thankfully, the Herero haven't attacked again. But more and more of our men are falling sick. The oppressive daytime heat, the sudden chill of the night, and the lack of food and water are doing the enemy's work. With more than a fourth of the men ill, we've now outgrown the makeshift hospital tent. Many of the sick, dressed in their filthy uniforms, lie in rows on the bare ground. A tent canvas, supported by long stakes, stretches like a roof above them, offering some protection from the sun.

The marines who are still able to function are so lethargic that there's little talk. "What's the use" has become the unspoken camp motto. Unfortunately, it's becoming my motto, too. Although I look at Hanna's picture every day, it's been awhile since I've written to her. I know I should, but I don't want to worry her with my despair, which I'm sure would shade anything I write. And what would I tell her?

My life is nothing but death and deprivation. Each evening, a few more bodies are laid to rest in the gray earth, the guns fire a final farewell, and the dirt is shoveled over the corpses. The gravediggers barely have the energy to make crude crosses and drag piles of brambles to protect the graves from scavenging animals.

The only sounds after the daily funerals come from the native drivers, who keep to themselves in a distant corner of the camp. Unmindful of our losses, they joke and laugh under the trees. Tonight, they're singing a chorus they learned from the missionaries. But it's not the time for music. An officer calls to them to hold their tongues. "Will jelle slap!" he hollers.

It's as silent as a tomb.

* * * * *

The major, who's a frequent visitor at the hospital, and several of the officers meet with the surgeons to discuss the situation. Nearly two-thirds of our officers and a third of the men are dead, wounded, or sick. And with typhus in the camp, those

numbers are bound to grow. We don't hold back on the grimness
of our predicament.

"It takes about a month for typhoid to run its course," Geier
says. "That means the first men to get sick are about halfway
through it. But we still have men in the earliest stages, and
more are coming down with the fever every day. And there are
likely to be relapses. It could be months before this ends – that
is if we have good water and better food. And protection from the
weather."

"Our orders are to hold this post," the major says, "but
without water, this is a death camp."

One officer suggests moving forward to find another waterhole.

"That would be suicide," Captain Dannhauer says. "Even
though the Herero seem to have retreated from the war for now,
we don't have enough able marines to fend off an attack should
Maharero change his mind."

The major nods in agreement. "We no longer have a fighting
army. This is a transport of sick soldiers, and we must act
accordingly." He makes plans to retreat to a better watering
place. We break camp the next day. The severely wounded and
sick are loaded into the wagons.

A few who are too ill to march but have the stamina to ride
are placed on the worn, rough horses. The rest of us march. It's
a slow, torturous journey.

A few hours into the march, one of the sick men screams out
deliriously and jumps from the wagon, landing on a few of the
men marching behind it. Before anyone can restrain him, he
runs, shrieking madly, into the bush. A few marines wearily
give chase, but they return empty-handed. To prevent further
incidents, the captain orders guards to surround each wagon. So
onward we march.

That night, I kneel beside a delirious patient to check his
pulse. He jams a gun barrel against my ribs. His face, contorted
by fever and pain, is inches from mine. "Back, you devil!" he
shouts. "I'm going to send you straight to hell where you and all
your kind belong."

Quelling the terror that threatens to paralyze me, I talk
to him calmly, like a mother to a small child. "It's all right,

Bernhard. It will be better soon. You just need to rest." I slowly reach for his gun. "Nobody is going to hurt you. Just trust me."

The anger in his eyes gives way to confusion as I take the gun from him.

I pull Arnold and the other orderlies aside. "We can't have that happen again. Next time it might not turn out so well."

"Should we take all their guns away?" Arnold asks.

I shake my head. "Only from those who are crazed. The others may need their guns for protection."

The next day, three of the sick die. We bury them, with little ceremony, in the bush. As we start to move on, one of the men in the ranks shoots wildly around him, screaming about a Herero ambush. Fortunately, no one is hurt.

A few days later, we finally reach a good water supply at an abandoned mission station. "There should be enough water here to wait out this cursed illness," the major tells the medical staff. "Do what you have to do to set up a hospital ward. The healthy men will camp up on that hill." He points to a small rise overlooking the station. "We can protect you from there. With any luck, the separation will keep the fever from spreading."

Geier and I tour the simple little church and what's left of the missionary's house, looking for the best location for our hospital. The church is pretty much intact, but the house has gaping holes in its roof and its doors and shutters are long gone. Broken furniture and debris litter every room. A pasteboard placard hangs untouched above the living room door. "Love Your Enemies," it says.

Despite the damage, we choose the house – it's bigger and it's closer to fresh water. And neither one of us is comfortable with bringing death into a house of worship. We help the orderlies clean the mess and then make up beds of grass and blankets.

Thankfully, the number of new typhus cases dwindles over the next few weeks, but healing is slow for those who already have the fever. Although we have plenty of water, our supplies are almost gone and the men have little to eat. The major consults with us regularly, assuring us that more supplies are on the way. The only other news we get is that the campaign has been halted. All of our divisions have been decimated by illness, and we have too few troops well enough to hold the line or continue pushing the enemy toward the east. We'll have to wait for the Kaiser to send more men.

That news makes the sick even more despondent. Hopes of a quick victory and a triumphant return home are dashed. "It's the way this campaign was carried out," one of my patients says. "If the main division had caught up with us like it was supposed to, we could have ended the rebellion weeks ago, and we'd be home by now."

Since the Herero have not attacked any of our units following the Easter ambush, I question whether there's even an uprising anymore. But I keep my thoughts to myself.

Fresh supplies arrive ten days later – mattresses, wine, egg whites, oats, bouillon, cocoa – a real feast. But the provisions do little to lift the spirits of those confined to the hospital. Every day brings another death, and the rants of the delirious sometimes make me question my own sanity. One of the sick, an able-bodied man who has traveled the world seeking adventure, insists that both of his legs have been shot off.

Another fear is that the medical staff will contract the fever or dysentery, which also is making inroads in the camp. Although he's still nursing his injured arm, Peter has taken on many of the duties of an orderly, but now he's showing symptoms of dysentery. It's hard to be optimistic in such surroundings. I feel as if we're all just shadows of life.

* * * * *

Now that the campaign is on hold and we're settled in one place, we're beginning to receive mail more regularly. I watch enviously as the men tear open their letters and pore over every word. Surely by now another letter from Hanna would have gotten through. But mail call after mail call ends with nothing for me. I remind myself that she hasn't received many letters from me either and vow to write more often.

Peter is riled by a letter one of his friends received. It seems that all anyone back home can talk about is the Russo-Japanese war. There's little mention of our efforts. And what little there is comes at our expense. If we were better soldiers, we would have whipped the natives by now. The folks back home can't understand why several hundred well-armed German soldiers haven't been able to put thousands of ignorant heathen in their place.

When Gerd comes to check on one of the old settlers, Peter shows him the letter. Gerd reads it and laughs. "What did you expect? All they care about back home is novelty. How many wives does the King of Siam have? That's what good Germans want to know." He hands the letter back to Peter. "And that's why the Englanders laugh at us. They couldn't care less about novelty. Their only interest is 'What use will this be to England?' That's how you build an empire." Gerd is still laughing as he heads out the door.

Today, I finally get a letter, but I have no time to read it. I tuck it in my pocket, a treat to be savored in private. Just knowing it's there brightens my rounds, which seem to be taking twice as long as usual. Another man has died. But others are getting better, I remind myself. With Hanna's letter nestled in my pocket, I refuse to give in to the melancholy that pervades this place. I actually smile – for the first time in weeks.

At last I finish my rounds. I take my worn blanket and head out into the chill air of the evening. I breathe deeply, ridding myself of the foulness of the hospital. I clear some of the gray seedpods from beneath a camelthorn tree and settle down to read Hanna's letter. I pull the envelope from my pocket and sniff the smell of home. I carefully break the seal and remove the letter. Each word breathes new life into my memories of Hanna. "My dearest Kov, how I long for your return. When you left, I lost not only my husband but my best friend and confidante. . . ." The ink blurs as if a tear has smudged it. I kiss the spot as if it were Hanna herself.

"You're always in my thoughts. Until I can hold you again, I will keep you in my heart. You are a good man – one I'm proud to call my husband. Don't let this war corrupt that goodness."

My own tears blot the paper as I finish reading the letter. My tears are not so much because I miss Hanna but because I realize I'm no longer the man she remembers. And I know I can never be that man again. I sit there, clutching her letter to my heart. I hear the dry branches in the thicket snapping with cold. And I see the vultures circling in the sunset sky. But my thoughts are far away, in another time, in a little house in Fürth.

The loud wail of a sick soldier brings me back to reality. I watch as two men dig yet another grave in the cemetery. From the camp above, I hear the bittersweet ode of men longing to be home:

But it will never be my fate.
I must wander through the world.
Home sweet home, you are always in my mind.
Home sweet home, to you I give my greetings.
I join in quietly on the final refrain:
Cherished home, hail.
In the distance, hail.
Hail in the distance,
Cherished home, all hail.

MOVING ON

I watch with mixed feelings as the last of the sick are loaded into the train cars at the station in Windhük for the slow trip home. I wonder how many of them will make it to Swakopmund, much less to Germany. A lot of the men have recovered and have already moved on. Peter left with a scouting unit a few weeks ago. Geier is leaving Windhük today to escort the sick to Swakopmund. Some of the other surgeons are going with the major, who vindicated himself in the public eye in the Easter battle and is now the leader of all the Marine Expeditionary Forces in southern Africa.

As the train pulls out of the station to begin the long descent to the ocean, I breathe a sigh of relief. For the first time in ages, I feel clean – at least physically. My stomach is full, and my throat no longer burns. I have a few days of rest before my new assignment begins. I need it.

If only I could cleanse my mind as easily as I wash my hands and uniform. Troubled by the deaths and brutality I've witnessed, I long for someone to talk to who could give me comfort. I think of my rabbi from Fürth, of Christof, and of Hanna. The rabbi wouldn't understand what I'm going through, but he undoubtedly would have some words of advice. Christof, with his knowledge of history, could help me make sense of it all. And Hanna could hold me, soothing away the specters of death that haunt me.

Refusing to give in to the guilt and depression that threaten me, I spend the next few days taking in all the changes that have occurred in the colonial capital since I was here in February. It seems like years, but it's only been five months. In that time, petrol-powered trucks have arrived on the rough streets, telegraph lines have been strung, new buildings erected, and now telephone lines are beginning to stretch across what's becoming a boomtown. Yet with all this growth, there are no synagogues and few churches. Ironic, I think, since the colony was first settled by missionaries.

South West Africa could do with a good dose of religious faith and the morality that comes with it. Instead, the colony is attracting adventurers, speculators, people of ill repute – from all over the world. Encouraged by newspaper reports that, after the war, tribal structures will be destroyed, the chiefdoms abolished, and all weapons confiscated, they want to get in on the ground floor of settlement. Lured by the thought of vast land tracts and free native labor, they hope to build their personal empires on the back of the German empire.

At times, I'm tempted to put down roots here myself. But then I think of my family. Papa's health is too bad for him to emigrate, and this country is still too wild for Hanna to be at home. White women – especially respectable ones – are scarce. As a result, several of the traders and early settlers have married into the ruling Herero families, something that doesn't sit well with the colonial officials. Our law requires them to recognize the descendants of legally married citizens – even those of mixed race – as Germans with full voting rights. That's a hard charge for people who see their race as superior to all others and who are afraid of being outvoted by "inferiors."

In addition to all the new settlers, thousands of troops have arrived from Germany, along with supplies and a general – Lothar von Trotha. Windhük is abuzz with talk of the general as expectations run high that he'll capture Samuel Maharero and the other rebellious chiefs within weeks. Arnold and I, along with several new surgeons and orderlies, have been assigned to the field hospital with Trotha's main division.

Captain Gansser, who's part of our new unit, says things will be different now that the general is in charge. A career officer, Trotha is known for his ruthlessness in quelling the

Boxer Rebellion and in suppressing several uprisings in our other African colonies. "It will take someone like General von Trotha to end this revolt," the captain says. "The Herero will only bow if they're forced to."

Müller, one of the home guard assigned to the division, nods in agreement. Most of the old settlers blame the uprising on Governor Leutwein's lack of firmness. Like the settlers, the governor believes in the colonial "law of existence." Simply put, that means the natives' right to exist is only justified by their usefulness to Germany. And of course, in the eyes of most of the settlers, their only usefulness is in giving up their land and cattle and accepting their role as laborers and servants.

But Leutwein wanted to let the Herero gradually get used to their new position. Urging the settlers to be patient, he insisted that, in time, the tribe's former independence would be just a distant memory. His plan was to sever tribal ties and to rule firmly but with some compassion.

"Any fool could see that wouldn't work," Müller says. "If we're going to take their land, we just need to get it done with."

"That's apparently what Trotha intends to do," Gansser says, repeating a report he heard of the general's first exchange with Leutwein. "When Governor Leutwein urged restraint, the general put him in his place, saying the Kaiser has ordered him to crush the uprising with any means necessary. Trotha reminded him that he knows the tribes of Africa, and they only respond to force. The general's policy is to use force with terrorism and brutality. He promised to annihilate the revolting tribes with streams of blood and streams of gold." Gansser smiles broadly. "That's the kind of leadership we need."

Müller nods approvingly. "The general understands lebensraum," he says. "If Germany is to remain strong, it must have more land for its people to settle. And if the natives won't give it to us, then we have no choice but to take it. It's survival of the fittest."

I ponder their words long after the captain and Müller leave. When they think of "streams of blood," they interpret is as the blood of the Herero, not of German troops. What they're forgetting is that Trotha, and the Kaiser, are willing to spend anything, including thousands of German lives, in their quest to destroy the tribe. My last conversation with Friedrich echoes through my mind. "Even if 2,000 German graves have to be dug here, the Kaiser will not give up South West Africa," he had said. Now Friedrich's bones are rotting in one of those graves. How many more graves will Trotha have us dig? Given the general's vow, there could be thousands more – both German and Herero. And what for? So the Fatherland can stand among the nations, head held high, and say, "Look at our great empire!"

* * * * *

It's in the height of winter that we prepare for Trotha's campaign against the Herero. Several months have passed since they last attacked a German settlement or military outpost. If it weren't for the general's grand scheme to cleanse the colony of their presence, I'd say the uprising is over. But what do I know? I'm just a doctor.

Headquartered at the fort in Okahandja, Trotha spends weeks drilling the troops and plotting strategy with his top officers. The general seems to revel in the irony of quartering in the home of Samuel Maharero and in the town that was the setting for the start of the uprising. It also was here that Göring first signed the treaty with Samuel's father, promising to protect the Herero from their enemies. It was here that Mr. Störmer opened a beer garden next to the Wecke & Voigts store, knowing he was encroaching on the sacred burial grounds of the Herero chiefs. And it was here that, according to some accounts, Lieutenant Zürn pushed Samuel and his men to take up arms against the settlers.

Regardless of its history, Okahandja is a good place to prepare for the final battle, as we have plenty of water and many of the conveniences of civilization. Best of all, the camel riders deliver mail on a regular basis to the town's post office, so I can catch up on my letters to Hanna, knowing I may not have the opportunity later.

Responding to the German residents' concerns that their Herero workers will run off, Trotha sets up a prison camp just outside the Okahandja fort for all the Herero living in the area. Whenever they're not working, they're imprisoned in the small camp that's bordered by barbed wire and the spiky branches of the camelthorn tree. And when scouting parties encounter peaceful Herero, they bring them in neck chains to the prison camp that lies within view of Moordkoppie, a rock outcropping where a band of Herero were slaughtered half a century ago while defending their lands from other invaders.

Soon, the small prison camp, located next to the stables, becomes a festering ground for dysentery as no thought was given in its creation to sanitation and proper drainage. Venereal disease also becomes rampant, thanks to our soldiers who freely use the Herero women.

As I see one of the officers emerging from the camp with a smug look on his face, I turn away, trying to hide my disgust. To hear most of the men talk, they view the Herero as little more than cattle. Yet they force the women to lie with them and then boast about their conquests. The conflicting standards make no sense to me.

Alexander Lion, one of the surgeons who recently arrived in the colony, tries to explain it to me. "It's a natural hunger they have," he says. "And like any hunger, it must be filled. Since they're separated from their wives and sweethearts, how else are they going to satisfy themselves?"

"We're not animals. We should be able to control our urges," I argue.

"Different forces are at play in times of war. These men are sacrificing their lives for the Fatherland. They're going to indulge themselves once in awhile." He smiles.

"But what about the women and young girls who are being raped night after night? Do they not matter?"

Alexander looks down at the ground. "I wish it could be otherwise. Unfortunately, it's the price of war. Their chiefs brought it on the women by rising up against the Kaiser. If anyone is to blame, it's the Herero headmen."

I shake my head in disbelief. "I've been here longer than you, and I've witnessed some horrendous acts on the part of the Germans. I often wonder which is the civilized race and which is the savage. If we keep making these excuses, we're in danger of losing our humanity."

Sometimes I think we've already lost it. The officers seem to be looking for reasons to kill the Herero prisoners. Any minor infraction or sign of disrespect is enough for the death penalty. The punishment is carried out on a makeshift gallows within view of the prison camp. The "guilty" are forced to stand on a wooden crate while nooses are tightened about their necks. Then a soldier kicks the boxes out from under them, leaving them to dangle a few feet from the ground until the next hanging. When we run low on rope, the soldiers use barbed fence wire to form the noose.

As the prison camp fills, the scouting parties stop bringing in new prisoners. Instead, they return with boastful stories of killing Herero. Today, one party came in after a few weeks in the mountains. They told one tale after another about how they shot a couple in the back, killed elderly women in their sleep and gunned down several women and a few men at a watering hole. They showed their "souvenirs" to back up their stories – fetishes, skin water bags, a few bones, and the brass and beaded hide bracelets and anklets from some of the women. I shake my head at such stories, not knowing whether to believe them. Sometimes, I think the men are just trying to outboast each other. But that doesn't make sense. These are stories of brutality, not valor. Why would anyone brag about such deeds?

Before we leave Okahandja, Trotha assembles the troops to tell us what's expected of us. Divided into seven units, we'll trap the Herero at Waterberg, where most of the tribe has sought refuge. The other units are already en route to the north and west of the region. We'll come up from the south. Together, we'll form an ever-tightening cordon that will keep the Herero from returning home.

"No quarter is to be given to the enemy," Trotha says, riding in front of us on his spirited horse. "We'll take no prisoners. All Herero, regardless of age or gender or guilt or innocence, are to be killed. We must exterminate them to ensure they never rise up against us again." Shivers run down my spine, but not from the cold. Surely this is just a rallying cry. He can't mean that we're to destroy an entire race of people.

A few days into our march, I realize that's exactly what he intends to do. We come upon what appears to be an abandoned village of Herero huts. One of the officers sends some troops to search the village. A few minutes later, a soldier reports that several old women are in one of the huts. A few of them are blind and one is so lame she can't stand.

"Just some helpless old hags," he says.

A few of the officers confer on what to do with them. "They're useless as prisoners," one of the lieutenants says. "Might as well put them out of their misery."

"Leave them be," another officer calls down to the men searching the huts. I start to breathe a sigh of relief until he adds, "Burn them with the village. There's no sense in wasting ammunition."

The soldiers don't even flinch at the order. Within minutes, they turn pieces of bush into torches and begin lighting the huts, including the one housing the women. The dry dung and branches catch quickly, sending up a rosy glow that stains the evening sky.

The killings bring back memories of the murder of the old couple in a similar village a few months ago. I had tried to block that incident from my mind, but today's act vividly revives it. At the time, I excused the shooting of the couple as an isolated incident and chalked it up to the madness of the long torturous march through the barren veld. But there are no such excuses for today's violence. The soldiers burned those women as casually as if they were burning trash.

I guess the horror I feel about the burning shows. That night in camp, Alexander claps me on the back. "This is war," he says. "People die. Like it or not, we have to get used to it."

I shake my head. "I've seen plenty of death. But this wasn't death – it was murder. I hope I never get used to that."

"You're a Jew, right?" I nod my head slowly, waiting for the inevitable insult.

"I don't hold that against you," Alexander says quietly. "My family is Jewish. I converted when I was sixteen."

I look at him in surprise.

"That's another story." He stretches his legs toward the fire. "What I mean is that this is no different than the Israelites' conquest of the Promised Land. God told our forefathers to destroy all the inhabitants so they could dwell in the land in peace. They were not to spare the elderly, the women, or the children."

I yawn tiredly. I've heard this excuse one too many times. "But the Germans already have a home. We don't need to take someone else's land."

"Ahhh, but you're wrong. God has richly blessed the Fatherland. We're running out of land in Europe. So as we multiply, it is our divine duty to civilize and people new lands."

The fervor of Alexander's words shocks me, and I have no response. I revert to small talk. "So where are you from?" I ask lamely.

"Berlin. My father is a banker there."

"You're not following in his steps?"

Alexander laughs softly. It's a hollow sound in the stillness of the night. "I'm the black sheep. Always have been. But after I converted, my family pretty much got used to me doing things my way. Besides, my brother is more than happy to continue in the family business."

"Why did you convert?"

"At first, I suppose I wanted to be like my friends. And I recognized I could have more opportunities. But then...." He pauses, staring into the fire, and shrugs uncomfortably. "I mean no offense, but converting just made sense – from a religious point of view."

"So do you feel more German now?" I ask, thinking back to the conversation I had with Epenstein.

"I've always been German – just as you're German. And I'm proud of it." He stretches. "We have another hard day's march tomorrow. We'd better turn in."

I try to sleep, but the image of the burning village plays over and over in my mind. As I think about it, I admit, for the first time, that I'm not proud of being German.

THE WATERBERG

We've been camped at Ombatuatipiro for several days. Though we have plenty of provisions, the waterholes have run dry, and the men and oxen are restless with thirst. Good waterholes are a short trek away – at Hamakari – but our scouts say they're heavily protected by the Herero. At this point, we're willing to take our chances. We can die of thirst. Or we can die trying to get to water. At least we have a fighting chance with the water.

But General von Trotha holds us back. Hamakari stands between us and the Waterberg, the last refuge of the Herero. Once our other divisions are in place to the west and north, we'll advance and force the natives deep into the waterless Omaheke to the east. The desert is to be their final executioner.

Ignoring my own thirst, I tend to several dehydrated men. "At least with no water, there's no typhoid," Alexander says. I try to laugh, but it takes too much effort.

"Look," Arnold says, pointing to the northern horizon. "The heliograph is signaling." I glance up in time to catch the bright flashes of light aimed at our camp.

"And over there!" Another orderly points to the western horizon. "The other divisions are ready."

We don't care that the news may mean battle. All we can think of is water.

The heliograph signals continue throughout the day, giving way to lantern signals as darkness falls. In the valley between us and the high ridge of the Waterberg, the whole of the Herero nation rests with its vast herds of cattle. Tens of thousands of men, women, and children. Their past and their future. I wonder what they must be thinking as they watch the lights blink from mountain to mountain.

While the general and officers plot battle strategy, the rest of us, driven by the desperate need for water, prepare to move. Men clean their guns. Fill their cartridge belts. Tend to the horses. Write what may be a last letter home. The medical staff is just as busy. Although the hospital wagons are mostly empty now, we know they could be filled with battle casualties tomorrow. We must be ready. As I check our supplies once again, I think of all the men who'd still be alive today had I had half of these medicines – and, of course, good water.

With nothing more to do, I write a quick postcard to Hanna. "We're likely to see battle tomorrow. I hope it will be the one to end this campaign. I'm so tired – of death, of the endless marching through the desert, of being away from you. When I return home, I'll never let you out of my sight."

We all turn in early, shivering in the cold. No fires are to be lit. And no singing is permitted. As if we had the voice to sing! I see a shadow move, and someone whispers, "Say an extra *Our Father* tonight. Who knows if you'll be able to tomorrow."

"Comforting thought," I mutter. "That will do wonders for morale." I lie there, trying to sleep, but my deep thirst makes it impossible. Every time I doze off, I swallow, and the pain wakens

me, so I lie there with images from the past few months flooding
my mind. Wasted cattle decaying in a clearing. Valleys blazing
with flames as the enemy tries to stop our advance. Waterholes
brimming with the rotting carcasses of animals. It's as if the
Herero are telling us, "This is our land. If you try to take it, we'll
make sure that what's left is not worth your effort."

Finally on the threshold of sleep, I suddenly remember: It's
the first day of Elul, the month of repentance. And here I'm
preparing for war.

Instead of the call of the shofar, I'm awakened shortly after
midnight by the command to advance. We're told we should
reach the waterholes at dawn.

The Witboois, the sworn enemy of the Herero, ride ahead as
our scouts. The cavalry goes next, followed by the artillery. The
hospital and supply wagons keep a safe distance behind. We
must be close enough to be of some good but far enough back
to be out of harm's way. Our advance is noisy – what with the
horses snorting in the cold, the jolting of the wagon wheels, and
the occasional cracking of a whip.

Just before dawn, we reach the broad, sandy riverbed of
Hamakari. Thick brush separates the dried-up river from the
waterholes. The wagons are ordered to remain here with the
oxen harnessed – in case we need to make a hasty retreat. The
elliptical balloon that marks the battle headquarters is quickly
raised above General von Trotha's wagon as the cavalry moves
into the brush toward the water.

I wait quietly with the other surgeons and orderlies, thinking
of nothing but slaking my thirst. At last, the morning breaks
as the sun makes its presence known. Its rays streak the sky
with rosy stripes of light that intensify as the sun climbs over
the eastern horizon. Its light transforms the rugged landscape,
chasing away the dark shadows. Forgetting my thirst for one
brief moment, I'm awed by the stark beauty of the setting.
Instantly, I'm struck with guilt for thinking about beauty when
we're so set on destruction.

A gunshot shatters the morning peacefulness. And another.
Followed by a torrent of shots and screams that splinter the
air. The cavalry is under attack. My first thought is not of the
wounded. Rather, it's disappointment that the water, which is so
near the animals can smell it, is so out of reach. For more than

an hour, I hear nothing but the whistling of bullets, the hissing of grapeshot, the cries of dying men, the horrific shrieks of the Herero. But as I wait, all I can think about is how thirsty I am.

Finally, the troops get a few of our big guns in place and start firing them, along with the cannon, toward the invisible line of the enemy. The Herero swiftly clear a path for the cannon, moving to the sides to attack our men. Standing back from the fray, Trotha has the heliograph signal to the other units to begin the attack. No flashes of light respond.

The sun is high in the sky, and its heat is oppressive here in the riverbed where there's no shade. The oxen bellow hoarsely for water, kicking up a thick cloud of dust that hovers over the clearing. The drivers struggle to keep the animals from surging forward toward the scent of the waterholes. We're plagued by large flies, biting at our hands and through our white medical coats. Swatting away another fly, I look up, trying to get a sense of time. Through the dust, I see vultures circling, waiting for their feast of flesh.

The orderlies run toward the line to bring back the wounded. I help the other surgeons set up the operating tables and assemble our tools. All the time, we're swatting and swearing at the swarms of flies. "Hardly the place to do surgery," Alexander mutters.

With still no response from the other divisions, Trotha orders the artillery to open in full fire. The blasts thunder through my head, drowning out all other sound. I can see the surgeons' mouths moving, but I hear no words. I can hardly think as my head throbs with the heavy percussion of the guns. The first of the casualties begin to arrive. I mechanically motion to the orderlies to lay them in the shade of a wagon flap. While some of the surgeons begin operating on an officer, I quickly examine the others the orderlies bring in. Most of them, including Captain Gansser, are already dead.

With nothing left to do here, I grab my bag and run toward the line with Arnold. More of the men may survive if they can get medical attention earlier. Arnold leads me to a man who's bleeding from several wounds. I kneel down and try to stanch the blood, even though I know it's futile. The white blanket Arnold had laid him on is already stained red. The soldier tries to speak and a wild look enters his eyes. Then he falls back limply. He stares sightlessly at the sky. As I close his eyes, I wonder how many more men I'll usher through death's door.

Arnold awkwardly lifts the man to carry him back to the clearing, but I move on. A small Herero child lies wounded next to the cannon. His thin bare arm braced against the wheel, he looks straight into my eyes in a silent plea for help. As I start toward the child, Major Stühlmann stops me. "Let the little worm die," he says during a lull in the firing. "You heard the general's orders. Nothing living is to be spared."

I reluctantly drop back to help Arnold carry the fallen soldier. The big guns are silent, but bullets continue to whizz through the bush. As we approach the general's wagon, I hear someone shouting, "We've got men dying of thirst. And the animals can't hold out much longer."

The general's response is lost in wild yelling and another volley of shots that rips through the clearing. Arnold and I drop the dead soldier and dart to the bush for cover. I quickly remove my white coat; it's too visible a target. I watch helplessly as the hospital wagon is riddled with a hailstorm of bullets. The surgeons grab their guns and hit the ground. A deep blood stain spreads across the back of the senior surgeon.

Everyone in the clearing – from the general to the drivers and secretaries – throw themselves to the ground, firing toward the attackers. The Herero edge closer through the bush, taunting us and constantly shooting. We answer with a barrage of our own.

At last, the enemy retreats. As the officers regroup in the center of the camp, I join the rest of the medical staff. The senior surgeon has been shot through the shoulder, but he'll live – barring any complications. We quickly move the dead and wounded into the wagons when the order comes to advance. We're taking the waterholes!

Driven by thirst, the men and the oxen surge forward, determined to break through to the water. Like wild creatures, the troops hurl themselves toward the Herero, who fire and run.

Shouting curses and continuing to shoot, our men push through to the clearing with the wagons close on their heels.

Late in the evening, we form our wagenburg around the waterholes as small parties of Herero warriors shoot at us from the cover of the bush. Some of the troops form an outer perimeter, holding the enemy back, while others cut the spiky branches from thorn trees to erect a stockade. The oxen bellow for more water. But the holes, which have watered the Herero herds, will soon run dry if we don't carefully ration the water. The earth, trampled and overgrazed by the Herero cattle, offers the horses and oxen no sustenance.

It's well past midnight when I finish my last surgery. I look at the wounded lying on the ground and shake my head. Many of them will be dead by daylight. I shiver in the cold. Again, we have no fires. The orderlies, lanterns in hand, creep from patient to patient, offering them a precious sip of water.

I'm exhausted when I finally pull my blanket around me, but I know there will be no sleep. The Herero continue to fire at us, their guns flashing continually in the dark. And occasionally, our men fire back. At long last, the guns fall silent. The silence is more frightening than the shooting. What are they planning? Are we to be overrun in the night?

In the distance, I can hear the confused lowing of large herds of cattle and another sound like thousands of feet running. The sounds grow fainter, moving away from us toward the glow of a large fire that lights the eastern horizon. Too tired to sort it out, I wait listlessly for morning.

As the sun shines on a new day, our scouts return with surprising news. The Herero have fled. The scouts bring with them a young emaciated Herero woman, who was too weak to keep up with the tribe. Trotha calls for Manuel Timbu, a Cape Bastard, to translate as he interrogates the starving woman. A few minutes later, Timbu leads the woman, her "Christian" dress in tatters, from the general's tent, followed by a young soldier.

"Let's see what you're made of," the soldier says, handing his gun with its attached bayonet to Timbu.

The native shakes his head. "I could never do such a thing to a woman," he says. "Why not let her go? What harm can she do?"

"You heard the general." The soldier laughs. "Here, let me show you what a good German can do." He pulls the woman away from Timbu and, without warning, drives his bayonet through her. He laughs again as her body goes limp. He removes the bayonet, letting the woman crumple to the ground. Waving the bayonet, dripping with the woman's blood, in front of Timbu's face, the soldier jeers, "See, that's how it's done."

I watch, stunned, as the men who had gathered for the spectacle turn away with grins on their faces. The woman's body is left to rot. "How can a man do such a thing?" I ask myself. "And the others, how could they just stand by?" Then I hear another voice in my head, "You were there watching, too. And what did you do?" I feel my stomach rising to my throat. I'm going to be sick.

The general storms out of his tent, cursing the Herero. Seeing their escape as his failure, he insists that we should pursue them immediately. Captain Max Bayer reminds him that we have heard nothing from the other divisions. Besides, our men and animals have reached the limits of their strength. We can't go on today.

So the troops rest. But there's no rest for the medical staff as we tend to the sixty men who were wounded in yesterday's battle. They lie on their blankets on the bare ground; there's no grass for even makeshift mattresses. Although we've stretched a tent canvas above them, the winter sun beats through it, heating the ground and anything that touches it. And the flies are everywhere, creeping into the men's wounds, resting in their crusted eyes, even lodging in the corners of their dry mouths. The orderlies patiently move from man to man, picking away the insects, only to have more swarm in as soon as they move on.

At noon, news finally arrives from the other divisions. Two have defeated the enemy. The third held its position but suffered heavy losses. They confirm that the Herero – all 60,000 plus their enormous herds – are fleeing toward the Omaheke. But Trotha doesn't see it as a victory. He dwells on the possibility that they may regroup, what's left of them, at the last waterholes before the desert.

While the general plots how to finally end the threat of the Herero, several of our troops continue to gather fallen comrades from the bush, piling them unceremoniously beside a tree in the middle of the camp. Hooded vultures, which have already feasted on the corpses, circle high above us in the sky. A few perch in the tree, their bald pink heads turned brazenly toward us as they wait for a chance to feed. Peter shoots at one. Squealing loudly, they fly off. Within minutes, they're back.

"We need shomrim to watch over the bodies," Alexander says. But we have no men to spare to guard the dead.

In the afternoon, our spent oxen and horses paw furiously at the dirt, searching for food. All they find is dust. Their sad bellows and whinnies fade as they lose the strength to complain about their hunger and thirst. The stench of death and dried manure is stifling. As I look around the camp at the despondent men and the starving animals, I wonder, "If this is victory, how much worse is defeat?"

Tonight, we bury twenty-six men in the dirt beneath a tree.

In the morning, our entire cavalry – 200 men – ride out on half-starved horses with orders to pursue the enemy into the desert. Armed with guns and heavy clubs, they're told to show no mercy. No prisoners are to be taken. The general is determined that the Herero will not escape their God-ordained fate in the desert. It will serve as a lesson, he says, to the other tribes of the futility of rising up against the great German emperor.

The rest of us stay in camp, going silently about our tasks. I spend long hours taking care of the sick and wounded, but all I can think about is when I'll get my next ration of water. By now, I should be used to the constant burning of my throat, of my mouth feeling as if it's rusted shut. I can hardly remember a day when I wasn't wracked by thirst, when I had clean clothes and a comfortable bed. I try to think of home, of Hanna and David and Papa. But they're the memories of another man.

Four days later, a lone rider returns to camp. He's bent over his mount, an East Prussian horse that looks as if it will drop with every faltering step. "Water!" The sentry calls as he eases the rider from the saddle just as the horse stumbles to the ground. Arnold rushes forward with a lid of water. Major Stuhlmann and I step up to see if the man is wounded. It's Peter.

After taking a slow, long drink of water, Peter gasps, "I'm all right. But the others ... they're back there...."

"What happened, Corporal?" the major asks.

"No water, sir." Peter takes a deep breath. "Four days ... no water. The men walking ... most of the horses ... dead."

"And the enemy?"

"Gone. Or dead." Peter shivers convulsively.

The major calls for wagons to be sent out to retrieve the rest of the cavalry. Arnold and I help Peter to the hospital tent where he instantly falls into a deep sleep. I wish I could sleep too, but if the other men are in worse shape than Peter, they're going to need medical help.

We "rest" four more days, feeding on rice and the oxen that have died. Our other provisions are gone. And the little water that's left is vile, spreading dysentery throughout the camp. Thinking the war is over, the men yearn to go home. They've had their adventure. Now it's time to return to civilization.

Although there's been no mail since we left Ombatuatipiro and it's hard to say when we'll see the mail camel again, I write another letter to Hanna, letting her know I survived the battle. "Physically, I'm still whole," I tell her. "But I'm not the man who left you all those months ago. My hair and beard have grown long and matted. My clothes hang on my thin frame. I can't remember what it is to have a full belly. But the biggest changes are the ones that aren't visible. Being surrounded by death and killing does something to a man. I only hope that I can return home to you, and if I do, I hope you can still love the man I've become. Please forgive me my stubbornness and my selfishness. I should never have deserted you, my love." I close with the blessing of Elul: *"Ketivah vachatimah tovah."*

This morning, the news arrives that the Herero, what's left of them, have found some waterholes in the east and are camped by them. Enraged, General von Trotha orders us to break camp. "We will force them northward, deeper into the Omaheke and death," he vows. "Only then can our colony be assured of peace and prosperity."

And so we march, with our large supply train, devoid of supplies, into the broad steppes to the east. No white man has explored this region, so all we know is that there's little water. The trail is littered with death, testifying to the harsh power of the desert. The bloated carcasses of cattle. Decaying bodies of goats and dogs. Dead and dying Herero. The ever circling vultures. And the brazen hyenas that look up from their twilight meals to stare at us curiously before returning to their carrion feast. But we march on, trampling over the corpses and, too often, giving death a helping hand.

It's late and teeth-chattering cold when we stumble across a few waterholes marked by the glow of a small fire. From my wagon perch, I watch as the general and a few other officers ride over to the flames. One of the officers dismounts. A few shots ring out, and then we're ordered to make camp for the night.

We use the original fire to stoke small fires throughout the camp. As I bend to pull a burning branch from the flames to carry back to start my own campfire, I see the frail bodies of two Herero women, their faces wrinkled by time. Their story is clear. Feeble with age, the women could go no farther. They had lit the fire for warmth while they waited for death, which we obligingly delivered. The firelight plays over the blood trickling from the bullet holes in their heads.

I want to cover their bodies, to give them a respectful burial, but I dare not. I wearily return to my campsite and light the fire, trying to silence my conscience in the routine. But as I drift toward sleep, the realization of what I'm doing hits me. This isn't a war, nor is it purgatory. It's a modern-day crusade – as vile and violent as the ones that killed my forefathers. But this time, there will be no memorbuch. There will be no one to bury the Herero dead, to remember their names, to memorialize their lives. And this time, I have joined the crusaders. How can I ever atone for this evil?

THE END OF REASON

I wake early in the morning and lie quietly watching the last stars blink out as the grayness fades to the first pink of dawn. I don my military hat and beg forgiveness for praying without my tefillin. I begin to recite Psalm 27, the Psalm of Elul:

"The Lord is my light and my salvation; whom shall I fear? The Lord is the stronghold of my life; of whom shall I be afraid? When evildoers came upon me to eat up my flesh, even mine adversaries and my foes, they stumbled and fell. Though a host should encamp against me, my heart shall not fear; though war should rise up against me, even then will I be confident.... For He concealeth me in His pavilion in the day of evil; He hideth me in the covert of His tent; He lifteth me up upon a rock...."

I stop as a slight movement just beyond the edge of the camp catches my eye. That bramble bush a little way off – I swear I saw it move. I stare at it through half-closed eyes. There, it moved again! Then I see her, a Herero girl, stick thin, lying on the sand next to the corpse of a man. Watching for any sign of movement in the camp, she slowly pulls the thorny bush over her. A horse whinnies in the kraal, and the girl stops, feigning death. As silence returns, she once again inches the bramble over her body. At last, she lies still, her cover complete.

I admire her courage and wonder how long she can remain motionless with the finger-length thorns digging into her young skin. I know the general would expect me to report her, but I refuse to be responsible for her death. Let her have a chance at life, I think. One young girl left alone in the veld is hardly a threat to the mighty German empire.

As we prepare to break camp, I discreetly keep an eye on her hiding place. I hold my breath as a soldier wanders over to the bush and relieves himself on it. When he's done, he bends down to pull the beads from the corpse of a woman next to the girl. With his souvenir in his pocket, he whistles as he joins other soldiers rummaging the bodies strewn about, looking for signs of life to snuff out and mementoes to take home to loved ones. Another soldier finds a young Herero woman still breathing. He calls to the others as he lowers his pants and forces himself on the woman. She doesn't have the strength to whimper. I turn away as the others join him.

I help load up all the water we can drain from the waterholes, knowing we may not come across another one for days. As I bend down to lift up a barrel, I look out over the veld toward the soldiers. They laugh as they finish with the woman. One of them picks up his bayonet and jabs it into her limp body, slicing her open. I quickly turn back to loading the water.

Just before we leave, I wander over to where the girl is hiding and make a pretense of urinating. I bend down as if I'm picking something up, but instead I shove an apothecary bottle filled with water and a little packet of stringy ox meat and a bit of plinsen under the bramble. It isn't much, but it's the most I can do. As I start to stand up, I freeze. Inches away, a black mamba rises up within striking distance of the girl. I slowly pull out my revolver and shoot. The deadly snake trembles and then lies still. I look toward the girl. Her dark brown eyes peer up at me through the brambles. It's a look I will never forget.

As I turn away, I quietly say the *Tefilat HaDerech* for her: *"May it be Your will, Lord, our God and the God of our ancestors, that You lead her toward peace, guide her footsteps toward peace, and make her reach her desired destination for life, gladness, and peace.*" Somehow, I find comfort in knowing that this girl, at least, may live.

Toward midday, we come upon a place where the Herero had abandoned a herd of goats that were too weak to go on. A young Herero boy, about ten years old, sits dejectedly near the animals. Apparently he's lost his way. When he cries out in hunger, Timbu offers him some food. "No!" one of the lieutenants barks. "What are you thinking?"

"He's just a boy, sir," Timbu says. "And he's starving."

"He's the enemy. And we're all hungry," the lieutenant responds. "We should just kill him." He draws his revolver.

"Killing him would be a mercy," another officer says. "Why waste a bullet? Let the desert take him."

The lieutenant laughs in agreement as he holsters his gun. Some of the soldiers gather up the goats that are still alive or are freshly dead. We can use what little meat they offer. And so we trudge on through the deep sand and the scorching sun, hunting the living and killing the dying.

Consumed by hunger and a maddening thirst, we push on over this no-man's land, faint shadows of the men we once were. We move as if in a daze, going through the motions of life without really living. When I look around at what we've become, I once again wonder who is the more civilized. The German? Or the Herero? Yes, we Germans build houses and empires. But we rape and murder women and children. We kill the aged and the infirm. We trample their bones and leave their flesh for the beasts. All because we see them as an inferior race. One that stands in the way of our progress. Is this who I so desperately wanted to be? Is this why I left my family?

The sun is still high in the sky when we come upon a waterhole. Despite the earliness of the hour, we're ordered to make camp. We have no voice to cheer, but we drag ourselves to the hole to wait our turn for a drink of the water. We satisfy our thirst, ignoring the weak cries of a Herero baby lying nearby.

Turning away from the waterhole, one of the men stumbles on the baby. He stoops to pick it up. "Lookie here," he croaks. "A baby baboon!"

His comrades laugh hoarsely.

"Here, catch!" he hollers, tossing the baby like a ball to one of his friends. The friend almost drops the baby, who cries pitifully. "Throw it here!" another man says. The game ensues as more soldiers join to form a circle, throwing the baby from one to the other as if he were a ball. I start to say something, but one of the surgeons puts a restraining hand on my arm. "Let them have their fun," he says. "Besides, it's too far gone to feel much pain."

"He is a baby," I scream silently to myself, "a child as human and as feeling as yours." But I stand passively in line, waiting to get water for some of the men who are too dehydrated to get their own.

Eventually, the baby's cries stop, and the men grow weary of their sport. As a few of them begin to walk away, the one who started it all grabs his bayonet. "Throw it here," he calls. "Let's see if I can catch it with this."

A few of the men lay odds on whether he can make the catch. Then the soldier holding the baby laughs and tosses the infant in the air toward the point of the bayonet.

I turn away in disgust, both at myself and the soldiers.

In my dreams that night, the soldiers are once again roughly tossing a baby from one to the other, but this time I join them. One of the men misses, and the almost lifeless infant falls to the ground. The soldier laughs as he picks the child up and throws him to me. I smile in triumph as I catch him. Then I look down into the bloodied face of my little David.

I wake in a cold sweat, too disturbed by the dream to even think of sleeping again. The rest of the camp slumbers as the fires grow dim. I quietly get up and creep to where the body of the mangled baby lies. And just as silently, I hurriedly dig a hole in the sand with my hands – barely big enough to hold the infant. I lay him to rest, covering his broken body with the gritty dirt and a little bit of brush. I search for the words to say. All I can remember is: "*And the Lord will always guide you, and satisfy your soul in scorched places, and resurrect your bones. Rest in peace until the coming of the Consoler Who will proclaim peace.*"

I scrub my hands with sand and return to the embers of my campfire. The burial can't undo what has happened, but at least I feel a little more human. I have a lot to repent of this month.

At last, a supply train catches up with us, bringing us fresh horses, provisions, and medical supplies. But best of all, it brings

mail, including a letter from Hanna. So starved for news of my
family, I rip open the envelope, barely noting that it was sent
two months ago. With the first sentence, I know this is the letter
I've been dreading since I left home. Papa has died. "He went
peacefully in his sleep," Hanna writes. "I think he knew his time
was near. In his last days, he had so much to tell me – stories
about you and your mother, his dreams for David. He loved you
very much, Kov. It troubled him that he wasn't able to see you
one more time to tell you how proud he was of you."

The words sear my heart. I have done nothing to make Papa
proud. Had he seen me standing by, condoning with my silence
the atrocities we have committed against an innocent people, he
would have turned away in shame. I have brought disgrace on
my family.

In mourning and in torment, I rip the left side of my uniform,
not caring that it represents everything I've lived for. If I could, I
would strip these cursed khakis from my body and run naked
into the desert, begging God to cleanse me from the touch of
death that covers every inch of my flesh. Instead, I whisper
the prayer of mourning: *"Barukh atah Adonai Eloheinu melekh
ha'olam, dayan he-emet."* I bow in grief, dry-eyed. I have no tears
to shed.

* * * * *

The long trek and the polluted water are taking their toll as
once again typhoid rages through the troops. We set up camp on
a high plateau where there's a little water. General von Trotha
stations small units to guard the known waterholes that border
the Omaheke and sends out a cavalry to push any remaining
Herero into the desert. The smaller units, many without doctors,
are strung across the veld. In a gesture of personal atonement, I
volunteer to ride from unit to unit, caring for the sick.

"Whoaa," Alexander tells me. "That would be suicide, given
the shape you're in. You've been out here twice as long as the
rest of us, and it's taken quite a toll on you physically."

I shrug. "Somebody has to go. It might as well be me. Besides,
I'd rather be healing people than trampling over their bones."

I pack my saddlebags and head out in the morning with
Arnold and one of the Bastards, who will serve as our guide.

We face into the bitter wind that blows incessantly across the veld, whipping the sand into our faces. Even as leathered as my skin is, the sand feels like stinging needles. I pull a kerchief up over my nose and mouth to protect them from the sand. Conversation would be pointless, even if we had the voice for it. As we ride, we're constantly reminded of the desperation of the fleeing Herero. Fresh waterholes have been dug as deep as twelve meters, but from the looks of them, most of them came up dry. The bloated carcasses of cattle and goats litter our path. And too often, we come across the bodies of Herero, mutilated by the vultures and other wild creatures.

Day after day we ride, from one parched unit to another, tending the sick soldiers. The worst cases are loaded into wagons for the long tortuous haul back to Windhük. "What's the use?" I wonder. Many of them will be corpses long before the wagons arrive in the capital.

At night, I sit silently by the campfire, watching the flames struggle against the wind. I hate the nights. Too cold to sleep, too exhausted to do anything else, I lose myself in my thoughts. At times, I feel as if I'm standing on a precipice with one foot reaching into the abyss of madness. All I have to do is step forward and let myself fall – blissfully and irretrievably – into the innocence of insanity. It beckons like a sweet endless sleep, a realm of no guilt or accountability, so inviting ... so enticing. As I lean forward to escape reality, to escape myself, someone always pulls me back. Standing firmly on the precipice, I turn toward my rescuer. It's Papa.

"You must not do this," he says as he relentlessly pulls me toward safety. "Think of Hanna and David."

"I am thinking of them," I cry. "They would be better off without me. Hanna should be free to love a man deserving of her."

He ignores my outburst. "And what about your forefathers? Is this how you honor us?"

I hang my head in shame. Papa lifts my head and looks into my eyes. "Yaakov, you can't undo what is past. Neither can you escape its consequences. But you will find peace in repentance and forgiveness. I forgive you. Now you must forgive yourself."

"I wish I could, Papa. But I have witnessed too much. And with my silence, I have condoned it. How can I repent when every day I must stand by and watch such evil without saying a word? My fate is sealed. Now I must live with the choices I have made." I fall into a dreamless sleep.

With Rosh Hashanah almost upon us, I rise long before the sun streaks the sky with its dawn light. I find a spot in the veld, not far from our small camp, where I will be undisturbed. Standing alone in this vast expanse of land, I wrap the tefillin about my skinny left arm and my forehead. I cover my head and mechanically say the prayers of repentance in preparation for the new year.

For as long as I can remember, I have spent the last week of Elul going with Papa to the synagogue before first light. There, the shofar would call the faithful of Israel to repentance. After chanting Psalm 27, we would pray the selichot, the prayers of forgiveness, and recite the thirteen attributes of God, as a reminder that, regardless of what we have done, He will forgive those who seek His face.

Papa took teshuvah, the return to God, very seriously, so the new year was always a solemn, pious occasion at our house. The joy of Rosh Hashanah, Papa said, was in knowing that we were starting again with a clean slate and that God had written us down for a good year – a promise that would be sealed at Yom Kippur ten days later.

This morning, I try to focus on the meaning of the words as I say Psalm 27. I make it as far as *"Hide not Thy face far from me; put not Thy servant away in anger; Thou hast been my help; cast me not off, neither forsake me, O God of my salvation."* Suddenly, tears stream down my face. The tears of mourning I couldn't shed when Papa died. The tears of anger I was forced to hold back when I saw the baby being tossed about like a ball. Tears for the unforgivable acts I have witnessed without protest. Tears of self-disgust that I feel every moment I wear this uniform. Tears for the man I once was. Tears at the realization that I have lost myself in this war.

Wiping away the wetness, I continue my preparations for the new year, reciting the attributes of God: *"Merciful God, merciful God, powerful God, compassionate and gracious, slow to anger, and abundant in kindness and truth, preserver of kindness for thousands of generations, forgiver of iniquity, willful sin and error, and Who cleanses."*

Just as I finish, the sun breaks the horizon, painting the sky in pink and violet. I look out over the stillness of the veld, thinking back on the past few months. If this was my testing in the wilderness, I have failed miserably. A deep sadness settles over me as I resign myself, like my forefathers, to wandering aimlessly in the desert. There can be no teshuvah for me, at least not this year. God may be merciful, but I cannot ask for that mercy if I can find no forgiveness within myself.

Having made all of our rounds and with my medical supplies spent, we join a provision train loaded with food and ammunition. Rosh Hashanah begins tomorrow at sunset. But of course, I'm the only one who recognizes today as the eve of the beginning of a new year, so there are no celebrations as we continue our wanderings in the wilderness.

It's a relief to have some decent food for a change, and the heavily guarded train offers us some protection, as well as companionship. Not that I have much to offer these days in the way of conversation. But listening to other people keeps my mind off my inner turmoil.

I wake up well before dawn the next day and slip away for a bit of solitude in preparation for the new year. As a child, I once asked Papa why we prayed before the sun woke up. He tousled my hair and said, "It's at this time that we can come the closest to God."

I look up at the graying sky, longing for that closeness I felt all those years ago. But there is nothing. I feel as if Heaven has turned its back on me. Nevertheless, I knock at the gates with my prayers. Facing east, I recite what I can remember of Psalm 145, ending with:

"The Lord upholdeth all that fall, and raiseth up all those that are bowed down. The eyes of all wait for Thee, and Thou givest them their food in due season. Thou openest Thy hand, and satisfiest every living thing with favour. The Lord is righteous in all His ways, and gracious in all His works. The Lord is nigh unto all them that call upon Him, to all that call upon Him in truth. He will fulfill the desire of them that fear Him; He also will hear their cry, and will save them. The Lord preserveth all them that love Him; but all the wicked will He destroy."

I stop short at the *"wicked will He destroy."* I have mouthed those words all my life as part of the ritual of teshuvah. The few times I reflected on what I was saying, I thought of the wicked as the enemies of God's people. Until now, I had never considered that I might be counted among the wicked. Without finishing the Psalm, I say the chatanu: *"We have sinned, our Rock, forgive us, our Creator."* But the words cannot undo my deeds.

As we ride along today, I amuse myself by watching the antics of the children of one of the native drivers. After all the dead Herero children I've seen, it's refreshing to hear youngsters laughing and playing. When we're moving, the driver walks beside his oxen, his whip over his shoulder. His wife keeps pace behind him, carrying a chubby toddler in a shawl tied to her back. The other three children walk, single file, behind their mother in descending order.

I'm amazed that the children, even the smallest, keep pace without any complaint. Perhaps the secret is in the family pipe. From time to time, the father draws on his tobacco pipe and then passes it back to his wife. Without missing a step, the wife takes a draw and hands it back to the oldest child, who in turns hands it off to the next in line. Finally, the youngest one gets his turn and then runs it back up to his father. I smile, for the first time in months, at this ritual that binds the young family together.

On the second day after Rosh Hashanah, we come to a broad river bed beside a waterhole. As the others water up, I walk along the sandy river looking for some sign of flowing water. But all I can find is a ribbon of wet sand. It will have to do. I pick up a handful of stones and toss them, one by one, into the dampness. It's a far cry from the annual tashlikh Papa and I did together on the banks of the Pegnitz, casting smooth pebbles into the river to symbolize the casting off of our sins as we prepared for Yom Kippur. As I stand there throwing rocks at the darkened sand, I feel foolish. My guilt is too heavy to be lightly cast aside.

A few days later, Arnold complains of chills and numbness – the first signs of typhus. I can't say I'm surprised, given the dirty water we've been drinking and all the typhus cases we've treated over the past several weeks. With my medical supplies gone, our only option is to get back to the main division as quickly as possible. I don't need Arnold's death on my conscience, too. This circuit ride was supposed to be my atonement, not his punishment. "How long will it take for us to reach the camp?" I ask our Bastard guide.

"About four days, sir," he replies.

"Is there no shortcut?" I enquire hopefully.

"There's one up ahead, sir. We should reach it tomorrow. If we take it, we could cut a day from our journey. But there may not be any water."

I shrug. "We haven't had much water along this trail anyway. We have to get Arnold back to camp before he's too sick to ride."

I explain the situation to the major in charge of the supply train. He gives us some provisions and what water he can spare, before wishing us godspeed.

The sun is high above us when our guide veers off the track, heading out across the veld. Arnold and I listlessly follow. Racing against the onslaught of the fever, we make few stops throughout the day. And the breaks we do take are brief.

It's well after sunset when we come to an old campsite. The guide insists that we give the horses a rest. I start to protest, but then I glance over at Arnold, who is almost doubled over in his saddle.

I dismount and help Arnold from his horse. "Please start a fire while I tend to him," I tell the guide. I lower Arnold to the ground, pillowing his head on his saddle. He's burning with fever. Feeling responsible for his condition, I bundle both our blankets around him and give him the last of my water. Too cold to sleep, I huddle close to the fire, turning to check on my patient every time he moans. He finally settles into a deep sleep, leaving me to my thoughts.

Staring into the flames, I do some mental calculations. It's Erev Yom Kippur, the eve of the holiest of holy days. If I were home, I'd spend tomorrow requesting forgiveness, doing charitable acts, and feasting in preparation for the day of fast. Still unable to sleep, I write another quick note to Hanna by the light of the fire. Again, I beg for her forgiveness – even though I feel unworthy of it.

As soon as the sky lightens, I say my prayers and wake the guide. "We've got to get moving," I tell him.

He grumbles but gets up and saddles the horses. He and I half carry Arnold to his horse and help him mount. As we ride along, Arnold occasionally dozes off, leaning precariously from his saddle. I reach over, supporting him until he shakes himself awake enough to ride on without help. Taking care of him helps me keep my mind off my burning throat. I try not to swallow. But sometimes without thinking, I give in to the urge and then groan in pain.

Hearing the sound of hooves coming up behind us, the guide and I look over our shoulders. "There are three men, sir," the guide calls to me.

Instantly alert, I shake Arnold, trying to raise him from his deepening stupor. It would be pointless to try to outrun anyone, given Arnold's condition and the weariness of our mounts. I turn my horse around to face the newcomers and reach for my gun. It's hard to tell if the men riding toward us are friend or foe. They're wearing German uniforms, but that doesn't mean anything as the Herero often wear uniforms they have taken from dead soldiers.

The men remove their hats and call to us in German. As they ride closer, I recognize Peter. He's much thinner, and his face is almost black from all the weeks of being in the desert sun. He offers me his water-sack, which I gratefully accept. His companions help Arnold from his horse so he can get some water. After a brief rest, they lift him back into the saddle and secure him. Together, we ride on.

I call for a break shortly before sunset. Peter looks at me quizzically as I pull my surgeon's coat from my pack and put it on. "Please look after Arnold," I tell him. "I'll be back shortly."

I walk up over a rise until I'm out of sight of the others. I cover my head and wrap my prayer shawl about my shoulders. Recalling the Kol Nidre prayers that bridged Erev Yom Kippur with the holy day itself, I face north and recite, "*We have sinned, our Rock, forgive us, our Creator.... May all the people of Israel be forgiven, including all the strangers who live in their midst, for all the people are in fault.*"

I modify it slightly and recite it two more times, "*May all the people of Israel and Germany be forgiven, including all the strangers who live in their midst, for all the people are at fault.*"

I sigh as I finish my prayers. By this time tomorrow, my fate will be sealed for the year. I remove the prayer shawl and yarmulke. Still wearing my once-white coat, I head back to the others and mount my horse for the final leg of our journey.

It's late when we reach our division, which is camped alongside some dried-up waterholes. A bitter cold wind picks up, chilling me to the bone. I'm settling Arnold in the field hospital when Alexander comes in. "I heard you had returned," he says. He takes a hard look at me and orders one of the other surgeons to tend to Arnold.

Drawing me to the fire, Alexander notices my surgical coat and smiles. "Not quite a kittel," he says, "but it works." He looks down at my feet and nods approvingly. "At least you kept your boots on."

I give a semblance of a smile. "I can go without food, water, and marital relations for Yom Kippur, but this year I'll have to break the bans on working and wearing leather shoes."

He wraps a blanket around me, whispering the new year greeting "*Shana tovah*" in my ear. He brings me a bit of half-cooked rice and sits down next to me. I push the rice away.

"I know it's the fast, but you've got to eat," he says, placing the food next to me. "God will understand. Besides, you've been nearly fasting for the past few months."

I give in and eat. When I'm finished, Alexander looks at me intently. "Are you trying to kill yourself, Kov?" he asks. "Because if you are, it looks like you're doing a pretty good job of it. At this rate, you'll not live to see another year."

I'm too tired to argue. "*Ketiva ve-chatima tovah*," I mumble, wishing him a good year. I curl up in a tight little ball beside the fire and sleep.

TO THE LIMITS

The cannons boom, shaking the ground with their thunder. I shiver in the cold and put my hands to my ears in a futile effort to block out the noise. I scream, and someone shakes me.

"Kov! Wake up!"

It takes me a minute to recognize Alexander, who's kneeling above me in the darkness. Then I hear the cannon again. "Are we under attack?" I ask.

Alexander shakes his head. "It's only thunder. But we've got to get to higher ground in case it floods."

"What day is it?" I ask as I stumble to a stand. The sky is black with clouds that roll over each other in the fury of the coming storm. The wind begins to pick up, howling about us in an unearthly voice.

"The fast is over. Now hurry," Alexander calls to me. "Leave your things. The orderlies will move them."

I stand numbly as the wind pushes against me. The gates of prayer have closed. I look up at the black sky, feeling as if God has turned his back on me. The rain begins to fall, the huge drops splattering against my face.

Alexander grabs me and hustles me up the hill to where the rest of the camp is moving. Lightning lashes across the heavens, illuminating the gray rain against the blackness of the sky. We barely have time to set up a bit of a canvas shelter before the rain pours down in sheets, flooding the area around the waterholes. "At least we should have water again," Alexander says with a wry smile. "Whether it will be safe to drink is another question."

Fighting the wind, he struggles to start a fire and coaxes me to sit close to it. But even with the heat of the flames, my teeth chatter in the cold dampness. I huddle in my blanket, trying to get warm. What I wouldn't do for a hot bath right now.

Seeing one of the orderlies darting into the field hospital, I think of Arnold. I should have checked on him. But instead, I've been worrying about my own comfort. I shrug the blanket off and start to stand.

"Where are you going?" Alexander asks.

"I've got to see to Arnold."

"The others are looking after him," he tells me. "You've got to take care of yourself, or you'll be as sick as he is. And then what good would you be to anyone?"

I nod and sit back down. "I must look pretty bad the way you're fussing over me."

"To put it bluntly, you're not much more than a walking skeleton." He hands me his shaving mirror. "Here, look at yourself."

I reluctantly look at my image. I don't recognize the gaunt face with its sunken eyes that stare passively back at me. A dark beard emphasizes the hollows of the cheeks. Unconvinced that this is really my reflection, I attempt a smile. The face smiles back garishly. I quickly return the mirror to Alexander. As I do, I glance at my bony calloused hand. It looks more like a claw than a human hand.

Alexander, who has been watching me, arches his eyebrows.

"You're right, Doctor," I mumble. "I look like death."

"You rest. I'll get you some dinner." He pulls his blanket around my shivering frame and makes me lie down.

When I wake, it's early evening. The rain has stopped, but the wind bites through the woolen blanket and my threadbare uniform. "Eat." Alexander hands me a bit of half-cooked rice and tough meat. "It's not much, and it could be the last you'll get for a few days. Our supplies are gone."

As I sit there chewing the meat, I look out toward the eastern horizon where the sky is ablaze with great clouds of smoke and flames. Alexander follows the direction of my gaze. "The Herero are burning any fodder so there will be no feed for our horses and oxen," he said.

"So we're still pursuing them?"

"Yes. To the ends of the earth, it seems. Major von Estorff and some of the other officers have urged the general to negotiate with the Herero, but Trotha insists they must be annihilated. The major has taken some of the troops on ahead of us." Alexander puts another piece of wood on the fire, sending sparks heavenward.

We sit quietly, lost in our own thoughts.

Finally, I break the silence. "How's Arnold?"

Alexander stretches his legs toward the fire. "He's delirious. A few others also have the fever. They don't have the strength to go on, so they're being sent back to Windhük tomorrow."

"Good." I look wistfully toward the horizon. "We should just call it quits and all go back. We've done what we set out to do. We don't need to bury the rest of the Herero, or more of our own troops, in the desert."

In the morning, I help the medical staff settle Arnold and the other sick men into the wagons for the long trek back to civilization. We give them what water we can spare. We don't have any food to give them, but they should meet up with the supply train that's supposed to be heading our way.

We stay in camp a few more days, waiting for the supply wagons to catch up with us. Thanks to the rain, the waterholes are replenished so we have enough water, if we carefully ration it, to last us a little while longer. With most of the sick on their way to Windhük, the surgical staff has little to do, so Alexander forces me to do nothing but sleep and eat.

When we finally break camp, I feel like a new man – almost. But my renewed energy is quickly sapped by the rigors of the march. By the second day, what little water we were able to carry from the camp is gone. And so far, we have found no waterholes.

This morning, we ride along the dry bed of the Eiseb River. Despite the recent rain, the land is parched. We come across a few waterholes shortly before noon. But like the riverbed, they're dirt dry. We rest as several of the soldiers dig the holes deeper in a desperate, futile hunt for water. They finally give up, flopping on the cracked, leathered earth, exhausted by their efforts. With no water, we can't even cook our rice. The horses, more desperate for water than we are, paw at the dust. Their mouths are too dry to chew the sharp, coarse grass.

When we start up again, we walk beside the horses so as not to exhaust them. Wearily, we trudge through the deep, blowing sand as the sun beats down on us unforgivingly. Driven by hunger and thirst, we march – mirages of life. Night falls, replacing the heat with a cold that the wind drives through our thin uniforms. Numbed by the elements and the endless trek, I hardly notice when my horse trips on a rock until he nearly pulls me down on top of him. I straighten myself and try to coax him up, but I have no voice. My throat feels as if it has been glued shut. So I stroke the horse while tugging gently on his reins. Finally, he struggles to his feet, and we limp on.

All around me, men and horses stumble on the stony path, cursing and snorting in the darkness. At last, the order comes to stop. A scouting party will go on ahead to look for water, but the rest of us can rest. With only a few fires for warmth, we lie beside our horses on the rocky ground. We're too tired to care.

Several hours later, we mount the rested horses. The scouts have found water. The moon rises over the steppes, lighting our path with its silvery blue glow. We ride silently, shivering against the wind. I try to ignore the dry burning in my throat and the hunger gnawing at my stomach, focusing instead on the stars scattered across the heavens. I remember the wonder I felt as a boy looking up at the night sky. The magical dazzle of the stars. The pearly stare of the moon. The awareness of being a tiny part of this great immensity.

My horse whinnies and picks up his gait. Off in the distance, the limey soil glows like white marble in the radiance of the moonlight. In the midst of it lie three dark pools, framed by a few trees and towering termite hills. The moonglow works its magic, transforming the tiny desert oasis into the ruins of an ancient city square.

The men stir in their saddles as we approach the long-anticipated water. The lead horses whinny as they reach the first hole, but they turn away and move on to the second one and then the third. A few of the men murmur, wondering what's going on. Then we smell it. Death. The holes are brimming with the rotting carcasses of cattle. The foul odor breaks the spell of the nighttime magic. We slide off our horses, which stand with their heads drooping. The men, fighting fatigue and the weakness of starvation, lean against their guns for support.

"How dare they?" one of the officers rails against the Herero. "What right do they have to contaminate the waterholes?"

I lower my head to hide a tired sardonic smile. We're pushing them to their death in the desert, and then we complain when they fight back with the only weapons they have left.

The general orders us to move on. With no water, it will be better to ride in the cool of the night and then rest in the heat of the day. So we saddle up and resume our sleepy march, stretching out single file over the steppes. What little energy I have ebbs quickly under the strain of the continued trek. A deep lethargy settles over me as the rocking of the saddle lulls me into a dreamlike state. Occasionally, my horse stumbles, jolting me to consciousness. I jerk awake and look around, trying to get my bearings. The man in front of me slumps precariously to the side. His horse falters and drops to the ground, groaning. Half awake, the man struggles to free himself from the saddle. As the rest of us ride past him, he urges his horse to its feet. But the horse is spent. The man wearily shoulders his pack and pushes onward on foot. Before long, half the troops are reduced to infantry.

All along the path are signs of the desperation of the Herero flight. Embers of small fires. Discarded clothing. Books from the missionaries. Wasted animals slit open to claim their last reserves of moisture. Bodies of the weak and feeble. My eyes take in the desolation, but I'm too emotionally spent to care.

A reconnoitering party comes back with the news that Major von Estorff's division has surprised the enemy. After a short skirmish, our troops pushed the Herero deeper into the Omaheke.

But it's still not enough for General von Trotha. We will continue our pursuit, he says. Our victory is not yet complete.

The next day we come to the waterholes of Osombo-Windembe and meet up with what's left of Estorff's division. Despite the general's order, Estorff has taken a lot of Herero prisoners. Many of them are too weak to continue their flight. Others surrendered, claiming they weren't involved in the fight. All of them begged for German mercy.

With Estorff's reinforcements, Trotha decides to make one last stand to eradicate the enemy, who are at what is reportedly the next, and final, waterhole. After watering the horses and drinking our fill, we rest. Tomorrow we'll prepare for battle.

The general orders a dress parade the next afternoon so he can review the troops. Trying to ignore a throbbing headache, I join the rest of the officers and troops forming ranks across the broad clearing. Those of us who still have horses mount our thin, shaggy steeds. The others line up on foot. The cannons are wheeled to the center. In our baggy, tattered uniforms, we're only a semblance of the force that attacked the Herero at Hamakari. It's hard to believe that was less than two months ago. It seems as if we've been marching in the bone-strewn desert for years.

As we wait in formation, the Herero prisoners – men women, and children – are dragged out in front of us. I gasp at their emaciated bodies as they huddle together. The campaign has taken an even greater toll on them than it has on us. I try not to look at their ghastly forms, but my curiosity gets the better of me. I find it hard to believe that any being could still function in such a condition. I stare at their shriveled skin stretching tautly over their bones – a macabre rendition of living skeletons. In contrast, even the sickest German soldier I have treated would look fat and healthy.

General von Trotha rides slowly between us and the prisoners, sitting erect on his horse. "Guten tag, men!" he calls out.

"Guten tag, your Excellency!" we respond.

The general proceeds to rally the troops, praising us for our perseverance, our service to the Kaiser, our dedication to duty. He then stresses the importance of what we're about to do, the final battle against our enemy. And then we can return home to our families, he says, heads held high, knowing we have fought with honor.

He motions to his aide, who hands him an official-looking document. Turning to the prisoners, he says, "I the great general of the German troops send this letter to the Herero people."

He reads from the document: "The Herero are no longer German subjects. They have murdered and stolen; they have cut off the ears, noses, and other body parts of wounded soldiers. Now, out of cowardice, they no longer wish to fight. The Herero people must, however, leave our land. If they do not do this, I will force them with the cannon. Within the German borders, every Herero, with or without a gun, with or without cattle, will be shot. I will no longer accept women and children. I will drive them back to their people or I will let them be shot at."

Trotha hands the document back to his aide as his eyes sweep over the prisoners. "These are my words to the Herero people. The great general of the mighty German Kaiser."

The general nods to the chaplain to begin a religious service. A big, strong man, the chaplain stands behind a wagon chest draped with a red cloth. In addition to his uniform and riding boots, which are in much better shape than most of ours, he wears a gold chain with a cross. As the other men sing "We Come to Pray Before a Just God," I awkwardly try to mouth the unfamiliar words. I don't know why I try to fit in anymore. They all know I'm Jewish. And, frankly, I don't care. I close my mouth and sit in silence as the singing continues, steadying myself as I sway in the saddle. Alexander gives me a worried look. I smile weakly in response.

At last the hymn ends, and the chaplain begins to speak, justifying the war and tomorrow's battle. "Savage by nature, the Herero have rebelled against the civilizing authorities that God has set over them," he says. His words come to me as if through a dense fog. "And in their rebellion, they stained themselves with blood – the blood of German martyrs brutally murdered in their beds and fields. Now, the Almighty has given us the sword, which we are to use to punish the enemy for rising up against the superior race He has sent to teach and guide them. May every one of us wield that sword honorably to the glory of God and the Fatherland."

I try to sit erect in the saddle as the throbbing in my head and a sense of lethargy make it harder and harder to focus on what is being said.

"We are coming to a serious hour," the chaplain continues. "It may be that some of us will not live to see another day. So let us prepare today to seek the face of God that He might bestow on each of us His eternal holiness. Let us commit ourselves to Him who promises the faithful everlasting peace and rest. And in so doing, let us strive to become better and braver before all the nations of the earth – for the world belongs to the noble. Thus saith the Lord."

Ignoring Alexander's insistence that I rest, I spend the remainder of the day, along with the other medical staff, tending to the men weakened by the long, waterless march. Several of the men are severely dehydrated and aren't fit for another march, let alone a battle. A few are showing signs of typhus. Short of a long rest and plenty of food and water, there's not much we can do for them.

Despite my pounding headache and deepening lethargy, I spend the evening hours in somber preparation for battle. Alexander brings me some dinner, but I wave it away. Even though I've eaten little that day, I have no appetite.

"You've got to eat something, Kov," he tells me sternly.

"Yes, Doctor," I say jokingly. I take a few bites. "Satisfied?"

He shakes his head and stokes up the fire.

In the last light of the day, I write another quick note to Hanna, assuring her of my love and begging her forgiveness. Although I love her as much as ever, the memory of her is fading. With every day that passes, I'm more convinced that I'll never hold her in my arms again nor look on the face of my son. I'm resigned to this fate. It's what I deserve for abandoning my family.

The moon has risen, lighting our way, as those of us with Trotha's division set out in the night. Estorff and his men are to stay at the camp a few more days before heading south to garrison some of the other waterholes. The general ordered Estorff to hang the male prisoners at dawn and then force the women and children into the desert. At least I'll be spared that spectacle.

Riding along the top of a low ridge, I see the shady lines of hills, rolling out in the soft moonlight from the broad valley that lies below us. The sandy bed of the Eiseb River forms a bright stripe wending its way through the valley. We ride for hours, searching for signs of the Herero. With each new summit, we're sure we'll see them.

The moon sets, and the sun rises. And we ride on, continuing our hunt. The sun climbs higher in the sky, its heat radiating around us, making our throats ache for water. Yet still we ride, single file, pressing toward the next height. In the heat of the day, I begin to shiver, confirming what I've feared for the past week. I have typhus. But this is no place to be sick, so I keep quiet, forcing myself to push on with the rest of the men.

As I approach the highest peak yet, I see the gunners up ahead removing the dust caps from the artillery. In the distance, a few shots repeat against the hills. We pick up the pace, sure the battle is on at last. At the top of the peak, I look out over the barren valley. It appears to be devoid of life. Then in the distance, I see it. A small dark cloud of dust swirling swiftly toward the horizon, marking the passage of what's left of the Herero into the deepest reaches of the Omaheke. There will be no final triumphant battle. The Herero, like the Sicarii besieged by the Romans at Masada, have chosen their own path to death.

We rest by their still-burning fires and the waterholes they recently abandoned. Once again, we're sure the war is over. There's no need to chase ghosts in the desert. But General von Trotha isn't satisfied. We must make sure the Herero die in the Omaheke, he says, otherwise, we'll never be able to live in peace. We must continue our pursuit, he orders.

So after filling our watersacks and resting a bit, we once again mount our weary horses and trek deeper into the desert, hoping the general soon sees the folly of our chase. Late in the afternoon, we cross over the sandy Eiseb. It had seemed so much closer when we were looking down on it in the moonlight last night. Close to the riverbed, we come to some old dried-up waterholes. The ground is scarred with at least a hundred fresh holes dug by the Herero in a desperate search for water. Some of the holes are more than twelve meters deep, but they're all dry.

Then we get the news we don't want to hear. These aren't the last waterholes, after all. Our scouts report that the Herero are camped by a watering place five hours from here. They assure the general that it is, indeed, the last water in the Omaheke. So in the cool of the night, we mount our horses again and ride on, intent on forcing the Herero even deeper into the desert while replenishing our own water supplies.

As we ride in the moonlight, a stifling heat rushes over me. I pull at the collar of my uniform, trying to loosen it. If I could, I would strip my clothes off so the night wind could cool me. Almost in a daze, I look at the men riding near me. They take on dreamlike proportions, growing and shrinking in size. I shake my head, trying to clear my thoughts. We've left graves all along our trek. I don't want mine to be the next. But perhaps this is what I deserve – a final resting place in these desolate steppes that give no rest in life. I laugh out loud at the irony, surprising myself with the strange, shrieking sound that echoes through the valley.

Alexander rides up beside me. "Are you all right, Kov?" he asks hoarsely.

"I'm fine," I lie.

We reach the watering place in the morning, eager to refill our water sacks and slake our thirst. But like the previous waterholes, these too are dry. We stand on a lonely hill, looking out over the Omaheke. In the distance, two dust clouds mark the trail of the Herero as they plunge deeper into the vast wasteland. They have split into two groups, one heading north and the other northeast. Death lies in both directions.

I fight back a surge of emotion as I gaze out over the sandveld, watching the remnants of this once-great nation vanishing into the horizon. Many of the men around me cheer hoarsely, thinking that this means they can go home as triumphant heroes. I lower my head in shame, feeling neither heroic nor triumphant.

Alexander gently slaps me on the back. "Why so glum?" he asks. "It's over. You'll be holding that son of yours in no time."

I try to smile, but I don't share his enthusiasm. Considering General von Trotha's ruthlessness, I'm not so sure the war is over. And I still have four months left on my tour of duty. Besides, even if I could go home tomorrow, I'm not sure I would make it. I've seen typhus claim too many men. I'm also not sure I should go home. I can't go back to my old life pretending I'm the same man who left there in January. I'm afraid that every time I embraced Hanna, my mind would be filled with memories of Herero women being raped and murdered. And how could I look my son in the eye when he asks me about my service in South West Africa? I would be haunted by visions of thousands of Herero children dying in the desert.

We sit wearily around the dried-up waterholes while the officers discuss our next course of action. The break is sorely needed. A fourth of the men have come down with one illness or another, but we have no medicine to give them. Everyone is exhausted. Half of the horses have fallen. And the men who have been forced to march have worn through their boots. Their feet are bleeding, pulpy masses of flesh. Since the nearest waterholes are a twenty-four hour trek behind us, more men are sure to fall ill. And some will die.

Trotha finally yields to the pressure of his officers and advisers. We will give up the pursuit. But he asks for volunteers to pursue the Herero even further into the desert. I'm amazed at the number of men who step forward. The general chooses the healthiest ones with the best horses for the mission, giving them what little water can be spared. He orders them to poison any waterholes they find and then wishes them godspeed.

Even though there's no water, the rest of us are to set up camp here in the desert where we'll wait for the scouts' return. Our presence here, Trotha says, will keep the Herero from returning.

I join the other surgeons in setting up a makeshift field hospital. Beads of sweat drip from my forehead as I begin to make my rounds. My hand trembles as I examine my first patient.

"Doctor, you don't look so good," the man tells me.

"No, I'm not...." I collapse to the ground.

* * * * *

The next thing I know Alexander is lifting me into a wagon. I try to sit up, but he pushes me back. "It's good to see you're still among the living," he tells me. "You had me worried for a few days. I hope you have the strength to make it back to Windhük."

I fall back against the hard floor of the wagon. "Please write to Hanna," I ask him.

He nods.

"Tell her I died. It will be easier that way."

BOOK 4

Jahohora

RESURRECTION

The man picks me up and carries me to his wagon. I've never been in a wagon before. He tells me to lie down. He puts his coat around me to keep me warm when the sun sleeps. The wagon begins to move. It shakes so much I think it's going to break. My body bounces against the wood. It hurts. I can feel the pain in my bones. I bite my lip so I don't cry out.

The man talks to me in Herero. I try to open my ears to hear him. Maybe it will help me forget the pain. But his words are lost in the noise of the wagon wheels hitting against the rocks. I close my eyes, hoping I can sleep.

The wagon hits a big bump. I bounce into the air and fall back down, screaming with pain. I open my eyes. If that was a dream, it was too real. The wagon stops. The man turns around and looks at me. He holds a jar with a fire in it so he can see in the darkness. It's like the jar the snake hunter gave me. Only bigger. And with two shiny sides. This must be what Tate called a lamp.

"Are you all right?" the man asks me in Herero. "Can you sit up? It might be easier."

I slowly sit up and crawl until I'm leaning against the side of the wagon. It hurts so much when I move.

The man smiles at me. "We'll be home soon."

I wonder what "home" is. I know it's not my home. I don't have a home. Not anymore.

I'm almost asleep when the wagon stops again. The man jumps down from the wagon and calls out to someone. I hear strange noises and see lights. I try to see where the lights are coming from. They aren't stars. And they're not fires. All I see is the dark shape of a house. I can't see the house very well in the dark. But it looks big. And it's square. Don't white people know that snakes like square houses?

The man carries me toward the house. I hear another voice. It's a woman. She talks with white people words. I close my eyes when we go inside the house. There's too much light. It hurts my eyes after the darkness outside. The man puts me down on something soft. I open my eyes very slowly. A white woman is bending over me. She doesn't look happy.

She turns away. I hear her talking to someone. I don't know her words. But her voice is hard. Yesterday, I would have been scared. Now, I'm too tired – and I have too much pain – to be afraid.

When the woman comes back, she's not alone. A Nama woman is with her. The Nama's eyes get big when she sees me. The white woman tells her something. The Nama shakes her head and backs away from me. The white woman says the words again. The Nama woman slowly comes toward me and picks me up like I'm a baby. I know she doesn't want to touch me. I can tell by the look on her face.

She carries me into another house. There's no outside between the two houses. She carries me from one house right into the other. The white woman comes behind us. She makes the wall move to hide the doorway. I can't see into the other house anymore.

The Nama woman tells me to stand up. She takes off what's left of my skin dress and drops it on the ground. The ground isn't dirt. It's covered with something smooth and hard. She kneels on the ground and starts to take off one of the beaded ankle cuffs Mama made for me. I pull my leg away. She grabs my leg and holds it still. She takes the cuff off and reaches for the other one.

"No," I say. "Mama made these for me. They show I'm a Herero woman."

"Those are the old ways," she tells me in Herero. "You can't go around half naked. You must dress like a good Christian woman now."

Christian? I don't know that word.

The Nama woman stands up and takes off my wrist cuffs. She drops them on the ground with the skin dress and ankle cuffs. The white woman picks up my clothes and puts them in the fire that burns in a hole in the wall. I reach for them. The Nama woman holds me back.

Tears fill my eyes. "They're all I have from Mama," I tell her.

The Nama shrugs her shoulders. But she looks at me sadly. "You must forget the past," she says. She reaches for the jar tied around my neck.

"What's this?" she asks.

I grab it away from her. "The white snake hunter gave it to me. It's so I will always have water."

"You can keep it," she says. "But you can't wear it around your neck. I'll put it in our room for you."

Room. It's another word I don't know.

The Nama woman pulls me over to a big, big pot filled with water. She makes me sit in the pot. The water is hot. I get very scared. I think they're going to cook me. I try to get out of the pot. The Nama woman holds me down while the white woman rubs me with cloths dripping water. The rubbing opens my sores. It hurts. A lot. She rubs me so much I think my skin is going to fall off. Then she rubs my head hard. I try to pull away. The Nama woman holds me too tightly.

Finally, the women let me go. I stand up and step out of the pot. I'm so tired I almost fall. The white woman holds me. The Nama rubs me with another cloth. It's bigger. And it's not wet. When she's done, she throws it in the fire with my skin dress. The cloth has blood all over it.

"You can sit down now," the Nama woman tells me. She puts something sticky all over me. It burns.

I try not to cry.

"It's all right," she says quietly. "It's medicine. It will help heal your sores."

"White people medicine?" I ask. My voice is a small whisper.

She smiles and nods.

I pull away from her. Tate said white people's medicine poisons the Herero soul. It's too late. The medicine is all over my body. I try to rub it off. But it doesn't come off.

"Stop that," the Nama woman says. "The medicine is good for you."

The white woman pulls something over my head. I can't see. I try to get it off.

"Hold still," the Nama says. "It's just a nightgown."

Nightgown? I don't know that word either. I wiggle my head up through an opening. The nightgown is long, like my skin dress. But it covers my chest. My neck. And my arms. And it's not skin. It's soft. It looks like clouds.

The Nama woman helps me stand. She shows me a long shiny thing. I jump when I see her standing in it. How can that be? She's standing next to me. What kind of evil magic is this?

She laughs softly and points at the shiny thing. The Nama in the shiny thing points back. "Don't be afraid," she says. "It's not magic. It's a mirror. And that's you."

I look at the other person standing in the shiny thing. She's like the bony carcasses I saw in the veld. Huge sores cover her skin. They're bleeding. The blood drops onto her white dress. She scares me. She looks like death. I hold my hand out to keep her away from me. She holds hers out toward me. I step backward and fall.

The Nama woman picks me up and carries me to another house. Again, we don't go outside. Instead, we go up and up and up. There are many houses here. All on top of each other or next to each other. The Nama carries me to a house that's on top of all the other houses. She puts me down on something soft and pulls a big cloth over me. It's very warm. This house is darker than the others. It makes me want to sleep.

The Nama woman won't let me. "You must eat," she says. She feeds me warm water. But it doesn't look or taste like water. It's brown. And it has pieces of meat in it. It's been a long time since I've eaten anything but dried berries and uintjes. The food is very good. But I can only eat a few bites. I'm too tired and weak to eat any more.

I lie back and close my eyes. Sleep comes quickly.

I sleep and sleep and sleep. But it's still dark when I open my eyes. I look around, trying to see where I am. I should be walking. I don't want the soldiers or the Herero hunters to find me. I sit up. I'm not on the ground. And this isn't the veld. Or home. I think very hard. I remember a dream I had. About a white man taking me to his house. And two women putting me in a cooking pot and trying to take the skin off me. I remember a very bad shiny thing with a hide-covered skeleton. The women told me I was the skeleton. I lie back down. It was just a dream. I close my eyes. Maybe I'll have a better dream.

Someone shakes me gently. I open my eyes. A Nama woman is bending over me. I don't know her. But I think I've seen her before. She smiles. I try to get up. She puts her hand against me. "You can sit," she says. "But no standing. You're not strong enough."

Her voice scares me. It's the voice from my dream. She's the one who tried to cook me. I move away from her.

She laughs. "You don't have to be afraid of me." She holds a gourd to my lips. "Drink," she says. "We need to fatten you up. You're skin and bone, child."

I take a drink. I taste little bits of meat. After a few small sips, I turn away. I'm too tired to drink more. The woman shakes her head. "You must drink it all."

I drink it and lie back. The woman softly rubs my head. "You poor child," she whispers as my eyes close in sleep.

* * * * *

A small noise wakes me. I look around. I can't see much in the twilight. It will be dark soon. I need to walk. I've been in this hiding place too long. The Herero hunters might find me. I sit up and look across the veld. But there's no veld. I'm in a strange square house. And I'm lying on something high above the ground. I slide down until my feet touch the ground. It's covered with something soft and warm. I look down at my legs. The sores have almost healed. I hold my hands out. The sores there are almost gone, too. I must have been sleeping for a long, long time.

I stand and look around the house. It has many things I don't know. I try to find the doorway. I see an opening up high. But it's not a doorway. It doesn't touch the ground. I walk over to the opening. Something covers it. Something I can see through. Like the jar the snake hunter gave me. I stand very, very tall so I can look through the opening. I almost scream. The opening is very high above the ground. It's as high as the trees. There's no way to get out of the house. I can't jump that far.

I hear a sound behind me. I turn to look. The wall is moving. It was hiding the opening. A Nama woman comes in from another house. She has food. She smiles when she sees me. "Good. You're up, " she says. "You must be getting better." She makes the wall move again so it hides the opening. "I'll put your food here on the table." She puts the food on something by the high opening. That must be a table.

The woman talks to me while I eat. "You had me scared. I thought you were never going to wake up. You slept for many days."

"Where am I?" I ask. "And how did I get here?"

"Don't you remember? Herr Jurgen brought you here in his wagon. He found you in the veld. You were dying."

I dreamed that a white man put me in a wagon. Am I still dreaming? I touch my face to make sure my eyes are really open. "Is he going to send me to the death camp?" I ask the woman.

She laughs. "No. You will work for the Jurgens. They'll take care of you. And give you a home." She smiles. "They took me in a few years ago. They are good Christian people. Many Herero and Nama work for them. But the others live in huts on the farm. You and I are the only ones in the big house."

She walks around, moving things. "This is our room." She points to a big thing against the wall. It's like the thing I've been sleeping on. "That's the bed where I sleep."

Room. Bed. Farm. There are so many new words. I try to remember them all.

The woman moves something on the table. It's the jar the snake hunter gave me. "You can keep your things here."

"What do I call you?" I ask.

"Marthe."

"That's not a Nama name. And it's not Herero," I say quietly. "Who is your family?"

"My family is gone. And my village. The soldiers burned it." She sighs. I see sadness in her eyes.

"I thought the Nama were friends to the white people," I say.

She sighs. "That was yesterday. When the Nama saw how the big chief of the white people was killing all the Herero, some of our warriors rose up against him. So the big chief said all the Nama should be killed, too. The Nama chiefs made a treaty with one of the other white chiefs. He said if we promised not to fight the white people again and gave the soldiers all our boom sticks, we could keep our villages and our cattle. Our chiefs did what he asked. But then the big chief sent the soldiers to burn our villages and kill our warriors. The rest of the Nama were sent to the death camps. I ran away before the soldiers burned my village. The Jurgens gave me a home."

Marthe lights a small fire in a jar and puts it on the table. "But that's the past. Now, we have only today." She sits on her bed. "What's your name?"

"I'm Jahohora, the daughter of Mutihu and Tutejuva. Tate is a great healer," I say.

"Frau Jurgen will give you a new name. A Christian name," she tells me.

"What is this 'Christian'?"

"It's the way of the missionaries. You have a lot to learn." Marthe laughs. "Where is your family now?"

"I don't know. I've been looking for them for a long, long time." I tell her about hiding in the mountains. About Tate and Mama going for water. And the sound of the boom sticks. I tell her about running into the Omaheke to find my uncles who joined Maharero. About all the death. And the snake hunter. I tell her about wandering in the veld. About meeting the Herero hunters. Rubbing the poison plant into my skin. And still not knowing what happened to my family.

"The postman might know," she says.

"The postman?"

"He's a missionary. But he's a Herero," she tells me. "He goes to the white people's farms, preaching to their Herero and Nama workers. He knows all the Herero and Nama who survived and where they are. The white people like him because he helps us become Christians. We like him because he brings us messages about our families."

"Will he come here?" I ask.

She nods. "He will be here before the rainy season." Marthe picks up my empty gourd. "Too much talk," she says. "It's time to sleep."

MY NEW HOME

"Penee." I open my eyes. Marthe is bending over me. "Penee," she says again, "you need to get up and eat."

I sit. "Why are you calling me Penee?" I ask.

"That's your name."

I shake my head. "My name is Jahohora."

She smiles. "Frau Jurgen gave you a new name. A Christian name. It's Petronella. But I'm going to call you Penee. It's shorter. And it fits you better."

"I don't want a new name. I like Jahohora. It's the name Tjikuume gave me."

"No one can take that away from you," Marthe says. "But Frau Jurgen will call you Petronella. You'd better get used to it." She watches me eat. "When you're done eating, you must get dressed. Then I'll show you the rest of the house. And you'll begin your lessons."

"Lessons?"

"All the things you need to know to work in the white people's house." She leaves the room while I eat the rest of my food.

When Marthe comes back, she has a long cloth. "This is for you. It's your new dress."

"I can't wear that." I back away as she brings it toward me. "It's the color of kudu. I'm from the Omukuatjivi clan – the people of the kudu."

"You must forget the old ways, Penee. They're gone. We must live by the white people's way."

I let Marthe take off my nightgown and pull the dress over my head. The dress is not skin, but it's heavy. It covers all of me. It's like Marthe's dress. But not as fat. I don't like it. I sigh. I will learn the white people's way. But I'll never forget the past, I tell myself. If I forget the past, I will forget my family. And the ancestors. I must never do that. Without them, I will forget who I am.

Marthe shows me how to make the wall move. She tells me it isn't a wall. It's a door that lets us into the rest of the house. She takes me through many rooms. She gives me words for all the things I see. It's a lot to remember.

She leads me outside to a small square hut. She opens the door. Inside is a seat with holes in it. She shows me how to pee like white women. I laugh. Why do they need a house just for peeing?

"It isn't right to show your body," Marthe tells me. "It also isn't safe. Especially if white men are around. Even Herr Jurgen. When white men see women uncovered, they act like animals."

Marthe lifts her dress a little. She has many more dresses under it. "That's why I wear so many petticoats," she says. "They make it harder for the white men to make me lie with them. Frau Jurgen is a good woman. But she would make me leave if I have a baby without a husband. I don't want to leave here. This is my home. It will be your home, too."

I begin to like my new home. I'm never hungry or thirsty. I'm warm at night. And I'm not alone. I slowly learn to live the white people's way. When I'm with Marthe in our room, we use Herero words. I have to speak the strange words of the white people in the rest of the house. They are hard words to say and hear.

I do many things for the Jurgens. I help Marthe clean the house, wash their clothes, and cook. I also milk the cows and play with the Jurgens' children. I like playing with Johanna and Lukas. But it makes me sad. They remind me of Karemarama and my young cousins.

Life is good at the Jurgen house. As long as I do what Frau Jurgen tells me. She's as hard as the words she speaks. I'm afraid she'll send me to the death camps if I don't do everything she wants. She's always telling me to hurry, to stop being lazy. "If there were a fire, everything would be burned up by time you got there," she says.

When we're alone in our room, Marthe tells me I'm no longer the proud daughter of an important healer. "This may be your home," she says, "but you must not forget that you're a servant here. You must move quickly, like a servant." She smiles to soften her words. "Frau Jurgen is a good woman, and she has a heart. But it's made of stone."

We both laugh.

The next day, I walk faster when Frau Jurgen needs something. I still hold my head high and stand tall. I may be a servant, but I am a Herero.

German soldiers often stop at the Jurgen house. Sometimes, it's just one or two. They come for food and a place to sleep. Or to get a new horse. Other times, there are more. And they have Herero they're taking to the death camps. The soldiers come in the house to eat with the Jurgens. But the Herero stay outside. They're chained together. I never see them eat. Most of them are very skinny. Like I was when Herr Jurgen met me in the veld.

I feel sorry for the Herero. I want to feed them. And I want to look at them to see if I know them. Marthe tells me I must stay away from them. "There's nothing you can do to help them," she says as we make dinner for the Jurgens and their guests.

I help Marthe carry the food into the dining room. One of the soldiers watches me as I serve everyone. I don't like the way he's looking at me. I want to leave the room. But Frau Jurgen likes for Marthe and me to stay in the dining room while they eat. Someone might need something.

The soldier asks me for more water. His leg touches mine while I'm filling his glass. Then he wants more meat. He puts his hand on my arm and thanks me when I put another piece of wildebeest on his plate. A little later, he drops his fork on the floor. "How clumsy," he says, looking at me. "Would you get a clean fork for me?" I give him another fork and then bend down to pick up the one he dropped. He rubs his leg against my body. I jump up and quickly move to the other side of the room. He smiles and continues to watch me.

I see Frau Jurgen looking at him and then at me. I hope she doesn't think I like him watching me.

As soon as the meal is over, I go to the kitchen to clean up. Marthe can clear the table. I don't want to be near that soldier. Someone walks into the room behind me. I turn, thinking it's Marthe. I start to smile. I stop when I see it's the soldier. He looks around. "We're alone," he says. "Good."

He walks toward me. I want to move away from him, but there's no place to go. He puts his arms on either side of me, holding me against the worktable. He rubs his body against mine. I can feel a hardness rising between his legs. I'm so scared I'm shaking.

He laughs. It's the sound the soldiers made when they raped the girl in the desert. It's an ugly sound. Like a hyena crying.

"There's no reason to be frightened," he says quietly. "I think you're beautiful. I want to show you how you make me feel." He bends down until his mouth covers mine. He pushes his tongue between my lips. I bite down as hard as I can. He cries out and slaps my face. Hard. I scream and scream and scream.

He slaps me again. "You little – "

"That's enough." Frau Jurgen's voice is cold and hard. Like iron.

The man backs away. "She – "

Frau Jurgen silences him. "Petronella, go to your room. And you" – she looks at the soldier as if he were a snake – "you get out of my house. Now."

I run to my room, holding my cheek where the soldier hit me. No one has ever hit me. It hurts more than anything I can remember. Marthe is right behind me. "Let me see, Penee." She gently pulls my hand away from my face. She shakes her head. "I'll be right back."

She comes back with a piece of uncooked meat. "Hold this to your cheek. It will take the sting away." She makes me lie down. "You rest. I'll be back after I've cleaned everything up."

I lie on my bed, watching the sunlight fade with the day. I'm scared. Scared that the soldier will try to hurt me again. Scared that Frau Jurgen will blame me for what happened. That she'll think I wanted the soldier to touch me. I'm afraid she'll make me leave. I don't want to lose another home. I bury my head in my pillow and cry.

I'm almost asleep when Marthe returns. She's not alone. Frau Jurgen is with her. "Sit up, Petronella. Let me look at your face," Frau Jurgen says. She holds up a lamp. I see anger in her eyes. I don't want her to be angry with me. She rubs her fingers over my cheek. Her touch hurts. I try not to pull away.

"It's swollen," she says. "But your jaw isn't broken. Open your mouth."

I do as she says. She holds the light closer so she can see inside my mouth. "And no broken teeth. Did he touch you anywhere else?"

I shake my head and start crying again.

"Hush," she says. "There's nothing to cry about."

"But I don't want you to send me away," I say. I wipe the tears from my eyes.

She sits on the bed beside me. "No one is sending you anywhere. This wasn't your fault, Petronella. I don't blame you. But you must be more careful. I'm not always going to be there to protect you. Do you understand?"

I nod my head slowly. "I'll go into the veld and get more of the poison plant to rub on my skin," I tell her. "Then the soldiers will leave me alone."

Frau Jurgen smiles. It's a small smile. But it's the first smile I've seen on her face.

"You don't need to do that again," she says. "From now on, you'll wear more petticoats under your dress. Lots of them. That will keep you safer."

The next morning, Marthe helps me dress. She gives me more and more petticoats until I have seventeen under my dress. They're very hot and heavy. Marthe laughs when she sees me walk. "Look," she says. She points to a mirror. I see a very fat Petronella. The skinny Jahohora is gone.

* * * * *

Frau Jurgen decides I must learn to read and write the words of the white people. I don't know why I need to. I have no one to write letters to, and I'm too busy to read books. But if she wants me to learn, I will. I sit with her when she teaches her children, Johanna and Lukas. They think it's funny that they know more than I do. They make it a game to test me on my words and numbers.

Frau Jurgen ends the class early today. "We'll have a guest for dinner tonight," she tells me. "He's a doctor who used to be a German soldier. I want you to help Marthe serve."

I shake my head. Ever since the soldier hit me, Frau Jurgen lets me go to my room whenever strange men come to the house.

"It's time for you to get over your fear," she says. "Herr Jurgen says Doctor Wolf is a good man. He won't hurt you."

I don't mind helping Marthe prepare the food in the kitchen. It's just the two of us. But when it's time to serve, my belly feels funny. My hands shake as I smooth my skirt over my many petticoats and tighten the kerchief wrapped around my hair. Marthe smiles at me. "You'll be all right," she says. "I won't leave you alone."

My hands are still shaking when I pick up a heavy tray of meat. I hope I don't drop it. I carry it close to my chest and walk very slowly into the dining room. I set the tray on the table and look up – right into the dark eyes of the Jurgen's guest. My heart beats loudly. I know those eyes. But I don't know the face. I quickly look away. My whole body feels like it's shaking as I cut the meat and serve the Jurgens and their guest. The man thanks me and then turns to talk to Herr Jurgen.

At the sound of his voice, I run from the room. I lean against the wall so I can listen to him without staring. I want to hear his voice rising and falling like Tate's when he talks to the ancestors. "Petronella!" Frau Jurgen comes out after me. "That is no way to behave. You've got to put this fear behind you. What must Doctor Wolf think?"

I hang my head. How can I tell her I'm not scared? That I could never be scared of this man? I didn't run out of the room because I was afraid. It was because I was excited. If this man is who I think he is, I owe him my life. I don't know how to tell Frau Jurgen what I'm feeling. "I'm sorry," I say instead.

I keep my head lowered as I quietly follow her back into the dining room. I feel the man's eyes watching me as I finish serving everyone. Does he know me? I stand back as the Jurgens and their guest eat. Whenever he's not looking, I watch him. His face is fuller, and the hair on his face is shorter and thicker. But I'm sure he's the one. He's the snake hunter.

I wake early in the morning and look out the window in my room. I can see the snake hunter. He wraps a leather strap to his left arm and another one around his head. He puts a blue and white cloth around his shoulders. He rocks back and forth. He's talking, but there's no one to hear him. I smile. He's talking to his ancestors. I pick up the jar he gave me in the desert. I tie it around my neck and hurry down to make breakfast. I wear the lavender jar all through breakfast. It hangs down when I serve the Jurgens and their guest. But he doesn't look at it.

After breakfast, I pack a bundle of food for the snake hunter. He will have to ride far before he comes to another house. I see him saddling his horse, so I hurry outside. He looks up and smiles. I feel very shy as I give him the food. He smiles again and puts it in a pouch tied to his saddle. I try to think of words that will make the snake hunter recognize me. I want him to know who I am. I want him to know I remember him. But he's getting on his horse. He's going to ride away. I have to do something quickly. I pull at his shirtsleeve. He sits in the saddle and looks down at me. I untie the leather string that's around my neck and give the jar to him. He looks at the jar and then down at me.

"*Mukuru ngakare punaove*," I say softly. It's my prayer for him.

His eyes open wide as he looks at me closer. He puts the jar in his pocket and pats it. A big smile covers his face. He remembers me. That makes me happy.

"Thank you, Petronella," he says. "That's a good name for you – the little rock that endured the desert."

THE POSTMAN

It is almost the rainy season. Marthe is very excited. The postman is coming. He'll have church services in the Jurgens' field for the Herero and Nama from all the farms near Otjiwarongo. "It will be like a big feast," she says.

We're busy for many days before the postman arrives. Frau Jurgen wants us to make lots and lots of food for the services. "The Africans need full bellies so they can listen to the Word of the Lord," she says.

"What's the Word of the Lord?" I ask.

She seems surprised. "It's the Bible. It's the most important word there is. It's why I want you to know how to read. I want you to be able to read the Bible for yourself."

By the time the postman comes, I'm as excited as Marthe. I can't wait to meet this man everyone talks about. I'm surprised when I see him. He's old. Not as old as Tjikuume, but older than Tate. He moves slowly and stiffly. His eyes are kind, but sad. The hardness of his life shows. Until he smiles. Then all I see is goodness.

He sits down with me the night before the church services are to begin. "It's good to meet you, Petronella." He smiles at me. "Marthe tells me you are the daughter of Mutihu, the healer."

I nod. "Do you know Tate?" I ask.

"I met him many years ago in the chief's village. He was a wise and good man."

"Do you know what happened to him and Mama?" I almost hope he doesn't. As long as I don't know for sure, I can think that some day I'll find them.

Kukuri – that's the postman's name – looks at me sadly. "The soldiers were hiding by a waterhole. When Mutihu and the others went to get water, the soldiers killed them."

"What about Karemarama and Tuaekua Ehi and all the others?"

"The soldiers climbed the mountain and killed them all," he tells me gently.

I swallow hard. I knew they were dead. But hearing it makes it real. I don't want to believe him. "How do you know these things?" I ask.

"I learned of them from Vijanda."

"Vijanda? He's alive?! Where is he?"

Kukuri puts his hand on my arm. "I met Vijanda in the death camp at Shark Island. He told me about the ambush at the waterhole. He escaped. After hiding for several days, he went to the top of the mountain. He found the others and buried them. He stayed on the mountain for a long time. When he came down, the soldiers made him a prisoner and sent him to the death camp." His eyes look into the distance. "Shark Island is a horrible place. No one leaves it alive."

"You did."

He looks down at the ground. "That is my sin," he says sadly. "I asked to go to Shark Island – not as a prisoner, but as a missionary. But I wasn't strong enough in my faith to die there with my brothers and sisters. There was so much death. People starving. And freezing. And working until they dropped. And when they died, their bodies were thrown into the great river for the sharks. Then they were forgotten. As if they had never lived. I couldn't take it. I had to leave."

It's hard to sleep that night. I think about Kukuri's words. And how my family was killed. I should have gone back to the Okavaka instead of trying to follow Maharero into the Omaheke. I would have found Vijanda. If I had been with him, maybe he wouldn't have left the mountain. And he wouldn't have been sent to the death camp.

Tears fill my eyes. I can finally cry. For Mama and Tate. For Ramata and Karemarama. For Vijanda, Tuaekua Ehi, and Karikuta. For Uapiruka and the children we will never have together. I cry for the ancestors who've been forgotten. For all the Herero who died in the Omaheke and the death camps. And for the few, like me, who survived, to wander through life in a land that's no longer ours.

I think about the years I walked through the veld, feeling so alone. But I had hope then that someday, somewhere I would find my family. That hope died with Kukuri's words. Now, I am truly alone.

A NEW GENERATION

The next time the postman comes, he has more news for me. The Jurgens think it's time for me to marry. And he has found someone for me – Fredrich Kandija Kandukira, a Herero man Kukuri is training to be a traveling preacher. "Herr Jurgen has met him and approves," Kukuri tells me. "Fredrich will be a good father to your children."

I smile at the old joke. "But I'm already promised," I say. "To my cousin Uapiruka."

"Uapiruka is not here," he tells me gently. "You must move on with your life, Petronella. It is what your parents would want."

"I don't know this Fredrich. He's not of my mother's clan."

"In all my travels, you are the only one of your mother's clan I have met or heard about – other than Vijanda," Kukuri says. He looks around to make sure no one else is listening before he speaks again. "The Herero are too small in number for us to hold to the old ways of marriage. The young people who survived – like you and Fredrich – must marry outside your clans if we are to become strong again. You must do this for your family, and for our people."

I think about Kukuri's words. There's wisdom in them. "Yes," I say. "I'll marry Fredrich. And we will have children to rebuild our houses."

And so I become Mama Penee, the wife of Fredrich Kandija Kandukira, the traveling preacher. Together with the other survivors, we raise up a new generation of Herero. A generation without a yesterday. A generation born into a land of strangers.

My children have no tjikuume to name them and give them their first cow, no tjikuu to teach them praise songs or the way of the ancestors. They have no cousins, no uncles, no aunties.

There is no holy fire outside our little square house where the ancestors wait to talk with us at dusk and morning twilight.

My children go to the missionary school where they are taught about Njambi Karunga, the creator of all. They also are taught that Njambi created the Herero to work for the white man. I look at a picture in my son's schoolbook. It shows a white overseer telling the black workers what to do. I flip through the pages. Every picture is the same. Every word teaches that a good Herero is one who works hard for the white man. There are no pictures of Herero taking care of their own cattle. No pictures of Herero families living and playing together. No words saying the Herero were once a free people who cared for their own land and decided their own tomorrow.

In their schoolbooks, my children's tomorrow is already written. Like their tate, my sons will be sent to work in the white labor camps far, far away. And my daughter, like me, will clean the white man's house and raise his children.

I put the book down. It makes me sad. This is not the world I want for my children and grandchildren. But what can I do? I'm one woman. I close my eyes to look back over my yesterdays, to find the wisdom of my ancestors. But it's not Mama, or Tjikuu, or any of the others from my family who visit my thoughts. Instead, it's the two women sitting by the fire in the Omaheke. "Someone must live to tell our story," they tell me. "You must teach your children and grandchildren the way of the Herero. It is why you lived when so many others died."

And so I teach my children, and their children after them, about Njambi Karunga calling the first mamas and tates from the omumborombonga tree. About the Herero wisely choosing the cattle. About the days before the white people, when Hereroland belonged to the Herero. About their ancestors and the price they paid when they tried to keep their land. I teach my children, and their children after them, to walk tall, with their heads held high. Yes, today they may be the white man's servants. But they are Herero. Someday they will be free again. And when that tomorrow comes, they must know how to think, and live, like a free people.

* * * * *

It's been many, many years since the postman told me the fate of my family. Even though I believe him, there are moments when I still let myself think, "What if he was wrong? What if Vijanda wasn't the only one who escaped?" I know my family is gone, but I find myself looking at faces, hoping to see a cousin, a brother, or an uncle or auntie. Sometimes, I think I see someone

I know. I look again and see only a stranger. The disappointment hurts as much today as it did all those years ago when Kukuri first told me what I already knew to be the truth.

My search was a slow one when my children were growing up. My days were filled from the sun's waking to its sleeping with working for the Jurgens and raising my children. But on those rare days when I went into Otjiwarongo, I looked at every Herero face, hoping to find someone from my past. And when we moved to Okakarara so we could have cattle once again, I thought there would be more faces to search. But Okakarara is a tiny village far from the other settlements in the Waterberg Native Reserve. I quickly learn all the faces. There's no one from yesterday.

It's Friday, the best day of the week. It's the day my grandsons come home from school. For two whole days, I'll have them to myself. For two whole days, I will not be alone. Even though Fredrich is too old and weak to work in the labor camps now, he's rarely home. He finally does what Kukuri trained him to do all those years ago, going from one settlement to the next, preaching the Christian Gospel. Sometimes I go with him. Not because I want to hear him preach. But because I want to see new faces.

I'm sitting on the ground outside our little house, my bright patched skirt spread out around me. Little Kapombo sits on my skirt, snuggling up close to me. "Tjikuu," he asks me, "when are Mama and Tate coming home?"

"Soon," I tell him. I know it's a lie. His tate works far, far away in the labor camps in South Africa. And his mother – my daughter – works for a German family in a village a few days' walk from here.

I hear a wagon bumping over the rough ground. I look up. We get few wagons in Okakarara. I'm surprised to see Fredrich driving the oxen.

"What are you doing?" I ask as he stops the wagon in front of our house.

"I've been asked to go to Otjimbingwe. I thought you might like to come with me," he says. Otjimbingwe? That was the village of our chief. I haven't been there since I was a girl.

Maybe Tate's cousin is still there. Or his cousin's children. "Of course I want to come with you," I tell Fredrich.

I ask a neighbor to watch my grandsons and milk my cows. I quickly pack a few things for the trip. I smile when I catch myself singing the old praise songs. As we bump across the veld in the wagon, my excitement grows. But I remind myself of Kukuri's words, preparing for more disappointment.

Otjimbingwe is not the village I remember. Its roads are filled with white people driving cars and trucks. Herero hurry to get out of their way. There are electric lines, and lots of big houses and shops. But some things haven't changed. I see two white policemen holding a Herero down on a whipping bench. A small group of whites and Herero gather to watch the flogging.

"What did he do?" Fredrich asks a Herero standing near the crowd.

"He was speaking English," the man says.

Fredrich pulls me away from the crowd as the flogging begins. Under South African rule, Herero can speak German or Afrikaans. And we can speak our tribal languages. But we cannot speak English. That's a special language only for the white people. I hear the man's screams and the slap of the whip as Fredrich and I walk away.

Fredrich goes into a shop that sells to Herero. I wait outside. There's so much I want to see. I stand straight and tall, with my good dress covering my many petticoats. I look across the road to where a Herero man is loading a wagon. Even though he's older, he's very strong. Something about the way he moves reminds me of Tate. His wagon loaded, the man turns briefly toward me. I see his face.

"Ramata!" The name comes to my lips before I think. I run across the street, ignoring the cars and wagons. I'm afraid that if I don't hurry, my brother's face will fade into that of a stranger.

The man stops and stares at me. I search his face. There's no recognition in his eyes. My run turns to a walk. I say the name again. It's more a question than a greeting.

"Do I know you?" he asks.

"You are Ramata Eliphas Mutihu?"

He nods.

I want to run to him and hug him and never let him go. But I hang back.

"Penee!" Fredrich calls to me as he crosses the road. He looks from me to Ramata. "Is this man bothering you?" he asks.

I laugh. "No," I say. "This is my brother."

Ramata stares at me. "Jahohora?" he whispers.

I run into his open arms. We hold each other tightly. There are tears. Lots of tears. But no words. At last, we break apart. "How?" we both ask at the same time.

I tell him my story – my escape from the mountain, my journey into the desert, my search for our family.

He tells a similar story. He was watching the cows in the clearing when he heard the shots that killed our parents. Like Tate told him to, he ran and hid. After many days, he came back. He found the bodies of Mama and Tate and the others. In the darkness of the night, he buried them near the waterhole. The next day, he climbed the mountain. He found Vijanda sitting quietly beside the grave he had dug. "The soldiers killed them all," Vijanda told him. "Even the baby."

Ramata stayed on the mountain with Vijanda for many days. The deaths of Tuaekua Ehi and Karikuta made Vijanda like a crazy man. Sometimes he talked about killing the soldiers. Other times, he wanted to find his parents and join Maharero. And there were times when he acted as if Ramata wasn't there.

is ready

When Ramata woke one day, Vijanda was gone. Ramata walked to the edge of the mountain and looked across the veld. But he could see no sign of Vijanda. Then he searched the mountain. Thinking Vijanda might have gone back to his village, Ramata went there. The village had been burned.

"What about Tjikuu?" I ask.

Ramata shakes his head. "All I found were burned bones. I buried them beside Tjikuume."

Ramata continued to our village. It had been burned, too. He was returning to the mountaintop when a farmer found him. The farmer was going to give him to the soldiers, but Ramata talked the man into letting him work on his farm.

I stay with Ramata until Fredrich is done with his preaching. It's hard to leave my brother when I've just found him. As Ramata hugs me goodbye, he promises to visit me soon. "We can't lose each other again," he says. "We have already lost too much."

* * * * *

It's the last day of school for the boys, so I'm cooking their favorite meal over the fire. Kapombo and Luther run into the yard and throw down their bookbags. They look at me and grin, as if they have the biggest secret in the world. "What are you smiling about?" I ask them. "You can't be this happy just because school is out."

Kapombo shakes his head and smiles even bigger. "It's a surprise, Tjikuu. A special surprise."

"A surprise? For whom?" I ask.

"For you!" Luther shouts. He starts to tell me more and then puts his hand over his mouth. I turn around and see Jesaiah behind me. He's shaking his head at his younger brothers. He stops when he sees me looking at him.

"What are you boys up to?" I ask him.

"Nothing, Tjikuu." Jesaiah was never a good liar. The boys run off to play before I can ask them more questions. I turn back to my cooking.

"If it weren't for that dress you're wearing, you'd look just like Tjikuu cooking over that fire," a voice says behind me.

Ramata! I spin around to see my brother standing next to the house. My grandsons are peeking around the corner. So this was their surprise!

"Did you know about this?" I ask Fredrich when he joins us later for dinner.

He smiles in that quiet way he has. Then he looks at Ramata. "Have you told her yet?"

"Told me what?" I glance suspiciously from my husband to my brother.

Ramata holds up several travel passes. "Tomorrow, we're going on a trip in my wagon. You, me, Martin, and the boys."

"Martin? But he's working in the mines in South Africa." I look at Fredrich. "And what about you? Aren't you coming?"

"One question at a time," Fredrich says. "Martin should be home late tonight. He got leave so he can go on this trip with you. And, no, I'm not going. I have to meet with the bishop. Besides, this is a trip you need to make with your brother and the boys."

"Where are we going?"

"To the Okavaka," Ramata says quietly.

We set out before the sun wakes the next morning. My son and grandsons stretch out in the back of the wagon. I sit on the driver's perch with my brother. We are silent as the oxen pull the wagon across the veld. No words are needed. Sitting next to each other after all these years is enough.

When Ramata is ready to speak, he says, "I should have asked you before.... Are you all right with going back?"

"Yes," I say. "I've wanted to for many years. But I wasn't sure I'd find it. That was so long ago." I look across the veld, seeing many yesterdays. "What about you? Have you been back?"

He shakes his head. "I was afraid to go. I wasn't sure I was strong enough." He wipes the tears from his eyes. "But it's time ... now that I've found you."

We sit arm in arm as the wagon bounces over the veld, sharing our memories. Our tears flow freely as we approach the waterhole at the base of the Okavaka.

Ramata helps me down from the wagon and leads me to a spot covered with rocks. Stooped with age and grief, we stand before the grave of our parents. My son and grandsons stand beside us as Ramata and I, through our tears, tell them of Mutihu and Tutejuva. We tell them how they died so their children, and their children's children, could live.

Ramata and Martin go to the wagon and return with the horns of several cattle. They place the horns on the grave. It is now a proper burial site for an important healer of the Herero.

"Do you want to go to the top?" Ramata asks.

"Yes!" the boys shout.

I shake my head. "If you think it was hard for Mama Uajoroka to climb that mountain, just imagine me trying to crawl up it in this dress and all these petticoats." Ramata and I both laugh at the memory of Auntie crawling up the path and threatening to make Tate or Uncle Kozondanda carry her up.

"You'll be all right down here by yourself?" Ramata asks, as he slings his pack across his back. "We won't be back until tomorrow. But there's plenty of food and blankets in the wagon for you."

I laugh. "If I could survive two years in the desert, I'm sure I'll be all right for one night in the wagon."

When they come down the mountain the next day, the boys beg to go on to the Waterberg. Ramata looks questioningly at me.

"Why not? It's good for them to learn their history," I say. "They won't get it at the white man's school."

So we journey on, bouncing in the wagon as its wheels slip into the old ruts that still scar the veld. As we come to the broad plain that spreads beneath the towering rocks of the Waterberg, I once again see the soldiers blink their star words across the night sky. I watch the flashes of lightning and hear the rolling thunder of the big guns. All those yesterdays ago, I saw it from the safety of the Okavaka, not understanding the death the lightning and thunder brought. Today, I tell my grandsons of the sacrifices of Mama Uaporimana and the other eighteen women who gave their babies' milk to the warriors so the Herero nation could live a few days longer. I tell them of that day that was the beginning of the end of a free people.

The boys cut through my memories, begging to explore the cemetery with its engraved headstones and crosses marking the graves of German soldiers. They read the red stone monument memorializing the German lives that were lost at the Waterberg.

"Tjikuu, where is the monument for the Herero?" Jesaiah asks.

"Here," I say, placing my hand on my heart. "And here. And here. And here." I put my hand on each of my grandsons' hearts. "You must never forget."

We stop at Ramata's house before going home to Okakarara. He has one more surprise for me.

He gets his pack from the wagon and sets it on the ground in front of his small square house. He pulls two pieces of wood from the pack. One is crumbling with age and ash. The other is an old branch of the omumborombonga tree. "They're from the mountaintop," he says quietly. "From our holy fire."

We sit around the fire circle as Ramata strikes Mama's firestones, sparking a flame with dried grass in a hollow branch. The holy fire comes to life as the sun slips behind the mountains. Ramata drinks from a gourd and spits three times. He hands the gourd to me. I drink and spit and pass it on to Martin and then to my grandsons.

Ramata turns to the fire. He tells the ancestors that he, Ramata Eliphas Mutihu, the son of Mutihu, the healer, and Tutejuva, is now the keeper of the fire. "It has been many years since we gathered at the fire of Mutihu," he says. "But we have not forgotten you. Even though our house has been diminished, we are still here." He looks at my grandsons. "And we will be here for many tomorrows."

I sit tall as Ramata says my name, "Jahohora, daughter of Mutihu and Tutejuva." Then he introduces my son and my grandsons to the ancestors.

Tears run down my cheeks as yesterday meets tomorrow. I am happy. Very, very happy. The circle of my life is complete.

Kov

WAKING TO LIFE

I'm trapped in a nightmare that I can't wake up from. One minute, fire is burning through my veins, consuming my organs. The next, ice floes freeze me from the inside out. And everywhere I turn is death. I walk chest-high in mutilated black bodies. In front of me, hooded skeletons hang from ropes. A wind kicks up, driving the sand into my eyes. I gag at the nauseating smell of rotting flesh assaulting my nostrils. I hear Hanna calling my name, but her voice gets fainter and fainter as it's lost in the thunder of artillery. A cannon ball crashes to the ground, splintering a pile of corpses into a shower of disjointed bones.

Something moist pushes against my cracked lips. I taste it, trying to remember what it is. Water! I swallow thirstily. The cool trickle feels like the sharp thorns of the bramble as it courses down my throat. I push it away. Someone holds up my head, forcing me to drink. I struggle as if I'm drowning. Voices buzz around me, their words a senseless hum. Once again, I hear Hanna in the distance, but the voices continue to crowd around me, overpowering her faint call.

"Be quiet!" I scream, covering my ears with my hands. The voices ignore me as if I am nothing.

I open my eyes to blurred images; the lines and colors bump into each other in a splash of blurred shapes. I try to make sense of the figures hovering about me, to attach the sounds I hear to some of the images. But it takes too much effort. I close my eyes and let the darkness envelope me once again.

I'm back home, smiling as I watch Hanna rocking David in Mama's old wooden rocker. A loud knock rattles the door. I get up just as three soldiers burst through the door, their bayoneted guns drawn. "What do you want?" I ask, trying to keep my voice calm.

"You are Jews." It is a statement, not a question.

"We are good Germans," I say.

"You're Jews." One of the soldiers spits on the floor as another one rips the mezuzah from the doorpost. The commanding officer points his gun at my chest.

"Yes, but we are good Germans. I'm an army doctor." I look down, surprised to see that I'm wearing my dress uniform. "See?" I say, pointing to the insignia of the snake wrapped around a pole.

"You make a mockery of that uniform," the officer says as he rips the insignia from my sleeve.

I back up, shielding Hanna and the baby. The two other soldiers search the house, overturning tables and throwing books and dishes. Hanna clutches at the back of my jacket as her china crashes to the floor.

"What do you want?" I repeat.

"We have orders to purge the Fatherland of all inferior races. We need more room for good Germans," the officer tells me.

"But we're good Germans," I protest.

"You're Jews. You know you're not wanted here, yet you insist on staying. Taking up space and jobs that belong to Germans." The officer looks inquiringly at the soldiers who have finished ransacking our small quarters.

"Nothing of value here," one of them says, "except these tin soldiers." He's examining the pieces of Papa's collection. He puts a few of them carefully into a pack.

"Put those back," I demand. "My father made those." Again, Hanna tugs at my jacket.

"Your father did nice work for a Jew," the soldier says derisively as he packs up the rest of the collection. He looks around disdainfully. "We're finished here."

I hear the gunshot just before the bullet tears through my abdomen. An unbelievable pain sears me as I drop to the floor. I try to stanch the blood with my hands.

"Kov!" Hanna screams. David cries as Hanna moves toward me. But one of the soldiers restrains her. The other tears David from her arms and throws him to the floor, stomping on him until his cries stop. Hanna sobs, watching helplessly as David's blood mingles with mine on the floor. Her sobs turn to anger as the soldier who's holding her begins to grope her. She kicks him and struggles violently. He slaps her, laughing when I try to reach her. I don't have the strength to stand up, let alone protect my family. I lose consciousness as the beasts begin to rape my wife.

I come to in the cemetery where Papa now rests beside Mama beneath the snow. I brush away a tear as I look at his tombstone. I should have been here when he died. I had no business going off to South West Africa. The earth shifts beneath me. I lean against the headstone to steady myself, but it breaks in half. I lose my balance and fall to the ground. Instead of landing in the blanket of snow, I crash into a tangle of bones and rotting corpses. I scream as I try to get up. But the more I struggle, the deeper I fall. The bones bury me, blocking out the gray light of winter. Someone grasps my arm.

"Yaakov, what are you doing here?" It's Papa. As my eyes adjust to the darkness, I make out his shape. "It is not your time for She'ol."

"They've killed me, Papa." I hold up my blood-soaked hand.

Papa shakes his head. "They can't kill your soul unless you let them. Open your eyes, my son. You don't belong here. Not now. Reclaim your life. Go back to Hanna and David."

"I don't deserve to live, Papa. I abandoned my family."

"Nonsense," his face is next to mine, his dark eyes pierce me with their intensity. "It takes courage to live in the midst of hate. And it requires strength to keep that hatred from eating your soul. You have both within you, son. You must tap into them, letting them grow and flourish from the inside out. In doing so, you will find atonement. Now, get on with your life."

"But. . . ."

Papa puts his finger to his lips. "There are no excuses. Live the life God has blessed you with. Go."

Papa's shape disappears into the inky blackness of the grave. "I will look for you in Olam Ha-Ba," he calls to me faintly.

"In the World to Come," I whisper in agreement. I open my eyes, and a bright light washes over me.

"Kov, can you hear me?"

I look up into Alexander's concerned face. "Where am I?" I whisper.

"You're back with the living," he responds. "I was afraid we'd lost you." I try to sit, but he gently pushes me back. "Take it easy. You're very weak."

Slowly, I get my bearings. I'm on a real bed in some kind of hospital. And everything is clean. I look at Alexander questioningly.

"You're in the hospital in Windhük. You've been here for more than a month," he informs me.

"A month?" I shake my head in disbelief. "What are you doing here? Is the war over?"

"I was assigned here when the Herero were defeated. The uprising is over, but the soldiers are rounding up what remains of the enemy and sending them to concentration camps."

"Concentration camps?" The term is new to me.

"They're prison camps modeled after the ones the English used in the Boer Wars. We're basically 'concentrating' hundreds, if not thousands, of Herero into small prison camps here in Windhük and along the coast," he tells me as he checks my pulse.

"I thought General von Trotha said the Herero would be killed if they returned."

"He did. But there was a bit of an uproar about it because the settlers were being denied their cheap labor. So the Kaiser ordered Trotha to set up concentration camps instead." Alexander feels my brow. "That's enough talk for now. You need to rest."

The next day, Alexander delivers a pile of letters from Hanna. I look at them in surprise. "I thought you were going to tell her I had died."

He busies himself checking on Max Bayer, the patient in the next bed. "That was the request of a fevered mind," he mumbles. "I know how much you love her."

I push the letters away. I can't deal with them yet.

I spend the next few weeks eating and sleeping and building my strength. I also catch up on the news with Max. Although he served as a captain in General von Trotha's division, I hadn't really talked with him until now. He was sent to the hospital to recover from typhus; then the doctors discovered he had a heart condition. Now, he's recuperating so he can go home.

"I wish I could stay here to see this thing out," Max tells me.

"What do you mean?" I ask. "I thought the war was pretty much over."

"The Herero uprising has ended. But now the Witboois and the other Nama tribes are revolting. They're smaller, so it shouldn't last too much longer." He sighs. "I'm looking forward to getting home. But I'd like to finish what I started."

"What are you going to do when you go home?" I can't bring myself to even say the word Germany.

"I hope to remain in the military," he said. "I guess it's in my blood. My father was a major in the Prussian army. I also want to write."

I quirk an eyebrow.

He smiles sheepishly. "I'd like to write about my experiences here. What about you? Are you going to stay in the army?"

"No, I've learned that army life is definitely not for me."

"So you will get a post in a nice hospital back home?"

I hesitate before answering. "I haven't figured out yet what I'm going to do," I say softly. "But I'm not planning on returning home." It's the first time I've voiced my intentions.

"What about your family? Or am I prying too much?"

I look down at the white bed sheet. My silence is answer enough.

* * * * *

My body is beginning to recover, but my soul remains torn. As soon as I'm able, I take daily walks around the small hospital and out into the so-called garden. I'm reminded of my walk with Hanna through the lush gardens at Juliusspital that fateful day when she agreed to be my wife. It seems so long ago – more like a wonderful book I read than something that really happened to me. I was a different man back then. A young, brash know-it-all who thought the world would mold itself to his bidding.

As I walk, I look for answers, or at least a little clarity. I'm sure of two things: I love Hanna so much it hurts. And I can never live in Germany again. So how do I reconcile these two truths?

It's not that I hate Germany. But I've come to realize Papa was right. Germany is not – and never can be – my Fatherland. Yes, I have some great friends who are Germans. And there are German leaders, like August Bebel, who speak out against the dangers of a racial pride that flows forward from the Crusades to be fueled by today's "science" of eugenics. A pride that's the foundation of a national policy that says all other people, by divine right, are to be valued only for their service to the German empire. And if their best service is extermination, so be it.

This time it was the Herero and the Nama. How do I know that, in the future, it won't be the Jews again?

I can't take that risk nor, by my presence, condone such a
policy and the actions that spill from it. My months in the desert
have taught me that. But if I don't return to Germany, where do
I go? Although the beauty of the African desert has grown on me,
staying in South West Africa would be as bad as going home. It's
now German soil.

I could explore other parts of Africa. Perhaps some of the English areas like Cape Town, Walvis Bay, or even Bechuanaland.
But from what I've heard, these are still wild areas that can take
their toll on the hardiest of people. How can I ask Hanna to give
up the comforts of home? To leave her family? What do I have
to offer her other than a broken man? I don't have the right to
demand that she leave everything that's dear to her to join me in
a foreign land where white women are scarce and Jews are even
more of a rarity.

Yet I can't imagine my life without her. She's my future. And
I fear for her and David, who's growing up in a country that
will never accept him. Like Papa, I want to spare my son the
disillusionment of the false hope that it can be otherwise.

Alexander joins me in the garden. I wish I could share my
thoughts with him. But I don't think he'd understand. He's still
blinded by hope.

I finally begin to read Hanna's letters. They're filled with her
love and the antics of our son. His first tooth is coming in. He's
beginning to crawl. He can say "Mama." I pore over her words,
which are filled with the normalcy my life lacks. Her days are
spent chasing after David, working in the garden, and canning
vegetables.

She also has found a trove of tin figures Papa had made,
along with notes on how to paint them. She plans to finish
them, keeping some of them for David and selling the rest to
supplement my military pay. "I can see you frowning right now
at the thought of your wife working," she writes. "This isn't a
financial necessity; it's a joy. Painting these little soldiers Papa
made brings me closer to him and to you. Besides, I'm trying very
hard to be a woman of valor." I smile at her reference to Proverbs
31, which Papa recited to Mama every Friday night before the
Shabbat meal.

After reading Hanna's letters, I walk in the garden, thinking
about how I should respond. I must let her know what's in my

heart. I owe her that. But I can't find the words to explain my feelings. Instead, a restlessness falls upon me. And with it, the need to escape the sterile walls of the hospital, if only for a few hours.

Dressed in my uniform, and with Alexander's stern orders not to overexert echoing in my head, I leave the confines of the hospital for a leisurely walk through Windhük. Without thinking, I head up the hill toward Alte Feste. The walled fort gleams white in the summer sun, like a jewel crowning the growing city. My trek up the hill is interrupted by the sight of an encampment of at least a hundred hovels made of sacking and salvaged planks, all surrounded by a double strand of barbed wire. A few soldiers guard the only entrance. This shantytown of pontoks must be the concentration camp. It sits in sharp contrast to the grand building taking place throughout the town.

I watch in astonishment as a heavy wagon rolls slowly toward the entrance. Instead of oxen, a line of half naked Herero women pull it. Still weakened from their flight into the desert, the women don't look strong enough to push a baby pram, let alone pull the overloaded wagon. As they reach the entrance, one of the women trips on a rock and falls. A soldier rushes forward, his sjambok raised high. The other women step passively out of the way to avoid the sting of the whip as it lashes repeatedly against their fallen companion. They look at anything but the skeletal woman lying motionless in the dirt as the soldier yells and beats her.

I see her blood pooling in the dust and wonder why she isn't screaming in pain. The only reason that comes to mind is that she's already a shade of death. There's not much more the soldier can do to her.

Without thinking, I step up to him and catch his arm. "That's enough," I say softly but firmly. I stare, unflinchingly, into his eyes, half expecting him to turn the sjambok on me.

Sweat beads on his forehead as he snarls at me. But apparently, he's had enough, too. He lowers the whip and looks around. The other women are watching him. To show he still has authority, he kicks the nearly lifeless body of the fallen woman out of the way and orders the others to get back to work. They grab hold of the rope and pull with what strength they have left.

As the wagon lurches forward out of the gate, I kneel beside the beaten woman. I pick up her arm to feel for a pulse, ignoring the curses of the soldier. It reminds me of the time I lifted the arm of a skeleton back in my early years of medical school so I could identify all the bones. The woman's pulse is so faint I can barely feel it. I try to lift her. Even though she has wasted away to almost nothing, I don't have the strength to carry her. Helplessly, I sit by her side as her last breaths make their escape, freeing her from further torture.

I shake my head, amazed at how the Herero are being treated. Then I notice the gallows in the camp. The corpses of several men hang awkwardly from the nooses. The extermination order may have been lifted, but we're still bent on destroying what's left of the Herero nation. Sickened by what I've seen, I retrace my steps to the hospital.

By the time I get back, I'm exhausted, both physically and emotionally. Alexander sees me as I limp through the door. He motions for an orderly to bring a wheelchair. I plop heavily into the chair without protest. Alexander follows me into the ward and helps the orderly lift me into the bed. He watches as I drink a little bit of water.

"I told you to take it easy, especially in this heat. You've probably set back your recovery by several days, if not weeks." He shakes his head. "It's true what they say about doctors being bad patients – at least in your case."

I wake hours later from a long nap, feeling slightly better. I reach for the glass of water on the little stand next to my bed, scattering Hanna's letters. I've got to write to her. I can't keep putting it off.

Max helps me prop up in bed and gives me a few sheets of paper and a fountain pen. "My dearest Hanna," I write. "Forgive my long silence. I've been laid up with typhus for a few months now. The fever was almost too much for my body, which was already exhausted, dehydrated, and malnourished from the trek through the desert. But I guess my time on this earth is not yet up. I'm recovering now and will be back on my feet soon.

"The best medicine I could get would be to hold you and our son. But that's not to be for at least several more months. Although my year of service is about over, doctors are still very much needed here. The Herero – those who have survived, that is – are coming in from the desert and being forced to live in filth in concentration camps. If they have any chance at life, they will need medical care. We...." I pause and scratch out the "we" before continuing. "I owe them that."

"My heart begs me to return to you, but my soul reminds me I have a debt I must pay to these people. I wish I could tell you when I'll be home, but after all I have witnessed, I'm not sure Germany can ever be my home again. Every time I think I've seen the worst man can do, I am proven wrong.

"I have sorely failed you, my Eshet chayil. You deserve so much more than what I have to offer. I will understand if the waiting grows too long and lonesome. Please, don't think you must be chained to an absent husband. Do what you think is best for you and David. *Rabot banot asu chayil v'at alit al kulanah.*"

A tear smudges the page as I assure her of my love and sign my name. I put the letter in an envelope, handing the pen back to Max. There, it's done. I've opened the door for Hanna to find a man worthy of her. While my heart breaks at the thought, part of me hopes she steps through that door. It would be a just punishment for my selfishness.

BACK AT WORK

It's with heartfelt sadness that I tell Max goodbye. He's finally strong enough to make the sea journey home. While I'm happy for him, I'll miss him. He has become a good friend. As he packs up his things, he asks me if there's anything he can take back to Hanna.

"I plan to do some traveling," he tells me. "It would be no trouble for me to stop in Fürth."

I give him the shawl I had bought for Hanna a year ago in Madeira. The bottle of wine I got for Papa is long gone.

His bags packed, Max gives me a firm handshake. "It was a pleasure meeting someone as principled as you," he says, looking me in the eye. "I hope someday you'll return home. The Fatherland needs men like you."

I smile. "Good luck with your writing. One of these days, I'll be reading a book by you, and I'll tell my children I knew the author."

Within a few days of Max's departure, I join the hospital staff. It's a temporary assignment until my next orders come through. It feels good to be working in a real hospital and to be caring for others instead of worrying only about myself. In my spare time, I volunteer at Eingeborene Lazarett, the "native hospital" set up next to Windhük's prison camp in response to the townspeople's concerns that infectious diseases will spread from the camp into the nearby neighborhoods.

Surrounded by thornbush fencing, the hospital is made up of a number of kraals in which the prisoners are separated by disease type. Inside each kraal are open-sided military tents and a bunch of pontoks, slapped together with wood, sacks, and corrugated iron. The biggest kraal is devoted to free native women and Damara and Ovambo workers. Even though these tribes have not risen in revolt, the colonial administrators are taking no chances. With the Herero all but decimated, the Damara and Ovambo are needed to build roads, railroads, and government buildings. The colonists fear that if they're not locked up, they would return home to their families and herds. And the colony can't prosper without forced labor.

While the "free" workers are a little healthier than the Herero prisoners, the biggest difference I see is their identification. The Herero are forced to wear metal tags, emblazoned with "G.H.," indicating they are Herero prisoners of war. Recognizing that those who escape might be able to remove the tags from around their necks, General von Trotha suggests tattooing identification on each Herero.

"We brand cattle," he says. "Why can't we tattoo the prisoners?" His staff officers protest the idea, saying it isn't practical.

The conditions in the camp worsen as hundreds of Herero are brought in. With no room to build more pontoks, thirty to fifty prisoners are forced to share each small hovel. Many of the Herero are hardly recognizable as human. Captured after months of barely surviving in the desert, they are mere skeletons. Young mothers, on the verge of death, hold their babies to their withered breasts in a vain effort to keep the little ones alive.

Despite their physical condition, the prisoners – men and women, old and young – are forced to carry loads heavier than them, from early morning to late at night, under the whips of the German overseers. On General von Trotha's orders, the only food they get is a handful of rice, salt, and water. They eat the rice raw as they have no pots to cook it in. Although the colonial government is making money by hiring the prisoners out to the railroad and settlers, Trotha insists that no resources can be drained for their care.

That attitude of neglect has turned the concentration camp into a cesspool of viruses that claims several lives a day and threatens the health of anyone who works here. Dysentery, influenza, pneumonia, scurvy, smallpox, syphilis, tuberculosis, venereal typhoid – it's all here. Death has become a way of life, whether by disease, exhaustion, or the gallows. The dead are carted out daily to be dumped in a mass grave outside of town.

Since the German doctors don't want the post, I volunteer for a full-time position, hoping I can bring a bit of humanity to the camp. It isn't easy. Brutality is routine in this place where the Herero are driven like cattle, fed like cattle, and buried like cattle.

I've just finished for the day and am heading out of the camp to return to my quarters. Hearing a baby cry, I turn around. Several frail Herero women are carrying heavy sacks of grain on their heads. One of them has the crying baby tied to her back. As the mother instinctively turns toward her baby, the load of grain shifts and the woman loses her balance. She falls to the ground, spilling the grain. Yelling angrily at her clumsiness, a corporal steps up and sjamboks both the mother and the baby for several minutes. The baby wails, but the mother, her eyes wide with fear, only whimpers. When the beating stops, she slowly struggles to her feet and raises the heavy load back onto her head. Fighting to conceal the pain, she continues her work.

Tears well up in my eyes as I turn away. I should have done something, I think as I walk back to my room. But what could I do? I'm no Moses. I can't take on the Pharaoh's guards. If I raise too much fuss, they might close down the hospital or send me back to Germany. What good would that do? The brutality would just continue, and there'd be no one here to soften the impact of the blows when the wounds become infected. No, I must go about my duties, doing what I can, and once again seeming to condone the atrocities with my silence.

A letter is waiting for me when I get back to my quarters. It's from Hanna. With trembling hands, I open it. "My beloved, I will be as honest with you as you always are with me." I stop, dreading her next words. I kick off my shoes and sit down on the bed, preparing myself for the worst. I take a deep breath and continue reading:

"It's not easy being separated from you or raising our child without his father. But as I reminded you in the gardens of Juliusspital, life is rarely easy for a Jew. You warned me then that we might have to be separated for years or live in a place far from Germany. Kov, home is not a place; it is you. Home, for me, will always be with you.

"I realize you have changed. How could you not? I've changed, too. Motherhood has a way of doing that. But my love for you has only deepened. If we must be separated for a few more months, or for several years, so be it. I will live embraced by our love and the knowledge that we will be together again."

Tears flow down my cheeks as Hanna's love uplifts me from across the miles. I hadn't realized how much I needed the steadfast assurance of that love.

My newfound optimism is challenged the next day when the soldiers bring in another group of Herero. Word quickly spreads through the town that there are a number of children among the new prisoners. Settlers and soldiers pour into the camp to inspect the children, especially the boys. They claim the healthiest ones to serve as their Bambusen. The young children cling to their mothers as the Germans pull them away. The mothers watch helplessly as their young sons and daughters leave the camp, knowing they will never see them again. The children are to become slaves to their German masters. At least they are spared the death of the camp, I remind myself.

I've heard stories about the Bambusen. Some of them are educated and treated well. But others are used harshly in their new homes. The attractive ones are often forced into the sex trade and are in demand in a thriving pornographic business.

I find myself having to turn a blind eye more and more as time passes. Soldiers and settlers have free access to the girls and women, who make up the largest portion of the concentration camp. Some of the girls get pregnant, but many develop gonorrhea, which they then spread to the few Herero men who manage to elude the gallows. Soon, most of them are sterile. General von Trotha welcomes the development; in his eyes, it's the continuation of his plan to exterminate the tribe.

With thousands of Herero packed into the confines of the Windhük camp, potential troublemakers and the strongest of the prisoners, along with many of the new arrivals, are sent on to the concentration camps in Swakopmund and Shark Island. I see the fear in their eyes when they learn their destination. While death is a reality at the Windhük camp, it is a near certainty at Swakopmund and especially at Shark Island, an outcrop of rock near Lüderitz buffeted by the harsh Atlantic winds.

In Windhük, there's some hope. The climate is more what the Herero are accustomed to. And if they escape, they're closer to their traditional lands. But Swakopmund and Shark Island are far removed from the interior Hereroland. And from what I hear, the German soldiers at those camps are as brutal as the weather.

News of the harsh conditions at the concentration camps has spread to Germany, but it's greeted more with curiosity than with protest. Hanna mentions it in her next letter. She has seen a postcard showing ten "Hottentots," as the Germans often call the Nama, being hung on a single gallows. I know which one she means. I've seen it in the stores in Windhük. The popular postcard shows some of the condemned men, nooses about their necks, standing stoically on packing cases as they wait for a soldier to kick the wooden boxes out from under their feet. Others writhe in the prolonged death struggle caused by the short drop. A German soldier tugs at the legs of one of the men in an effort to hasten death.

"What crime did these men commit?" Hanna asks. She mentions some of the other postcards she has heard about, like the pornographic ones of young Herero girls. "I don't understand the attitudes that encourage such pictures. Although I'm sure these images make the good German frauen uncomfortable, they laugh about them. It's as if these girls aren't human because they're of a different race.

"I mentioned this to Captain Bayer when he visited the other day. He chuckled and said I sounded just like my husband. He had the kindest words for you and spoke of your high principles. I must confess, I swelled with pride." She thanks me for the scarf and then tells me of a newspaper article questioning why the

German troops aren't following the Geneva Convention in their treatment of the Herero and Nama prisoners.

It's a good question. According to the Hague agreement, which the Kaiser signed a few years ago, only combatants can be confined to camps – and then only as an "indispensable measure of safety." That means women and children can't be treated as prisoners of war. The agreement also dictates how prisoners must be treated. They're to be paid regular wages for their labor. Their work can't be excessive or related to military operations. And they are to be housed, clothed, and fed on a par with the soldiers. If German soldiers were treated the same as the Herero prisoners, Germany would have no army.

General von Trotha repeatedly justifies the camp conditions. "It goes without saying that war cannot be waged according to the Geneva Convention," he insists.

But we're no longer waging war. The Herero and the Nama have surrendered. They've asked to live in peace. Our idea of peace is condemning them to death camps.

RETURN TO SWAKOPMUND

Seeing an opportunity in the number of infectious diseases afflicting the prisoners, the medical community in Germany petitions the government to set up research laboratories in the camps. Given my university work in bacteriology and experience in the colony, I'm assigned to the new lab being built at the concentration camp in Swakopmund.

I travel to the coast with Alexander, who's shipping out for home. His company makes the train journey over the mountains far more pleasant than the one that first brought me to Windhük. Although the train cars still aren't that comfortable, more stations have been built along the tracks, so food and water are plentiful. There's also no danger of attack.

It's evening when we step off the train to spend the night at one of the stations. I breathe in the high mountain air, welcoming the evening coolness after the heat of the day. The setting sun softens the harsh landscape, draping it in subtle shades of pinks and purples.

"This country does grow on you," Alexander murmurs.

"Yes, it does," I agree.

We get our food and head back outdoors to eat under the evening sky. I look up, spotting the first star of the night. "You know, after all the months of living in the open, I sometimes feel too confined inside. It's almost like being in a prison," I say.

"I know what you mean. I'm not sure I will adjust to living in Berlin again," Alexander murmurs. "There's something to be said for living off the land. I think it makes one stronger and healthier."

We sit quietly as the sky darkens. A full moon hovers on the horizon, its glow reflecting against the smooth face of the mountains. As the stars pierce the darkness with their intense points of light, they seem to be just overhead. "Look!" I point as a falling star streaks across the sky.

Alexander sighs. "I will miss this. I can understand why you want to stay in Africa."

* * * * *

We taste the salt air of Swakopmund long before the train pulls into the station a few days later. As we leave the depot, we look around in disbelief. The sleepy town on the water's edge is not so small anymore, and it's bustling with activity. A train station that could rival many German depots is nearing completion. The main road is lined with new stores, banks, and hotels. The tired wooden houses that greeted me a year ago sparkle with bright colors and new red roofs. Stately manors are under construction.

I'm so busy taking in the sights that I don't notice the truck speeding toward me until Alexander pulls me to safety. "Where did that come from?" I ask, trying to compose myself.

Alexander laughs. "This is definitely not the quiet little town I remember."

Agreeing to meet for dinner, we part ways. He heads toward the busy pier, while I make my way to my new quarters near the Swakopmund concentration camp. The first thing I notice are the gallows, strung with five naked men. The condition of the corpses suggests they've been hanging there for a few days. I want to look away. But the grotesque image, presented as normality, draws my gaze every time I try to glance at something else. I hurry into the makeshift barracks and stow my bags in the quarters reserved for the medical corps.

Knowing that we may never see each other again, Alexander and I share a somber dinner. We focus on small talk, reminiscing about the months in the desert and old acquaintances. As we lift our steins, the conversation turns to the future.

"I envy you the work you'll be doing," Alexander tells me. "Who knows, you may discover a cure for tuberculosis – or better yet, a vaccine."

"That would be great," I say. "But all I care about is improving the life of the poor people condemned to those camps. If I can help save even one life, I'll not think my work here has been in vain." And then maybe I could forgive myself, I think, for the man I shot and all the times I stood by silently, watching the Herero suffer the basest inhumanities.

Alexander puts his stein down a bit loudly and leans toward me. "The camps are inhumane. There's no excuse for how we're treating the prisoners. And there's no reason to imprison the women and children."

I nod in agreement. "Why is no one doing anything? We would never treat English or French prisoners like this."

"Major von Estorff and some of the other officers have started to protest. And the missionaries are stirring up fervor in Germany with their reports. They also are getting German churches to send clothing and supplies for the prisoners," Alexander sighs. "Surely the Reichstag and the Kaiser will yield to the pressure and set the Herero and Nama free. They're a broken people and pose no threat to the colony now."

"I hope you're right," I say as we leave the restaurant to walk toward the pier.

"I've heard rumors that General von Trotha is being recalled," Alexander says quietly.

"But when? I've heard those rumors for months now. Tomorrow wouldn't be too soon."

"The question then is who replaces him. A change in leadership isn't always a change in direction. Many of our career officers share his ideas. They look at this as a race war that can only end with the destruction of one of the races. They claim coexistence would be impossible after all the hostilities," Alexander says.

"But they're the ones that made this into a race war," I protest.

We've reached the harbor. Strings of lights twinkle on the water, outlining a number of steamers and ships. The waves crash rhythmically against the pier. The long beam of light from the lighthouse plays across the jagged coastline, warning ships to keep their distance.

Alexander smiles as he shakes my hand. It's hard telling him goodbye. We've had our disagreements, but we have shared much over the past year. It's as if I've known him a lifetime.

"Thank you," I tell him.

"For what?" he asks.

"For saving my life. For helping me keep my sanity. For understanding." I laugh, trying not to get too emotional.

"Just doing my job, Doctor." He also seems to be trying to hold his emotions in check. "Keep in touch, Kov."

I nod. "You too."

As I start down the street, Alexander calls after me, "Kol tuv."

I turn and wave. "Shalom," I respond.

* * * * *

I quickly learn that my idea of medical research is far from the reality of what's happening in the Swakopmund camp. I had thought we would be taking samples from the sick prisoners to look for cures for them. Instead, the researchers are infecting the "healthy" ones with smallpox, typhus, and tuberculosis. The aim is not to relieve the prisoners' suffering. Rather, it's to reinforce the German ideas about race while finding medical solutions for the troops and the people back home by using the Herero as lab animals. The scientists can do research here that they'd never be permitted to do in Germany.

The Swakopmund camp is smaller than the one in Windhük, but the death toll is just as high, if not higher. Most of the prisoners are Nama, who surrendered following negotiations that guaranteed them peace in their homelands. But as soon as they laid down their weapons, they were rounded up and sent off to the camps. Many of their leaders were executed for treason. Others were shipped off to Shark Island after a few months here.

The ones who remain in Swakopmund are forced to work in the icy waters of the Atlantic, hauling rocks to build a better harbor.

Disease is rampant, largely because of the design of the camp, which is located next to the military stables. All the excrement from the stables flows into the prison camp, along with the waste from the medical lab. Flies infest the place, carrying germs from one person to the next. It's as if the intent is to kill as many of the prisoners in as short a time as possible.

Unlike last year, I pay little attention to the High Holy Days. A few mornings, I wake early enough to say the prayers of repentance. But what good are prayers when I can't change my actions? My fate is already sealed for another year. I've resigned myself to that fact. But I haven't entirely given up hope.

The news I've been waiting for comes in November. Now that the war is officially over, General von Trotha is being recalled. He's to be replaced by Governor von Lindequist, who served under Leutwein, the former governor. Perhaps Lindequist will be more compassionate.

When the new governor arrives from Germany, he assembles all the prisoners at Swakopmund. Dressed in his best uniform with his stout chest covered with bright medals, Lindequist addresses the starving, half-naked people.

"His Excellency, the Governor of German South West Africa, greets you," he calls out pompously.

The prisoners stare straight ahead.

He ignores their passionless faces and promises that the innocent ones – those who did not murder farmers and traders – will be set free again as soon as all the Herero still in the bush surrender.

"I guarantee they will be treated fairly," he says. "And those of you who work hard and show good conduct also will be treated well."

After the speech, I return to the lab. It would be great if conditions improved in the camp. But I have come to put little stock in the words of colonial leaders. "We'll see," I murmur under my breath.

* * * * *

I peer into a microscope at a slide of a tissue sample taken from a woman who died from tuberculosis. One of the other researchers opens the door. The foulest odor I've ever smelled fills the room. I gag, covering my nose with my handkerchief. "What is that stench?" I mumble.

One of the new assistants smiles wryly. "Dr. Fischer has returned."

"Dr. Fischer?"

"Eugen Fischer. He's a scientist from one of the universities back home."

"I know who he is," I say. "I met him when he first came. But what does that smell have to do with him?"

"He wants to take some Nama and Herero skulls home for his eugenics research," the assistant says. "He's having the women prepare them for shipping."

I'm familiar with the bone shipments. Several anthropologists have requested native skulls and other body parts. One of them, Professor von Luschan, director of the Ethnology Museum in Berlin, even put together guidelines for soldiers and German travelers on how to properly pack the bones they pick up in the desert or unearth from Herero graves.

But that doesn't explain the smell. I rub my eyes, which are tired from straining through the microscope. I stand up and head for the door.

"You don't want to go out, Doctor," the assistant says. "It's not a pretty sight. And the smell is even worse out there."

I shrug, opening the door.

"Just remember, I warned you," he calls after me.

Ignoring him, I head into the camp. I almost double over from the foul odor. Once again, I cover my nose with my handkerchief, but the smell is overpowering. I hold my breath, taking quick gulps of air only when I absolutely have to.

Following the stench, I come to a group of women sweating over a large pot of water that's boiling on an open fire. What I see stops me dead in my tracks. One of the women is dropping the severed heads of prisoners into the boiling water. After awhile, a few other women pull the heads from the pot. Most of the flesh has boiled away, but bits of meat still cling to the bone. And the eyeballs bulge garishly from the skulls, which are given to other women to finish cleaning. Using shards of glass, they dig out the brains and cut the eyes and remaining tissue from the bone – all under the watchful gaze of Fischer. The skulls are left to dry in the hot sun.

I look back at the pot of boiling water as one of the women cries in agony. The head of a little boy is lowered into the pot. I leave as quickly as I can, trying not to vomit until I'm out of sight of the women and the guards. I knew that child. He was born from the German rape of his mother. Like other mulatto children, he was chosen for one of Fischer's medical experiments. I had watched him try to play even as the sickness Fischer infected him with slowly destroyed his small young body. I had seen his mother starve herself so she could give him a little more food each day. When he died, she had no tears to shed. She just sat there, holding his lifeless body until a soldier tore him from her arms and forced her to go back to work.

I shake my head in disgust. What kind of men kill children in the name of science? What kind of men make women do such a thing to the bodies of their loved ones? And what kind of nation lets them do it?

Hoping to wash the macabre image from my mind, I head back to my quarters for a shower. I scrub my skin until it's raw, but I still feel unclean.

In the evening, I take a long walk past the German cemetery at the edge of town. In a sandy, windswept field beyond the cemetery is the burial ground for the concentration camp. Row upon row of unmarked mounds form a sharp contrast to the neatly tended colonial cemetery with its ornate headstones and mausoleums. The desolate field is a silent memorial to the senseless tragedy of the Kaiser's colonial policy.

This past year, the Swakopmund camp has averaged about a thousand prisoners. According to our medical records, eight hundred have died, and their bodies – at least the parts that haven't been shipped to German universities – are buried here in this veld. Until today, those numbers were just statistics to me.

I shudder as the image of the little boy's severed head flashes before me. The thought of our brutality overwhelms me as I turn away from the burial ground, blinded by my tears. I have lived too long if this is what the world has come to. I bow to the ground, feeling very old and very helpless.

RESIGNATION

Walking back to my quarters, I finally make up my mind about the future. I must resign my commission. I have no business serving in the German army. In the past, I made excuses to justify the horrors I silently witnessed, but there are no excuses that can justify the living death of the camps. And my idealistic thoughts about being able to improve the conditions of the prisoners were the stuff of fairy tales.

In the morning, I write to Hanna about my decision. "I can't be a part of this butchery any longer," I tell her. "When I signed on to work at the camps, I thought I could help find cures that would relieve some of the suffering of the Herero and Nama. But that's not the kind of research that's being done here.

"I find it impossible to work with Dr. Fischer and the other scientists who are using the prisoners like animals. I fear where their studies may lead. Convinced that the Germanic race is genetically superior to all others, Fischer is bent on proving his theories. He takes countless photographs and meticulous measurements of all the prisoners, but he seems most interested in the mixed-race children who are the result of the soldiers' 'use' of the Herero and Nama women. If his research were only photographs and measurements, I could put up with it, even though I don't find his theories credible. But the more he 'proves' the inferiority of his subjects, the cruder his methods become.

"I often wonder how respected men of science can devote precious time and resources to such racial quackery when there are real problems they could be solving. The only answer I can find is that this irrational research is an attempt to provide a 'scientific' cover to justify our national chauvinism and greed. Whatever the reason, it doesn't bode well for Germany's future."

I lay out my plans to Hanna, asking her to sell Papa's property so we can use the money to start afresh someplace in Africa. We will make our own future, far away from such hatred. Maybe then I will at last find peace.

* * * * *

The sun rises early over the veld, waking me with its brightness. Stretching lazily, I listen to the bird chorus singing around me. Odd, I think. In all those months of marching with the marines and the army, I don't remember hearing bird song. Perhaps I just wasn't listening. I'm beginning to realize I really didn't see this land before. In the last few weeks of traveling by myself, I've been amazed hour after hour by the country's wildlife. Its vegetation. Its diversity. Where once I saw desolation, I now see a landscape teeming with life. The giraffes and wildebeest grazing in the distance. A warthog ambling alongside the road. Baboons watching me with their passive curiosity.

I leisurely eat my breakfast and clean up. It feels good to be on no one's schedule but my own. I saddle my horse and head deeper into the interior, following the trail that's been forged by settlers, traders, and the army. I have no set destination. This quest, which began with my resignation from the army, has a dual purpose – to find direction for the future and to reclaim the humanity I buried in the desert.

Along the way, I've visited with several settlers and missionaries. Their stories convince me I can't stay in South West Africa. While some of them lament the fate of the Herero and Nama, too many applaud the actions that allowed Germany to "civilize" the territory. And a few of the settlers boast of the part they continue to play.

I was at one of the stations the other day when a group gathered around a leathered man telling how he had rounded up several Herero hiding in the bush. "They were paper thin," he said, "which made me wonder how many I could kill with one bullet. So I stood them single file, front to back all the way down the line. Then I took my gun and shot at the heart of the first one."

"How many did you kill?" someone asked.

"How many do you think I got?"

While some of the men began shouting out numbers, a few looked away, apparently discomfited by the conversation. But no one reproached the settler.

He ended the guessing. "Seven fell," he said. "But I had to waste a few bullets finishing two of them off."

I quickly paid my bill and left the station.

Thinking back on the incident, I'm once again ashamed by my own silence. These actions stem from the same hatred and bigotry that have fueled anti-Semitism over the centuries. This is a bond I share with the Herero, so why do I keep quiet? Is it cowardice? Or is it the fear that if this hatred were deflected from the Herero and Nama, it would once again be aimed fully at my people? I hope my silence is born of cowardice. I can live with that shame more easily than I can with the alternative.

I come to a fork in the road. If I head northeast, I'll retrace the path I took with General von Trotha toward Hamakari and Waterberg. I close my eyes, trying to block out the images I've tried so hard to keep in check. I have no desire to go there again. So I head northwest toward Otjiwarongo, a place that has no memories for me.

As the sun sinks toward the horizon, I come upon what looks to be a prosperous farm. Following the custom of the land, I stop and ask if I can stay the night. After putting my horse in the kraal and cleaning up at the pump, I join Herr Jurgen and his wife for dinner. Jurgen is asking me about my experience in the war when a Herero servant, dressed in a drab cotton gown with a kerchief tied about her head, enters the room with a heavy tray of meat. Her dark eyes meet mine when she sets the tray on the table. She carefully carves the beef and puts several pieces on my plate. I smile at her before responding to Jurgen. The servant blanches and runs from the room, her multitude of petticoats swishing loudly.

"Petronella!" Frau Jurgen goes after the servant. I can hear her sternly scolding the woman in the next room.

"Please excuse Petronella," Jurgen says. "She's afraid of strangers, especially German men. Not that I blame her, given what she's lived through."

I look at him questioningly.

"I found her several months ago in the desert. She was hardly alive. She doesn't say much, but apparently she survived on her own in the desert for two years after her family was killed." Jurgen shakes his head. "And then last month, a soldier tried to rape her. Here, in my house." His disgust is obvious.

He butters a big slab of crusty bread. "My wife and I have taken in several Herero and Nama. We see it as our duty to civilize them and raise them up to be good Christian souls. It's difficult, though, when Germans act like such beasts."

Frau Jurgen rejoins us, followed by a quiet Petronella. The young woman keeps her eyes on her work as she serves the Jurgens. Out of curiosity, I study her, surprised to see she's much younger than I had first thought. She's barely a teenager, and yet she had the wits to survive the nightmare the Germans unleashed on her people. I wish I could hear her story.

Realizing I'm staring, I look away. Now I feel her watching me.

After dinner, I discuss farming with Jurgen. What it takes to start a farm. The challenges. The best methods. Crops that are in demand. He suggests a few places I should look for land.

"This territory is getting a little too settled for me," I say diplomatically.

He nods in agreement. "I know what you mean. If I were a young man just starting out, I would consider Bechuanaland. It's an English colony, but they welcome settlers from other countries."

"Bechuanaland? I heard some of the Herero went there."

Jurgen misunderstands the reason for my comment. "Yes, Samuel Maharero and the few who survived the march through the desert are rebuilding their herds there. But they're no longer a threat. We've knocked all the fight out of them."

After a bit of polite conversation, I excuse myself and take my bedroll outside to sleep under the stars. Gazing up at the night sky with its swirling colors of galaxies, I think of the possibilities of Bechuanaland. Perhaps there I could make amends to the Herero for my role in the war that rendered them landless.

With a newfound sense of direction, I rise early in the morning to say my prayers. It's time for a new beginning.

I'm saddling my horse after breakfast when Petronella comes out to me. She walks slowly, her head held high. She shyly gives me a packet of food. I smile my appreciation and stow it in my saddlebag. As I mount, she tugs at my shirtsleeve. She removes a long leather cord tied around her neck and hands it to me. It's attached to a small empty apothecary bottle. Puzzled, I examine the lavender-tinted glass before turning back to Petronella.

"*Mukuru ngakare punaove,*" she says softly.

Recognition dawns as I look into her eyes – those eyes I saw peering up at me through the brambles in the aftermath of Waterberg. I smile and pocket the bottle. It's the one I had filled with water and left for her in the desert.

"Thank you, Petronella," I say. "That's a good name for you – the little rock that endured the desert."

As I ride off, my vision is blurred by tears of gladness. God heard my prayer that day in the wilderness. And He answered it.

A NEW LIFE

I nervously watch as the passengers of the English steamer spill out onto the pier in Walvis Bay, searching for Hanna and little David in the growing crowd. I wonder if I'll even recognize them, but then I realize there probably aren't too many young women traveling alone with a toddler.

I wanted Hanna to wait until I had a farm established in Bechuanaland, but she would have none of it. "My place is with you," she wrote. "If we are to make our home in Africa, we will build it together." I still have my doubts about exposing her and David to the hardships of wilderness life. But I know from experience that Hanna is capable of anything she sets her mind to.

An elegant young woman in a stylish walking suit catches my eye. Surrounded by settlers and harbor workers, she looks out of place. But she walks confidently, drawing more than one admiring stare. She nods politely as a knot of men parts to let her pass. That's when I see the little boy toddling beside her, his small hand firmly clutched in her gloved one.

I watch a moment longer, taking in the serene beauty of my wife and the wonder of my son. Then I push forward, madly shouting her name. Hanna looks up and smiles brightly.

Forgetting my nervousness, I hug her. I hadn't realized how lonely I was or how much I missed her until this moment.

Hanna is the first to break the embrace. She steps back slightly, straightening her hat. Noticing that some of the men are watching us, she blushes and laughs softly. "You need to meet your son." She bends toward the boy. "David, this is your father. Remember the man in the photographs?"

He nods at her solemnly and then looks up at me with big eyes. They are Papa's eyes.

I reach down to pick up my son for the first time. He strokes my face with his hand and then rests his head on my shoulder. I smile at Hanna. With my free hand, I wipe a tear from her eye before extending my arm to her. "Shall we go, Frau Wolf?" I ask brightly.

After checking in at a hotel near the harbor, we explore Walvis Bay together. I carry David, who squeals at the flamingoes that flock around the shallows like herds of cattle. We marvel at the scarlet salt flats. Hanna's gaze is captured by the rusted orange dunes rising up on the horizon. "This land is so strange ... and yet so beautiful," she murmurs.

Over dinner, we discuss our plans. We'll take the steamer to the Cape and then travel inland to Bechuanaland. It will be a long journey, but fortunately, it's winter, so it shouldn't be too hot. And we'll have plenty of food and water. Hanna's eyes dance with excitement. I hadn't realized how adventurous she was. I smile across the table at her, marveling at her capacity for life and the miracle of her love for me.

It's late when we go to our room. Tonight, I am once again a clumsy bridegroom, and Hanna is my blushing bride.

* * * * *

Creating a farm in the wildness of the veld isn't an easy task. Hanna and I work from dawn to dark taming our land and building a small house. Although we're anxious to move from the confines of our Cape wagon into a real house, we take a much needed break so I can begin the real work that brought me to Bechuanaland – offering my medical services to the Herero. I set up a meeting with the old chief, Samuel Maharero, at his hut in Serowe.

Having never met the chief, I'm not sure what to expect. Will he consider me an enemy? Or another condescending German intent on taking something from him?

When I arrive at Samuel's hut, he greets me warmly. "It's good of you to visit, Doctor," he says in perfect Deutsch.

"Please, call me Yaakov," I respond.

Samuel offers me tea, and we engage in small talk. "So you're a German?" he asks.

"No. I was born in Germany, but I'm not a German."

Samuel smiles approvingly. "I thought not," he says. "You don't use fancy titles and try to make yourself better than the Herero."

"We're all just people," I say, "regardless of what titles we claim or the color of our skin. It's a lesson too many never learn."

The chief nods in agreement.

I take a deep breath and plunge into the reason for my visit. "What the Germans did to your people was wrong. I'm sorry to say that I helped them by serving as a doctor in their army. I can't undo what has been done, but I would like to make amends in the only way I can. I want to work as a doctor for the Herero."

"What price must we pay?" Samuel asks.

"All I want is your permission. My wife and I are starting a small farm here in Bechuanaland. It will be enough to support us."

"How many cattle do you have?" he asks.

"Ten to start with."

"You'll need many more," he says.

The chief studies my face while he ponders my offer. He finally speaks. "You will become my doctor. My heart has not been strong since we were driven into the desert. And you may be a doctor to the other Herero – not because they need it, but because you need to do this thing. For your services, I will give you my red cow with the white band."

I know better than to protest, so I accept his cow, which, to a Herero, is the greatest gift that can be given.

Samuel pours another cup of tea and then settles back on his stool. "The Germans think they have defeated me," he says softly. "They've killed most of my people. They've taken our cattle. And they've stolen our land. But I am still Samuel Maharero, the son of Maharero. Some day, I will be gathered with my people in the land of my ancestors. These are things the Germans can't take from me."

I'm surprised at the lack of bitterness in his voice. "You don't hate the Germans?" I ask.

"I'm an old man who has become wiser with age," he says. "German, Herero, Nama, even the English – not one of us is different when it comes to greed. But in the end, each of us chooses his own path in life. I choose not to be eaten by hatred."

Riding toward the homestead Hanna and I are carving out of the wilderness, I reflect on Samuel's words. I, too, have chosen my path. "I am Yaakov," I say loudly, laughing when I startle a flock of weavers. "It's a good name for a Jew who happens to live in Africa."

I can almost hear Papa chuckling in the distance.

* * * * *

Hanna's eyes shine in the flickering candlelight as she waves her hands over the candles, welcoming the first Shabbat in our new home in Bechuanaland. She covers her eyes with her hands as she says the traditional prayer: *"Barukh atah Adonai, Eloheinu, melekh ha'olam asher kidishanu b'mitz'votav v'tzivanu l'had'lik neir shel Shabbat."*

"Amein," David and I say together.

As my father before me, I turn to my wife and chant the *Eshet Chayil.* "An accomplished woman, who can find? Her value is far beyond pearls," I begin. The words of Proverbs 31 take on new meaning as I look at Hanna's sun-freckled face and calloused hands. She has never looked more beautiful.

As I continue reciting the verses, I think of all the weeks she has been here beside me, building our home in a strange land. After a full day of back-breaking work, she would go to bed in the wagon, kissing me goodnight with a smile. There were times when I wanted to quit, but her calmness kept me going.

Only once did she complain. That was when she discovered some of her mother's china had broken on the long trek into the interior. Tears rolled down her cheeks as she held the pieces in her hands. She smashed them into the ground and ran toward a cluster of sweet-thorn trees.

I checked the rest of the china and found most of it was intact. I showed the dishes to her when she returned about twenty minutes later. "Thank you," she said with a tired smile. "But they are just things. What is important is that I am with you and David."

I watched while she cleaned up the broken pieces. "Stop lazing around," she said, blushing. "We have a home to build!"

My voice breaks as I think about how blessed I am to have such a wife. I swallow and continue with the proverb:

"Strength and honor are her clothing, she smiles at the future. She opens her mouth in wisdom, and the lesson of kindness is on her tongue. She watches over the ways of her household, and does not eat the bread of idleness. Her children rise and praise her, her husband lauds her. Many women have done worthily, but you surpass them all. Charm is deceptive and beauty is vain, but a woman who fears God shall be praised. Give her of the fruit of her hands, and let her works praise her in the gates."

The candlelight plays over Hanna's contented face as I stand behind David to give him the Shabbat blessing. Laying my hands on his head, I pray, *"Ye'simcha Elohim ke-Ephraim ve'chi-Menashe."* Hanna joins me for the rest of the blessing:

"May God bless you and watch over you. May God shine His face toward you and show you favor. May God be favorably disposed toward you and grant you peace."

As we're going to bed, Hanna reminds me that Elul starts next week. "And by the way," she says, "you're going to be a papa again."

Holding her close to me in bed, I look up at the ceiling, smiling broadly. God has indeed blessed us. And next year is sure to be a good year.

A COUNTRY OF OUR OWN

The world has become a new place in the years since Hanna and I first planted our roots in Bechuanaland. While the powerful nations of the earth fought the Great War, we built our herds and raised our family, far removed from the bombs and fighting. And when the guns fell silent, I must admit I took some pride in seeing Germany kicked out of South West Africa and Kaiser Wilhelm forced from the throne. The last of the concentration camps would finally be emptied.

Samuel, who had sent his men to fight with the South African troops, saw it as a chance to go home. At first, the South African leaders, the new rulers of the former German colony, gave the ailing chief permission to return to Okahandja. But just as he was preparing to leave, Samuel learned the offer had been revoked.

The chief sits looking westward out over the veld when I come to check on him. "How are you doing?" I ask.

"The pain grows worse," he says, putting his wrinkled hand over his heart. He waves me away when I pull out my stethoscope. "There is nothing you can do for it," he says with a look of longing in his eyes. "I had hoped to end my days in the home of my ancestors. Now I know I will breathe my last in a land of strangers." The chief sighs deeply. "But in death, I will rest with my fathers."

As I ride home across the veld, I look up into the endless blue sky, musing over the differences between Samuel and me. Although my ancestors have been buried in German soil for nearly a millennium, it is not the land of my fathers. I have no need, no desire, to return to the country of my birth – neither in life nor in death. This place, where Hanna and I have carved out a new beginning for our family, is where I belong.

After dinner, I sit in my favorite chair by the fire. Amichai, our youngest, sits on the floor playing with Papa's tin soldiers. I can hear Anna and Elise singing in the kitchen as they wash the dishes. David has his nose in Max Bayer's book. It's the copy Max sent me before the Great War began – the war that ended his life.

"Don't believe everything you read in that," I tell David. "When you're done reading, we'll talk about what really happened."

I smile contentedly as I tackle the pile of newspapers that's been growing by my chair.

"I don't know why you bother," Hanna says, looking up from her knitting. "It's all old news by time it reaches us. The world has already moved on."

"That's no reason to be uninformed," I tell her as I flip through one of the newspapers.

A headline about the Kaiser living in exile in the Netherlands catches my eye. Wilhelm is trying to denounce his abdication, saying it was forced upon him by Germans who had been "egged on and misled by the tribe of Judah.... Let no German ever forget this, nor rest until these parasites have been destroyed and exterminated from German soil."

He recommends a worldwide pogrom as the "best cure." The Jews are a "nuisance that humanity must get rid of some way or other," he says. "I believe the best would be gas!"

Will the hatred never end? I throw the newspaper in the fire, watching as the Kaiser's words disappear in the flames. My disgust melts as I glance at the mantle and my eyes take in the lavender apothecary bottle I had once given to Petronella. For our family, it has become a symbol of hope, of endurance, of God's deliverance.

I step outside into the winter chill and look up at the night sky exploding in the light of thousands of stars. The soft lowing of the cattle thunders in the quiet of the veld. I'm reminded once again of God's promise to Abraham. It is a promise that has been handed down through the generations. But here in this African wilderness, I finally feel the power, and the comfort, of that covenant. My children and my children's children will grow and prosper in this land, far from the hatred of the kaisers of this world, the dangerous science of the Eugen Fischers, and the greed of the people who feed on that hatred and "knowledge."

I reflect on the journey that has brought me here to this country where Hanna and I will someday rest in the sands of the Kalahari. The words of the Psalm come to mind:

"They wandered in the wilderness in a solitary way; they found no city to dwell in. Hungry and thirsty, their soul fainted in them. Then they cried unto the LORD in their trouble, and he delivered them out of their distresses. And he led them forth by the right way.... He turneth the wilderness into a standing water, and dry ground into watersprings. And there he maketh the hungry to dwell, that they may prepare a city for habitation; and sow the fields, and plant vineyards, which may yield fruits of increase. He blesseth them also, so that they are multiplied greatly; and suffereth not their cattle to decrease."

Lost in my reverie, I don't realize anyone has joined me until Hanna drapes a coat across my shoulders. "You'll catch cold out here," she says.

I smile my appreciation and pull her close.

She lays her head against my shoulder and looks up at the sky. "This is home," she murmurs.

I feel a small tug on my shirt. "Look, Papa! A falling star!" Amichai points to a brilliant streak across the sky. "Can we find where it landed?"

Hanna and I laugh. My son's zest for life amazes me. He definitely lives up to his name, which in Hebrew means, "My people are alive."

It is the name Samuel chose for him.

Epilogue

General von Trotha nearly succeeded in his efforts to exterminate the Herero. Over a span of just a few years, more than 60,000 Herero, or 85 percent of the tribe, died. While thousands were killed by German troops, countless more met death in the desert or German concentration camps. The remnants were forced to work for German settlers or condemned to a life of exile in surrounding countries. As for Samuel Maharero, he was allowed to return to the land of his fathers only in death.

Although these events unfolded more than a century ago, the children, grandchildren, and great-grandchildren of the Herero who survived still live with the consequences of the genocide. Once a proud, powerful force in the land that was to become Namibia, today the Herero make up about 10 percent of the Namibian population. Much of the land their herds once grazed is still farmed by the descendants of the German colonizers. And for more than a hundred years, many of the bones of their ancestors, collected from the death camps or dug up from their graves, have been the "property" of German universities and museums. Twenty skulls gathered for Dr. Eugen Fischer's research were finally returned to the Herero in October 2011. One was that of a four-year-old boy.

Germany partially apologized in 2004, accepting "political and moral responsibility for the past and colonial guilt." While it has given generously to Namibia in foreign aid, Germany refuses to pay reparations for a genocide it has yet to officially admit.

In 2007, members of the von Trotha family met with Herero leaders to offer their own apology. "We all bear the same family name and that is reason enough to deal with historical facts associated with General Lothar," Wolf-Thilo von Trotha, chairman of the von Trotha Family Association, said at that meeting. "We, the members of the von Trotha family, are ashamed of the terrible events that took place a hundred years ago. We deeply regret what happened to your people and also to the Nama and Damara – the cruel and unjustified death of thousands of men, women, and children."

Author's Note

While Kov and his family are the stuff of fiction, many of the people he encounters are as real as the events that shape this story. Take Alexander Lion, for instance. Born into a Jewish banker's family, he converted to Catholicism at the age of sixteen. He served as an army surgeon in German South West Africa during the Herero uprising. After the war, Alexander and Maximilian Bayer, who was a captain under General von Trotha, joined forces to found the German Boy Scout movement. Alexander continued his military duties in World War I, receiving the Iron Cross for his service. But despite his conversion and service to the Fatherland, Alexander was branded a Jew in World War II and arrested by the Gestapo. He was one of the fortunate ones. He survived.

Returning from Africa with a heart condition, Maximilian went on the lecture circuit and wrote romanticized books about the Herero uprising. Ignoring his health, he continued his military career. He was killed by a sniper's bullet on the Western front in World War I.

Jahohora is based on a real Herero girl by that name who survived two years in the desert after her parents were killed when they went for water. Like the girl of this story, the real Jahohora rubbed her body with a poisonous shrub to ensure no Germans would rape her. When she was taken in by a German farmer, she was stripped of her identity and renamed "Petronella." Years later, Jahohora was reunited with her brother, the only other survivor of her family. Along with their children and grandchildren, they made the trek to the waterhole where their parents were killed. They continued on to the Waterberg and then reignited the holy fire.

After South Africa replaced Germany as the colonial power in South West Africa, Jahohora made it her mission to teach her children and grandchildren the lessons of the ancestors and what it means to be Herero. Such lessons were the seeds that took root against apartheid in South West Africa and grew into demands for independence. In planting and nurturing those seeds, Jahohora and others of her generation truly became the mothers of modern-day Namibia.

Years of research went into the telling of this story, which was first inspired by Kapombo Uazuvara Ewald Katjivena, Jahohora's grandson. Guided by his grandmother's life, Kapombo became a SWAPO freedom fighter. He engaged in a war of words to persuade other countries to force South Africa to grant independence to South West Africa, which it had taken over following Germany's defeat in World War I. Forced into exile during the long struggle for freedom, Kapombo could not be with his beloved grandmother when she died.

Some of Kov's story follows the flow of Gustav Frenssen's *Peter Moor's Journey to Southwest Africa*, a novel loosely based on a composite of several German soldiers' experiences in South West Africa. Whereas Frenssen's fiction, which proved quite popular in Germany in the first part of the twentieth century, was light on research and heavy on racist justifications, my account is heavily researched and argues against those racist attitudes that eventually culminated in the Holocaust.

I would be remiss in not acknowledging all those who helped me with this research. I owe Kapombo a huge debt of gratitude for sharing his grandmother's story and making me aware of the first genocide of the twentieth century. He spent countless hours explaining the importance of the holy fire, the ancestors, and the essence of being Herero. This book also could not have been written without the help of the Paramount Herero Chief Kuima Riruako, Dr. Hoze Riruako, and Belinda Veii Riruako. The three of them were my go-to sources on Herero customs and traditions. For Kov's story, I must thank Martin Berman-Gorvine and Dr. Martin Evers for their insight on Jewish traditions.

Lastly, I thank my family for their encouragement and for putting up with an absentee wife, mother, grandmother, and daughter as I was working on this project. Most of all, I thank my husband, Job Serebrov, for his patience, his willingness to be my sounding board, and his perseverance in tracking down answers to my research questions.

About the Author

A N AWARD-WINNING journalist with a passion for history, Mari Serebrov has authored a variety of books, including *The Life and Times of W.H. Arnold of Arkansas*, the historical novel *Mama Namibia* and a children's book, *Jahohora and First Day*. She also contributed to *The Grandmother's Bible* and has co-authored a number of church resource books and the historical novel *The Fugitive Son* with her mother, Adell Harvey.

Because of her work in calling attention to the first genocide of the 20th century in what was then German South-West Africa, Mari was named the literary laureate of the Herero Tribal Authority in 2013. She and her husband, Job, have two children and six grandchildren.

Visit us at
www.KamelPress.com/Serebrov
to see more from this author!

Lightning Source UK Ltd.
Milton Keynes UK
UKOW04f1930180717

305584UK00001B/68/P